Elquin

Rose Sweetwater

ELQUIN

© 2015 by Rose Sweetwater Publishing

All rights reserved.

Rose Sweetwater Publishing

6742 Webber Rd. 270266

Corpus Christi, TX 78414

www.rosesweetwater.com

https://www.facebook.com/authorrose

Library of Congress publication date is available upon request.

Library of Congress Control Number: 2015915448

Rose Sweetwater Publishing , Suffolk, VA

ISBN-13: 9780991648610

ISBN-10: 0991648617

For my family,
the joy of my heart, the light of my being, and the legacy of my blood,
I love you all.
Uncle Brent, you're awesome.

For my family,
the joy of my heart, the light of my being, and the legacy of my blood,
I love you all.
Uncle Brent, you're awesome.

To control human nature, man created limitations, restrictions, and boundaries. When we take a moment to step back and simply allow ourselves to be, we let go of preconceived notions and explore all the universe has to offer. Fear of what and who we are only limits the potential of what and who we can become.

Author Unknown

Those Who Ponder

Age of the Enlightened

Contents

Elquin

Prologue

A crowd gathered, with eager anticipation on every face. There wasn't even standing room along the marked-off section of a wheat field in Marthasville, Missouri. Reporters were focused in front of their cameras, and researchers poured into the field by the dozens. Several helicopters made passes overhead, and officials worked tirelessly to control the growing crowd.

A crop circle formation had appeared earlier that morning as owner Billy Napper walked toward his barn to feed his hens. Instantly he froze as two balls of white light moved in synchronization at opposite ends of his wheat field. After approximately three minutes, the balls vanished, and Billy stood there awestruck. He walked slowly into the clearing, and his jaw dropped when he discovered an intricately carved circular pattern of rings that appeared to close in on themselves several times over. The rings wove outward into a space about 200 feet wide and 375 feet long. Billy wasted no time contacting the authorities. Less than twenty minutes after he'd dialed 911, several different agencies pulled onto his property.

There were onlookers, believers, worshipers, and spectators, all appraising as much of the clearing as they could possibly see. *You'd think we'd won the lottery or something*, Billy thought to himself as he thrashed into his front door and plopped down on the couch. He looked through the window and past the crowds where he could see into the clearing. In the middle of the field stood two men. They seemed to be chatting casually about the latest crop circle formation as they pointed and recorded information on their instruments. Since the early 1990s, the world had all but turned a blind eye to this strange phenomenon.

"Must be better than examining crop circle photographs from the seventies," Billy said. "I hope they get this circus over with quickly."

The shorter of the two men was about five feet eight. He had broad shoulders and a muscular build. His rich russet eyes were complemented by deep-brown hair, and his skin was the exact color of the Sahara Desert at dawn. He was explaining that their crop circle examination team was the perfect cover for those who still believed. His eyes scanned the growing crowd approvingly.

"That is not your concern at the moment, Vishnu," the taller of the two men said. He was about six one and muscular—almost to the point of a body builder. He had ochre-brown eyes and chocolate-brown hair. His skin was tanned to the color of antique gold, and his manner was harsh and disapproving.

"They call me Taren here," the shorter man interrupted. "I'd much rather you used this title instead."

"My apologies…Taren. That is none of your concern. You have a job to do at present. This was not a simple social call. You have to gain the information we need from their government facilities. This planet is more like our home than any of the others we've encountered. Take this," the taller man said as he placed a small black box into Taren's hands. "Record the information, and report your findings. You have one year."

Taren took the box willingly and started walking away, but turned before his first step. "This planet has sufficient resources to share. Is it necessary to destroy its inhabitants to gain what we need?"

The taller man's brows drew down, anger flashed in his eyes, and he growled and spat through his teeth. "Vishnu, this is not about you! Your continued tolerance for this world is incomprehensible and not at all conducive to our mission here. If you cannot or will not see the benefits of our occupancy, you will be replaced. Your position on the council is assumed and will not deter the decisions of the whole—"

"I understand my objective, Locknoff." Taren cut him off again with anger in his voice now. "I am capable of completing my mission. I am simply stating the obvious."

"Be that as it may, Taren, your opposition is being noted."

With a low growl, Taren answered, "You'll have my first report within a month." He then turned and walked away.

Hmm…maybe they did find something, Billy thought as he watched the man walk away. "Now that would be something," he remarked before turning his attention to the television.

One

CHANCE ENCOUNTER

A man walked hastily through the lobby of a crowded hotel. Without realizing, he entered the hotel's casino wing. He turned to gauge the position of his pursuers and stumbled into a blackjack table. Regaining his footing, he looked up briefly and moved swiftly past the slot machines and card tables. Although the casino was hosting an unusually large night crowd, the man spotted his pursuers effortlessly. When he glanced back, two men were closing in on him from both sides of the coin slots. The four men were dressed in black-and-white army fatigue pants and black T-shirts. He was sure of their identities because of the clothing they wore.

The pants were held in place with black belts, each with a gold buckle bearing a symbol: one large star that took up the entire right half of the buckle, and three smaller planets of varying sizes in the shape of a triangle. The planets were on the top left of the star. The largest of the planets was bluish green with white clouds. The second, closest to the star, was blue and pink with white clouds. The third planet was the farthest from the star and red-orange. Under the planets were the letters *R* and *T*, which aligned perfectly one on top of the other and centered to the right of the *E*.

The man increased his pace as he scanned the crowded room for another exit, spotting one leading directly to the parking lot. With fear in his eyes, he turned to see that he was still being chased. Suddenly, he stumbled and fell over a large decorative plant, a crystal cylinder falling out of his pocket and landing to the right of the plant.

A woman bent to help him up as she came in through the sliding-glass doors. "Oh my goodness, are you OK?" the woman asked, helping him to his feet.

"Yes, thank you," he said as he looked anxiously behind him for the location of the men following him. To his surprise, they turned and left the chase just as the woman's friends also rushed to his side. Feeling safe for the moment, the man climbed to his feet, holding the woman's hand. He quickly scanned the room again for his pursuers and smiled, seeing no one.

"Do you need any help?" the woman asked, her eyes darting everywhere as she searched for a casino attendant.

"No!" he responded, loudly enough to regain her attention. He then leaned forward and kissed her gently on the lips. He began to pull away, but suddenly grabbed the back of her head and pulled her closer for a more passionate kiss. The woman didn't resist, but her eyes bulged in surprise to her own reaction.

"Thanks again," the man said on his way out the door. Shocked and out of breath herself, the woman was speechless. She followed and watched the man run through the casino parking lot. Her friends joined her with equally shocked expressions as they looked on.

The man noticed two of the four men coming toward him from the rear of the parking lot. He stopped suddenly and took up a defensive stance, at which point he noticed the other two men coming toward him from the hotel's front entrance, which was to the left of the parking lot. He ran directly for the two men in front of him at full speed.

One of the men behind him lifted his hand to speak into a walkie-talkie. "He's charging," the man said with amazed disbelief. The women reached the parking lot in time to see the man leap forward and bend at the waist just seconds before reaching two arms that threatened to clothesline him. As he rolled onto the ground, he grabbed the ankles of one man, pulling him down as well. Just before rolling onto his side in an effort to get up, he kneed the fallen man in the face, breaking his nose. The second man reached for him as he stood, but missed his opportunity, as he rolled to safety and got up.

The men faced each other, and the fight began. They both kicked and blocked at the same time, forcing their legs to touch with a force that might have sent a person on the receiving end of it ten feet back. The other two men quickly joined in the fight, but it was apparent that the stumbling kisser was capable of holding his own, as another man fell to the ground after being kneed in the chest and hit in the back of the head with a double fist. As the man leaped forward toward his third target, he was sideswiped by someone who knocked him onto the ground.

Others quickly surrounded them and placed the kisser under arrest. Both his hands and feet were bound behind his back with a set of oversized copper bracelets and anklets. There was a bridge between the cuffs connecting all four of them together, requiring his legs to be bound bent toward his hands. There were tiny, blue lights along the length of the bridge that connected the cuffs together. Once the man was secured, they placed him in the back of a SWAT truck and pulled away.

Small clusters of people gathered to watch the man being carried away. They all gasped at the scene and wondered what he had stolen. One of the woman's friends looked at her and said, "Well, Jen, at least you gave him something to think about on those long, lonely nights locked away in a jail cell."

"Shut up!" she replied a little too loudly, blushing red as the other women joined in with laughter.

"I knew I shouldn't have let you guys drag me out tonight."

"Well, you certainly wouldn't have been able to make some weirdo's night had ya stayed in, would ya?"

"Yeah, 'cause they're all attracted to me, right?"

Again the women burst into laughter as they continued on into the casino.

"At least he was cute," one said.

"I wonder what he did," Jen continued, "and why the hell I kissed him back like that."

"It's just your body's way of protesting," another commented through laughter.

"Protesting?"

"Yes. If you gave in to simple pleasures more often, you wouldn't have let him touch you like that, no matter how cute he was. I on the other hand may have," she said with a smirk, and the women burst into laughter again. The ladies enjoyed each other's company, laughing and joking through drinks and games, as Jen had provided plenty to discuss. A couple of hours later, Jen decided to leave the casino.

"Why?" a friend complained. "We'll knock it off, won't we, girls?"

"Speak for yourself," another added. "Little Miss Perfect deserves it."

Jen sighed. "Come on, guys. You know I've got to get back on the road tomorrow, and I'm not feeling so good right now..." The ladies looked questioningly among themselves before turning toward Jen with calm faces so fast that she almost imagined the brief exchange.

"You know you should have flown," one of the women complained, cutting her off.

"I know. I just get so sick the moment I get on a plane that it's not worth it."

"Don't worry, Jen," the woman who'd called her Miss Perfect said. "I've got to hit the sack too. Long day tomorrow. The day before the concert is always the worst. Come on. You can give me a ride."

The two wished their friends a good-night and retired for the evening. As time continued forward, another woman left, and only three of the original six women remained in the casino.

The short drive with her friend was not enough to make Jen feel any better, so she headed for the shower when they walked through the door. As she wiped the mirror clear of condensation and examined her reflection, Jen sighed and pulled her toothbrush out of the bag. She brushed her teeth quickly and, once finished, wiped her mouth and reexamined her reflection. Meeting her own eyes, Jen moved closer to the mirror, frowning. For some reason, her eyes seemed brighter around the pupils. Jen blinked several times as a response to the sudden blurriness she experienced. Exhausted, she shook her head as her vision returned. "I've got to get more sleep."

Donning her nightgown, Jen made her way to bed, turned out the light, and climbed in contently. Sleep found her quickly.

◆ ◆ ◆

Standing in the driveway of a large suburban home, Jen looked around, confused. *Where am I*, she wondered. *I've never been here before.* The surrounding homes were all brick. "Suburbia...what the hell."

Jen took a step toward the house and was suddenly standing in the master bedroom, watching a couple kiss. She closed her eyes tightly, wondering how she got here and hoped they did not see her. Abruptly she opened her eyes at the sound of voices.

"Have a good day," the woman said, walking past Jen without acknowledging her presence.

Jen now realized that she was dreaming and followed the woman to the front door. She watched her get into a car and drive away. Jen's curiosity was fueled only by the fact that the woman was wearing a US Air Force uniform. She lifted her foot in an effort to follow her further, but was interrupted by the sound of voices coming from the bedroom. Lowering her foot, she turned to walk back into the bedroom, but found that she was suddenly standing in the master bathroom right behind the man. She was confused. He was watching a group of people in the mirror. Jen squinted, looking into the mirror. *No,* she thought, *not in the mirror. They're on the other side of the mirror.* Jen raised her eyebrows and stepped closer. She suddenly froze as she really got a good look at the people. Before she could find her voice, one spoke.

"What knowledge have we gained so far?" a feminine voice asked. The males on the other side of the mirror appeared to be aged with long, white hair flowing down their backs, some even touching the floor. Simple white bands were wrapped around their heads. The backs of the bands appeared to be braided into several strands of hair that flowed down to the floor. The women too had long, flowing, white hair that appeared to touch the ground; however, their foreheads were adorned with intricate strands of braided hair. The braids connected to the sides of their temples and then flowed freely from there.

All of the individuals had eyelashes but no eyebrows. Their eyelashes were the same shade of white as their hair. On the sides of their faces where ears would normally be, there were several rows of arched bands that encircled a triangular shape that appeared to have no entry or exit point. Their eye colors varied in shades of brown, from zinnwaldite to fallow. The bridges of their noses were covered in several tiny layers of miniature scales. The skin on their faces was varying shades of tea green, with lips that were a darker moss green. Their skin resembled the texture of a morning-glory- flower.

"To date," one of the males said, momentarily bringing Jen out of her examination of them, "we know that Earth holds a molecular structure similar to our own." He pressed his hand on the table in front of him, and an image of Earth appeared along with an earthlike planet Jen had never seen before.

"The protective layer around it," the man continued as he gestured to the magnetic field around the planet, "provides adequate safety for its resources. Additionally, the behavior of its star suggests that this planet is safe from implosion for perhaps another several thousand epochy. With the information Vishnu has provided, we have an accurate composite of the natives' military behavioral patterns. Combined with what we have already discovered through informants placed on this planet, I would say we are victorious well before the battle commences." Pleased with himself, the male sat back, smiling.

Jen was surprised by the form this dream had taken. She stepped closer to the mirror to see the others better, but stopped short and gasped when she saw the features of the man sitting in front of her. He was the strange man that had kissed her in the casino earlier tonight. Gasping, she woke, sitting up swiftly and examining her surroundings.

"You OK?" a familiar voice asked. "Sorry, didn't mean to wake you."

Jen recognized the voice of her friend Cara Johnson. She was just getting into bed and was wearing a pink-and-white tank top with matching pajama pants.

"Yeah, I'm OK." Jen shook her head. "You didn't wake me. I just had a…dream."

"Oh, you wanna talk about it?"

"No," Jen replied as she got out of bed. She walked out of the room, heading for the kitchen. *What the hell was that about?* she wondered while gulping down a glass of water. *I didn't understand any of it. The only thing I can figure is that somehow the man from that casino is involved with this. But that can't be—I don't even know him.* She visited the lavatory once more before returning to bed. Moments after she closed her eyes, dreams overcame her.

◆ ◆ ◆

Jen found herself flying over a vast body of water. The light from a not-too-distant star reflected her image off the water's surface. Looking past her reflection, she could see movement beneath the surface. Several gray-and-white clusters were moving in unison with her. Curious, she looked closer and saw a school of creatures that had an almost disklike shape with tree-limb patterns sticking out of the rounded middle. The animals reminded her of jellyfish, but she'd never seen jellyfish move this way. They were moving in a circular motion, almost like saucers flying underwater. The closer she got to them, the closer they seemed to get to her, until suddenly several jumped at her.

Jen moved back swiftly, barely missing the creatures' advances as their attempts continued. She suddenly found herself on the beach, gasping. It didn't take long for her to notice her surroundings. The sand was Nassau blue. There were vast hills as far as she could see, and the trees were a mixture of green, white, and blue. Their limbs all pointed upward with blossoms that reminded her of broccoli. The planet was close enough to its star that Jen felt like she could reach out and touch it. Strangely, she did not feel like she was in an inferno. The temperature was comfortable, but she noticed goose bumps on her arms as the wind blew.

Taking a step further to investigate her surroundings, Jen found herself at the base of one of the far hills. There were voices coming from the top of it. Looking in that direction, she noticed two people… *Wait, not people. They're different.* They looked like the individuals she'd seen in the mirror. Suddenly, Jen realized she could get as close to them as she wanted without them noticing her, so she took a step closer and was directly across from them, watching as they looked down at something.

They both had long, white hair, but it was held away from their faces. The female had a crown of braids that hung from her hair onto her forehead. It almost covered her eyes. Both were wearing black pants that covered the heels of their shoes, and matching jackets that covered only the top half of their arms. The jackets were held closed by several golden wires and polished jade stones. There was little difference between the designs. Both individuals were covered from head to toe in blue, as they had been digging in the dirt. Directly at their feet sat a large, cylinder-shaped, silver contraption that had a white glow coming from its core.

"It needs to be replaced, Skyke," the male said. "That makes seventeen all together." He looked out over the hillside. "If they are not replaced soon, it will mean a loss of two centimeters. It's hard enough to keep these running. We may not have time to post anymore if the rate of consumption persists."

"I know, Madafski."

"We have to inform the council. Our increased demand is pushing the current resources beyond their capacity, even with farming twenty-four planets."

"We may have to consider the possibility of—"

"No," Skyke cut him off. "We cannot abandon our home, not until we have completely lost the battle. We will just have to keep farming until we find a suitable replacement to run the generators."

"OK, then what do you propose we tell them?"

Skyke sighed. "The truth. But we'll have to make them see the importance of finding a more suitable replacement."

"I've heard news that scouts just found a deposit of detritus on Oororah-9."

◆ ◆ ◆

Jen woke with sweat-drenched pajamas. Getting her breathing under control, she decided that she'd had enough rest for one night. She immediately got up and gathered her things together. It took several trips, but she soon had everything neatly packed in the trunk of her car. When she returned to get dressed, Cara was awake.

"Is everything all right, Jen?"

"Yes." After a long moment, she explained. "I'm just having a hard time sleeping tonight. I'm gonna get on the road. Maybe I'll get back in time to catch that frat party Zackary has been going on about."

"You don't have to go, Jen. Your dreams won't scare me off."

Jen smiled and looked at her friend. "I know, Cara…it's just…these dreams make no sense to me, and I have no idea what they mean. I'm sure they're important, but I just don't know how, and I'm convinced that I'll have another one the minute I close my eyes."

"Why don't you tell me about them? Maybe I can help."

"Remember the dream I had about your parents when we were in high school?"

Cara nodded, remembering the warning Jen gave—that her parents were going to win the lottery and meet with an unfortunate accident two weeks later while the family was on its way to a vacation in Fiji. When they'd actually won, Cara claimed to be sick and convinced her parents to stay home with her rather than taking the planned trip. On the day of their scheduled flight, the plane was hit on takeoff by another trying to land. Investigators said the weather had made visibility difficult.

"Yeah?" Cara raised an eyebrow.

"Well, it's not like that. I feel like it's important, but I just can't see how. I've been dreaming about an alien world, and that guy we thought was crazy just might be from there." Cara's eyes bulged as she suppressed a laugh, but she could not help smiling slightly. "See?"

Cara breathed deeply. "It's not that I don't believe you. It just sounds a bit…off, that's all. I mean, aliens, Jen. Come on…maybe your dreams are a bit off because you're exhausted. You've been having long days since you got here, and driving all the way here was a big factor."

"I know it sounds crazy, Cara, but I feel like they're important somehow." She shook her head. "I just have to get going, Cara. It's not too early for me to get on the road, and I couldn't sleep a wink, even if I tried." She shrugged.

"All right, but I want you to be careful. I couldn't forgive myself if something happened to you."

"I know. I'll be careful."

Cara walked her friend to her red Honda. Yawning, she hugged Jen and said good-bye.

Jen smiled. "Get some sleep."

"The minute you're out of sight."

They hugged again, and Jen started her long drive back to Florida.

Two

CONFINED

The SWAT truck pulled up to a remote area in the desert. The door opened, and the bound man was carried into the facility with an individual holding each of his limbs. With lowered brows, he noticed where he was. The building appeared to be a warehouse from the outside. It was nestled deep in the hillside and taller than any factory he'd ever seen. There were six floors and more tiny windows than any one place should have. As he was pulled into the building, he noticed that they were one-way viewers, and from this side, it appeared as a wall of glass.

When all the men were inside, they shuffled him down a long hallway to the right of the main entrance. This hallway had several small rooms, each with a tiny window of its own and a keypad entry. At the end of the hall, he was carried through a set of double doors. This portion of the building looked more like a research facility and also had several smaller rooms. The man was pulled into one of them just a short distance from the entrance and placed into a large metal chair, where his binds were removed.

He was swiftly cuffed to the chair, his hands and feet immobilized. The chair was in the middle of the room. A woman covered from head to toe in white scrubs approached the man and turned on a digital handheld device that beeped and flashed red. The device was quickly passed over the man's head and chest, but it did not change in size or color. Puzzled, the examiner reviewed his entire body, stopping at the man's neck when the machine gave off a constant beeping sound while flashing yellow. The examiner called for the authorities who were chatting outside of the door.

"What's the problem?" they asked with surprised expressions.

"It's not here," she replied, confused.

"Impossible," a man said in a deep, raspy voice as he entered the room. "I scanned him myself, just before he entered the casino."

"Locknoff!" the bound man screamed angrily, shaking the chair as his fists rumbled in anger.

"You must return for it," the woman said, interrupting him. "There's no time to lose."

Locknoff looked at the man bound in the chair with pitying eyes. "You left me no choice, brother. Taren, I am sorry for your suffering."

He then swiftly walked toward the door with several other men following close behind. As they reached the doorway, the woman asked, "Where is the scan of the woman? Without the orb, that will be our best starting point."

Locknoff turned and responded coldly as he looked at Taren. "An adequate scan was not possible. The orb is our only chance now."

The woman's brows lowered, but she said nothing. Locknoff and the others walked out of the door, and the woman walked over to Taren and took a vial of his blood. She handed it to an assistant. "Scan it. I want to be thorough." The assistant nodded and took the blood away.

Locknoff walked into the security screening office and looked around. It was stocked with so much high-tech equipment that it could protect a small bank, rather than a hotel. At his side were two other men from the capture team. One had a bandage under his eye, decorated by a purplish-blue bruise. A security officer directed them all to a monitor without saying a word. He loaded the entire evening's security footage, and Locknoff directed him to begin at the point when Taren had entered the casino. They watched Taren's actions up to when they saw him stumble over the plant. When they spotted the cylinder, Locknoff ordered the security officer to pause the tape.

"There!" he said a bit too loudly while pointing at the screen. "Where is that?"

"Near the parking entrance of the casino," the security officer replied.

Locknoff hurried out of the office with the other men close behind him. As they entered the casino, people started to stare and whisper at the sight of the bandaged man. Two of Jen's friends noticed them and started laughing. The men ignored the whispers and snickers as they headed directly for the plant. It did not take long for them to find the cylinder. When they did, however, they quickly noticed that its contents had been removed.

Locknoff growled loudly and clinched his fist around the cylinder. Suddenly his cell phone rang. "Taren has chosen to make this more difficult," he said through clenched teeth while grabbing the cell phone from his pocket and checking the number. "Return to the security tapes—we must have missed something. Find whomever he's touched."

The men hurried toward the security office as Locknoff answered the phone. "Yes Sariah," he answered angrily.

"We may have a problem," a feminine voice replied. "It looks like Taren has given the orb to one of the casino guests. A young lady who is one of a group."

"We will find her," Locknoff replied impatiently.

"Hurry," Sariah replied, "there's no time to lose."

"Would you like to do my job, Sariah?" Locknoff growled.

"I'm sorry. I—"

"I can handle my responsibility," Locknoff interrupted. "Just be sure you're ready when we get back. The council is waiting for an update." Locknoff shut the phone without waiting for her response. He then hurried back to the security office.

As he entered the secured area, Locknoff noticed that his partners were shaking hands with the security officer. They had several papers in their hands and were headed toward the exit. He waited patiently for their reunion, knowing some progress had been made. Locknoff was handed the papers a short distance from the door, and the three men walked out together. They stopped just shy of the lobby and began discussing the photos on the pages Locknoff now held. The first was of a woman with ash-brown hair that flowed just past her shoulders; she had royal-blue eyes and cheeks the color of pink rose petals. As Locknoff reviewed it, one partner pointed at the photo and said, "This is the woman Taren kissed, and the others were traveling with her. Three of them are still in the casino."

Locknoff looked briefly at the other five photos. Three of the women had dark-brown hair and brown eyes, one had black hair and brown eyes, and the other had green eyes and jet-black hair. He returned to the first photo and stopped, looking over it once more, and then headed for the lobby. The other men followed quickly after him, saying nothing.

When he reached the front desk, Locknoff asked to see the manager after placing the stack of photos on the desk. The attendant quickly called the manager and stepped slightly to the right to help the next customer in line. The moment the manager saw Locknoff and the others, she directed them to follow her. Locknoff grabbed the pages and complied.

"How can I be of assistance, Locknoff?" she asked once inside her office. "Please sit." She gestured to a couple of chairs on the other side of the desk as she took her seat. Locknoff handed her the photos.

"We need to find them."

"Certainly. Let me check the guest log." The manager turned to her computer and compared the photos against the guest log. She recognized only one of the six women and explained while printing off an information page.

"This young lady," she said, holding up a photo of the woman with jet-black hair and green eyes, "is Emily Townsman. Her license is registered in Los Angeles, California. Her hotel registration was part of a flight and hotel package online." The woman pulled a sheet of paper from the printer. "Her address is 3300 Overland University Drive, Los Angeles, California, 95151. She is registered as a guest here until noon tomorrow. Her room number is 417. As far as the other women…" She stopped, holding one of the photos. She turned it around to show a woman with brown hair and eyes and pointed to the printed line of information at the bottom of the page. "This one is Cara Johnson. Her license is registered here in New Mexico. The address is a short distance from here. The rest of them are not in our database."

Locknoff took the photos and printed information away from the manager and said, "Thank you, Feleet. You've been more than helpful."

"You're very welcome, Locknoff. Please let me know if you need anything else."

Locknoff and the others stood to exit the room. "Call me the moment Emily Townsman returns to her room."

"What now?" the bandaged man asked as they headed for the car.

"The council will decide, but I have a feeling we will be on recovery tonight."

Locknoff used the drive back to consider the day's events.

Three

REPORT

Ten twenty was what his watch displayed when Locknoff answered his students. "Time plays no part in the evaluation of a crop circle. Its investigation will always begin the same."

Suddenly, a crop circle began to form to the left of the small group of students. The students were speechless, and Locknoff focused his attention on the bending corn. The formation was fairly complicated yet simple. It resembled a corsage as the lines spiraled outward and then looped several times over. Locknoff wasted no time deciphering the message after one look at the completed formation. He called his assistant and released the class. "I need to make some phone calls. I'll be back as soon as I can."

"OK," responded his assistant, a tall, slim man just out of the acne phase. He wore a goatee and had auburn hair. "I'll get some readings before the press shows up."

Locknoff walked away with a concerned look in his eyes. He pulled the cell phone from his pocket. *Something had gone terribly wrong, that much was clear, but what?* he wondered.

"What is it, Ahdortee?" he asked, answering his phone midring.

"I'm not sure. Taren has left the house. He appears distressed. He's taken only one small bag. I don't think——"

"Follow him!" Locknoff shouted, cutting her off. "I'll be there as soon as I can." He boarded the first flight out of Spokane Washington, bound for Bethesda, Maryland. The flight offered him a unique opportunity for a nap, and he rested comfortably until the plane touched down.

"What's your location?" he asked Ahdortee while starting the engine of a rental car in the airport parking lot.

"Taren has just been joined by his assignment at a Rickmen's restaurant down the street from her employment," Ahdortee replied.

"Listen to the conversation. I'll be there as soon as I can." Locknoff placed the speaker on and listened in on the conversation while driving to meet Ahdortee. "Follow her," he ordered when Taren's wife got up to leave. "He's not likely to leave her now. I'll be there shortly."

When Locknoff pulled up, Taren was racing to catch his wife.

"Fall back," he told Ahdortee. "I'll handle this."

"We don't know——" Ahdortee began.

"*Fall back*, Ahdortee! We know he's running——that's enough for me." Rather than stopping her car, Ahdortee continued driving, and Locknoff pulled up to the curb directly across the street from a dry cleaner.

With no time to lose, he opened a small briefcase, pulled out a modified .357 with a silencer attached, and picked out a bullet. First he touched one of several in a row. They each had a rounded top and bottom. After a half second, he picked up a bullet from the second row. This row had bullets with rounded tops and arrow tails. Without hesitation, Locknoff loaded the round and fired the shot just as Taren's wife opened the door to step inside the cleaner. Locknoff returned the weapon and waited as Taren caught his wife and pulled her inside the cleaner.

Locknoff did not leave until Taren pulled away, at which point Locknoff headed for Cyder Memorial Hospital. Ahdortee joined him a short while later. The two waited patiently for the woman's body to arrive at the hospital morgue. When it did, they walked over to the information area and asked to speak with Dr. Kelly Morintine, who met them eagerly.

"How may I be of service to you, Locknoff?"

"A female body was brought in a short while ago. We need a scan."

"OK, I'll only be a few moments. Please wait for me here," Morintine said, gesturing to the waiting area behind them. Locknoff raised an eyebrow briefly but otherwise said nothing. After forty-five minutes, the doctor returned.

"Come with me," he ordered. Locknoff and Ahdortee exchanged a brief look but followed as directed. The three entered the morgue, and Locknoff was surprised to see that the woman's body was lying on a table, as if being prepared for an autopsy.

"What is this?" Locknoff asked angrily, pointing to the body.

"The military is here. That's why it took so long for me to get in here. They're conducting an autopsy." Locknoff and Ahdortee both looked at the body a moment longer before turning their attention to the doctor for his explanation. "The examiner has taken a break, and the guards are more interested in the soccer game."

"Where is the scan?" Locknoff asked.

"That's why I came to get you. On my way to retrieve the blood, I saw this," the examiner said while holding the dead woman's mouth open. "I would be glad to retrieve it now if you'd like, but I doubt it would do any good."

"No," Locknoff replied, looking intently at the spot on her tongue. He sighed. "Don't bother." He turned to walk away, but he was stunned into stilled silence with the doctor's next statement.

"There's more." Morintine held up an incomplete autopsy report. "I'm not sure if this matters, but she was pregnant." Locknoff looked up from the report with lowered brows and an expression of shocked disbelief. "Will you need the body?" the doctor continued.

"No." Locknoff's expression was agonizing for a brief moment as he looked at the doctor.

"Too much time has passed. The fetus will have been affected as well," Morintine said as Locknoff headed for the door. "Is that even possible?"

Locknoff paused a moment. "There's no other explanation than what we have in front of us, Doctor. I gather it's a question for the medical staff to answer." He turned and continued on his way.

Ahdortee had to be called twice as Locknoff exited the morgue. Her form was frozen, expressing just as much shock and disbelief at the doctor's words. Locknoff pushed a button on his phone as they exited the hospital.

"He's headed your way! Flush him out. We'll meet you there."

Locknoff and Ahdortee took the first flight to Ruidoso Downs, New Mexico. Locknoff knew that because of his actions, Taren would more than likely want to get in touch with the council. *And there was only one place he'd be going*, Locknoff said to himself.

The hotel parking lot was full by the time they arrived. Locknoff grunted, frustrated. "The concert...this crowd will make it more difficult to isolate him."

They headed for the lobby and reached it in time to see Taren go into the casino. Locknoff pulled out his phone, flipped it open, and held down a button until Taren was no longer in view. A blue light began to flash on the screen, and he told the four men following Taren to pull back. "We'll cut him off in the parking lot." Locknoff heard a report that Taren was charging. He ran at full speed the moment Taren was in his view.

◆ ◆ ◆

The short drive back was not enough to relieve his frustration, so when Locknoff returned to the compound, he walked directly over to Sariah's workstation with a glance at the clock. At this hour not many were about the facility, so he would have a private conversation. He turned on her screen.

"Greetings, Locknoff," Bathmantu said as the council meeting room became clear on the other side of the screen. "We have been waiting anxiously since Vishnu's report."

"What did Vishnu report?" Locknoff asked dismissively, cutting Bathmantu off.

"Patience, my friend. The council will be joining us momentarily. There is time. How is your health? It's been a long time since we've spoken."

"My health is of no consequence at the moment, Bathmantu. I simply must do what is necessary for Elquin."

"Indeed. However, you must keep up your strength in order to be of service to anyone." Their conversation was cut short as the other council members joined Bathmantu.

Once seated, they all looked to Locknoff as Elitar began.

"Greetings, Locknoff. What have you to report?"

Locknoff recounted the day's events with great detail. When he was done, he asked, "What report has Vishnu given?"

"Vishnu—" Bathmantu began.

"Why did you feel it necessary to kill his assignment without speaking to him first?" Nesset angrily interrupted

"Nesset," Locknoff replied shortly, "I was unaware of the circumstances to which Vishnu was running. However, my actions were nothing short of routine. Do not question me as if I were a young one on trial for misbehavior. I share my brother's loss just as you do—perhaps even more so."

"Yes," Skyke said, interrupting him, "we must discuss this new circumstance."

"Later perhaps," Bathmantu added. "We must pursue the orb."

"Later!" Skyke yelled, shocked at the interruption. "Vishnu has sent the orb on an unauthorized path with a simple request. We should honor his wishes."

"And we shall," Madafski replied. "However, we must have all the facts. Retrieve the orb. I fear there is more to this than a lost child."

"He is not seeking justice," Nesset said coldly. "Only our discussion of the latest developments. Do we not owe him this?"

"He knew the necessity of his assignment," Bathmantu said angrily, "and he has chosen to make this more challenging. We owe him nothing. We must find this girl."

"Enough!" Elitar interrupted, sternly cutting the conversation short. "We owe Vishnu more than we can give for his loss, and we will do as he has asked. However, Madafski is right—we need the orb. Retrieve it with haste, Locknoff. We haven't a moment to lose. We have lost another seven meters. Something must be done soon, or all is lost."

"Are there limits to my retrieval methods?" Locknoff asked expectantly.

"The orb was designed based on Vishnu's microbes alone. We haven't time to alter it," Elitar replied. "Retrieve it as you see fit, but keep in mind, Locknoff, you do have options. Sariah can work wonders around the microbe's design. Report back once you have the orb."

"What of Vishnu?" Nesset asked.

"Vishnu is not himself," Bathmantu replied. "He cannot be trusted to—"

"Once the council has decided to agree to his terms," Nesset interrupted, "he will be more willing to—"

"No," Elitar said, cutting her off. "Bathmantu is right. Vishnu must stay where he is for the moment. Find this woman, retrieve the orb, and report back."

"I shall," Locknoff replied. He signed off. With a sigh, he turned to leave and saw Sariah staring at him, her eyes judging.

"Taren is not untrustworthy," she said somewhat angrily as Locknoff exited her workstation.

"I will have a space of my own, Sariah," was all he said in response before walking out of the room.

Sariah plopped down at her workstation and repeated to no one, "He can be trusted." She looked at a photo on her desk of two young Elquin girls laughing. Running her fingers along the length of one of them longingly, Sariah was reminded of the first time she'd met Vishnu.

Four

OBLIGATION

Sariah sat behind her workstation looking through records and organizing patients' information based on their transport statuses. Her
crown of braids overlapped at the corners and appeared as three sepa-
rate crescents that almost covered her eyes. Her hair fell loosely down
her back. The bright star of Elquin shone through the hexagon window
onto her desk and arms. The star's rays made her arms darken into a
yellow-green pattern. She looked up at the sound of laughter as two
individuals entered her space.

"You're not afraid, are you, rookie?" the taller of the two asked.
He was dressed from head to toe in garb that made him look like a tree
trunk. *Today's tree must be midnight blue*, she thought. On the left side of
his shirt was an embroidered section with what looked like a horned
bird's skeleton whose wings were extended. His long, white hair was
pulled back with a band across his forehead. He was an ERT (Elquin
Recovery Team) Sariah recognized.

"First assignments always bring up undigested meals," he said, "but
for most, the meals have already been consumed." They both laughed
and looked at Sariah, who raised a brow.

"Sorry," the taller man said. "The rookie's going out today and
needs to be cleared."

"Is there something I should know, Master Locknoff?" Sariah asked skeptically.

"He was sick at council this morning."

"But I'm fine now," the rookie said, enthusiastically cutting him off.

"All the same, we should take a look at you," Sariah responded. "This way," she said as she walked over to a table and patted it while looking at the rookie. He appeared to be just a few years younger than Sariah, who had just joined the medical staff after only recently completing her master's training. The young male was fairly muscular for his age and wore a pair of black pants with army boots. He had on a black belt with a gold buckle. A black T-shirt completed the outfit. There were white letters over the left breast that read ERT. Above the letters was an embroidered symbol of two doves facing each other, interlocked at the neck. His white hair was pulled back and braided into a single long braid that dangled just past his shoulder blades.

"What's your name?"

"Vishnu," the rookie replied. "This is my first official assignment." He smiled proudly.

"I gathered as much," Sariah replied with a smile of her own. "Lie back and try to relax." Sariah walked to the end of the table and pushed a button. A large arch that was attached to the head of the table and along its width passed over him, displaying an array of lights. It stopped at the foot of the table and displayed a digital image of his body into the air. She pushed another button, and the muscles were removed. She pushed yet another button and revealed the body's inner systems. Sariah enlarged the midsection for a few moments, examined it, and then pushed a button on the table to remove the display while replacing the arch. She then motioned for Vishnu to get up.

"Nothing appears to be out of order, though I would suggest a good meal and a couple hours of rest."

"See?" Vishnu said, looking at Locknoff smugly. "I told you I was fine."

Laughing, Locknoff hit him on the back. "Well, better to be safe. I'd rather not have my strongest rookie in a pieleen down because of illness."

The two men walked out of her office, and Sariah went back to work. Moments later, she was interrupted again by a much older female dressed from head to toe in blue. The white braids on her forehead were wrapped with gold strands, and ruby stones were woven through them. She moved with a grace that demanded respect.

"Am I interrupting something vitally important, child?" she asked expectantly.

"Zeeporah!" Sariah exclaimed, jumping to her feet. "No, I was just organizing some responsibilities. How may I be of assistance?"

Zeeporah nodded her head briefly in response to Sariah's greeting and said, "I need to speak with you regarding an important matter. Is there a private space here?"

"Yes, this way," Sariah responded, leading Zeeporah into an office space just past the last of several worktables. When the passageway closed behind them, Zeeporah settled in one of the chairs and began to speak.

"There has been a development on Oororah-9. Diplomacy has failed us, and the council has decided against farming. A ship is leaving to retrieve our stationed members there later today. Your presence is requested on the planet to aid the injured."

Sariah gasped, her mouth falling open. She changed three different shades of green. Zeeporah cleared her throat, and Sariah regained herself.

"Oororah...9?" she said questioningly.

"Yes, the station is being evacuated, but battle has left them without a medical officer. You are—"

"My sister," Sariah interrupted, "has she been evacuated?"

"No, the council has been taken. The ERT has been called on to retrieve them and any others under duress. You're welcome to deny the assignment, but—"

"No," Sariah exclaimed. She took a deep breath, settling herself at the look in Zeeporah's eyes. "No, I would be delighted to help."

"Then it's settled," Zeeporah said, satisfied. Getting to her feet, she continued, "Prepare yourself. The ship leaves in three hours."

Shock covered Sariah's face once again as Zeeporah walked out of the medical facility without another glance in her direction. Sariah stood there unmoving for several moments until she remembered she'd forgotten to breathe. Her assistant called to her.

"What is it?" he asked, taking in the look of despair on Sariah's face.

"I have been called to assignment on Oororah-9."

"Oororah-9!" he gasped, horrified. "But wha—"

"I will be leaving in a few hours," she said. She shook her head. "Don't worry, dear Churvack. Another medical officer will replace me shortly. I do not anticipate being gone long, seeing as Oororah-9 is being evacuated."

"Evacuated!" Churvack gasped again. "But your sister…"

"Will be returning to Elquin soon," she managed to say with confidence. "As will I. See that my station is running at full order during my absence, Churvack. I'm counting on you."

"And so it shall," he responded with a nod, confusion clear across his features.

Sariah hurried to gather her things so she could be ready in time for the ship's departure. She found concentration difficult, as her thoughts kept returning to her younger sister, Youkoni. Youkoni had only recently joined the council and had been called to Oororah-9 within days of her nomination. "No," Sariah said aloud, denying the thoughts that threatened to claim her sister's life. "She will make it home alive. I'll make sure of it."

She took time to visit the archives and talk to whomever she could with regard to the situation before boarding began. The time passed as a blur for her, and Sariah still had more questions than answers, but nothing kept her from boarding the ship when the time came.

It was unlike anything she'd ever seen. From the outside, the ship appeared to be a vast sphere with legs and webbed feet. The inside was breathtaking. There were rivers and streams, landscapes and moons, buildings, bridges, and roads. Sariah was breathless. It resembled a small world inside, and she briefly wondered how it was constructed. She was directed to her rooms, which were to the left of the ship's entrance. They wound upward and to the left of what resembled an orange willow whose branches just barely touched the ground. Sariah could see the willow from her rooms and wondered how her sister was holding up. Without time to consider much, she was interrupted by a knock on the door.

"Enter," she said with a sigh. Sariah turned to see a young Elquin whose braids crowned her head in a way that outlined the beauty of her dark-auburn eyes.

"Pardon the interruption, Master Sariah, but your presence is required in the medical bay."

"Thank you..." she responded, unsure of the young Elquin's name.

"Deverah," the young Elquin said.

"Thank you, Deverah."

Sariah followed Deverah hastily, wondering what could be so important that required her presence so quickly, until she remembered Zeeporah's words about Oororah-9's medical officer. *Maybe I'm the only officer on board as well*, she thought. When she reached the medical bay, she was surprised to see so many staff about. They all seemed busy as they hurried along. *Preparing for the effects of war*, she thought glumly.

"Sariah!" a familiar voice called sternly. She turned to recognize her childhood friend.

"Tomahbare!" she said excitedly as she ran toward him. She threw her arms around as much of his large frame as she could and asked to his well-being.

"We must speak," he replied with concerned eyes as he led her to the medical officers' work space.

Behind closed doors, Sariah asked, "If you're here, Tomahbare, why am I needed?" Confusion was clear across her features.

"I'm stationed on the ship, Sari. Your duty is Oororah-9. Although I still do not understand why you're the one to...There's been a complication, Sariah."

"I know about the council's condition," she said. "Zeeporah was all too happy to lay that one on me."

"Ah, yes," he said, nodding as if he now understood. "Well, prepare yourself. Things have been deteriorating rapidly. Two council members have been killed."

Sariah's breath stopped instantly as she gasped. Her eyes grew, and goose bumps rose on her arms. She gave Tomahbare a pained look.

"As far as I know," he said, watching her expression, "your sister's still alive. Rest assured, the ERT will bring her home safely."

"Of course," Sariah replied, but the pain was still there.

"It shouldn't take long for us to reach Oororah-9. You'll see her before you know it."

"I can't stand it, Toma. She's too young for this mission. She's barely had time to grow into her crown."

"She was ready for that crown six moons ago, Sariah. She may be your younger sister, but she is not exactly a young one." Sariah sighed as Tomahbare continued, "She's of the Grendore bloodline."

Her mood shifted suddenly to one of pride, and her back straightened. Tomahbare smiled.

"Strong of will and mind," he continued. "It's only natural that the council saw her potential. She has been through much. You both have, and it's only made you stronger. She will draw on your strength, as you have drawn on hers, and you'll both make it through this."

"Is that an official reading then, Tomahbare?" Sariah asked, smiling.

"Ha!" he replied. He kneeled in front of her and looked into her eyes. "I do not need a reading to see your future, Sariah. Your hearts sing to me. They always have. You'll make it back. You both will."

Sariah was speechless as she looked at him. She saw the warmth in his eyes and knew he was right. There was no point in dwelling on the negative. Her sister would make it home...somehow. She threw her arms around him again.

"Thank you, Toma. I'm glad you're here. This journey will be less painful now."

"You're welcome," he replied, putting his arms around her. "Whatever you need."

Sariah looked at his warm almond eyes and knew his hearts called out to her as well. At the sound of his name from the other side of the sliding doors, Tomahbare stood, pulling her along, not taking his eyes off of her, and said, "We shall have a meal together upon your safe return."

"Indeed," Sariah replied, smiling. She lifted onto her toes, kissed his cheeks, and returned to her rooms.

The ship did not take long as Tomahbare had promised, and soon Sariah found herself sitting on board a shuttle bound for Oororah-9. The ride was smooth until the pilot was forced to maneuver around the oncoming burst of energy rounds being fired from the planet's surface. Sariah held on to the thought of her sister safe and sound on the surface, just waiting for her to arrive. Within minutes, the shuttle touched down on the edge of the Elquin campsite, near the heart of Oororah-9.

Five

CAMPED

Clouds of white, orange, and red filled the sky as far as Sariah could see. She noted brilliant colors of orange, green, gold, and blue within the surrounding forest. She barely had time to glance as she was ushered toward the building, passing huge mounds of various sizes, silver in color to match the dirt. In the distance, Sariah could hear sounds of weapons being fired, which would explain the clouds of smoke rising from various areas within the forest. Sariah's attention returned to the path ahead.

Directly in front of her was a mountain that stretched toward the sky. The rich, silvery dirt almost gleamed in the sunlight. To the right of the mountain sat a large, cone-shaped apparatus with intricately cut grooves spiraling along the top and point of the cone. It stood dusty with a silvery shine that had the consistency of powder. To the left and right of the large tool laid several long pipes with oversized pottery bowls connected to them somehow. The bowls were big enough to hold several individuals. Small tools lay tossed about on the ground.

"A mine," Sariah said aloud as she connected the images in front of her with the memory of mining tools used by her brothers before they'd joined the battle efforts. Doors opened out of nowhere, and a frenzy of movement surrounded her. Standing tall, Sariah focused on the path ahead. Stepping into the mysterious mountain, she was suddenly reminded of how many wonders the universe held.

The room was shaped like an oval. There were double doors about three hundred yards from the entrance and several smaller doors to the left and right of them. The floor was covered with a painting of Elquin, its bright star, and all twenty-eight moons currently under her reign. The painting looked like a masterpiece and appeared to account for all the lifeless stars in the sky as well. Sariah was reluctantly drawn away from her observation while hastily being led to the medical facility.

When she walked inside, her eyes widened, and she gasped. The room was bright, almost as bright as the Elquin sun. Several Elquins lay on the floor. All seats were taken by the injured or the dying. Moans of what could only be taken for agony were heard echoing throughout the small space. There were four worktables, but each was occupied. All three medical staff members were examining digital images of Elquins projected from the tables.

Suddenly all the staff rushed over to a worktable in the far left corner, leaving their patients where they lay for the moment. Alarms sounded and blinking lights echoed.

"Everyone ready for transport are to leave with me," said the young Elquin who escorted Sariah.

A flood of movement began as Elquins started heading toward the exit. Most appeared to be comfortable. Four, however, had to be carried out on floating tables. Sariah's survey of the remaining injured was interrupted when she saw the blinking lights. A patient's projected image causing the alarms displayed two large hearts on either side of his lungs, which were in the center of his chest. Sariah's brows lowered as she looked on. The heart on the right was enlarged and pulsing uncharacteristically faster than normal. The heart on the left was barely pulsing due to the spikes that seemed to be shooting out of every direction. They were seemingly sourced from within. The spikes moved outward several centimeters for a short moment, and the patient howled in agony.

One of the staff injected an orange liquid into the arm of the patient, and one of the others held his hand and started speaking in hushed tones. "We are doing all we can, but the pebble is expanding. We'll have to work delicately as we remove the thorns we see. Rest, and all will be well soon."

Sariah had seen this happen before; it was during her final lessons. She was confronted with a test patient who had been injured on the battlefield, carried to safety by one of his battle brothers. The pebble had entered his leg. The medical team had been unable to do anything but keep the splinters cut before the pebble unexpectedly burst, and he lost his leg. The students had had a difficult time deciphering how to remove the pebble safely. It was determined that the pebble had lodged itself so deeply in the muscle that nothing short of slicing it off would be effective, because the splinters just grew larger every time they were cut. Eventually the pebble had burst.

Wasting no time with formalities, Sariah stepped over a young female who lay on a padded mat. She grabbed two syringes off the tray beside the worktable, knocking the medical staff member who had given the injection out of her way, and then injected a black, misty substance directly into the center of the patient's spiky heart. Sariah followed that with injecting the other heart with a green substance. She stepped back and looked at the floating image.

"How dare you!" the attending staff shrieked at her. "Who are you to—"

She cut off, turning to watch the alarms and images. Within seconds, the right heart was beating at a slower rhythm, and the left heart began responding to the reduction in pressure caused by the pebble. The injected nanoids removed the individual spikes from the pebble's base and worked to destroy the pebble itself from within the heart. The steroids decreased the pressure on the other heart, and the patient's breathing became less labored.

"Get him to a shuttle," Sariah barked at one of the staff members, "and see to your patients. I am Master Sariah of the Grendore bloodline, and I will see these injured Elquins to a shuttle within the hour." Scrambling to their tasks, the staff complied without another word.

Sariah's mood lightened as the day progressed. Her patients were stabilized enough to be transported off the planet, and she found that the worries she'd had about her sister were lessoned by her workload. The injured came in waves, as she wasted no time getting her staff to focus on the task at hand.

"What happened to your last master?" she asked, taking a break after the tenth group of patients was transported out. Dorlam, a middle-aged Elquin who'd recently lost half the length of his hair and never saw fit to tie it down, was one of the second rotating staff members. His hair shifted as he turned to address her.

"Master Sunden of the Albitroin bloodline was lost in a battle that took place fairly close to this installation. He felt it necessary to treat patients who could not come to him. When the soldiers finally encouraged the Oororan fighters to pull back, we found him. Half his body was lost to an energy blast from close range. The attack was short, but cannon fire kept us from getting close enough to assist him before it was too late. He saved forty-three Elquins that day, and we have not had time to mourn him."

"We will," Sariah replied. "In time we will mourn them all."

"Yes, Master Sariah, I believe we will," Dorlam replied.

Sariah saw to patients until there was no one left before retiring to her quarters. Her fatigue was distant in her mind as she worked to shelve her belongings, which had been brought directly to her room by one of her staff members. She knew her time would be short lived here, but she was determined to be as comfortable as the situation would allow. Sariah worked swiftly.

Forty-three lives, she thought. *Sunden was proud. Everyone knows you don't run into a hopeless situation without all the facts. But what else was he to do? Lives were at stake. He's saved hundreds in the past by staying where he was needed most. I aim to save everyone left on this world, my sister included. We will leave this rock together.*

Sariah found sleep easily that night and rested well. When morning came, she moved swiftly to get back to work.

Sariah's days were filled with the injured, her nights tormented by images of her sister mutilated. She woke often throughout the night, gasping at the sight of her sister's limbs spread across the camp. Once, her head sat on top of a tree. Seventeen others decorated the woods; all were members of the council that had been taken during negotiations with Oororah-9 representatives.

On the morning of her fifth day, when Sariah walked into the medical bay and saw four injured ERT members, she gasped. Many of the fighters and civilians had been evacuated. However, injured ERT meant things were taking a turn for the worse. Keeping her emotions in check, Sariah spoke.

"What happened?" she asked calmly, moving to perform her normal tasks of the morning.

"We were on a recovery mission," the patient responded. She was a young Elquin. Her long, white hair was pulled into one braid that dangled to her waist. She wore a headband and ERT uniform. Her rank was difficult to determine because her uniform was stained with blood from her injuries, but Sariah could see the emblem on her belt buckle that indicated her veteran status.

Six

TRAIL OF DEATH

"We found the location of the council."

Sariah froze.

"We were injured during the rescue."

"They're here?" Sariah asked with no attempt at masking her excitement.

"Not all of them. We were able to recover seven of the—"

"Rashanah!" Locknoff interrupted her as he walked into the medical bay with Vishnu close behind. Rashanah's eyes lowered, and Locknoff spoke directly to Sariah. "We've rescued nine council members. Four were killed in the attempt, and four are still being held. We have been given one day to evacuate everyone else. If we have any hope of recovering the other four members, we must comply."

"There is a young female on the council," Sariah says. "She is—"

"Your sister was not one of the recovered," Locknoff interrupted. "Nor was she among the dead. For now, we have to assume she is alive. You and your staff are to report to the shuttle bay by midday."

"Master Locknoff," Sariah said calmly, "may I speak with you privately?"

"I'm sorry, Sariah, but I have many things to address at the moment. We will speak once the evacuation is complete." Locknoff turned for the door.

"I will not leave without my sister!" Sariah shrieked angrily. "I did not come all this way to leave her here."

"You endanger her life and yours by staying," Locknoff replied as he turned to face her with a look in his eyes that said she should understand.

"Master Locknoff," Sariah said calmly, her emotions now under a bit more control, "there are some things more important than even my own life."

"Would you put the other council members' lives in danger just to recover your sister?"

"I cannot leave without her," was Sariah's only reply.

Locknoff opened his mouth, prepared to address her again, when Vishnu suddenly spoke. "Master Sariah, I will bring your sister home... on my honor."

"Please," Locknoff said, looking wide eyed at Vishnu, "we must keep Elquin safe from further political distress, which means following procedure. We will do all we can, Sariah, and perhaps you will be reunited with your sister sooner than you think, but now you must go."

Sariah looked at Vishnu for a long moment with pleading eyes and then relaxed as she took in his expression. "On your honor," she repeated softly. Vishnu nodded. "Her name is Youkoni," Sariah said. "She's young, very young. She has never cut her hair, so the length reaches past her knees. Return safely." Sariah then turned and headed to her rooms.

While looking over the photo once more before placing it with her belongings, Sariah suddenly became aware of screams coming from all over the camp. Gripping her belongings tightly, Sariah ran out to the main doors of the building, trying to see what had happened. She froze in fear where she stood. There, on the ground just three feet from the monstrous doors, lay a head. His silvery white hair was blowing in the wind. Sariah recognized the face as Ahovin of the Tocowie bloodline.

Ahovin was the senior council member assigned to the Oororah-9 embassy mission. He was one of the oldest Elquins Sariah knew. He had taken this assignment as a sign to others of the dire need for resources. Many saw the wisdom in his decision. Youkoni was one of those inspired by him, and she'd joined the council when he'd come out of retirement to go on this mission.

Within seconds, twenty ERT surrounded Sariah.

"Fan out!" Locknoff barked. "Check the tree line, five thousand yards. Ahdortee, Fandore, Porock, Jussalte…" Two females and two males stepped forward at the sound of their names. "Get everyone else to the shuttle bay. We leave immediately. Vishnu, load up. We bring our remaining council with us now! Oororah-9 has shamed itself in this act of treason, and I will not stand by and let them continue to kill Elquins."

Sariah briefly locked eyes with Vishnu, a look of panic and pleading in her eyes. He nodded, and she slowly turned to join the gathered Elquins preparing to head for the shuttle bay.

The trip to the shuttle bay was somewhat different than the path Sariah had taken when she'd arrived. Due to the evacuations, there was a permanent boarding site just under a mile away from the building. Sariah had insisted on keeping one full day's rotation of medical staff members on Oororah-9, so when she was instructed to evacuate, she and the six staff members were hard pressed to get out in time. Satisfaction overwhelmed her as she looked through the group walking in hurried paces and noticed that all six remaining staff members had moved fast enough to make this trip with her. That feeling did not last long, however, as she noticed the concerned looks of the ERT that escorted them.

The four ERT had surrounded the group, one on each corner of the walking Elquins. They were all dressed in black from head to toe. Their shirts were tucked into their pants, and black vests covered their insignias. Each one wore a belt that held a large disk in back with a staff peering through either side of it. The staff seemed to be molded to the shape of their waists, and the belt buckle had the ERT emblem. Every vest pocket was bulging.

After what seemed to be a very short time to Sariah, the group halted. Sariah's gaze shifted to the front, where she could see that two ERT were discussing something. The conversation took only seconds, and then everyone was hurried off the path and instructed to get down. From her view, Sariah could see the shuttle bay. *Wow, we must have been walking faster than I thought. What's the hold up?* she wondered.

There were five shuttles. They looked like oversized pebbles, each one with its doors open. There was slight movement inside. The bright red-and-blue flashing lights behind the entry pathway indicated that the shuttle was preparing for departure. Sariah began to speak but quickly thought better of it when she noticed the ERT were suddenly armed and looking intently at the trees between the second and third shuttles. To Sariah's horror, several Oororan fighters were setting up to fire at the shuttles.

The weapon was difficult to handle. It took three of them just to hold its legs, and another four to hold the mounting device. When they had determined where to place it, they put the legs down and collectively picked up the mount. It was secured on top of the legs with care. The weapon was large and shaped like a cylinder. It was camouflaged to resemble the surrounding forest. Sariah instantly thought of the mounds she passed on her way into the medical facility. She dove onto her belly when she heard the energy burst from the ERT weapon next to her. She watched in horror as the blue-and-white light burned the individuals around the cylinder. The weapon was knocked onto the ground, and part of it was simply gone.

There was nothing she would do. The Oororans were preparing to kill them all. After the initial blast, the fighters were on guard. They had sensed exactly where the burst had come from and were now focusing their attack on the gathered party. Sariah wished she knew what was happening with her sister. She wanted the opportunity to say goodbye if this was her last moment to live.

Elquins fell dead on every side of her. Treating the injured as she inched forward, Sariah began to feel sick to her stomach with fear for them all. There was nothing more she could do. Suddenly energy bursts seemed to come from every direction at once; bright lights were everywhere. Sariah looked up in time to see that a tree directly behind the ERT standing beside her was blasted. She was flung through the air and...darkness.

No, Sariah cried internally. *Youkoni...I will see you safely home...
Youkoni...*

The darkness was all around her, and all she could hear was the rhythmic beating of her hearts.

Seven

Reunited

Suddenly Sariah could hear ringing in her ears. Abruptly, shouting overtook the ringing. She tried unsuccessfully to open her eyes. She could hear someone calling her name. A few more tries, and she could see. Youkoni was kneeling over her, her face troubled.

"Sariah," she crooned. A smile covered her stressed features. She bent down to hug her sister, and they were both encircled in Youkoni's long, unkept hair. Youkoni was stressed and dirty, but happy. She pulled Sariah up into a sitting position and smiled. "You look tired."

"And you look like you've been sleeping on a bed of leaves and dirt half your life," Sariah replied. Silvery dirt covered Sariah and Youkoni as they reached for each other again to embrace, laughing. Before either could say another word, Vishnu knocked both of them to the ground. His arm covered his face as he shielded them all from the force of a deadly spear.

He had a round disk on his arm. Sariah noted that it looked like the disk she'd seen earlier on the ERT belts. The disk was somehow extended on all sides. There was a pebble formation that encircled it, making its shape big enough to shield his head and chest. Sariah scrambled to her feet and threw herself at Youkoni, protectively shielding her as best she could while watching Vishnu. She noticed other ERT and Oororan fighters engaged in close combat. Most of the Elquins still alive ran or helped one another to the safety of the shuttles.

Sariah locked her eyes on Vishnu as she heard the loud thud that was his shield falling to the ground. With wide eyes she watched as Vishnu tumbled to the ground. He rolled backward and landed in a crouched position. He maintained the grip on his staff, only it was pulled into two equal halves. There were knives on each end of the two pieces, which curved up and slightly inward. Vishnu brought his hands around in time to block a deadly blow to his neck.

With a twist of his right wrist, he sliced the top end of the spear pointed at his neck. He then spun to the right, slicing what remained of the staff. As he came back around, he moved closer and continued slicing with every pass. After his third spin, he crouched with weapons in hand and arms back. The bloodied Oororan fighter stood motionless for a moment and then fell forward piece by piece. Vishnu looked expectedly to his left and right but saw no others advancing on him. He turned and walked toward Sariah and Youkoni but froze at their expressions.

He put his staff back together by retreating the knives, interlocking the two pieces at the ends before replacing it on his belt. He then walked toward them hurriedly. As Vishnu bent to help them up, he was attacked from behind. A very large Oororan fighter wrapped his arms around Vishnu's waist and pulled him up into the air. Vishnu leaned forward, bending at the waist. His feet made contact with the ground, but the fighter still had a tight grip on him, squeezing with all his strength.

Vishnu twisted upward and brought his elbow around swiftly to strike the fighter in the head. He quickly repeated the strike with his other elbow. The fighter did not seem stunned at all, so Vishnu repeated his strikes several times using all his strength. After the third strike on either side, he then bent to roll on the ground. As he came around, he had the fighter's leg securely in his grip, trapping him. Vishnu pulled swiftly, and both Sariah and Youkoni cringed from the tearing and ripping sound that escaped the fighter's limbs. Vishnu came around with a final elbow to the fighter's chest and head. There was no more movement from the fighter afterward, so Vishnu got to his feet, helped the females up, and swiftly headed for the shuttles.

Several paces from the ship, however, Vishnu stopped suddenly. To his left, a fighter was tangled with Locknoff in close combat. Vishnu motioned for Sariah and Youkoni to get down. He moved quickly and silently behind the fighter, who had Locknoff secured in a headlock and was now reaching for his knife. With his left hand, Vishnu swiftly lifted the fighter's head. He placed his arm under the Ororoan's neck, completely cutting off his air supply. The fighter went down within seconds, and Locknoff sat up just in time to catch the knife as it left the fighter's hand. He tossed it swiftly behind Vishnu's right shoulder, hitting another fighter in the head, effectively ending his advance.

Vishnu held out his hand to help Locknoff up. Locknoff smiled, took his hand, and spoke while getting to his feet. "I'll remember next time to look to the east. Ha, guess you've earned that."

Vishnu looked down at his hand with wide eyes. There in his palm lay a belt buckle with the ERT emblem. Vishnu smiled proudly and placed it in his pocket.

"Congratulations, brother," Locknoff said, hitting him on the back.

Vishnu turned to look at Sariah and Youkoni. "Master Sariah," he said with proud confidence, "it's time to leave this rock."

"With pleasure," she responded breathlessly, walking toward them. Sariah stopped at the shuttle doors, turned to Vishnu, and said, "Thank you. I am more grateful than you will ever know. Perhaps I can repay your bravery in time."

"There is no need for repayment, Master—"

"Please call me Sariah."

"Sariah, I have simply done my expected duty. Please think no more of it."

She turned to Youkoni, who had come to her side, and they both looked at him with gratitude.

"As you wish," Sariah said and turned to board the shuttle, wrapped in Youkoni's arms.

◆ ◆ ◆

Sariah blinked away tears as she remembered her sister. "No," she said aloud. "He may be a lot of things, but untrustworthy is not one of them."

Sariah was confident now; she would help Taren somehow. She understood his loss almost better than anyone. They'd both struggled after the death of Youkoni, but she'd never had the opportunity to repay him for his bravery that day. She would today; somehow she would ease his suffering.

"But how?" she asked no one, walking toward the room he was being held in.

As she reached the door, Locknoff walked up behind her and peered into the small window on the door. Taren was pacing back and forth across the small space, anger clear across his features.

"Try as you may, Sariah, but he won't tell you a thing. I intend to fix what he has done."

"How?" she interrupted.

A cruel smile spread across his lips, and he raised an eyebrow.

Sariah sighed. "By killing more humans," she said in a disgusted tone.

"It is because of his actions that more will die," he said, gesturing to the door. "You need not worry, Sariah. I intend to…" He trailed off as his phone rang, and his gaze fell on the caller ID. "Yes, Feleet," he said, turning away from Sariah.

She looked at Taren longingly as she tried to think of a way to help him.

"Good," Locknoff said, interrupting her thoughts, "we're on the way. Detain her if she tries to leave before we get there." Locknoff ended the call and looked Sariah in the eyes. "I will handle this as I see fit. Just be ready when we get back." He walked away and began yelling names: Ahdortee, Porock, Jus...

Sariah stopped listening when Taren's gaze fell on her. She took a deep breath, typed in a code on the keypad, and opened the door. Taren turned away from her and continued his pacing. When the door closed behind her, his angry gaze looked past her at those guarding the door. She turned her head slightly and sighed at the ERT standing there.

"Taren," she said, claiming his attention. His angry gaze fixed on her, and she stepped back slightly.

Taren sighed. "I'm not going to hurt you, Sariah." His eyes were slightly softer, but anger still burned in them.

"Taren," she repeated, swallowing the lump in her throat, "what do you know about the orb?"

Eight

The Orb

"The orb," Taren replied, confusion replacing anger for the moment. "Yes."

"Well, it was designed to respond to my genetic microbes."

"Yes," Sariah said encouragingly.

"I'm the only one who can remove it from the host while they still live. What's your point, Sariah? We both know what I did with it."

"The orb," she began in a lecturing tone, "is a protein-based data synthesizer. It obtains information through its link to the host's central nervous system. The orb distributes its components throughout the host's body until it reaches the most powerful nerve endings. It then releases the components its design requires. The host responds by providing the answers from collected memories or the input of outside influences, like the information your assignment provided for the council."

"I understand the mechanics, Sariah—what's your point?"

"My point," Sariah said with a hint of irritation at the interruption, "is to remind you of its flaw."

"Flaw?"

"Yes. The orb was designed shortly after diplomatic relations began on Oororah-9. After its successful trials were conducted on Ratier, informants were sent to Oororah-9 to search for detritus deposits. The Oororans were confident in our inability to locate the detritus deposits on their world and only agreed to the council's initial terms."

"We could look," Taren said, sitting on the edge of the bed and focusing on Sariah's words as she sat down.

"Yes, but if we found any, we were to negotiate terms of extraction. It was difficult in the beginning because traditional methods yielded very little, if anything. After six months, the council approved the orb's use. Bathmantu was assigned to one of the local villages. He befriended many Oororans within the surrounding villages and developed a close bond with one of the young females there, Naubo of the Dracora tribe.

"She was beautiful, even for Oororan standards. She was Persian orange and had large, brown locks that hung down her shoulders. The top of her head was decorated with shorter brown locks and the leaves and branches of the nearby forest. Her eyes were shaped like a large cat, the color of almonds. The tops of her ears were pointed, and they curled toward her flowing brown locks. On either side of her neck were several rows of almost fishlike gills that she often kept hidden under her long hair.

"She had a thin line of eyebrows and a row of dark-brown dots under each eye that arched to the tip of her eyebrows. From the base of her nose to the tips of her ears was a thick, ropelike patch of skin embedded in her cheeks. Shortly after their relationship began, we found three cerium deposits. The sites yielded more on the surface alone than Elquin had found in any single mine under her reign.

"Oororah-9's panel of officials were shocked, to say the least, and reluctantly agreed to the mining of only two of the three discovered sites. They then forbade any friendship between our worlds. Naubo was ordered to relinquish her relationship with Bathmantu. The council ordered Bathmantu to retrieve the orb without incident. However, Bathmantu found it impossible to get near her. He had no choice but to wait for an opening, lest he risk war between our worlds. He'd tried several times but was forcefully refused a meeting with her.

"After roughly forty-five days, Bathmantu returned to the Dracora and asked to say good-bye to Naubo. He said that he'd been called back to Elquin. He was once again refused but informed that she was ill. The village did not know what was wrong with her, only that her strength decreased by the day and that her eyes let off a strange glow. Everyone was kept away for fear of her illness spreading. He was turned away with weapons when he said that he didn't care if he got sick.

"Taking a longer path through the forest than necessary to consider his options, Bathmantu stumbled upon a lake. He looked up to find Naubo sprawled on top of a rock by the river, with her toes dangling in the water. The edges of her long, brown hair lightly brushed the ground. When Bathmantu approached her, he was shocked to see her condition. Naubo's skin was a pale champagne, her ears drooped, and her pupils were glowing a bright Maya blue. 'Bathu,' she cooed, smiling when she saw him. Bathmantu froze midstride. She'd just called him by the youngling name his mother used often. He'd never told her of it.

"He walked toward her cautiously, now eager to ask where she'd heard the name, but when he did, Naubo just smiled and looked at him. She told him she didn't know. She'd just woken up one morning and knew, as if it was part of her own memory. She then described his childhood home with perfect accuracy. Bathmantu was stunned and intrigued. He stepped closer to her, but she waved him back, saying that she was struck with a strange illness. Bathmantu shrugged and moved closer still. He kneeled next to the rock she lay on and looked into her eyes.

"It was then he realized that the brown in her eyes was still there. The blue seemed to be glowing from behind her pupils. She was near death, he realized, and the orb was the source of it. With frantic determination, he pulled her close and kissed her. He was too late. Her exhausted body gave its last breath. With her limp body in his arms, he held her tight and cried. Bathmantu wept until he heard the village protectors approaching. He released her body, gently laying her back down on the rock. While doing so, he noticed her mouth glowing bright blue.

"Bathmantu parted her lips slightly to investigate further, and the orb lifted from within her body. It moved approximately five inches upward and hovered. Bathmantu encased the orb, put it into his pocket, and kissed Naubo once more on the head. He laid her back down on the rock and turned to leave, but he stopped instantly as he came face to face with a six-man patrol unit. Their expressions of horror at what they'd just witnessed mirrored his own feelings at what he was responsible for doing to her.

"Bathmantu bolted through the woods. Not wanting to be responsible for any more death and desperately needing some answers, he ran. When he could no longer run, he hid. When he could no longer run or hide, he faced his pursuers, the very beings he'd befriended. Despair tugged at his hearts but lessened slightly when he noticed that only four of the six now pursued him. *Two must have returned for reinforcements*, he reasoned. It would only make matters worse if he did not make it back to the Elquin council. He pulled the knife from his boot and hid behind a sharuba tree."

"Sharuba tree?" Taren interrupted skeptically. "What's a sharuba tree, and how do you know so many details about his assignment? You didn't get to Oororah-9 until I did."

"You forget, Taren, Youkoni was my responsibility long before she was yours. When diplomacy failed on Oororah-9, I wanted to know why." Sariah sighed. "I had to take the chance presented to be on the extraction team, Taren. She was my sister."

"I know, Sariah...I know."

"I reviewed the orb text before we left for Oororah-9 because I had to know more about it, along with Bathmantu's experience. That which was not scrolled, I squeezed out of him personally. I figured knowing the details would help me understand how to counter the orb's behavior to our benefit later. And a sharuba tree is the main source of sustenance for many of the tribes in the Bouju forest on Oororah-9." Sariah gave Taren a look of annoyance and said, "Please let me finish before you ask any more questions. It's frustrating."

"All right, all right," Taren said, throwing his hands up defensively, gesturing for her to continue.

"The blue-green leaves of the sharuba tree worked well to hide him from the protectors. He concluded he would face them individually and set out on his first target. The males all had features similar to Naubo's, but their ears were pointed more upward than back, and they had two rows of braided flesh looping from the base of their noses to their ears. Many of them kept their hair short. The protectors, however, wore it long and free flowing. Some braided their hair, but most were not. They often decorated their flowing locks with twigs, leaves, or thongs constructed from tree vines or the large leaves of healthy trees.

"The protectors were scattered but could still see each other, for the most part. They could not see much below the waist, however, because of the forest growth. Bathmantu crouched as low as he could beside one of the trees. He then leaped for the feet closest to him. As the protector fell, shocked, Bathmantu lunged at his head and stabbed him in the neck before he could regain his bearings. Bathmantu hurriedly crouched behind a nearby shrub. The other three males gasped and hurried to their fallen brother when he did not get up. With shrieking agony, they let out a wail that made Bathmantu cover his ears in pain. With renewed determination, they set out to find him. Separating again, they leaped forward in a sprint, aware of every single movement within sight.

"Bathmantu ran after them as quietly as he could. He lunged forward, leading with his knife when he was close enough to touch the male in front of him. As the male turned to the approaching shift in wind, he had time only to see the knife piercing his left eye socket as Bathmantu landed on his chest, pushing him to the ground. As they both fell, Bathmantu rolled, pulling the agonized man on top of him and breaking his neck in one swift motion. Bathmantu tossed the body aside and retrieved his knife. The leader called for the trio to stop when he heard a thump and turned to see only one other behind him.

"'Mickrey! Mickrey!' The lead male shouted frantically, looking about.

"'He has fallen, Kuopo,' the other said, stopping when he reached his side. 'We must stay together.' With a nod, the two men started walking swiftly in the other direction.

"'*Bathmantu!*' Kuopo cried after walking three hundred yards. 'Face me with honor, demon, for you have brought death to our people, and now it is your time to die.'

"Bathmantu inched closer to the edge of the tree limb he'd climbed onto when he saw that the two men had turned around. This time he was almost completely camouflaged by the swirling green hues of its branches and leaves. He held his long, white braid in his teeth to keep it from dangling loosely.

"'What is it you want from us? Why did you bring death to our people? Why do you befriend us only to bring us misery? How does it end? Have you poisoned our lands with your digging, as you have poisoned our maeeling?'

"Bathmantu froze. He did not know many words in the Oororan tongue, but he knew that one. He'd often heard it mentioned by the council; it meant princess. *Naubo was to be presented before the council of elders as the next representative of Oororah-9*, Bathmantu thought. *That's why she seemed prized among the villagers; that's why she had protectors. What have I done? Mercy...I didn't know...I didn't know. How are we going to fix this?* Bathmantu gently touched the pocket holding the orb. *No, it is already done. This will mean war; I have to get back to the council. They must know of this.*

"'Why do you hide, coward?' Kuopo continued, questioning the air. Gracefully, Bathmantu stood, released his braid, and tucked the thick blade of his knife between his teeth. He leaped for a tree limb that hung slightly over his pursuer's head. When he grabbed it, his body moved swiftly forward, knocking the male six feet back into a thorn tree. With a hard thud, the tree shook, and the body went limp. The man's midsection surrounded the eighteen-inch thorn that now stuck out of his stomach. The orange tree trunk was now covered in his blood. Bathmantu rolled to the ground, dodging the spinning spear Kuopo had lunged at him.

"His shrieking howl ripped through the air. Bathmantu's eyes watered with the pain of not protecting his ears as he watched his opponent. Desperately he searched for a way to release his agony. *How long can he hold his breath?* he wondered. 'I'm sorry about Naubo,' Bathmantu said. 'Her death was unintentional.'

"'Speak not of the maeeling, plague,' Kuopo interrupted. 'Your sorrow is for naught! You bring pain and suffering to us all, and now you must die.' Kuopo charged Bathmantu with knife in hand, and Bathmantu ran toward him. The two engaged in close combat, slicing and kicking at each other. Both were equally diverted. The two were of similar strength. But only one could walk away.

"Within the span of one breath, Kuopo brought his knife arm above his head and swung at Bathmantu, who blocked Kuopo's attempt and turned his back to him while stepping into the side of his striking arm. Bathmantu pulled Kuopo's arm straight down over his shoulder and then turned slightly to drive his boot knife into Kuopo's heart just below his stomach. Bathmantu dropped to his knees and sighed as Kuopo fell. He was now responsible for five deaths. 'Plague indeed,' he said aloud. 'I don't know how it ends, friend, but I do feel sorrow at what has happened here.'

"Kuopo and Bathmantu had become friends before the digging commenced, and it was that closeness Bathmantu used to get past the protectors whenever he needed to see Naubo. That, and the fact that she thought their presence was a waste of time. She would always wave them off at the first sign of Bathmantu's approach.

"Sprinting for the council, Bathmantu darted unchallenged across the forest for over three miles. When he reached the outer ring of the camp, he started shouting orders for defensive positions to be held. Bathmantu did not stop to explain himself, and fighters all but ignored his warnings as they looked in the direction he'd come from for signs of pursuit.

"Once inside the camp, Bathmantu explained what had transpired to his fighters' master and gained permission to seek out the council. When he found them, he explained Naubo's fate, her parentage, and the orb's actions. Upon completing his report, it was decided that he would be safer on Elquin. His ship was the last to depart Oororah-9 before the council was taken.

"Bathmantu's warning about the Oororans' howls did not aid the council. Before his departure, they'd set out to diplomatically resolve tensions with the Oororan officials. Although their initial meetings went without incident, they refused to incorporate protection upon hearing of their disadvantage. It was said that any action to block the Oororans' instinctive behavior would cause distrust on the part of Elquin, and war might then be unavoidable."

"But war was inevitable after Bathmantu's killings, right?" Taren interrupted again.

"It was the ultimate result when the council would not give up Bathmantu to be punished by Oororah-9 law. I had briefly worked with Zeeporah on the dynamics of the orb when I received the council's account. What we eventually discovered after Oororah-9 was that the orb feeds off of the host's energy emissions. When the orb is set on a path, the answers trigger its overactive proteins, which is why it must be removed from the host within thirty days."

"And why your reports contain more information than necessary."

"The orb will automatically reissue request when it obtains its objective."

"Meaning?" Taren asked, confused.

Sariah sighed. "It will seek responses to its molecular design by supplying its host with knowledge of its parentage." Sariah continued when Taren looked as if he was going to attempt solving the Elquin shield problems all by himself. "The host will experience memories of the orb while it remains within the body." Taren's eyes widened. "If nothing is offered, the orb embeds itself within the information pathways of the host, overwhelming it and denying protein to the host body. The host decreases its overall functions due to the lack of blood flow. Over time, the host will die if the orb is not removed."

"I don't understand. How can we carry the orb without being affected like our assignment?"

"Because it is designed based on your protein molecules, your memories, if you will. Your central nervous system can provide the answers to any memory it constructs because it was designed using those events."

"Before I left Elquin," Taren said, "I was told that the orb was designed closer to my microbes than any others."

"I wish you knew more about the orb before you took the assignment," Sariah said, shaking her head. "The orb can be designed based on anyone. It seems that you were selected for this assignment rather than given the option to refuse."

"They believed my hatred for this world's past actions would cement my loyalty to the assignment."

"I'm sorry, Taren."

Silence lingered for a long moment between the two of them as Taren stood and resumed his pacing.

"Wait!" Taren shouted, turning to Sariah. "This means..."

"This means," she said while getting to her feet, "that you have approximately two weeks to find her before the orb kills her."

"Why so little time?"

"Because she does not have the answers to the questions the orb was designed to ask. It will not take long for the orb to review all the questions it was assigned, and even less time for it to review your memories."

"Wait a minute. You intend to let me out of here?"

"I do not believe Locknoff will bring her here for me to remove the orb. I will do what I can, Taren," she said, looking at the ERT standing at the door, "but that won't be much."

"I don't need much," Taren said with a smirk.

Sariah walked to the door and paused before opening it. "She may not have two weeks, Taren. I'm not sure what's going on, but the energy readings from the orb are extremely high. She's headed east."

"Is my bag here?"

"Yes, it was retrieved from the hotel in the hopes of recovering something useful." Sariah turned to look Taren in the eyes. "The numbers 57381 will open the door. You may have to bring her back here, Taren, if for any reason you cannot remove the orb."

"No!" Taren growled. "She's not a part of this mission."

Sariah sighed. "Taren, I will not let harm come to her. Locknoff knows the risks, which is why he has already set out."

"I will not kill another innocent woman, Sariah. I will find a way to—"

"What? Remove her memories of meeting you, or whatever you have to do to retrieve the orb? She will forget only that which pertains to Elquin. Your road to retrieval cannot be erased. Will you hide her from the battle if it is decided to move forward with the current plans? You may need help, Taren. Bring her back here where you'll both be safe. Or have you forgotten their capabilities?"

"I've not forgotten!" Taren shouted. "If I have no other option, Sariah, I'll consider your request." He took a breath. "As you said, she'll be of no consequence once the orb is removed."

Sariah turned to the door, input the code, and left the room. She walked back to her workstation and dug through the desk until she came upon a small box. She pulled it out and opened it. Inside was a cased syringe; connected to it was a gelcap filled with green liquid.

"If you have no other choice," she said aloud. She closed the case before placing it into Taren's bag. She printed off copies of the photos Locknoff shared with the council and put them in the bag as well.

Nine

Recon

"Ahdortee, Porock, Jussalte, with me. Celtine, Rashanah, guard that door until she comes out of there," Locknoff ordered, pointing at the room Taren was in. Locknoff headed for the exit.

The ride to the hotel was long and silent. Locknoff sighed when they reach the hotel. He desperately hoped to get this task over with quickly. Locknoff pulled up to the curb and into the valet parking area. The four exited the black SUV and walked toward the glass doors. As he passed the parking attendants, Locknoff pointed to the car and yelled, "Leave it right there!"

When the valet tried to protest, walking around to the driver's side of the SUV and quoting hotel policy, Locknoff gave him a look combined with a growl that had the valet back up several paces. The young man agreed to the demand without further protest.

The lobby was a bustle of activity. Locknoff was not surprised. For some reason, humans seemed more alive at night in this city than anywhere else. The Elquins walked past a set of elevator doors to their right and a variety of potted flowers and mirrors to the left. They came to a halt at the customer service desk and asked to see the manager.

Kathrin Brown was the name on her ID tag. The woman looked to be in her late twenties, and her dark-brown hair was pulled in a tight bun. She had earrings that brushed her shoulders lightly, resembling large teardrops. Kathrin's skin reminded Locknoff of molix fruit, and her gaze was fixed on the computer screen in front of her. Kathrin had a look that suggested she was trying to fit guests in places that did not exist, between floors that would not appear.

"I'll be with you in one moment," she said without taking her eyes off the computer screen. After several more moments of typing, Locknoff began to get impatient. Before he could voice his opposition, however, Kathrin sighed and looked up. Her eyes widened when she took in the four of them. "How may I help you?" she nearly whispered.

"We need to see your manager."

"One moment please."

Kathrin disappeared for a moment and returned with a woman she introduced as Feleet. She was roughly five feet six and had a similar skin tone to Locknoff's. She wore her long, brown hair loosely curled, and the smile on her face seemed glued there. Feleet's smile was brighter than a summer's day when she looked at Locknoff.

"Right this way." Feleet motioned them into her office, stumbling backward over a small trash can as she led them through the door. Porock and Jussalte shared a brief look and then smiled as Locknoff whispered, "Not a single word," while leading them behind Feleet. Ahdortee looked at him with a face that portrayed no emotion for a moment, but even she could not resist a smirk at his expense.

As Feleet closed the doors, Locknoff asked, "Did the others return to the room with the one registered?"

"No," Feleet said as she walked around to her desk, "only the two that were in the casino when you left."

"In all likelihood," Ahdortee offered, "the girls that left together are still together. I believe the other woman lives close by."

"You may be right," Locknoff replied, "but I would hate to lose this opportunity to question them. And I would also hate for them to warn the others before we get to them. However, the one unaccounted for concerns me. She could be with either of them." There was no need to clarify which one he meant.

"What room did you say they're in?"

"Four seventeen, the second room off the elevator to the left."

"Get me a two-man security escort. I'd rather have their cooperation from the start."

"All right," Feleet responded. She pushed a button on the phone at her desk. "I need a two-man escort team in my office immediately."

"Would you like me to send a squad, Miss Feleet?" a male voice replied.

"No, two will suffice," she said, releasing the button.

"Will you be needing the tapes, Locknoff?"

"No, but I will need their phone signals blocked for a time after we leave."

"Will you—"

A tap on the door interrupted her question. Everyone looked toward the sound.

"Come in," Feleet said softly.

The two-man security team opened the door, looked over the five individuals briefly, and walked into the office.

"Take these people to room 417 and assist them in their investigation," Feleet ordered.

"Investigation?" one of the security men questioned with lowered brows.

"Yes. I'm sure you were informed of the incident we had in the parking lot this evening."

"Yes, but—"

"Some of the guests are being questioned about the matter," Feleet said sternly, interrupting his protest. "You are to take them directly to room 417, do as they instruct, and return to me the moment they are finished with the guest. Is that understood?"

"Yes, ma'am," they replied in unison.

Without another word, both men stepped into the hall and headed for the elevators. Ahdortee, Porock, and Jussalte followed quickly behind them. As Locknoff headed out the door, Feleet grabbed his massive arm, looked into his eyes, and said, "Safe journey, Locknoff."

He looked at her for a moment and half smiled. "Thank you, Feleet," he responded, gently removing her hand from his arm. He turned and headed after the others.

Locknoff reached the group as they were getting onto the elevator. He stepped in and looked at the closing doors. Wasting no time with pleasantries, he spoke to the security officers while removing a weapon from the holster at his belt. It resembled a 9-millimeter, only it had a longer barrel and silver stripes along its side.

"When we get to the room, inform the guest that we are investigating the disturbance in the casino from earlier this evening." Locknoff pushed the magazine release button and briefly inspected the silver bullets.

He then put the magazine back into the weapon and looked at the visibly shaken security officers, who asked with wide eyes while staring at his weapon, "Are you f-from the FBI?"

Locknoff drove the bolt home and said, "You will then wait outside the room. Your responsibility is to ensure that no one gets in or out, unless it is one of us. Do you understand?"

As Jussalte's, Porock's, and Ahdortee's bolts were all sent home, the security guards jumped in unison and shook their heads in agreement. The elevator doors opened before another word was spoken.

Exiting the elevator, the security guards focused on the decor rather than the individuals they were escorting. The walls were divided by darkly stained crown molding. The top half was covered in purple-and-gold flowered wallpaper, and the bottom was painted gold. Paintings hung between light fixtures spaced several feet apart on the wall, and the floor was decorated with a purple carpet that was littered with gold vines and flowers. The carpet was centered on a Naples-yellow marble floor. Crown molding framed a tray ceiling, which housed decorative golden light fixtures that were also spaced several feet apart throughout the length of the hall. The group hastily made its way to room 417.

As the security officers approached the door, light gleamed off the golden buttons on their otherwise white, collared shirts. Timidly the taller of the two knocked on the door and looked to Locknoff for instructions.

"Who is it?" came a soft feminine voice.

"Hotel security," he whispered. He blurted out what they wanted so fast that the only reply was "What?"

Nearly knocking them both to the ground, Ahdortee shoved her way to the door.

"Hotel security, ma'am," she said. "We apologize for the disturbance, but we need to speak with you regarding an important matter."

The loud click as the doorstop caught the opening door was enough to draw everyone's attention to the big, brown eye that appeared at the opening. "Disturbance?"

"Yes, ma'am, may we come in for a moment?"

The eye swept across the six individuals briefly before the door closed and completely reopened a moment later, revealing a young woman with long, brown hair. She was dressed in a dark-green tank top with matching pants. There were white flowers down the side of her pants and along the neckline of her top. The woman stepped aside, revealing two others in the room.

The room had two large beds equally spaced on a golden carpet with purple spirals throughout. The blankets were also purple with golden spirals. There was a set of both purple and gold curtains on the opposite side of a small table and two large chairs. Decorative light fixtures were in between the two beds and in the far corners of the room. A desk along the wall housed a beautifully designed golden lamp, a desktop computer, and a wide chair on wheels.

There was a small desk in between the beds that held a clock radio and a wireless phone. Each bed held several pillows that were obscured by the women who sat on them, looking intently at the newcomers. Across from the beds was a large flat-screen television housed in a darkly stained wardrobe that spanned from the desk down the other side of the wall, next to a small dry bar with a brown-and-black countertop. Atop it sat a coffee machine, several cups, an assortment of coffee and hot chocolate, as well as condiments.

The two women stood as the four ERT members entered the room. Locknoff recognized the three women from the security photos, but only knew one as Emily Townsman. His attention turned to her green eyes, which were bright against the white robe she wore.

"What's this about?" she asked, addressing Ahdortee. Porock and Jussalte stayed close to the door as Locknoff and Ahdortee moved in a bit closer to address the women. As Locknoff spoke, the woman who opened the door moved closer to join the conversation.

"My name is Jonathan Grady," Locknoff explained. "These are my partners. Angelia Sival," he said, gesturing to Ahdortee. "And Gabriel and Thomas Blackard," he continued, swinging his hand toward the others. "We represent a private investigation firm. You came across a man earlier this evening who is the subject of an ongoing investigation. Unfortunately, he gave one of you something of great value to us."

"No, he didn't," the woman who let them in said, interrupting him as she sat on the edge of the bed closest to the door. "He didn't even touch us. Well, he kissed Jen but—"

"Jen?" Locknoff interrupted.

"Jennifer Braxton, one of our friends who was here earlier," Emily said. "She helped him up when he fell, and he kissed her and said thank you, but he didn't give her anything either."

"What we're looking for," Ahdortee said, "is very small. He may have slipped it into her pocket or something. She wouldn't even know it was there if she wasn't looking for it."

"Angelia is right," Locknoff protested. "She could go for months without even knowing it was there. Do you have any idea where Jennifer may be right now? We really must speak with her."

"She left hours ago with Cara," the third woman said with a shrug. "She said she wasn't feeling well." Ahdortee and Locknoff shared a look, surprise clear on their faces. "What is it you lost?" the woman asked as she reached down to search her bag. Long, brown hair hid her features. Another moment and she pulled out a cell phone. Tucking a few strands of hair behind her ear, she said, "We can call and have her check her pockets to see if it's in there."

Locknoff gave Porock a quick glance and then returned his attention to the woman. "That isn't a good idea," he protested, raising an eyebrow. "It's a very dangerous piece of equipment. It would be better if she didn't even know she had it. What we need to know is how to find her, preferably before she finds it."

"Well," Emily said with a gesture to the other woman, "as Amy said, she left earlier with Cara. I'm not sure where they are now, but Jennifer's staying with her until after the concert tomorrow. Do you know where Oliveton Park is?"

"Yes," Ahdortee said.

"Cara lives three blocks from the main entrance on Elfmen Street; it's the fifth house on the left, number 2734."

"Hmm...that's strange," the third woman said, looking at her phone. Everyone turned to look at her.

"What is it, Kim?" Emily asked.

"My phone...the signal..." Her brow turned down in confusion. "It just...disappeared."

"That tends to happen sometimes in this area," Jussalte said. "It's not all that uncommon for signals to come in and out from time to time in this area."

Kim seemed to accept his explanation reluctantly. "Oh," she said, frowning.

"All right then." Locknoff turned for the door. "If you hear from your friend, please let hotel security know, and remember not to tell her about the danger."

"Don't worry," Emily said, smiling while following him and Ahdortee to the door. "We won't say a thing."

As she closed the door behind them, Locknoff heard one of the other women speaking.

"Well, this sucks."

"What now?" Emily responded.

"My Internet's down too. I don't—"

The door shut, cutting off the rest of the conversation abruptly.

"Take them back to Feleet," Locknoff ordered, gesturing with his head toward the security guards. "Tell her we'll need the entire floor blocked until further notice. The sensor you placed will only block their room, so they will need to be monitored when they are not on this floor." Porock and Jussalte bowed their heads slightly, gathered the security officers, and headed back downstairs.

Locknoff grunted with satisfaction as he and Ahdortee exited the hotel and he saw the black SUV still parked where he'd left it. "Hun," he said, smiling, "and he wants to save them. What a waste of perfectly good resources."

Porock and Jussalte joined them as they reached the vehicle. Porock was grinning from ear to ear, and Jussalte was trying so hard not to laugh that it looked like he was in pain.

Locknoff sighed. "What is it?"

"She wants you to know," Porock explained, "that her hearts await your command."

Jussalte burst into laughter so loudly that the valets standing nearby all jumped and looked at the closing doors of the vehicle. Even Ahdortee could be heard snickering.

"It will take a miracle," Locknoff said quietly, "to discourage that one." He then pulled away, frustration clear on his features.

"Are you quite finished?" he growled at Jussalte.

Clearing his throat, Jussalte responded, "Yes, Master Locknoff."

"Good. Let's retrieve the orb and get back. I have questions for Taren that cannot wait until morning."

Ten

Rude Awakening

Jennifer gasped as she awoke. She instinctively moved her hand to her head. It throbbed, her clothes clung to her body drenched in sweat, and hair stuck to her head in several places. She was exhausted, more exhausted than she'd been the night before when she'd finally decided to pull into a hotel and get some sleep. It was only out of desperation. Her lids had become so heavy she fell asleep twice behind the wheel before deciding to pull into a hotel.

She knew it was the dreams; they felt so real to her. Almost as if she was actually experiencing the things she saw. But how could she? There were no such things as aliens or life on other planets, unless you were in Hollywood. As she stood, a trickle of sweat ran down her back. She could feel it touch the inside of her butt. *Ugh*, she thought, sighing as she made her way to the bathroom. She stopped at the dry bar and downed a couple of complimentary aspirin, turned on the coffeepot, and pulled her bag of toiletries out of the suitcase.

Jennifer started for the phone to call Cara and the others, but she decided against it when she realized the time. It was only 6:45 a.m. Cara might be awake, but the others would still be asleep. *No matter,* she thought, *I'll call them when I'm dressed.* She jumped in the shower and sighed as every one of her muscles relaxed under the water pressure.

Her head was starting to feel better. *It's too bad I'm not a writer, because I could write a killer movie out of these crazy dreams.* She could remember every last detail from the moment she'd closed her eyes.

It was like she'd gone through a portal and come out in another world. The first time she'd opened her eyes, she saw a room bustling with activity. The beings were definitely not human. They looked like the same creatures she'd seen in the house with the strange man who'd kissed her. There were so many of them here that she gave up on counting them. Jennifer could see their alien features clearly as she searched the crowd. Most of them were dressed in a kind of clean garb from the neck down.

Jennifer froze when her gaze settled on a male and female standing within close proximity. They were the same two she'd seen before. She started to make her way toward them, but somehow they seemed so far away now. They were near the front of the crowd. She squeezed through effortlessly, seemingly unnoticed, and froze as she reached the clearing toward the middle of the crowd. Jennifer was awestruck.

In front of her on an oval-shaped table sat a large, silver disk. It was roughly two feet wide and had a transparent, cylinder body. Its length was about five feet, and the top end was covered with the same silvery disklike shape. Suspended in the middle of the cylinder was a misty form. On either side of the cylinder stood the two individuals she'd seen on the hill not so long ago. Both were intent on their work, and as they pushed buttons simultaneously, more mist began to fall.

Each time the mist fell, it joined within what was already in the cylinder. The mist started falling faster and faster. As it fell, the color changed from clear to silver, then cyan, next was morning blue, and finally a bright blue. The mist started to spin, casting blue light throughout the room. Everyone was bathed in blue until suddenly the light retracted into the misty form, which was now an orb. Jennifer was astonished. She stepped closer to get a better look at the orb and was jolted awake by what sounded like thunder. Her head was pounding so hard that she didn't even try to move; she just closed her eyes again and found herself back in the world of dreams.

When she opened them this time, she was in the middle of some kind of battle. Strange vehicles flew overhead firing blue light at forces in the distance, both in the air and on the ground. Attacks were returned with blasts of gray and blue. Trees, dirt, and bodies fell all around her. Jennifer closed her eyes in an effort to escape the scene and found herself standing next to one of the alien males. It was dark, and he was with a group that was advancing through an elaborately designed building.

She followed them cautiously, gasping as they moved about. The walls were curved. Every room they went through seemed tall enough to host a giant, and all the walls led up to a portion of the triple-crescent ceiling. Jennifer reached a hand out to feel the brown texture on the walls and was surprised. It was bumpy in places but smooth in others. The small group passed through halls that led to rooms and mass gathering places.

The group she noted was all dressed in black. On their shirts, Jennifer could see what looked like a small, embroidered bird's skeleton. Two of them looked like they had horns on their heads. Everyone in the group had their hair pulled away from their faces in different fashions. Some had thongs; others had braids. The male she walked next to wore a dark-green band around his head and a single braid. Although she couldn't explain why, Jennifer felt an odd sense of security around him. It wasn't long before the group came to a sudden stop as it reached a room leading to a giant set of double doors. To the left and right of the doors were corridors. The group focused on the double doors.

They looked heavy to Jennifer and curved at its points, following the pattern of the ceiling. They were deep chocolate in color and had carvings of tulips along the top, bottom, and edges of both sides. In the middle of the doors and on either side, there was a pair of golden spears in the shape of an *X*. The bottoms of the spears were shaped like crescents, and there were gold tulips carved throughout the staff.

The group silently made its way to the doors with weapons in hand. The weapons the beings carried reminded Jennifer of shotguns. Silver triangles were along the length of the weapons, ridges along the grip, and six strange hollow holes toward the back. Jennifer tensed as the doors were pulled opened. Curiosity had her moving forward eagerly. When she saw what was on the other side of the doors, she gasped.

There were seven individuals in the middle of a dimly lit room. It looked like their skin was made up of purple, braided flesh. Even their eyelids looked to be made of braided skin. Their noses were different shades with one thick braid of skin that went all the way up to their scalps. Where lips would normally be, these beings had a single section of smooth unbraided skin that formed a *U*. It took more willpower than Jennifer thought she could muster to take her eyes off their faces when one of them raised their arms and began to speak. The voice was feminine, and as she spoke, her thick, black hair began to blow as if hit by a blast of fresh air.

"I am Kelentar. On behalf of Baitorus, we offer no further resistance. Our resources are yours. Please, stand down your attack. My people need suffer no more."

Two of Jennifer's group shared a brief look and then returned their glares to the female, who lowered her head and bent to one knee. Following her example, the others repeated in unison, "Our resources are yours," and all went down on one knee.

The leader of Jen's group, who was already in front, took one step forward. He was humongous; his hands were as big as Jen's head. If he were human, Jennifer thought he could easily pass for the world's strongest man.

"I am Master Locknoff of the Grokni bloodline. On behalf of Elquin, I accept your..."

Bright gray lights flashed from the back corners of the room, slamming into two of the standing party. Jennifer ducked behind the male she stood next to, who'd rolled onto the ground and come up with some kind of shield. It looked to her like a giant fan with a small disk in the middle. Jennifer watched as her group withstood blast after blast of the strange light. The four still standing came together to shield each other. At the first opportunity, someone fired a strange blue burst of light from behind a shield.

The kneeling group did not move. Suddenly the blasts stopped on both sides. Jennifer returned her attention to the aliens who'd replaced their strange weapons with some kind of knife. Locknoff looked at his group and said, "For the honor of Elquin."

They repeated his words in unison and went to meet the army of Baitoran warriors who'd come out of the dark corners to eliminate them all. There must have been twenty or thirty of them. Jennifer stopped counting as they began to fall at the hands of the shielded beings who swung, hit, and spun with their knives and shields.

Jennifer was astonished. It was like watching a movie play out right in front of her eyes. Every time one of the warriors fell, more filled in from the dark corners. Suddenly one of the shielded men fell. He'd made his way to one of the corners, fighting off everyone who entered. As the last warrior came at him, two of the kneeling Baitorans stood and drove a knife into his back. Before he'd fallen to the ground, the male Jennifer had been hiding behind forcefully tossed his shield at them, killing one of the warriors in his path, and leaped forward, somehow splitting apart his knife weapon and simultaneously decapitating both Baitoran in midair. As he came down, he rolled up into a crouching position.

Jennifer thought something about him was familiar, but how could that be? She didn't know any aliens. Suddenly she felt searing pain as her alien bodyguard was sliced across the back.

Jennifer gasped as she had woken up, and now she sighed, finding her surroundings more comforting than she ever had while traveling. Jennifer lightly touched her upper shoulder, interrupting the water's flow as she remembered feeling the pain. She frowned. With a sigh, she turned off the water and climbed out of the tub, happy they were only dreams.

After wrapping a towel around herself, Jennifer stepped up to the sink and wiped the condensation off the mirror. Her head felt so much better. She focused on her eyes. *Hmm*, she thought. They did seem a bit brighter to her but not much more than usual.

"Certainly not enough to be worried about it," she said aloud. She brushed, dressed, repacked her suitcase, and then headed down the stairs to check out. She wanted to be on the road as soon as possible. The moment she entered the lobby, her stomach growled as she smelled the eggs and bacon coming from the complimentary breakfast bar.

A quick bite won't hurt, she thought as she headed toward the aroma of bacon. Quickly finding an empty table, Jennifer shoved her suitcase underneath it and made a beeline for the breakfast bar. There were so many choices. Eggs boiled, scrambled, and fried. Bacon and sausages, hash browns cooked with real potatoes, onions, and bell peppers. Hot oatmeal, grits, and barley. Jennifer's stomach rumbled, and her mouth watered as she stepped forward to make her selection.

With great difficulty, she managed not to fill her plate to the point of spillage as she settled for waffles, eggs, hash browns, and bacon. After setting her plate down, she returned to the bar for orange juice. When she reached for a glass, a large hand reached ahead of her and grabbed it first.

"May I?" he asked, smiling as she looked at him in disapproval. Without waiting for her response, the man filled the glass and waited for her to take it. She looked at him for a moment, reaching for it, and then suddenly remembered the stranger who'd kissed her.

Pulling her hand back, Jennifer said, "No, thank you. The last stranger that offered me something gave me nightmares." She grabbed an empty cup and poured herself a glass of apple juice instead.

"Sorry," he said.

She offered him a smile and then continued on her way.

Eleven

FREEDOM

Taren stood for a moment, watching as Sariah left. His eyes moved past her and settled on the ERT standing guard at the door. Sariah's exit echoed throughout the small room, and Taren sat when the ERT followed her away. After nearly twenty minutes of inner contemplation, Taren decided he'd had enough.

He walked over to the door and peered through the small window. As Sariah's assistant walked past the door, he input the code she'd given him. The air locks released, and the door popped open. The assistant gasped at the sound and quickly turned to resecure it. As he did, Taren met him with an open palm to his midsection, knocking him back several steps. He struggled to regain his breath. As the assistant bent forward, Taren delivered a double-handed hammer blow to his temples, rendering the man unconscious. Taren caught his limp body before it touched the floor and dragged him into the room. He then secured the door and headed in the direction Sariah had gone.

Taren made it through the double doors, past the long hallway, and into Sariah's workstation without running into anyone. He grabbed his bag and hurried out the door. When he reached the building's entrance, however, he slowed his pace at the sight of two ERT. He felt a tap on his shoulder.

Sariah motioned for him to keep quiet and follow her. Taren raised a brow but didn't argue. They walked through a set of double doors directly across from the main entrance. Taren slowed his pace again, looking at the glass room the path had brought them to. It had two hospital beds in the center and several large machines that resembled giant metal spiders. Taren recognized them as the tools used to manipulate DNA. It made Elquins resemble humans.

"Taren, come on," Sariah beckoned. "It won't be long before Elious wakes up, and after what you did to him, he won't be in the best mood."

"You won't have to worry about Elious for a little while. He'll have a bit of a headache when he wakes up, maybe some memory loss."

"Still, we should keep moving."

Taren nodded in agreement and followed her out into a parking structure. She tossed him a set of keys.

"Safe journey, brother. May your hearts find peace in the journey ahead and maybe even a love to share in your bed."

Taren stumbled and turned to look at her with a raised brow.

"What?" Sariah responded innocently. "There will be more Elquins here soon, Taren, even if it's just to conduct mining. She will live on in your hearts, but it's time for you to start living for yourself. The Master Vishnu I came to know and care for would not linger in his loss. You made her happy, Taren, from the moment she laid eyes on you. You made her happy, and she died with more love in her heart for you than anyone she ever knew."

Taren searched Sariah's eyes a moment and then lowered his gaze. "Thank you, Sariah." He turned and headed for the corresponding sound to the alarm he disarmed with the key he now carried in hand. Taren followed the sound until he reached a chestnut-brown Jaguar XS convertible. He smiled and sighed and said, "She certainly will, Sariah. Thank you."

He started the engine and headed east. After twenty minutes of highway driving, Taren pulled into a rest area on Highway 93, unzipped his bag, and pulled out a cell phone. He put his thumb on the screen and removed it three seconds later. When he did, his print appeared on the screen. The phone analyzed it, marking several identifying spots. After a moment a woman's face appeared.

"Welcome, Taren. How may I be of assistance?"

"Locate the orb."

"Locating," the face responded, looking up and to the left of the screen. She blinked several times and said, "The orb is located on Great Bay Highway, moving south at seventy miles per hour, currently passing mile marker 8.50. Would you like to place a tracker?"

"Yes," Taren responded. As he proceeded toward the orb, he remembered happier times in the brief life he'd shared with Youkoni.

◆ ◆ ◆

Vishnu, as Taren was known on Elquin, had just returned from a mission on Starbane when he saw her for the second time. The first had been back on Oororah-9 when his squad rescued the council members held under duress by Oororan fighters. He'd recognized her by Sariah's description of her hair. It was very long and unkept. It flowed down the length of her body and wrapped around her like a blanket. She was beautiful…dirty and bound, but beautiful. As he helped her up and out of her bonds, Taren looked into her eyes and froze.

They were the most beautiful eyes he'd ever seen. Rich chestnut brown in color, they stared back at him intently. His hearts simultaneously skipped a beat. He found it difficult to pull his gaze away from her eyes, but did at the realization of hostility around her. He'd returned her safely to her sister as promised and was not sure when he'd see her again, but from the moment he'd laid eyes on Youkoni, his hearts belonged to her.

Today, however, she looked like the sun itself. She was dressed in the traditional blue of the council. The dress was long and sleeveless, gathered at the waist by a thick braid of golden fabric. Her shoulders were slightly covered by a layer of blue ruffles. An essence of confidence radiated from her so strongly that Vishnu had a hard time keeping his focus.

Her long, white hair floated over her ocean-blue dress. It was kept back with a small braid from each side of her hair that was joined in the middle and decorated with a golden spiral. Her crown of braids formed several single crescents across her forehead. They were so low that Vishnu could barely see her eyes. But see them he did. He smiled and wished he'd had the chance to freshen up.

Youkoni smiled when she saw him, and his ears began to twitch. She greeted him formally as she passed. "Good day, Vishnu."

"Good day, Youkoni. I trust your health is well?"

"Yes, thank you," she replied as she stopped to address him. Her gaze made him feel warm, and his hearts longed to be near her. Youkoni's dress left most of her arms bare, displaying her yellow-green and jade swirls. Vishnu searched for words but found it difficult to speak. His mouth was dry, and his thoughts were cloudy.

"How is your health?" Youkoni asked.

"Fine, thank you. But we are required to be evaluated at medical upon return from any mission. I trust it will go well."

"As do I, Vishnu." She smiled brightly and continued on her way. He returned the smile and watched as she disappeared around a corner.

"You really should ask her out, Vishnu. You two make a great pair."

Vishnu turned to see Locknoff watching him, watching her. "I will." He sighed. "As soon as I find the courage."

Locknoff eyed him skeptically. "So you can charge a herd of Angolore beast without backup, but you lack courage when it comes to females?"

"Not all females. That one."

Locknoff laughed and smacked him on the shoulder as they walked away. "Ah, young love."

◆ ◆ ◆

Locknoff was right, of course, even though Vishnu did not see her again for almost four moons. When he did, he didn't let his chance get away. Youkoni had come into the medical bay one day, while he was being evaluated after a mission to Ratier, to speak with her sister. As she walked toward the exit, Vishnu sat up, almost bumping his head on the arch arm, and asked her to join him for a meal. She appraised him for what seemed an eternity before answering, tilting her head and raising her left eyelid slightly wider, which caused the sunlight to momentarily gleam off her pupils, turning them into a rich liquid chestnut.

"It would do my hearts well to share a meal with you, Vishnu," she said softly. He was so taken with her eyes that he almost forgot she was waiting for a response. Sariah actually cleared her throat loud enough to remind him.

"Excellent," he said, "I'll see you later then."

Youkoni smiled and continued on her way. Vishnu lay back blissfully unaware of the bump he did received this time.

Sariah smiled and stepped closer toward him, saying, "Take care never to be the source of her tears, trainee, or no master will save you from my wrath." Vishnu's grin was humongous. "Come on," she continued while guiding his head under the arch and pulling on his hand to help him up. "The only ailment you have is self-inflicted. You're free to go."

"Thank you," he said with sincere gratitude in his eyes, the smile gone from his face.

"You're welcome," Sariah responded with a smile of her own.

"There aren't many I would approve of, Vishnu, but you seem to be capable of making her smile."

Vishnu's proud grin returned and lit up his face. Sariah laughed and returned to her work as he walked out of the medical bay.

That dinner led to the biggest merger of bloodlines Elquin had seen in a turnier. The wedding lasted so long, Elquins were beginning to think there was no crisis. Youkoni was eager to wed after Vishnu's proposal, due to her upcoming council mission, which was not far off and would take much longer than she'd wanted. The public announcement of their intent began the process. First, there would be a banquet in the capital, held by the council in their honor. Next would be the acceptance ball, followed by the mating ceremony, and finally the congratulatory banquet.

Twelve

MERGER

Elquin's capital city was enormous. It was built in the shadow of the planet's tallest mountain. Many of the buildings were oval shaped and had similarly shaped rooftops. Its design was meant to be a line of defense against the star's harmful rays. The energy collected was converted into power for the building. Vehicles of all shapes and sizes were designed with technology overhead to power them. Train rails made of paper-thin strips of a solid, water-like substance floated throughout the city. Spectators could be seen for miles as individuals made their way to the banquet hall.

The streets were paved in flowers, leaves, and vines from every known tree on Elquin. The road to the banquet hall was flanked on either side by brown trees that were covered in cauliflower-like buds. Elquins both young and old bordered the streets and alleyways as generations of Grendore and Ateenn bloodlines made their way to the hall. Behind the families came friends, neighbors, and patrons to join in the joyous festivities.

The procession ended nearly an hour after it began, and the guests were seated through the hall as the banquet began. Elquins of all ages wore their best and greeted each other eagerly, but they turned their attention to the council when the meals started to arrive. Shortly after the food was served, Elitar stood and addressed the crowd. A band of gold cloth that stretched around his head and folded into the free-falling strands in back held his long, white hair down. In the middle of the band was a fantastic display of planets. Seventeen in all, they surrounded a large planet that could almost pass for Earth's twin. With more land than water, the planet held so many brightly colored plants that a solar view displayed more pink than green.

With outstretched arms, Elitar addressed the assembly, his long, blue robe moving with him. "Greetings to all. We have gathered today to witness the merger request of Grendore and Ateenn bloodlines for the good of Youkoni and Vishnu." The crowd cheered, and several offered their early blessings before Elitar could hush them all. He looked to either side of him where they both sat, before addressing them and the crowd.

"The council smiles on this assertion and wishes you peace and happiness in your venture." He then looked to the high family gathered around the table. "What say you?"

As a large male seated next to Youkoni stood, Elitar sat. The large male wore his hair in a long braid tied back with a black headband. Across his white, sleeveless shirt was a black sash covered in golden embroidered sessile leaf plants.

Looking directly at Vishnu, he said, "I am Technon, the eldest living male born to my father. We are Grendore." He stretched his arm toward those seated on his side of the table.

"Our bloodline has brought honor to Elquin for generations. My great father was a contributor to the shield that protects her today. Our parents both gave their lives for the betterment of Elquin. My brothers and sisters each contribute to her success through their service to her.

"With the transitioning of our caregivers, the task of protecting and providing for my family falls to me and the others born to my great father. You come before us today seeking to remove a branch from this deeply rooted tree. What say you to the task of protecting and nurturing that branch, as it seeks to become part of the roots your bloodline has established in Elquin?"

As Vishnu stood, his gaze locked on Youkoni. He smiled and turned to address the Grendore bloodline. Technon sat and briefly hugged his younger sister before looking to Vishnu.

"Honor indeed, Grendore. I admire your strength in the face of such a challenge. I am Vishnu of the Ateenn bloodline. We too have a rich history of honor in Elquin. My father," he said while gesturing to the male seated next to him, "like his father before him and many generations of Ateenn blood, has spent an epochy protecting Elquin.

"My great mother was the chief scientist on staff when Elquin's shield was recalibrated. Our duty to each other and our fellow brethren has always been to protect and preserve our world and those within it. I have joined the efforts of my bloodline as a protector of this world, and I would do no less to protect and nourish your precious branch as it attaches to this tree rooted deeply in Elquin honor." Vishnu turned to Youkoni and smiled. She stood and returned the smile.

"Honored elders," he said, turning to address the gathered party, "we come to you free of coercion and request your blessing to merge our bloodlines, as our hearts sing to become one."

Vishnu's father stood, looked at Youkoni, and asked, "Young one, we have heard from your custodian, and we have heard from your pursuer. What I ask now is of your desire in this matter."

Youkoni smiled a moment, looking at Vishnu. "What I desire is to merge our bloodlines, honored one. I have found more than a heart song with Vishnu; I have found purpose."

"Then I give my blessing," he said, looking to Technon, who stood.

"I give my blessing."

"I give my blessing," came a feminine voice on the Ateenn side of the table.

"As do I," said Sariah.

"And I," others chimed in.

Within moments, every honored member was standing, and the merger was approved.

Joyous applauses came from the crowd and echoed throughout the hall. Vishnu and Youkoni took the opportunity to hug briefly before Elitar stood and raised his arms again. Silence overcame the hall quickly, and everyone took his or her seat.

"As the elders have decided, so shall it be. Let the merger commence!"

Cheers filled the hall once again, and the banquet continued well into the night.

◆ ◆ ◆

"What are you afraid of? It's not like she's gonna bite your head off," Locknoff teased.

"The lights," Vishnu replied timidly. "What if they're not bright enough for anyone to see?"

"They don't have to be bright; they just have to appear. Don't worry. Nature does that part for you."

"All the same, I'd rather not have a repeat of Porock's experience."

"Ha-ha-ha, you're much stronger than Porock, and Youkoni loves you, no worries. Now turn around so I can tie this properly."

Vishnu was dressed in a dark-red, sleeveless shirt and black trousers with a large black cloth belt secured at the waist. Across his chest, Locknoff was tying a black sash that had an embroidered tree wrapped in large, green vines along its length. His hair was thonged and braided.

"Don't worry, brother. You'll do fine. I'll make sure the lights are seen, even if I have to stand watch myself."

"Ha!" Vishnu replied skeptically. "If you can get past the bloodlines. I heard Grendore and Ateenn are both petitioning to stand watch. I wouldn't be surprised to see my father standing guard himself." They both laughed aloud.

"It's time," Locknoff said.

Vishnu took a deep breath and held out his hands, nodding. Locknoff placed a folded golden cloth in his upturned palm. Vishnu took another breath and stepped outside the meeting room he and Locknoff commissioned to prepare for tonight's events. He was one step closer to seeing his bride.

The short path to the meeting hall seemed endless as Vishnu placed one foot in front of the other. His boots echoed throughout the hall with every step. When he finally came upon a set of double doors, he paused, squared his shoulders, and raised his head. Members of his bloodline opened the doors simultaneously, and Vishnu stepped into the hall. He froze when he looked up, seeing Youkoni stepping clear of the doors thirty yards across from him.

She wore a deep-purple dress. The length was just past her heels. One side of the dress was split open to her waist, revealing a darker shade of purple underneath in the form of a miniskirt. Part of her leg was showing, and Vishnu could see her sandal straps, which were laced up her leg. Her shoulders were bare, and there were two crossing rows of three thin, black straps that seemed to hold the dress in place across her bust. The straps were joined in the back of the dress and were the only things shading her back.

The bust of her dress was covered with a black embroidered sessile leaf plant. Youkoni's long, white hair was adorned with purple and gold gems, free flowing in the back. Her crown was wrapped individually with strands of black silk and decorated with purple and gold gems. The braids of her crown almost covered her eyes, but Vishnu had no trouble seeing them, when he could focus.

In her hands, Youkoni held a folded cloth of deep purple. Directly to her left and his right was a flight of stairs leading deeper into the grand hall. Someone cleared his throat behind Vishnu, and he took a step forward, focusing on his path ahead. Youkoni smiled and started down her own flight of stairs. As they reached the bottom, they stood face to face briefly and turned toward Elitar, who stood at the head of the gathered council. To the right and left of Vishnu and Youkoni were family and friends dressed in their best. Their path to the council was clear, and they stopped four feet from Elitar.

The council members gathered around them as Elitar spoke. "The bloodlines have agreed to your request. It is with great pleasure that I proceed." He turned to Youkoni and said, "Please place the bloodline seal upon Vishnu's breast."

Youkoni opened the folded cloth she held and stepped closer to Vishnu. She placed the cloth at the top of his sash and secured it underneath. She then stepped back into her place. On the cloth was a small sessile leaf plant embroidered in black.

Elitar then looked to Vishnu and said, "Please place the bloodline seal upon Youkoni."

Vishnu stepped forward and unfolded the cloth he held and placed it around Youkoni's waist. She held her arms high, and he secured it behind her back, struggling slightly with her long hair. On the cloth was an embroidered tree wrapped in large, green vines. When finished, he stepped back into his place, looked at Youkoni, and smiled. A low humming radiated from them both, and Elitar's smile was one of a proud parent.

The council turned to face the crowd, and those in Vishnu and Youkoni's path moved to the left or right. Elitar raised his hands and said, "Let the celebration commence!"

Vishnu took Youkoni's hand, and they turned to face the crowd. Taking several steps to be clear of the council, they began to dance. Others joined in the dancing but did not speak to either of them.

Thirteen

Bond Of Love

The music radiated across the hillside as couples joined in the celebration. Vishnu and Youkoni seemed oblivious to the music as they
twisted and twirled to the sound of their humming hearts. It was not
until the music stopped and others cleared the dance floor that they
realized Elitar had spoken. Hand in hand, Vishnu and Youkoni turned
to Elitar and waited. Elitar's blue robes quivered with his laughter, and
it took him a moment to recover. After clearing his throat, he spoke in a
loud voice. "Tradition demands that your path now lead to the hillside,
where your merger will be completed in a bond stronger than blood.
Are the witnesses present?"

"Present and willing," came a feminine voice. Vishnu and Youkoni
both turned to see Sariah and Stofena standing at the edge of the parting crowd. Vishnu smiled at the sight of his mother, remembering the
conversation he'd had with Locknoff, and walked toward them, towing
Youkoni along. Without letting go of her hand, he hugged his mother
and then Sariah, and Youkoni did the same. Elitar continued speaking
as the brief exchange took place.

"Then with the council's blessing, go forth and return only when
the lights have confirmed the bond." The four exchanged quick glances

and walked swiftly out of the hall. The gathered crowd cheered the couple and followed at a hurried pace.

Outside the hall, flowers adorned the streets. There were so many flowers that the pavement could not be seen. At the road's end, flowers covered a wide path leading toward the hilltop. Vishnu and Youkoni exchanged a quick glance before starting up the hill. Amazingly, family and friends had taken up station on either side of the flower trail.

Vishnu and Youkoni walked the trail at a measured pace. Their witnesses followed quietly. After about a mile, the flower trail widened, and distant calls of congratulations could be heard from excited family and friends below. At the hilltop, Vishnu could see a white building. The witnesses stopped and sat on either side of the flower trail, which held two large chairs decorated with white cloth and flowers, and wished them luck.

"No need to stress," Stofena said as she took her seat. "We will call to witness as soon as the lights begin to show."

Vishnu looked to Youkoni. "Are you ready?" he asked.

"Yes."

They continued on the path until the witnesses could no longer be seen. The building came into full view then, and they happily walked inside. There was only one room in the tiny building. In its center was a bed shaped like a large lotus flower. The sides were covered in miniature lotuses, and the sheets held a floral design so realistic that only touching it would reveal the reality of its making.

"There is only one thing in the universe more breathtaking," Vishnu said.

"What?" Youkoni asked in a disbelieving tone as she looked at him.

Vishnu turned to look into her eyes. "You," he said as he wrapped his arms around her waist, pulling her close. He kissed her gently on the lips, and she returned the kiss while reaching up with both hands to touch his ears. Vishnu froze as she lightly traced them with her fingertips.

With trembling fingers, he reached around and removed her cloth belt. In response, Youkoni released one of his ears and unfastened his sash. All too quickly, her hands were back; this time they traced with more pressure. After a few minutes, his inner ear appeared to be hollow, and Youkoni drove her middle fingers through the opening. Vishnu gasped, and she pulled him closer for a kiss. Try as he might, but her fingers had his full attention. He felt like she was intruding into the very core of his being.

He closed his eyes in concentration and clenched his teeth together, determined not to scream or pass out as Youkoni's thumbs rubbed his lower jaw in a clockwise motion while she placed gentle kisses along his cheeks, neck, and chin. As she did, tiny blue veins came from deep within the core of his brain and attached like suction cups to her fingers. He wasn't sure if minutes, hours, or days passed before the feeling suddenly changed. It was like her presence within him was comforting rather than intrusive, almost like a support blanket wrapped around every part of his mind. Her presence was the missing link that made him complete. All too soon, she removed herself, leaving Vishnu wanting. He opened his eyes, and the very sight of her brought him peace.

Vishnu looked at her with wide eyes; hunger replaced fear within an instant. There was a hunger in his eyes so fierce that it needed to be attended to immediately, and Youkoni was the only one who could satisfy it. With a growl, he pulled her closer and began kissing her fiercely. When air was needed, they paused only to remove their clothing. Wasting no time, they made for the bed and continued where they'd left off. Their need for each other was primordial, and the responding presence brought a release of joy through them both that could only be expressed through a heart song.

◆ ◆ ◆

Vishnu lay there breathless and sweaty. Youkoni's long hair was sprawled all around him. She was under there somewhere, he knew, and he wanted to hold her. The buzzing of their hearts was loud enough to be heard for miles, and it took him no time at all to locate her. They lay in each other's arms, content. Youkoni's yellow and jade green overlapped Vishnu's moss.

"Are you all right, my love?" Youkoni asked, her voice cutting through the buzzing for the first time as she looked up at him.

"More than all right," he responded, smiling at her. "I'm…" He trailed off, looking at the little room's entrance. "Do you hear that?"

"Drums," they both exclaimed, sitting up.

"Not just any drums, Vishnu. Those are…" Youkoni trailed off as she and Vishnu noticed the glowing room for the first time. Every flower had a faint glow, transforming the little room into a glowing ball of white light. Youkoni and Vishnu looked at each other, smiling.

"How long do you think they'll wait before coming for us?"

"I'd rather not give them the opportunity," Vishnu said, getting to his feet. He grabbed Youkoni's belt along with his sash and reached for her hand. They walked around the little glowing room until Vishnu found a small opening in the flowers.

On the other side, they found a small pond. The same flowers lay all around it and in the surrounding forest. There were so many of them that it looked like a small, glowing cave. To his left lay the only color in it, a pair of black slacks, and a golden, sleeveless shirt with black boots. There was also a black, sleeveless dress with golden embroidery along the bust, and knee-high strapped sandals with three-inch heels covered in miniature straps as well. Vishnu set aside the things he carried with the clothing and walked hand in hand into the pond with Youkoni.

After a short time, they reluctantly climbed out and headed for their clothing.

Once dressed, the pair walked down the flowery path to their waiting witnesses and were delighted to see who was there.

"There you are," Vishnu's mother said, smiling.

"We thought you were going to stay in there through another moon cycle," added his father.

"Hello mother," Vishnu replied, smiling as he reached to embrace her, ignoring his father's statement. Stofena embraced him gently and looked to Youkoni.

"Greetings, Stofena."

"Welcome to the family," Stofena replied, embracing Youkoni. They were similarly dressed, only Stofena's dress had sleeves and rich blue embroidery across the bust.

"To what do we owe the—wait, did you say moon cycle? How long were we in there?" Vishnu asked.

"Four days," his father replied proudly. "And we've had to turn away your congratulators for two of them."

His mother interrupted. "The lights have been shining brightly now for three days. Congratulations."

"But we must be going," his father added. "I fear the council will want to come up and congratulate you next." Vishnu and Youkoni shared a brief look before starting down the path hand in hand behind Stofena, who stood just below her husband's neckline.

The flower trail was littered with gifts from friends, family, well-wishers, and admirers. Vishnu could see that some had waited until they could see the couple's return before placing their gifts along the path. This made their return trip slightly more difficult as the four climbed, pulled, and jumped their way back to the banquet hall. Well-wishing began as soon as the group came into view. No one stepped on the flowery path, but that didn't keep everyone from crowding into every available space around it.

Cheers broke out the minute the hall came into view, which erupted into a loud roar as they entered. Elitar was slightly irritated as he stood waiting with outstretched arms to greet the approaching honored guests, motioning for the council to stand. Slowly the crowd became quiet. When all was still and the newly bound couple stood above the crowd, Elitar spoke.

"Honored elders, bloodlines, and guests, we've gathered in this place to celebrate the bond of Vishnu and Youkoni. As we enjoy this evening's festivities, I challenge each of you to look upon them in peace and welcome their bond as you would that of your own parentage."

He then embraced them both and returned to his seat, where he removed his crown and dug into his meal. One by one the council stood before them and offered similar congratulations. By night's end, the couple had spent more time accepting well-wishes than celebrating, and each had a bad case of aching feet.

◆ ◆ ◆

Roughly eight moons after the merger, Youkoni was called upon to go on a diplomatic mission to a star system located on the eastern sublevel of Elquin's star, roughly forty light-years away. Although scientists knew of this star system, the interest in farming did not develop until after a transmission was picked up from a lifeless vessel outlining the region. It provided a general description of its inhabitants and the atmospheric conditions.

"I don't want to go so far either, love," Youkoni complained after Vishnu's initial objections. "But we all have to do our part if Elquin is to have a future."

"It isn't Elquin's future that I object," Vishnu countered. "I am concerned about you." He walked over to her and sat down by her feet, which dangled on the edge of the bed.

"I have been on eighty-three missions since Oororah-9, Vishnu."

"And none of them displayed the level of intelligence this world has," Vishnu countered. "Moreover, none of them has been able to respond to our probes, let alone launch one of their own with such accuracy. The atmospheric readings of this world are incredibly complex and may indicate a closer match to Elquin than any other star system we've encountered. The implications are incredible and may suggest a level of hostility we've never encountered before."

Youkoni sighed. "I'll be all right, love. You'll see. We both will."

"It's not my father I'm worried about either." He sat on the bed and looked into her eyes. "You carry more than Elquin's future when you travel, Youkoni. I cannot bear to think of you or our future young one in danger," he said, placing a hand on her midsection.

"Your father will see to our safety, Vishnu. Try not to worry so much."

"It is because of my father's presence that I can even bear the thought of you being so far away from me." He sighed heavily. "I know this trip is just an initial contact, but I want you to take great care, Youkoni. Stay close to my father and come home safely. I have not had my fill of you."

Youkoni smiled. "All right," she said, pulling him closer for a kiss that left him breathless and hungry for more. "And how long"—kiss—"do you think"—kiss—"it will be"—kiss—"before you've had your fill?"

"Not even after a thousand lifetimes," he responded and kissed her with a passion that left them both panting and fighting with each other's clothing. That was the last night they shared together before Youkoni journeyed to Earth.

The report of her death ripped holes through every part of him. Vishnu retreated into his duties for Elquin with a renewed passion unmatched by anyone in Elquin history.

◆ ◆ ◆

Overcome with a wave of physical pain brought on by his memory, Taren was forced to pull over. Simultaneously, the navigation voice began: "The orb has stopped on Interstate 15, at mile-marker 90. Do you wish to follow?" The pain had bound Taren so tightly that he was unable to answer. Within seconds he blacked out. *No*, he thought, *Locknoff cannot find her first...*

It was midmorning before Taren opened his eyes.

"Where's the orb?" he shouted too loudly while sitting up.

"Calculating," responded the feminine voice, its eyes pointed to the left briefly before speaking again. "The orb is located on Interstate 40, currently passing mile-marker 57. Do you wish to follow?"

"Yes," Taren shouted angrily, pulling onto the road with more force than necessary.

Fourteen

A Necessary Inconvenience

"What are we looking for, Ahdortee?" Locknoff asked.

"I'm inputting the address now," she replied, pulling a small computer from under the seat. A woman's face appeared on the screen.

"Good day, Ahdortee. How may I be of assistance?"

Ahdortee ignored the voice and pushed one of the keys on the notebook.

"Your destination is 4.7 miles from here. Turn right in 1.3 miles on Redden Street."

As the navigation continued, Locknoff asked, "What's with you females? How hard is it to understand that some males just aren't into bonding?"

"Because," Ahdortee replied sarcastically, "we want what we want, and apparently a heart song isn't always required."

"Turn left in 3.0 miles on Bannard Road."

"What are you waiting for, Locknoff? It's not like you're getting any younger. You've had many moon cycles unbonded. Why not share the rest of them with someone? She obviously adores you."

"*Because,*" he said, dramatically cutting her off, "Elquin's future demands my attention at the moment. When things settle down…"

"Your destination is on your right."

"Perhaps I'll consider...bonding." He pulled over to the curb and answered his ringing cell phone while getting out of the car. "Yes, Rashanah."

"Taren is gone."

"What!" Locknoff barked. "How!"

Ahdortee froze and looked over at him.

"I'm not sure. Celtine and I went to share a meal when Sariah left the room, and when we returned, her assistant was in the room passed out on the floor, and Taren was gone. I think he may have tricked him somehow."

"Ya think!" Locknoff shouted. "Where is Sariah?"

"Tracking the orb."

Locknoff stiffened, looked at the house, and asked, "Where is it now?"

"Traveling south on Highway 93."

"How long has he been gone?"

"No more than an hour. We were—"

"Why did you wait so long to call me?" Locknoff interrupted.

"We wanted to be sure he was not on facility grounds."

Locknoff took a deep breath. "Next time, call me immediately! Tell Sariah to have a workstation prepared for me when I get back. This won't take long," he said, looking at the front door.

"Yes, Master Locknoff," Rashanah replied.

Locknoff hung up and sighed heavily.

"What is it?" Ahdortee inquired, reading his expression.

"Taren has escaped."

Everyone gasped. Porock and Jussalte looked at each other.

"Where did he go?" Ahdortee asked.

Locknoff looked at her as if she was missing something obvious. "The orb."

She gasped as Locknoff headed toward the house.

"Let's find out what we can here. Perhaps we'll meet him there before too long. Porock, Jussalte, stay here. This won't take long."

Ahdortee joined him, and the others returned to the car.

A firm knock revealed one of the women Locknoff recognized from the security photos. She was dressed in a pink-and-white nightgown.

"Good evening, ma'am. My name is Jonathan Grady, and this is Angelia Silva. I apologize for the hour. We represent a private security firm investigating the disturbance in the hotel parking area earlier this evening. May we come in for a moment? There are a few things we'd like to discuss with you regarding the incident."

The woman's eyebrows drew down instantaneously.

"Now? What kind of things?"

Locknoff scanned the area quickly. "Just a few questions about what you saw, ma'am, and I promise we won't take up too much of your time."

The woman looked from Locknoff to Ahdortee briefly and then sighed. "I suppose a few minutes won't ruin my night. Come in."

"Thank you," Locknoff said as he and Ahdortee stepped through the door. "Is your name Cara Johnson?"

"Yes," she replied skeptically, raising an eyebrow.

"Forgive my forcefulness, ma'am. We've already spoken with your friends at the hotel."

"Oh," Cara replied, but comprehension did not touch her eyes. In fact, they looked more suspicious, if that were possible. "How can I help you?" she continued.

"Is your friend Jennifer Braxton here?"

"Jen…no, why?"

"We believe," Locknoff said, motioning to Ahdortee, "that the man you and your friends bumped into this evening may have given her something very dangerous. It is imp—"

"But he didn't," Cara said interrupting him. "He didn't give her anything. He only kissed her and said thanks for helping him up." She shrugged. "That's all."

Ahdortee could see Locknoff's frustration level rising and interjected. "What we're looking for is very small. It could fit into her pants or jacket pocket easily and be there for weeks before she even realized it."

"Well, she left a little while ago, but if you tell me what you're looking for, I'll call her and have her check her pockets."

"That wouldn't be a good idea," Locknoff said. "What he gave her is a very dangerous piece of technological equipment. She can activate it accidentally just by investigating it. It would be better if she was unaware of its presence."

"But what if she finds it before you find her?" Cara said with concern in her voice.

"I'm sure we will be able to find her quickly with your help, Cara, so there's really no reason for you to worry. We just need to know where she went."

Cara was quiet for so long that Locknoff began to wonder if she was even listening. After a few moments, she looked at him and asked, "What did he do?"

"I'm sorry?" Locknoff responded.

"The man from the parking lot. What did he do?"

Ahdortee and Locknoff shared a look before addressing her.

"He was caught stealing technological information from the hotel," said Ahdortee. When Cara's suspicious look did not change, she continued, "The technology he took was designed as a defensive mechanism for the hotel's vault security system." Cara's eyes widened. "Once activated, it destroys any IT-based equipment within several hundred yards, effectively disabling the vault through all but manual operations."

Cara was speechless for a moment, but she seemed calculating. Locknoff raised one eyebrow as he watched her.

"So," Cara said, sarcasm lacing every word, "this isn't about aliens or world domination or anything, huh?"

Locknoff met Ahdortee's eyes briefly, and they simultaneously chuckled. "Ha! Where would you get an idea like that?"

"I don't know," Cara replied, walking over to her small dining room table to retrieve a pad and pen. She shrugged. "Jen was going on about some dream before she left. I'm not sure what it was all about, but she woke up determined to leave. Said she couldn't sleep anymore, mentioned something about aliens." She laughed, shaking her head.

"Hmm…" Locknoff responded more to himself than to her.

"She's on her way back to school," Cara said while writing. "She attends the University of Florida. Jennifer is a fast driver, so I don't think it will take her more than a day to get there. If you don't catch up with her, she lives in the western wing of Freelance Hall, building B. They'll give you the room number at the dorm…"

Suddenly her words turned into a gurgle, and she hit the floor, clutching her neck with an expression of shocked disbelief.

"Get the blood," Locknoff said as Ahdortee stepped back away from the oozing pool. She looked up from the pad to see him wiping a triple-bladed weapon clean of her blood. The blades retracted, and he replaced the weapon underneath his clothing. Stepping over her body, Locknoff continued.

"We know where the orb's going. We'll head back and get some rest. There isn't much more we can do tonight. Get four tickets. We leave at first light. I must consult with the council about Taren's latest actions."

He returned to the car, and Ahdortee quickly retrieved a vial of Cara's blood before joining him.

"But I don't understand," Jussalte said, the lines on his forehead squinting with the effort of trying, transforming his already battered face into a mask of purple and yellow. "Why kill her? Wouldn't she be of better use as a prisoner?"

"Not necessarily," Porock responded while leaning back in his seat aboard the 757 bound for Florida.

"The little she did know could have done more harm than good in the end. Remember, the other one will forget what she knows as soon as the orb is removed, but if she dies beforehand, then her friend could become a liability. We must neutralize any possible threat before moving forward. All operations must be carried out without rumor of fact."

"What about Taren?"

"The council was clear. He is to be returned to headquarters and changed. We cannot—"

"Ahem," Locknoff muttered while forcefully returning his tray table into the back of Porock's seat, effectively ending his explanation.

Locknoff leaned his seat back as far as it would go and closed his eyes. Sighing heavily, he opened his eyes and reached for the button to call the flight attendant. Midway, however, Ahdortee put something black and smooth in his hands before leaning back into her own seat to catch a catnap.

"Thanks," he said, opening the cloth and placing it over his eyes. He could smell the herbs mixed in the cool cloth infusion designed to help with pain relief.

"You're welcome."

Locknoff tried but found it difficult to rest. His long day was further extended by the frustrating council meeting, which left him restless. Bathmantu had suggested Taren return to Elquin at once.

"We cannot," Nesset interjected. Nesset looked directly at Elitar when she spoke. "We're sending a fleet to Earth in less than a moon cycle. Vishnu is one of Elquin's most efficient protectors, and he is well informed of the situation at hand. We cannot afford to replace him now."

"He has disobeyed orders!" Bathmantu shouted. "And he is effectively delaying plans that have been in place for over eight pieleen. He dishonors Ateenn blood with every act. What would you suggest we do with him?"

"Has the decision to consider his request been eliminated by his recent actions?" Nesset asked calmly.

"His request...bah! We owe him nothing," Bathmantu said.

"We owe him," Skyke interjected in a lecturing tone, "the chance of a new beginning. The review he has asked for in no uncertain terms."

"There is no time for a review. We are beginning to lose centimeters daily."

"All the more reason to consider every possibility before moving forward," Skyke concluded.

"Madafski, Skyke," Elitar said in a rough voice, "run a diagnostic. We will discuss the matter in four days. For the time being, Nesset is right. Vishnu will be of better use where he is."

"Secured behind a door?" Madafski asked sarcastically.

"No," Locknoff said, speaking for the first time. Everyone turned to him then. "No," he repeated.

"Have you a better idea?" Elitar asked.

"Vishnu is angry but reasonable. If Sariah transforms him to his Elquin state, he will have no choice but to stay at headquarters for the time being, away from the humans. Moreover, his heightened sensitivity will allow us to resolve his recent transgressions and focus on the task at hand."

Everyone was quiet, and then Bathmantu sighed. Skyke and Madafski looked at each other questioningly, and Nesset looked as if she would cry. "I take it no one has any objections?"

Every council member replied in turn. Some said no; others simply shook their heads.

"All right then, we will reconvene in four days. Be sure Vishnu is here by then," Elitar said, looking at Locknoff.

Locknoff bowed his head slightly and logged off. *Considering his recent loss,* Locknoff thought, *Taren will suffer greatly for a time, but his Elquin form should remind him of his allegiance and keep him away from the humans... for now at least.* That was enough for Locknoff. He sighed again and adjusted his position in the seat.

Fifteen

MISSING CHORUS

After her third cup of coffee, Jennifer had no choice but to answer nature's call, so she headed for the nearest exit in search of a lavatory. Once the car was parked, she jumped out and bolted for the restrooms of a rest stop, nearly knocking over a slow-moving couple who seemed to be enjoying each other's company.

"Sorry," she yelled, glancing over her shoulder while making her way into the ladies' room. *I hope there's no line.* She thanked the stars as she rounded the corner to see two empty stalls. Leaping for the one closest to her, Jennifer unfastened her blue jeans, locked the door, and began relieving herself all in the same moment.

Ahh, she thought as her bladder emptied, relaxing every muscle in the process. Jennifer exhaled slowly and stood to replace her clothing, but she instantly fell back onto the seat. "Hmm," she said aloud as she registered the fainting feeling she'd just experienced. *Perhaps I should have something to eat too,* she thought. She slowly stood to replace her clothing. Gently, Jennifer applied her moist hands to her neck after washing them. The cool touch felt nice, and she reluctantly headed for the snack bar.

The rest stop was a full-service area, equipped with six refueling pumps, three different food bars, a gift shop featuring road maps, and a souvenir shop alongside a small video-game room. She chose the first place she saw: a sandwich shop. Although she wasn't hungry, she'd been on the road for hours and could obviously use a meal. After searching the menu for something that sounded appetizing, Jennifer settled on a meatball sub with Parmesan cheese, chips, bottled water, and a pickle. As she sat eating, she noticed a little girl standing in line with her mother. She clutched a doll to her chest and was covered from head to toe in red-and-white ruffles. The little girl smiled at Jennifer, who smiled back.

Jen's attention unwillingly returned to the strange dreams she'd been having. For some reason, she could not get them out of her head. She even tried calling her friends in an effort to focus on something else, but couldn't get through for some reason. Because none of them responded, not even Nancy, who would have certainly been on her way home by now. She figured they were all busy or at the festival. *I'll call them later*, she concluded. *Why am I having these dreams?*

What importance could they have? Who was she dreaming about? The beings in them were so real to her…in her memory, anyway. It was like they'd always been there or like she recognized them because she'd always known them. *There isn't a doctor on Earth who wouldn't admit me*, she thought, reaching for her water bottle. As she did, Jennifer's eyes focused on the condensation dripping on the outside of the bottle. Her vision momentarily clouded, and she blinked a few times and could see into another world.

Rain filled the bright-blue sky as Vishnu stood unprotected, clutching his pistol. The silver crescents gleamed in the light. He wore a beige, sleeveless shirt with brown cargo pants and black boots. In his other hand was a spear. It had an oddly shaped head. It was three dimensional with four equally raised edges. In between the edges and along the sides were miniature crescent-shaped hocks with edges facing inward. At Vishnu's feet lay the body of a Tishod fighter.

One half of its body from shoulder to ankle was simply gone. The leathery, gray face covered in a rough, sand-like substance held an expression of horrified disbelief. A sigh from behind made him shift his otherwise statue-like body. Vishnu's eyes stayed locked on the sporadic movement in the tree line ahead of him. Every few minutes he would see a head or two pop out from behind a tree and quickly retreat when their eyes met his.

"No worries, Officer Vishnu. I do not believe they will test their courage against you now."

Vishnu sighed and relaxed his shoulders slightly. "Perhaps. I'd rather not give them the opportunity to consider it."

"What are you doing, Vishnu? We don't aggressively defend against technologically underdeveloped species. You know that."

"Underdeveloped!" he yelled, turning to face Locknoff and holding the spear high enough for him to see. He pointed toward the building fifty yards away and said, "Did you see what they did to Afenah or Elaron or even Porock? He'll be lucky to walk away from this with even one heart intact, let alone two!"

"It was a skirmish, Vishnu. You know that. Barely worth the effort. They are simply trying to regain some honor. And Porock will be fine. The medical staff can remove the stick without causing any more harm and repair the damage."

"That isn't what I'm referring to."

"You have to talk about it, Vishnu. You lose more of yourself every day. Another six moons of this and there will be no turning back for you."

"I have no idea what you're talking about," Vishnu said, tossing the spear aside and returning his attention to the trees.

Locknoff peered at him suspiciously but said nothing. Sighing heavily, he turned to walk away but stopped when Vishnu spoke.

"I don't know how to go on without her," he said, pacing now as he watched the trees. "It feels like the very core of my being has been ripped from my soul. I love Elquin, and her existence is vital to our survival, but I'm not sure what it all means to me without her."

"You'll find another heart song, brother. You—"

"I've lost everything!" he shouted, interrupting Locknoff and pausing to stare him in the eye. "My chorus, my young one, my father, my mother..." He sighed and shook his head, not paying any attention to the tears that threatened to fall.

"Locknoff, I couldn't even mourn her...my own mother. I've been numb since the moment I heard the report. My mother's siblings had to perform the ceremony of passage for me. I couldn't even speak to return my own mother." He began pacing again. "The only time I feel purpose calling me is when I am actively protecting Elquin. I know of no other way."

Locknoff's expression remained encouraging, but it didn't touch his eyes. He placed an arm on Vishnu's shoulders to stop his pacing, looked him in the eyes, and said, "These beings will pay for what they've done, brother. By their own actions, they have left us no choice. New tactics have been approved, and we will enter their realm as one of their own. You will have the chance for revenge, Vishnu, and your loss will not be for naught. Your parents will live on through you, and Youkoni will always be part of you. I shall count the days until I can stand by your side at council for bonding."

"Bonding...I will never bond again."

As Vishnu blinked away droplets of rain and looked at the sky, Jennifer's vision faded, and she could see the condensation on the water bottle. Instantly, her hands shot up to either side of her head, responding to the agony brought on by her vision. She gasped at the pain, and tears rolled down her cheeks.

"Are you all right, miss?" the little girl's mother asked from her seat at the table across from Jennifer. After a few moments, Jennifer's gasps became pants.

"Yes. I'm fine. Just a migraine, I guess." A few minutes later, her pain subsided, and her breathing was normal.

"They're not friendly," she said aloud.

"What's that?"

Jennifer looked at the woman. "They're not friendly," she shouted.

"Who?" the woman asked, but Jennifer was already on her feet.

She'd taken her food and water mechanically. *Am I losing it,* she thought, *or is there really a battle brewing between some alien world and Earth? The government has been denying the existence of extraterrestrial life on Earth for years. Who knows? Maybe I'm not crazy after all. I'll have to speak with Lu.*

As she trotted past the crowded food bars, Jennifer fixed her vision on her car. She didn't even turn her head as she yelled "Sorry" to some guy she'd bumped into. The minute she stepped outside, her eyes started burning. It was so bright. She used her hands to shield her eyes. By the time she reached her car, tears rolled down her cheeks. Jennifer found her sunglasses, started the car, and drove off in the same minute. She was vaguely aware of a man standing a little too close to the car. She might have hit him if she was not paying attention to what she was doing.

"What the hell, dude? Do you want to get smashed?" she asked no one as she merged into traffic. Not more than a mile down the road, her cell phone rang. Jennifer stopped midrant to double check the caller ID. It was Nancy Peterson returning her call at last.

She smiled. "It's about time someone returned my—" was all she got to say before Nancy's words stunned her silent.

"Cara's dead…someone attacked her last night."

"Not possible. I was just with her all night. Well, I left at about two a.m., but she was going right back to sleep. She said so. I don't understand. What happened, Nancy?"

"I don't know, Jen. I guess someone else came to see her after you left, because the cops said there was no sign of forced entry. They sliced her throat, Jen. I can't get a hold of Kim or any of the others. I only came by because I wanted to see if you guys needed a hand with anything. Where are you?"

"I'm about to pick up Highway 75. I'll be home in less than an hour, Nancy. I don't know what's going on, but I'll call you back when I get there. Make sure the others are OK. Be careful. Call me when you get to the hotel. It doesn't matter what time. Maybe the others know something. I've been waiting for a response from them too."

"I will, Jen, and you be careful too. Good-bye."

"Bye."

Jennifer was numb. Here she was daydreaming about some alien world that may or may not exist, and her best friend was murdered without her having even an inkling of foresight. Focusing on the road ahead, she decided there would be no more distractions. No more dreams of crazy places and people if she could help it. She focused on her path, thought only of good times with Cara, and saw nothing but traffic and road signs.

As dusk settled into early evening, Jennifer pulled into the student parking area of the western wing. Slowly she got out of the car, grabbed her things, and went into her Freelance Hall apartment.

Freelance Hall held some of the more private studios on campus. Jennifer's room was small but spacious enough for two. She graciously paid the extra cost of not having a roommate. The walls were a warm milkshake brown, and the exposed brick framed two large windows. Jennifer favored simplicity and only had one or two paintings lining the walls. She had a queen-sized bed in the far right corner and a work desk in the other. Her lounge chair was big enough for two and looked comfortable enough to hold her hostage for hours. The hardwood floors made it difficult for her to hide her movements from others in the hall, but she liked the look and relief it offered her from seasonal allergies.

She turned on the news the minute she walked in the door and was shocked once again to hear the confirmation of Nancy's words. Jennifer, beginning to feel sick, ran to the bathroom. She lifted the toilet seat and unleashed a steady stream of vomit that lasted a good two minutes. Afterward, she brushed her teeth and jumped into the shower. Relief washed through her for a moment, and then grief overcame her, and she wept for her dead friend.

When the water turned cold and her shivering body protested her stance, she reluctantly got out of the shower, put on a robe, and made her way to bed. Minutes after she closed her eyes, a knock pounded on the door. She was beyond frustrated and wanted nothing more than to ignore the knock, but she knew it was a bad idea. Whoever it was sounded like he or she was not going to go away. So she pulled herself out of bed and dragged her feet to the door.

"What have we got, Ahdortee?" Locknoff asked, pulling away from the rental car parking lot. Ahdortee opened her notebook and pulled out a long cylinder canister. When she unscrewed the top, steam escaped as the seal was broken. Ahdortee pulled the vial of Cara's blood out, opened a pocket to the right side of the notebook, and inserted the vial.

"Analyzing," the voice said as the eyes looked to the left. Less than a minute later, a DNA strand appeared.

Ahdortee typed in "Jennifer Braxton," and a slew of information appeared on the screen. She scrolled down several lines and then said,

"Jennifer Braxton is in the third year of a six-year clinical doctorate program at the University of Florida. She is a member of Kappa Theta Nu, working toward a physical therapy degree and licensing. Jennifer lives in room 365B on the third floor of Freelance Hall. She is currently dating a Gamma Sigma who lives in the fraternity house on campus."

"How long before the orb gets here?"

"At her current rate of travel, about eight and a half hours."

"Good. Get a layout of the building." She nodded, closed the notebook, and looked at the road ahead.

In no time at all, they reached the general parking area in front of the Freelance Hall building. Ahdortee wasted no time exiting the car. As she left, Locknoff leaned his seat back and closed his eyes. Eight hours was plenty of time to get some shut-eye, he concluded as Ahdortee disappeared into the building. Jussalte and Porock followed his lead and settled down for a long wait.

Before long, Ahdortee returned, slamming shut the door and pulling her long, black locks into a thong.

"Filthy creatures. I don't understand how they still exist. They have no honor and will destroy themselves long before their star does the trick. We should not risk valuable Elquin lives on the creatures. Not one!"

Locknoff opened his eyes, took in Ahdortee's demeanor, and said with a smirk, "Does your honor need defending, Master Ahdortee?"

She released her hair, letting the locks settle a moment, and scowled at him. "My honor is intact, Master Locknoff. What I lack is the sympathy shared by so many for this primitive species." She sighed heavily. "No time for stating the obvious—it will be a topic for another day. Things should go quite smoothly tonight. There is a falling star or comet or something scheduled to fly close enough to Earth to see with the naked eye, so just about everyone will be gathering on the lawn to watch."

"Good. Our journey ends tonight, the moment she returns."

◆ ◆ ◆

A catnap later and Ahdortee was waking Locknoff. "The orb's arrived."

"Where is she?"

"Stationary on the third floor."

"Good. Let's go."

As the four exited the car, Celtine asked, "Are we to capture or retrieve the orb?"

Without missing a step, Locknoff answered, "Whatever is easiest."

Sixteen

TREASURE HUNT

The tires protested as Taren pulled away, leaving marks along the road. With his memory of the night's events placed aside for the moment, he was able to focus on the task at hand. He had to get to her before Locknoff did, or she wouldn't live to see another day. For hours he drove upward of twenty-five miles over the speed limit, stopping only to fill up the tank when he took the opportunity to get snacks and visit the lavatory.

Suddenly the feminine voice on his phone spoke out, "The orb has stopped. Do you wish to follow?"

"Where?"

"At 2.74 miles from this location between mile-marker 743 and 744. Do you wish to follow?"

"Yes." Taren was relived as he pulled into a rest stop and noted the orb's location inside. He saw no signs of ERT pursuit.

He parked in the closest spot and pulled out the picture Sariah had put into his bag to refresh his memory, because all he could remember about her was that she had blue eyes. Recognition ran through him the moment he saw her picture. He got out of the car and headed into the building, quickly scanning the faces he passed. No one resembled the woman he sought, so he moved his search along, staying close to the exit, reasoning that he'd catch her on the way out.

Taren didn't have to wait long, for as he turned from one direction to look in the other, the woman ran right into him. She didn't stop to look or try to pacify him in any way; she just yelled "Sorry" and kept running. It all happened so fast that by the time he realized it was her, she was out the door. Quickly he went after her, but she was already in her car when he got outside.

Perhaps if I stand in her way, he thought. But she was single minded, focusing only on the road ahead. She pulled out farther than necessary in an effort not to hit him. While Taren appreciated her actions, he needed to get her attention. Walking swiftly to his car, he made his way onto the highway, but she was already miles ahead of him. Irritated, he turned to his phone and said, "Locate the orb."

"The orb is merging onto Interstate 75. Do you wish to follow?"

"Yes." Taren felt a hint of irritation at his recognition of the woman, because he'd only seen her once and could not recognize her from his wife's circle of friends. After twenty minutes of driving, Taren was surprised that he'd still not caught up with her. "She's in a hurry to get somewhere," he said aloud.

Just then, the voice spoke. "The orb is exiting the interstate. It is merging onto Highway 4, southbound."

"Follow!" Taren shouted as he sped up, hoping to close the distance.

After fifteen minutes of driving, he noticed the destination: the University of Florida. *Interesting*, he thought. Finding his way to the general parking area, Taren chose a secluded spot in the far right corner and put on a gray hooded sweatshirt. He placed the syringe into his pocket and got out of the car.

Marching into the building as if he belonged, Taren paused and quickly scanned over the parking area. He noticed the presence of a long-haired brunette with a striking resemblance to Ahdortee and immediately made his way further into the building with a renewed determination to retrieve the orb quickly. He pulled out his phone, muted it, and pushed several buttons. After a moment, he located the stairway and headed up.

◆ ◆ ◆

Jennifer sighed as she realized who could be at the door. *I don't have time for this*, she thought. She opened the door, and in barged Zackary Mason.

"Good, you're back."

Jennifer walked past him to the bed and sat down. She picked up her brush and started brushing her hair mechanically. Zackary stood about five feet eleven, weighing roughly 280 pounds, with muscles pouring out of every available space in his clothes. He wore a navy-blue T-shirt that was two sizes too small, a pair of dark-blue jean shorts, and black-and-white tennis shoes. He looked at her for a long moment with lowered eyebrows and then asked, "You're not coming?"

She sighed, shaking her head. "I'm sorry, Zack, but I'm not feeling well."

"Not feeling well…but Jen, we've been planning this party for two months."

"You're gonna have to go without me, Zack. I've been feeling really sick for the past couple of days, and Cara was…" She paused, taking a deep breath. "Cara was killed this morning."

"Go without you?" he asked, not hearing the rest of her words. "You're my girlfriend, Jennifer. I expect you to be at my side when I need you, and tonight I need you."

"I'm sorry, Zack," she said, shaking her head, "but I'm not go—" Abruptly she stopped talking when he walked over and forcefully grabbed her hand midstroke.

He suddenly flung her through the air and watched as she came to an abrupt stop as her back hit the brick wall between her windows. Jennifer was stunned. Her entire left side was numb. Her head swam as she tried to understand what was happening. Zack closed the distance between them in two long strides. He pulled her up by her hair, ignoring her protest, and tossed her hard across the floor. The chair met her shoulder as she slammed into it with a grunt.

What's with him? she wondered. He never treated her this way before, no matter how important he thought his fraternity gatherings were. Then she realized—just as he landed a kick to her ribs, lifted her by the hair, and punched her repeatedly in the face—*I never gave him the chance. I always dreamed about what he would do and was always able to counter it somehow. I haven't dreamed about him at all.* As realization hit, she was gasping for air and holding her midsection tightly as he kicked her again. Jennifer wondered how long this would last as he reached down and grabbed her by the hair again—but was himself tossed halfway across the room by a force she did not see.

She didn't have the strength to look; all she could do was gasp. When she caught her breath, Jennifer noticed her left ear ringing. Her head pounded, her back was on fire, and a sharp pain extended from her neck to the top of her head. Stunned, she reached up and felt blood. She tried to focus but could only hear grunts. Before long, Zack fell to the floor. Her vision was getting blurry, and the side of her chest felt like a brick was sitting on top of a knife that was jammed deep into her ribs. Her back stung, and she knew she would fall if she even tried to get up. She turned her head in order to get a better look at whoever had helped her and was almost blinded by warm liquid as it came gushing down the side of her face. Jennifer blinked several times, and her savior bent to help her up.

She reluctantly moved to sit on the bed, and her savior disappeared into the bathroom. Jennifer heard the water come on and asked, "Brian, is that you? Thanks." She continued without giving him the chance to respond. "I don't know what happened."

"No." She heard an unfamiliar voice respond, "I'm not Brian." She blinked several times in response, trying to clear her vision, and took in her room for the first time.

Her bed was tilted slightly, her lamp was knocked on its side, the entertainment center was completely destroyed, and shelves lay broken on the floor, their contents scattered everywhere. Zackary was face-down on the floor, his large frame covering almost the entire length of the little room. If it weren't for the steady rise and fall of his back, she would have thought he was dead.

"I didn't think you'd mind my interference." Jennifer looked up to see a towel placed in her hands.

"Thank you. No, I don't mind," she said, wiping at the blood on her face. As she pulled the towel down, her eyes fell on a familiar face. Familiar because from the moment he kissed her, she could not get the image of his face out of her head. Familiar because everything that was happening to her was a result of her courtesy that day. She gasped, and her eyes grew about three inches. She tried to back away, but every muscle protested, and she found herself closer to him in spite of her efforts.

"Please don't freak out," the stranger said. "My name is Taren Waters, and I'm..." was all she heard as her eyes locked onto his, and she doubled over in a fit of pain. Jennifer squeezed her eyes shut and pressed her palms to her temples, but she couldn't stop herself from crying out. Although her eyes were shut tightly, she could see him clearly in another light. Taren was standing in a brightly lit bathroom with his eyes closed shut. He sighed heavily and opened them. What she saw next was shocking, but she could not look away, no matter how badly she wanted to run back to the present.

Seventeen

INFORMANT

Jennifer watched as Taren removed a small black box from his brief-case and placed it onto the bathroom counter with a look of deter-mination in his eyes. Inside, he removed a snugly fit cylinder-shaped crystal bottle. The bottle contained a dark-blue, misty orb. Taren re-moved the bottle from its sleeve carefully and then removed the top and bottom of the crystal casing, leaving the orb suspended in midair. He opened his mouth and breathed in deeply. The orb floated into his mouth and quickly connected to the tissue at the back of his throat. When he closed his mouth, the orb dimmed and disappeared complete-ly from Jennifer's sight.

Wearing nothing at all, Taren walked out of the bathroom and into the bedroom of what looked like a honeymoon suite where a young woman waited. Jennifer recognized her face from a dream she'd had once. The woman was lying between two decorative blue pillows on top of two larger-than-necessary white pillows, surrounded by lilies. At the foot of the bed there was a folded blue blanket nestling two kiss-ing swans that were adorned with red roses. Over the bed and hanging from the ceiling, there were white drapes that enclosed the shape of the bed with white-laced fabric. *Wow,* Jennifer thought. "So beautiful," she said absentmindedly, vaguely paying attention to Taren, who quickly made his way to his wife's side. She sat up to meet his piercing eyes and blinked, gazing back into them.

"I love you, Lilly," was all he had time to say before she pressed her lips against his fiercely. Taren wrapped his arm around her waist, pulling her into him while parting his lips as he met hers. Grabbing the back of her head, Taren used his free hand to pull her head closer to him and kissed her with a passion that might light the room on fire. Making use of the pillows, he then freed her lips, leaving her gasping, and moved on to her neck, where he kissed softly. She moaned slightly, and he moved down a bit farther to kiss her breasts. Taking them firmly in hand, Taren kneaded them and ran his tongue around her nipples several times before sucking on each of them in turn.

He moved down to Lillian's stomach next, where he kissed her gently, but did not stop kneading her breasts. He spent a few moments more licking and sucking on her nipples and then fondled every part of her he could reach. Making a full circle before returning to her lips, Taren looked into her eyes and smiled, then kissed her fiercely again, ensuring that his tongue, which was now saturated with a thin layer of sky-blue mist, touched the roof of her mouth. Jennifer's eyes bulged as she looked on. Before moving to kiss her neck again, Taren traced her lips with his tongue, which no longer showed any signs of the mist.

On the roof of Lillian's mouth, the blue orb had completely enclosed itself. Jennifer gasped as the orb moved swiftly through Lilly's tissues, leaving only traces of blue as it disappeared. Taren continued to make love with his wife, confident in the completion of his task. Jennifer closed her eyes and tried not to listen but could not help peeking when she heard voices. With lowered brows, she looked around and listened closely.

"The protective layer around it provides adequate safety for its resources. Additionally, the behavior of its star suggests that the planet is safe from implosion for perhaps another several thousand millennia.

With the information Vishnu has provided, we have an accurate composite of the natives' military behavioral patterns. Combined with what we have already discovered through informants strategically placed about this planet, I would say we are victorious well before the battle commences."

"Victorious?" one of the females interrupted in a suppressed tone. Jennifer recognized most of them as the beings she had seen before in the bathroom mirror not long ago.

"You presume too much, Bathmantu."

"Victory would suggest that the natives are not going to put up much of a fight. Do not forget the price we have paid getting to this point. Nor should you presume that our actions will not cost us dearly." Taren stiffened at her words and began to speak but was not the fastest.

"Forgive my insensitivity, Nesset," Bathmantu replied humbly. "I merely meant to point out the fact that Vishnu has gained access to an excellent source of information that will prove useful in the future."

"I—" Nesset began but was interrupted yet again.

"Is war the only option?" Taren asked. "Please forgive my interruption, Nesset. I only mean to point out the fact that we do have another choice."

"Vishnu," Locknoff cautioned angrily. "We must consider the greater good."

"Vishnu is right." One of the other males spoke for the first time, interrupting Locknoff.

"Casualties will affect both parties. I do not take honor in the eradication of a complete world. That being said however, we are running out of options. Earth is our final choice. We must move forward. If another opportunity presents itself, we will take it into consideration. For now, let's review the information Vishnu has provided."

"Madafski is right," Nesset replied, effectively ending the conversation.

Attention swiftly turned to the screen that held a DNA strand of information. The council reviewed the DNA buds one line at a time. The first line was Taren's DNA code, posing a question. The second line was Lillian's DNA, responding to the questions presented. The questions revolved around military weaponry and potential weapons, troop disbursement, and the strength of allies. Other questions referred to defensive capabilities and recovery strategy. The council reviewed the entire first page of DNA information prior to addressing Taren directly, at which point Skyke, the smallest female on the council, pointed out the relevance of the DNA buds that had been collected on the bottom of the screen.

"Vishnu," she said, looking at him, "you must take care to review the earthly wants of your human companion. It is absolutely vital that you maintain your cover."

Taren looked at the DNA information and replied, "Certainly," noticing that she'd been thinking about more romance and nights out.

"If you have nothing further to pass on," Elitar, the third male on the council, said, "we look forward to your next report."

"Indeed," Taren replied as he placed his palm firmly on the screen. After a few seconds, the screen disappeared, leaving a normal mirror behind.

Jennifer blinked and looked around. She recognized her surroundings. She watched the apparent conflict in the eyes of the man before her. Although he said nothing, clearly something was bothering him. She watched him closely as he looked adoringly at the photo of his wife. Jennifer remembered the woman she'd followed in a dream once before. She was intrigued, because that woman wore a military uniform. The female was about 130 pounds on a five-foot-five frame with honey-bronze skin and long legs. Her rich brown hair was pulled back and held up high above her shoulders.

As time passed, Jennifer's vision grew more in-depth, and she watched the pair grow in their marriage. Lillian enjoyed taking belly-dancing classes, and Taren had taken Skyke's advice about using the DNA scans to better understand her and the things that made her happy. Taren reported regularly to the council as Jennifer looked on; he continued to push his ideas of diplomacy. Taren recognized that he was growing fond of Lillian beyond the needs of his assignment and was having a hard time keeping it under control.

As Jennifer watched him, she came to understand that what she'd seen in his eyes before was conflict. At every meeting, she looked on as Taren continued his opposition to no avail. He was only encouraged to continue his surveillance and give timely reports.

One day, while Taren was preparing for a meeting with the council, he reviewed the orb's contents and discovered that Lillian was pregnant. Additionally, defense operations within the US government had been conducted in response to reports of alien sightings and encounters. In his opinion, an invasion now would not surprise the humans. Taren immediately turned off the screen, grabbed his keys, and called his wife. Jennifer followed him.

"Let's meet for lunch," he suggested.

"Sure," she replied, "I'll meet you at Rickmen's down the street from your office."

"OK, see you soon."

He grabbed a small gym bag from the hall closet along with his car keys and raced for the door. Jennifer had no choice but to watch. It was almost as if she was seeing his experiences through his eyes.

Taren drove as fast as he could without attracting attention to himself in his navy Corvette and reached the restaurant within ten minutes. He told the waiter that he was expecting someone and requested a private table. While Taren waited, he examined a tiny green capsule he held in his hand. Jennifer's surroundings shifted. She blinked as the scene changed to one of him staring out of a window, dressed in simple white scrubs, looking across the terrain of a snowy mountain ridge.

Behind the ridge, there was a humongous star shining as brightly as Earth's sun. It was barely hidden by the mountainside, and several gray clouds threatened to obstruct its visibility. Nesset stepped forward and began to speak. She was much younger than the vision Jennifer had had of her in the past. Her hair seemed shorter, and her crown was only two large crescent-shaped braids across her forehead. Encouragingly she said, "It's not too late, Vishnu. This task does not have to be placed on your shoulders."

"Then whose?" Taren asked skeptically. "Would someone else be better suited for this task because they have not lost a blood member to the humans?"

"That isn't what I meant, but yes," replied Nesset. "That too is cause enough to let someone else take on this burden. You have barely been home from the colonial wars a moon cycle, not to mention the fact that your bloodline has seen enough loss. I have seen enough loss."

Taren exhaled wearingly and turned to face Nesset.

"My loss," Taren said while placing a hand on her shoulder, "and your loss. They're reasons enough for my presence on this assignment, Nesset. If our world is to survive, something must be done sooner rather than later. I just wish there was another way. This form," Taren continued, looking at his chest in disapproval, "it's very restricting."

"I don't know…" Nesset began with a smile, but she was interrupted by Locknoff's entrance into the room, smiling and speaking as if there were over five hundred yards between them.

"Just coming to wish you luck, brother," Locknoff said, hitting Taren on the back. Locknoff was also in human form. "We leave at first light. Those humans won't stand a chance when we get to them." Locknoff looked over at Nesset, smiling. "Congratulations, Nesset, on your council nomination."

Nesset nodded. "Thank you, Locknoff." She then started toward the exit.

Taren looked in her direction with a raised eyebrow. "The council?" he asked in a surprised tone, reclaiming her attention.

"Yes, I too feel the need to do what I can for Elquin." She then turned and walked out of the room.

Taren and Locknoff made their way into the next room and swiftly took a seat at the foot of a large oval table, where several others were also seated. Both male and female genders of the human species were present. Bathmantu addressed them all.

"You've all been chosen for this assignment based on your success in the farming efforts. This assignment, however, may very well be your most challenging. Before you decide, consider the reality that many of you may not survive this task. Individual assignment requests have been placed before you." Attention shifted to the electronic headband that now sat in front of each individual. "Review them with the understanding that your decision to accept or reject them will not affect your individual stature or that of your bloodline in any way."

"Hmmph," Locknoff said in a hushed tone. Vishnu smiled, and Bathmantu continued.

"Provide a response as soon as possible, as time is limited."

Taren picked up the silver and black headgear in front of him and placed it on his head. A small piece expanded to cover his ears on either side of his head, and both eyes received a video feed from a small screen directly in front of them.

"Vishnu," a familiar voice began. Taren recognized the voice as Elitar, senior council member of Elquin. "You have been chosen for a vital part in the success of this mission: the surveillance and capture of intelligence from Earth's defenses."

Several colorful lights flashed across the table, which now held a floating 3-D image of a woman in a US Air Force uniform. Jennifer was stunned as she looked at Taren's wife. The woman's image spun slowly, and Elitar's voice continued.

"She is an intelligence officer in the US military. She recently joined the defense intelligence analysis center at Andrews Air Force Base in Maryland. Your molecules have been matched to the DNA specifications of her ideal mate." Taren looked over himself swiftly with a raised brow, poking here and there. "The information came directly from the source, so you need not worry about rejection." The 3-D image replayed the DNA scan in which the sought-after information was gathered. An image appeared directly in front of the table as the message ended.

"Vishnu of the Ateenn bloodline," Nesset said, "can the beings of Elquin count on your presence and experience in our quest for survival?"

"Yes," he replied confidently. The scene shifted again, and Jennifer was back in the restaurant, where Taren's wife has joined him.

"Hi, honey," Lillian said, interrupting his thoughts as she touched his shoulder. Taren closed his hand around the pill and simultaneously pulled her closer for a more intimate reunion. Lillian was not surprised by her husband's actions, although she did detect a hint of worry in his eyes. Without letting on to her perceptiveness, Lillian wiggled free of her husband's arms and sat down.

"So have you ordered yet?" she asked.

"Not yet." Lillian began to look over the menu when Taren suddenly said, "Let's go away this weekend."

She pulled the menu down slightly to look at him, raising one eyebrow. "Where did you have in mind?"

"Arran," he replied, smiling.

"Scotland," Lillian said, surprised, "you want to go to Scotland for the weekend?"

"Machrie Bay, to be precise."

Taren smiled, knowing she couldn't resist the chance to visit the magical island where they met while she was on an assignment for work. She'd run into him one evening while relaxing on the beach, and then again on the plane ride home.

"OK," she replied, barely hiding the excitement in her voice. "Is it too late to get tickets for this afternoon? I'm just about done. We had only one meeting today, and that's just ended."

"Nah, there is a flight leaving at two forty-five p.m."

"Excellent," she said, cutting him off and getting to her feet. "I'll meet you back at the house in twenty minutes."

"Are you no longer hungry then?" Taren asked.

"Hungry?" Lillian said. "Who can think of eating at a time like this? I'll see you soon."

She grabbed her purse off the table and darted out the door. Taren looked after her worriedly but said nothing. He simply grabbed his things, placed five dollars on the table, and headed for the exit.

Casually he walked out of the restaurant toward his car, giving her enough time to get hers started. As she pulled out of her parking space, Taren noticed a dark-blue BMW sedan pulling out in front of him. It turned in the direction of his wife's car, and he focused on the vehicle. Jennifer recognized the driver as one of the females who sat at the table across from Taren nearly a year ago back on Elquin. Taren started his car and raced after his wife, creating a miniature donut as he turned in her direction.

Taren was suddenly aware that the words exchanged between him and his wife may not have been between them alone. More importantly, the fact that he had missed a scheduled council meeting could only mean one of two things. One, the government was aware of him and his position was compromised. Or two, his assignment had discovered him and was now a liability. Either way, Lillian was in danger. Taren accelerated in an effort to catch her before she exited the car. He was horrified as she made an unexpected stop at the dry cleaner, a short distance away from the entrance at Andrews Air Force Base. Taren skidded to a stop and pulled over to the curb.

Jennifer followed as he got out of the car and raced toward his wife, who was now reaching to open the door of the cleaner. As Lillian stepped into the shop, Taren was aware that the blue BMW had not stopped. He reached her in time to catch her as she stumbled toward the floor. Taren made the connection at once, when he noticed something sticking out of her leg. It was a tiny arrow tail. Lillian had been shot with a nanobullet and would soon be in agony. She only had minutes left. When hit, the target is completely destroyed. Nothing survived.

Taren pulled his wife farther into the building and brushed the arrow tail onto the floor. There was no evidence of a rupture in her skin, which further angered Taren as he realized the type of bullet she was hit with. He looked at her with pitied eyes. Jennifer was tears as she watched them.

The woman behind the counter watched with lowered brows. "Oh my god, is she OK? Do you need any help? Can I call an ambulance or something?"

Taren accepted without taking his eyes off his wife, and the woman darted to the phone.

"I'm so sorry, Lilly," he said, shaking his head.

"What's happening to me? It hurts to breathe, and I can't move."

"You've been shot," Taren replied. "I'm so sorry," he repeated over and over again. As her breathing became labored, Taren kissed her gently on the lips. "I love you, Lilly."

"Taren, I...I...love...you," Lilly said between gasps.

"I know," Taren replied softly. "I'm so sorry," he repeated as she took her last breath.

Taren hugged her gently and reached into his pocket. Pulling out the green pill, he looked at it a moment, then placed it on her tongue.

Her body absorbed it instantly, leaving just a tiny green ink splotch on her tongue. Taren hugged her once more and gently placed her body on the ground as the paramedics arrived. He got into his Corvette and raced down the road. The driver of a black Lexus pulled away from the curb, heading in the other direction.

"Locknoff!" Taren screamed in anger, gripping the steering wheel tightly as he pulled away.

Eighteen

MISUNDERSTANDING

Driving without fear of pursuit, Taren went directly to the airport. He took the first flight to Ruidoso, New Mexico, and walked into the Chess Ling Inn. Taren asked the attendant for any room along the western wall of the hotel.

"Would you prefer a particular floor?"

"No, any room will do."

As the attendant took a few moments to enter Taren's requirements into the computer, he noticed that the hotel was surprisingly crowded.

"They're all here for the Annual Chestnut Concert," the attendant said, noticing his stare. Jennifer recognized the screen before her eyes, and her thoughts turned to Cara.

"Oh, thanks." Taren grabbed his key card and turned for the elevator. Once inside, Taren pushed the button to get on his floor. As he did, he noticed the number on his room key. It was the same room he was given when he initially came to Earth. He thought of that day.

Jennifer blinked away tears, and the scene shifted again. Taren was sitting toward the front of a shuttle, which held all of the individuals from the conference room and several others. All of them were in human form. The shuttle left the ship just outside of Earth's gravitational field. The shuttle had been built to resemble a falling star through a telescope, but was not exactly a deterrent, as this star had coordinates, and Earth's scientists had seen this particular phenomenon several times before.

"Occupants, prepare yourselves," one of the operators yelled out. "We must be fast, as this shuttle was designed to self-destruct soon after we land."

Tension filled the air and Taren seemed deep in thought when Locknoff hit him on the back with excitement.

"Don't worry. I've got your back, brother."

"Worried," Taren replied, shocked that his brother in arms would come to such a conclusion. "The only thing I'm worried about, brother, is you walking away with all the glory."

Taren and Locknoff both laughed as others joined in.

"Don't worry. I'll be sure to save some for you. We're a team, after all." Locknoff continued in a slightly more serious tone, "I'll be with you every step of the way."

"Hmm," Taren replied, "I'll be sure to look to the east."

"Ha. Look to the east indeed, brother," Locknoff replied as the shuttle escalated, entering Earth's atmosphere.

The occupants braced themselves for landing. After several minutes, the shuttle slowed in speed. Locknoff said, "Be ready. Our descent will give much away to the humans. We will have six minutes once we touch down. Leave nothing." Seconds later the shuttle came to a halt. Occupants stood, grabbed their things, and headed for the exit.

As the shuttle doors opened, a black truck pulled up. The letters SWAT were written on both sides of it. Two men stepped out, weapons in hand, and spoke to the gathered. "We have four minutes before the natives arrive. Several stargazers reported a falling star that slowed in speed as it descended to the ground."

"Let's move," Locknoff shouted. After the last person was out of the shuttle, one of the armed men pushed a button on two tennis-sized balls and tossed them, now blinking, into the shuttle. After several seconds, one of them exploded, leaving a cloud of blue smoke. The electrical equipment started to blink, some sparkled, and then all went blank. It took two and a half minutes for the shuttle's occupants to exit and board the truck. As they pulled away, Taren heard the blast of the second ball. This one exploded, leaving a fireball that extended upward roughly three hundred feet.

The truck pulled into the underground parking area of the Chess Ling Inn. Everyone was directed to a conference room, given a key, and told they'd be contacted within the hour. Taren looked at his room key and smiled. Five twenty-five happened to be the exact number of assignments he'd taken since he'd joined the ERT. Jennifer watched, astonished at the scene playing out before her eyes.

The low ding, as the elevator reached the fifth floor, reminded Taren of his current predicament. He stepped off the elevator and headed directly to room 525. He then threw his bag down and slumped on the bed, holding his head in his hands. After several moments he looked over at the clock, took a deep breath, and stood to face himself in the large mirror adorning the dresser. He pricked his thumb and logged in.

Nesset was pacing on the other side of the mirror. She stopped and sighed loudly, lowering her shoulders as she took in his appearance.

"What has transpired, Vishnu? The council did not receive your timely report. Locknoff was called to—"

"Locknoff should not have been involved with this matter," Taren interrupted angrily. "He has not regained himself. Why was he even called in?"

"What has he done?" Nesset asked calmly.

"Why was my assignment being followed?" Taren asked, ignoring her question.

"It was not your assignment being followed, Vishnu. It was you. Wait, why? What has happened? Why are you logging in from this location?"

"You have not addressed my question, Nesset. Why was I being followed?"

"Because of the nature of your assignment, Vishnu. You have been asked to pair with a human. That alone denotes caution, as our disadvantage in this form is too apparent. What has happened?" she asked again.

"Locknoff has assassinated my assignment."

"Why?" Nesset interrupted, confused. "Those were not his instructions."

"Because Vishnu was compromised, planning to run," Elitar said as he walked into the room. "He may have jeopardized all we've worked for."

"But why?" Nesset asked again, still confused.

"I didn't know it was possible," Taren said, more to himself, staring blankly through the mirror. "All this time spent investigating them, why wasn't I told this was a possibility?" he asked, looking directly at Elitar.

"What?" Nesset asked.

"She was pregnant," Taren explained.

Shock covered Nesset's face as she took in his words. "I…I don't know…I was not aware of—"

"Our reproductive compatibility is not an underlying factor in the decision to take this world, Vishnu," Elitar interrupted.

"What do you mean?" Taren challenged. "It changes everything. It proves that we are compatible in more ways than we knew. Sharing this world with the humans is more than considerable. It's possible for our immediate future and that of our offspring." Taren looked into Elitar's eyes a moment and saw knowledge. "You knew," he accused, stepping backward with a look of disgusted shock in his eyes. "How can you condone this?"

"I was aware of its possibility," Elitar began unapologetically. "Scientists working on the orb's molecular structure discovered the potential possibility long ago. That is irrelevant now, the council has decided."

"This is not a decision for you alone, Elitar. We must consider every possibility before sending more Elquins to their deaths."

"The decision was made over thirty leniors ago! The humans could not be reasoned with then, and they cannot be reasoned with now, or have you forgotten your own loss at the hands of the humans? Or Nesset's, for that matter." He gestured to a now-seated Nesset, who appeared confused.

Taren sighed. "I have not forgotten, Elitar, nor will I forget the loss I have now suffered under my brother's hand. Humanity is not the same as it was. Collectively yes, growth is necessary. However, there is so much more compassion for life among the whole that I believe our venture to exist among the humans would be profitable for both our kinds. We must at least consider the alternative."

"They would kill us!" Elitar shouted coldly.

"You don't know that, Elitar."

"Neither do you. We need your report to finalize the battle plans. What say you, Ateenn blood?" Taren was visibly taken aback briefly by the name Elitar used. Nesset looked up at him with lowered brows. Taren swept his palms along his face calmly and spoke, looking at Elitar.

"You may have my report when the council has discussed my opposition in light of the new evidence."

Nesset gasped, stood, and started to speak, holding her hands out to touch Taren as though there wasn't a world between them, but Elitar beat her to it.

"Vishnu..." he began but was cut off when Taren abruptly ended the conversation by logging out of the conference.

It wasn't long before he heard a knock on his door. "Hotel security," a voice announced. "Please open the door, sir, or we will open it by force."

Taren raised a brow, grabbed his wallet, and placed it in his pocket. He then took the orb casing out of his bag and slipped it into his pocket as well. He took the security lock off the door, stood beside it, and held the handle tightly. He opened the door slightly, then shoved it suddenly with all his strength as one of the men started to enter.

Taren stepped around the open door, letting the injured man fall to the floor. He pulled the other man into his knee and flung him across the room while rolling onto his side. He then pulled them both farther into the room and closed the door before walking out. Taren took the stairs, unwilling to wait for the elevator. When he got to the lobby of the casino, he was confused by the crowd but grateful for its presence.

Jennifer blinked and lowered her brows as she watched him stumble over the plant. She had not noticed before that he'd tossed the cylinder behind the plant. The next scene was all too familiar to her, and she closed her eyes in understanding and resignation. She understood now: Taren and Vishnu were one and the same, and not only did aliens exist, but they were here on Earth. She understood that she was currently in the presence of one of them. Jennifer blinked away tears, considering the possibility that Cara was one of their victims. She cried in resignation of the reality that she now held something they wanted.

Tears flowed from her eyes as she thought of Emily, Amy, Kimberly, and Nancy. Tears flowed from her eyes as she realized that she might be next. When Jennifer opened her eyes again, she was back in the present, but she didn't recognize her surroundings. Everything was passing by in a blur.

Jennifer tried to sit up but was quickly overcome by a wave of pain. She groaned, moving through it, and sat up, pulling her legs up into her arms. She placed her head on her knees and stared into the distance. After a moment, Jennifer blinked, realizing she was in a car with no memory of how she'd gotten there. Tears rolled down her cheeks, and a moan escaped her lips as she tried to adjust to the movements of the vehicle.

Suddenly all was still. Jennifer blinked, feeling someone touch her arm. She looked up. "It's all right," the now-familiar voice said. Jennifer instantly moved away. The other side of the car stopped her, and Taren got out of the driver's seat. He walked around to the back and got in. Saying nothing for a long moment, Taren just looked at her.

"Get it out of me," she sobbed. "Get it out. Just get it out," she said over and over again, holding her head down in defeat.

Taren grabbed one of her wrists, lifted her head, and looked into her eyes. "I'm sorry, Jennifer." He brought his lips to hers and kissed her gently at first, then more fiercely, pulling her closer to him.

Jennifer braided her fingers through his hair, breathing deeply. She returned the kiss in kind, moaning slightly as Taren moved his hands down her back, pulling her closer. When they were both out of breath, he released her, panting. Taren looked into her eyes, and Jennifer stared back at him. After a moment, she fainted. Taren sighed heavily and laid her down across the backseat. He grabbed the syringe Sariah packed, filled it with her blood, and wrapped a bandage around her arm. Moving swiftly now, Taren jumped behind the wheel and pulled back onto the interstate.

Nineteen

Cat And Mouse

Ahdortee led the way, as Locknoff, Porock, and Celtine followed her through the stairwell toward the third floor. The dorm was quiet, as she'd predicted, Locknoff noted, and the orb's signal was strong.

"Room 365B," she announced. As the four made their way onto the third floor, Locknoff glanced at the elevator, at the sound of the ding announcing the elevator's presence as they came around a corner. He grunted, seeing a couple enter the elevator, thinking it strange. The boy in sweats was actually carrying the woman rather than letting her walk. He shook his head and turned his attention to the others, who were slowing now having found the room.

Ahdortee took the lead, knocking once, twice, thrice, before lowering her brows and looking to the group, unsure.

"Miss Braxton, are you home? We have a few questions to ask you."

When no one answered, Locknoff lowered his eyebrows and ushered her aside. He kicked open the door and took only three seconds to evaluate the scene before running in the direction they'd just come. Zackary was beginning to stir.

"Where's the orb?" Celtine asked a drowsy Zackary. Ahdortee pulled out her cell and ran after Locknoff.

"She's moving fast. I don't understand."

"He has her," Locknoff replied angrily.

"Who has her?" Celtine asked, joining them.

"Vishnu," Porock responded.

"Good. This time I'll be ready."

"Call in a team," Locknoff ordered as they reached the parking lot.

"Give them the orb's coordinates, and place a tracker. He will not slip through my grasp again."

Locknoff started the car and proceeded down the road as Ahdortee spoke in hushed tones into the cell phone. Celtine and Porock pulled out their weapons and started readying them.

"He's fast," Ahdortee said as she opened her notebook and clipped her phone into place.

"He knows the jig is up," Locknoff said. "How long before backup arrives?"

"The Gainesville teams have been deployed. Ten minutes. He's twelve miles ahead of us."

◆ ◆ ◆

Jennifer opened her eyes; she was lying across the backseat. Every part of her hurt, but she felt human at least. *For now*, she thought, remembering her predicament and evaluating the scene around her. There was a black gym bag in the front passenger seat. Taren or Vishnu or whatever was driving down I-70 pretty fast. A bandage was tied around her right inner elbow, and she looked at it for a moment, confused. She couldn't remember getting hurt there.

"You scratched it on a tree last night at the viewing," Jennifer heard Taren explain. Her eyebrows turned down at him.

"You probably don't remember much though; we were pretty wasted last night." Taren chuckled dryly. "I'm Taren, by the way," he said, turning his head around briefly to look at her.

Tilting her head, Jennifer looked at him for a minute. "That's not how I remember it," she exclaimed and then turned her gaze out the window.

Taren was shocked; it was his turn to look at her with lowered brows. "What do you mean?" he asked, unsure.

"I remember everything."

"What are you talking about? How is that even possible?"

"Those aren't images one easily forgets," she said, looking him in the eye. "Or was I supposed to? Because if so, your thingy is broken." Returning her gaze out the window, she added, "Thanks...for earlier. I don't know what came over Zack." She wrapped her arms around herself, holding her ribs tightly, and sighed. "Where are we going?"

Taren was dumbfounded; he looked up several times. As he watched her through the rearview mirror, he wondered how she could possibly remember anything and why the hell he felt like he knew her. He immediately pulled the car to the shoulder of the road, turned to Jennifer, and asked almost accusingly.

"Who are you? How is it possible you remember anything? Where exactly are you from, and what is your mission here?"

Jennifer turned to Taren with a smart remark ready but shrank back a little at his tone and the look in his eyes.

"My name is Jennifer Braxton," she said sternly. "I was born in Lalin, Florida. My only mission is...or *was* to graduate with a 3.95 grade point average so I can be accepted to the number one physical therapy program in the country! As for the memory, assuming the loss of it could even be possible, I..." She stopped midrant and looked away from him.

"Go on," he encouraged.

Jennifer sighed. "I probably remember because I've always..."

"Yes," Taren prompted.

"I've always been able to dream about things. Well, that was before you put that thing inside of me. Now I'll be lucky to dream of anything at all other than alien worlds."

Taren searched her eyes for a moment but found only honesty. "I'm sorry," he said and pulled back onto the road. She reached a hand up to her pounding head for a moment and then returned her attention to the window. "You should probably have that looked at."

Jennifer looked down at her hand and cringed at the blood. She then noticed the wrapping on her arm again and asked, "What happened?"

Taren swallowed. "I wasn't sure if you'd make it. You weren't responding earlier, and I needed some of your blood...just in case."

"Oh...where are we going in such a hurry?"

"Nowhere in particular, just...staying in motion."

Jennifer nodded and closed her eyes, wiping a tear away before it could reach her cheek.

"I'm so sorry about all this," Taren said again.

"Did you kill Cara, my friend?"

"No, I spent the night confined. I came here looking for you the moment I regained my freedom."

"Are you going to kill me?"

Taren felt a twinge of irritation at the desire to reassure her but answered honestly. "No. The one responsible for your friend's death pursues us now."

Her eyes grew and she looked out the back window nervously.

"No need to worry. He's probably a good twenty or thirty minutes behind us, although that distance may have decreased slightly due to our stops." He shook his head. "You won't have to worry about them coming after you anymore, Jennifer. I have the orb now. Is there a place you feel safe going to? I'll take you there and drive away. You'll never have to see me again."

Jennifer looked at him and sighed. "There's no place safe for me now. He knows where my friends are, and one of them is already dead. There is no place for me to hide. If it's Locknoff who seeks us now, it's only a matter of time before he finds me no matter where I go. I am not safe until your council gets that orb back."

Taren snapped his head up in response to her recognition of Locknoff and the council, and comprehension filled his eyes. She might be right, particularly if there was a way for Sariah to know of her ability. "How much do you know about us?"

"Enough to know that you and Locknoff were friends at one point. What happened?" Taren sighed as he remembered, and then he explained.

Twenty

EARTH

"Locknoff," Taren began, "was to be my compatriot, my partner, of sorts. While I made contact with my assignment, he made sure our covers were in place. We were carpenters." He laughed dryly. "When I introduced him to Lillian, he was my brother, recently transferred. Our job was simple. Until the orb arrived...assimilate and report back to the council.

"Locknoff found pleasure in our advantages...or disadvantages, depending on how you look at it."

"What disadvantage?"

"On this planet, our emotions are enhanced almost five hundred percent." Jennifer's brows drew down. "This form dulls it a bit," he said, gesturing to himself, "but not much."

"All emotions?" Jennifer asked suspiciously.

"Yes. Anger, fear, joy, peace, happiness, et cetera. Additionally, because we have two hearts, our bodies can be pushed harder and further than any human body. The size of our lungs alone allows us to make better usage of the oxygen we take in here."

"What do you mean?"

"Well, the average human can sprint about 1.3 miles before getting winded. For one of us, it would take about seven miles before we would need to take a breather or even slow down. Like you though, we can train our bodies to be pushed further. A trained combatant on Earth could probably sprint about seventeen miles before needing to slow."

Jennifer gasped. "We don't stand a chance, do we?"

"Not on foot. But Earth is not defenseless." His tone changed, became saddened. "Our mental capability is evenly matched. Weapons could probably stand up to one another as well." He went quiet.

"So what happened with Locknoff?"

"He was angry at humanity and took pleasure in their discomfort at his hands. We first noticed it one night while returning to our car after a movie. He was enjoying the company of one of Lillian's friends, when a man came up to us with a gun and demanded our wallets, the ladies' purses, all jewelry, the keys to our car. Locknoff went to hand him the keys but intentionally dropped them near the man's feet. The man ordered him to pick them up and pointed the gun in our direction. As Locknoff bent to pick up the keys, I moved in front of the women. On his way up, Locknoff spun and punched so hard under the man's arm that he yelped and lowered his hand with tears in his eyes. I shoved the women down as the man uncontrollably fired a shot before releasing the weapon, his arm going limp. Locknoff came up and landed a hammer fist to the back of his head. The man fell to the ground unconscious, but that wasn't enough for Locknoff. You have to understand his training," Taren explained in response to Jennifer's horrified eyes. "Locknoff is a protector. When he's called in, the threat is completely removed, not neutralized."

"Whatever," Jennifer said sarcastically.

Taren continued.

"Locknoff beat him until his fists were bloody, and then strangled him until there was no life left in the man's body. When the council found out, they said he was simply performing his duties and ordered us not to draw attention to ourselves."

"What about the police?"

"Self-defense." Jennifer looked at him as if he were a misbehaving child who knew better. He shrugged and responded, "We have friends in high places."

Jennifer shook her head in disbelief.

"For some reason, Lillian's friend found him irresistible after that and felt the need to show her gratitude with…well, sex. It wasn't long before he started getting involved in extreme sports with her encouragement. Any sport, it didn't matter. He went from soccer, to football, and then rugby. Amateur fighting was next." Jennifer's eyes widened. "Oh, he didn't kill anyone. He just got a kick out of maiming them."

She rolled her eyes but looked on intently for the rest of the story.

"Locknoff took advantage of the emotional highs. If he was in a good mood, the person usually walked away with minimal damage. If not, they were out of the sport for at least six months. He would bring Anna back to the apartment—"

"Anna?" Jennifer interrupted.

"Anna Desai, Lillian's friend."

"Oh."

"Locknoff would bring her back to the apartment afterward and—"

"I get it," Jennifer said, tilting her head and rolling her eyes.

"Anyway, one day Anna mentioned that she'd been promoted and would be leaving for Turkey on a two-year project her company was working on. Locknoff was so attached to the emotional high he'd been accustomed to with her that the thought of losing it invoked such strong anger within him that she didn't waste time saying good-bye. He yelled at her the first time she brought it up. He destroyed every piece of equipment in the house, broke the furniture, and all but threw her out. Anna was head over heels for him, but she wouldn't test his patience. When he found out that she'd gone, he went into an emotional withdrawal so powerful that it threw him into a deep depression. He tried to find her, but Lillian wouldn't tell him where she was. When she threatened to end our relationship because of his obsession, he was forced to let Anna go."

"Why couldn't you just use the orb?"

"It doesn't work that way. It's preloaded with the task."

Jennifer nodded.

"It wasn't long before he started bringing girls home from clubs, bars, or even supermarkets in an effort to relive what he'd experienced with her. He couldn't do it, of course, because none of them cared for him the way Anna did. One night he was watching a science-fiction flick with one of his supermarket girls, and she made a wisecrack about aliens being senseless or bigheaded or something, and he lost it. Locknoff hit her and found a satisfaction so great in the emotional release that he couldn't help but do it again. When she stopped fighting, he raped her. By the time I got home, he was standing over her, screaming about how insignificant humans were and how their days were numbered."

"How do you know all this if you weren't even there?"

"I spoke to him about it briefly before contacting the council. I apologized to him then for not being a better compatriot. You see, I never interfered with his behavior because he always reminded me of why we were here. If he ended up killing someone, it was one less human to defeat in the end. He never let me forget the cruel nature of humanity, so I let him be. In the end, the woman had to be killed because our mission was at stake." Taren sighed, and Jennifer swallowed.

"Shortly afterward, Locknoff was reassigned to communications in Missouri. He got better with time, but he never truly got over the loss of Anna."

"Sounds like he was in love."

"I don't know about that. After his transfer, Locknoff found sex with Elquin women just as pleasurable. So he never touched a human that way again. He also never got over the fact that I was responsible for his transfer."

"Wait, I don't understand something," Jennifer said, lowering her brows. "Why wouldn't he try having sex with someone from your planet in the first place?"

Taren chuckled. "Locknoff has always been somewhat of a ladies' man. But sex without bonding or marriage isn't as pleasurable. It is one of the things that helps bond us to our life's mate when we find one."

"Why are your emotions affected so?"

"It has to do with the Earth's electromagnetic pull on us. Because humans are native to this planet, its effects are not so drastic. You're designed to coexist with the field, where we are alien to it, so its effects pull us against our own energy fields. I imagine the more time we spend here, the easier it will be to adjust to its influence."

"So how do you find them?"

"Who?"

"Your life's mate?"

"Oh, no," he said, shaking his head, "it's your turn. What do you remember about us...about me?" He looked in the rearview mirror at her reaction to his words and instantly regretted it, because she was staring at him. Her eyes were the exact color of the sky on the mountain ridge of Elquin's capital city. They were beautiful; he had a hard time looking away.

"I remember..." Jennifer began, and Taren returned his attention to the road ahead. "You fighting...a lot. Almost every memory I have is of you in battle. I'm kinda surprised you didn't kill Zack. How many invasions have you been a part of?"

"I've never invaded anything. I've been assigned to 525 farming efforts."

"Will they kill me?"

"Not while I live," Taren answered a little too quickly, looking directly at her through the rearview mirror. Although he'd said the words, he felt them more deeply rooted than any promise he'd ever made. Returning his attention to the road, Taren contemplated. *What am I doing? I must be crazy…I can't let her go. She knows too much. But if the council finds out, her life may already be forfeit.* He looked at her again. *No, I must get her away from the orb. It's the only way.*

"So, what are we going to do about it?" Jennifer asked, pulling Taren away from his contemplation.

"About what?" he asked, his expression a bit confused.

She pointed to the blinking gas light on the dash.

Taren sighed. "We have to stop. We have no choice."

A half mile down the road, a gas sign appeared. The pair looked at each other briefly and then headed off the interstate in search of a gas station. Taren hoped their pit stop would go unnoticed.

Twenty-One

Boxed In

Taren screeched to a halt at the pump and jumped out of the car. He
shoved the nozzle into the tank and swiped the card. It didn't matter
if it was traced at this point, because he had the orb. They were coming
to him one way or another. *But Jennifer*, he thought, *she can get off this
crazy ride.*

He looked up and saw her looking back at him. To her far left he
noticed a black SUV pulling into the gas station just a little too slowly.
"Hmm…" It no longer mattered what he thought; Jennifer would have
to stay on this ride just a little longer.

Taren replaced the nozzle, calmly walked back to the driver's side,
and got in.

"Stay down," he ordered. "Things may get a little dicey from here.
If you see an opportunity to get away, run." Instantly he regretted the
words, as the thought of never seeing her again slightly irritated his
stomach. He was happy she didn't ask for an explanation. She merely
nodded and moved quickly to get down and out of sight.

Taren pulled away so fast he left tire marks on the pavement and
nearly clipped another black SUV making its way into the station. Just
under a mile down the road, he came across three more black SUVs.
Weaving in and out of traffic, Taren made several turns in an effort to

elude them, but he found it difficult to shake his pursuers. Suddenly, he swerved to miss an oncoming car.

"Shit," he yelled, struggling to maintain control of the vehicle. The engine began making strange noises, the car backfired loudly, and the electrical components blinked. Taren had no choice but to pull over less than a mile down the road into a small wooded clearing in a public park, just as the malfunctioning car rolled to a complete stop.

When the car stopped, Taren hastily got out and ran to the backseat. Without a word, he reached for Jennifer. Panic overwhelmed her, and she shook her head, backing up. She tried to get the door open but found it impossible. Taren moved closer and forcefully grabbed her wrist. She screamed and tried kicking at him, which only made him move all the more urgently as he wrapped his arms around her frame and pulled her closer. Jennifer was out of breath and immobile, locked tight in his arms.

Her chest heaved as she tried to catch a breath, and he whispered to her, "If you are what you say, then watch and run when you can. I'm sorry about this."

"About what?" Her words were cut off abruptly as Taren applied pressure to her neck. Jennifer's body went limp in his arms as she fell unconscious, but she was not blind to the scene that played out around her.

Jennifer watched as Taren laid her across the backseat and pulled his gym bag out of the front. He opened it and removed a silver cylinder casing. He then removed a green pill from the bag, and Jennifer gasped, shaking her head, as she looked on. Taren looked at her unconscious body briefly and stuck the pill into his pocket. Sighing, he removed a roll of cash from the bag, and put it into Jennifer's robe pocket. He then zipped the bag closed, climbed out of the backseat, and turned to leave, but he stopped after two steps because he was surrounded.

Locknoff and Ahdortee were headed right for him. Porock and Celtine had taken up positions to his left and right, and several others surrounded them. Taren looked back at Jennifer's sleeping body briefly, but his attention was averted as Locknoff spoke. "Step away from the girl."

"She is no longer of interest to you."

Locknoff looked at Ahdortee, who lifted her cell phone toward Taren for a moment, and then nodded. When he returned his attention to Taren, Locknoff noticed the cylinder in his hands. Everyone stopped at Locknoff's signal, and he alone moved closer. He stopped roughly four feet in front of Taren and began pacing.

"Master Vishnu of the Ateenn bloodline..."

Taren lowered his brows as Locknoff spoke, almost growling at the name he used. Jennifer blinked as she watched the exchange between them.

"You've been summoned before the council to answer for recent actions." Locknoff stopped, pulled out his pistol, and continued. "As for the girl, well, I'm not inclined to leave any more loose ends."

"More?" Taren asked, stepping into his line of sight. With a raised brow, Locknoff continued. "Her friends...one of them we've not been able to locate. We aren't sure what she said to her while under the orb's influence. But thanks to you, we can find out." His focus was on the cylinder in Taren's hand. Locknoff looked at Porock, who started walking closer to Taren with the small party.

Taren raised his hands in surrender and said, "Brother..." Locknoff looked up, lowering his weapon, and held a hand up, stopping their advance.

"You have taken much from me. I will do as you ask, but I have removed the orb. The girl is close to death already, as you can see. Let her final moments pass in peace."

Locknoff looked at him for an immeasurable moment and then turned his attention to Jennifer and sighed.

"Your tolerance..." he said, shaking his head as he looked down at his weapon. He depressed one of the holes briefly and stepped closer to Taren, raised his weapon, and fired a shot around him at Jennifer. She gasped. Ahdortee and half the others echoed her protest.

"No!" Taren shouted, dropping to his knees in defeat. He scrambled to Jennifer's side and inspected the area Locknoff had hit. He sighed deeply when he saw a small prick on her skin. He checked her pulse and exhaled audibly.

"She still lives, as you can see, brother, but you're a fool if you think I'm going to let such a treasure slip by me even if she is practically dead. It seems this human is the only way to get you to cooperate. And if she survives, the girl may prove useful in the future."

Jennifer thought Taren looked numb as Porock and several others pulled him to his feet.

"That will no longer be necessary," Locknoff announced, walking away. "He will come on his own accord."

Taren grabbed his bag and followed. A small part of him was grateful for the tracer Locknoff had placed.

Jennifer was stunned at it all. She was angered that Locknoff would use her to control Taren. She was annoyed that it even mattered to her. She was afraid of what would happen to her in Locknoff's hands and terrified of what Locknoff would do to Taren if he found her alive and well. She knew what would happen if she went to the authorities. *Psych ward central*, she thought as she looked around, wondering how she would get home.

Roughly ten minutes after they had all gone, Jennifer woke with a gasp, sitting up. Strangely, she felt refreshed. Her bumps and bruises were still there, but she didn't feel so bad. Instantly she looked down at her leg and moved her hand over the area Locknoff hit. There was a small pin-sized prick in her calf. She sighed and reached into her pocket.

Taren had placed a stack of hundreds into her pocket. The tape around it read 10,000 in bright-orange print. She lowered her brows.

"How the hell does an alien just have ten thousand dollars lying around?" she asked no one. She looked down at her robe and sighed again. Looking around, she saw no one and jumped out of the backseat. She got behind the wheel and turned the key, attempting to start the car. It sputtered but did nothing more.

Dead, she thought as she looked down at the baby-blue robe she still wore. She replaced the cash, got out of the car, and headed toward the sound of oncoming traffic. *There has to be an office somewhere around here,* she thought. As luck would have it, she didn't have to walk long.

A park ranger drove up beside her and asked, with a look of shocked horror on his face, "Are you all right, miss?"

Am I all right? Jennifer said to herself, looking at him in disbelief. *I'm dirty, bloody, bruised, and dressed in a bathrobe. What the hell is he thinking?*

"Yes," she said calmly. "I just need a cab."

The ranger got out of the car and rushed to her side. "Who's done this to you?" he asked, ushering her to the door and scanning the park for any signs of trouble.

"My boyfriend...ex-boyfriend."

"Is he here in the park? What does he look like?" the ranger asked, grabbing his radio as he held the door open for her.

"No," she responded, climbing into the car.

The ranger nodded and got back into the car. "Do you live close by?" he asked as he started the car and drove away.

Jennifer was quiet. How was she going to explain all this? Quickly she ran through it in her mind.

My name is Jennifer Braxton. I was kidnapped by an alien who represents a race of beings intent on killing every last one of us. They put some kind of tracking device in my leg and...

She sighed. *No, that won't do. I can see the straitjacket now.*

"No," she said aloud. "I'm a student at the University of Florida."

The ranger looked at her even more sympathetically now and asked, "How did you get all the way here and dressed like that?"

"My ex-boyfriend beat me, and I blacked out. I'm not sure how I got this far out, but he is a Gamma Sigma Phi brother and may have had someone try to scare me by bringing me all the way out here. When I came to, I was lying across the backseat. There wasn't anyone else in the car."

"That's your car?" he interrupted, surprised.

"No, I've never seen it before today."

The ranger pulled into the station and ran to hold the door open for her. "What was his name again?"

"Zackary Mason."

"All right. It will take about fifteen minutes for the squad to arrive, but that ought to be plenty of time for me to make a circle. You can sit with Careen until I get back."

"Squad?" Jennifer asked, turning to look at him. A woman came out of the building then and waited at the top of the steps. Jennifer looked timidly at the ranger station, which was in a clearing just past the park entrance. It was a colonial-style cabin.

"Well, yeah, I can take the report, but a police unit will be needed if you want to press charges."

"Charges?" she repeated mechanically.

"Well, I didn't think you'd want to go to them," he said, gesturing to her robe.

"No," she replied, shaking her head.

"It shouldn't take long, and Careen might have something that fits you."

Jennifer nodded, moving closer toward the woman by the steps.

"Hey, Kendle, about the 2742…" The ranger spoke into his walkie-talkie as he headed back to the vehicle and prepared to drive away. Jennifer's attention was diverted as the woman came nearer.

"I am Ranger Careen Dailyn."

"Nice to meet you, Ranger Dailyn," Jennifer responded, holding her hand out. "I am Jennifer Braxton."

Ranger Dailyn smiled as they greeted each other. "Come on in."

The pair then made their way into the building.

Twenty-Two

SISTERHOOD

Jennifer sat waiting across from the police officer who'd introduced himself as Officer Lennon. Jennifer was dressed in a borrowed pair of sweats, with ten thousand dollars secured in her pocket. Careen was more than happy to offer her something other than a robe to wear. The wounds on her head were cleaned and bandaged. Dailyn informed her that because she was hurt and on public property, she could skip pressing charges but would have to give the police a statement of the facts.

"Whenever you're ready," Ranger Dailyn repeated.

Jennifer blinked and sighed, sitting up. She didn't want to be doing this. She just wanted to be in her own clothes and with her friends. It didn't even matter if she had to take an airplane back to Ruidoso at this point; she just wanted to be where she could say good-bye to her child-hood friend and sorority sister.

"I was having a disagreement with my boyfriend, and he attacked me. He threw me across the room a few times and kicked me. I blacked out after that and woke up here in that strange car."

"What did you guys argue about?"

"Does it matter, Officer Lennon?" Ranger Dailyn interjected.

The officer looked up from his pad. "If I am to be thorough in my report, I will need to know what the disagreement was about."

"He wasn't happy that I didn't feel up to going with him to one of his fraternity parties."

"Which fraternity?"

"Gamma Sigma Phi."

"Where did the argument take place? Were others around?"

"My dorm room, and no, I don't have a roommate."

Officer Lennon looked up again with one raised eyebrow. "Would anyone clean your room before you get back there?"

"No, but I could have Kevin fax you a picture of the damage. I'll need it for the insurance paperwork anyway."

"Who's Kevin?"

"Kevin Kingly is the dorm representative. He works the evening watch at the front desk in Freelance Hall."

"All right. Is there anything else you'd like to share?"

"That's all I remember," she said defensively.

"All right. I understand you do not want to press charges."

"No."

"Then you may be on your way just as soon as we complete a rape kit. And may I suggest that at the very least, you get a restraining order against Mr. Mason and maybe the fraternity. Understand, it's not an arrest warrant, but it can give you a layer of protection."

"I don't think he—" she began and then stopped midsentence at his accusing stare. "All right…you make a valid point."

Forty wipes, swabs, and photos later, Jennifer found herself in the back of a cab headed for Freelance Hall. She'd decided to get the restraining order for Zackary only. In the end, she didn't need the entire brotherhood after her. Relations between the houses were always civil, although this would certainly shake things up a bit, as there was no way Kappa Theta Nu would just stand by and allow one of their own to be treated this way, particularly when it contributed generously to battered women's recovery projects around the country.

Before long, Jennifer walked into the front door of Freelance Hall. Kevin gasped at the sight of her.

"Are you all right?" he asked, moving toward her.

"I'm fine, thank you," she responded, continuing forward.

"You're not allowed up there yet."

Jennifer stopped. "What? Why?"

"The police were here not twenty minutes ago."

Jennifer's eyes widened. "That was fast."

"Yeah, seems your Officer Lennon has serious issues with Sigma Phi. His local counterparts were all too happy to serve the protection order, I heard."

"Wow."

"Yeah, and Lu wants to see you."

Jennifer closed her eyes and sighed. She wanted to see Lu too, but on her own terms. "Where is she?"

Kevin stepped back and motioned to the elevator.

"How long has she known?"

"You've been missing for almost twenty-four hours. She saw your room, and Grand Master Allen was called over just after the cops left."

"Thank you, Kevin."

"You're welcome."

As Jennifer entered the elevator, her stress level decreased. She would not have to explain the protection order. *Would Lu understand?* she wondered. *Would she even be able to help?* The low ding as the elevator reached the top floor reminded Jennifer that she was about to meet with her sage mother. Jennifer wished she'd dressed more appropriately.

Exiting the elevator, Jennifer was met by two beautiful redheads. The women who stood before her were wearing long, green dresses, which complemented their eyes and flowing red locks. The dresses were identical, gathered at the waist. They were cropped at the shoulders and adorned with a large sorority crest in the center, a fully bloomed white rosebud with a yin and a yang at its center. Behind the bud was a pair of crossed swords with black hilts. Centered between the hilts was a dove in flight, clutching a scroll. To the left and right of the petals were crescent-shaped leaves. Underneath it all was a ribbon that read Kappa Theta Nu. The women were so similar that it would be difficult for someone not to notice that they were twins, perhaps even identical.

"Welcome back, sister," one of them spoke. "This way please." They both turned and headed down the hall.

The hallway was painted khaki and decorated with large portraits of women dressed in similarly styled outfits, each one a primary color. Jennifer followed the women quietly, and after a few yards, they came to a set of double doors. The twins stopped, bowed their heads slightly in respect, and pushed the doors opened. As they disappeared into the room, Jennifer took a moment to examine it before walking in.

They must have been accepting pledges, she concluded based on the decor. Several draped cloths hung from the ceiling to the floor. They were draped in the pattern of a large rosebud, with only white toward the center. The outside petals were of primary colors. Each cloth bore a large crest identifying the sisterhood. Less than three feet from the center, Jennifer heard a masculine voice.

"There. She lives, as you can see."

"Yes," replied a feminine voice sternly. "But not without blemish."

Jennifer squared her shoulders and made her way into the bud's center.

On the floor was a large crest four feet in diameter. Across its center was a large fabric scroll pulled open. From end to end, the scroll overlapped parts of the crest. The scroll had golden doves on the top and bottom of each corner. In front of the scroll and centered with the crest was a white pillow large enough for someone to sit comfortably. To the left and right of the pillow stood pillars, which held large, white candles. The fire had recently been extinguished. Jennifer knew by the smell lingering in the small space. Centered between the pillow and scroll was a large, oval-shaped crystal bowl. To each side lay a sword. Its points just barely touched the fabric's edge.

"Welcome back," the female said with outstretched arms. She stood about five feet five, with dark-blond locks extending down her back. She had a dark-brown complexion, and her eyes were green. She wore a long, white dress, with thick ropelike straps and a golden belt buckle fastened around her waist. On her buckle was a dove in flight, clutching a scroll. Jennifer crossed and made a point of stepping around the large scroll to embrace her.

"Thank you, Sage Mother Luania. I—"

"What is the meaning of this protection order?" the male interrupted. "How dare you bring dishonor on Gamma Sigma Phi."

Jennifer opened her mouth to speak, but Luania beat her to it, pressing a finger to her lips. "You would deny me the opportunity to assess my dear one, Joshua?" she asked accusingly, turning to face the man.

Joshua stepped back at her glance, and Jennifer saw that he was dressed in a dark-blue suit. He had on a blue-and-black striped tie, and his jacket bore a crest on the left breast pocket. It was a silver shield with a black border. In the center was a large sword. Its length ran throughout the shield. The hilt was black and ran above the shield slightly. Centered behind the shield was a pair of large wings. In the middle of the shield and on either side of the sword was a winged gargoyle, growling and clutching a scroll. Under the shield was a ribbon with the words Gamma Sigma Phi.

"No, Luania, I was just..."

"Get out!" she ordered. "You have worn out your welcome, Grand Master. You will receive answers to your query within the hour."

He squared his shoulders. "I expect you will deliver them personally, Luania."

She lowered her head slightly, and Joshua returned the gesture and then turned and walked out of the room without another word.

"Come with me," Luania said, disappearing behind one of the draped cloths. As Jennifer followed, they walked in silence until Luania closed a door behind them.

"I don't know what..." Jennifer began but cut off quickly at the look of disapproval in Luania's eyes. She sat down at the worktable in the far left corner of the room and looked to Luania, lowering her eyes quickly as Luania began disrobing. She was completely nude under her robe, and it must have been chilly.

After a few minutes, Luania joined her, dressed in a yellow top and dark-blue jeans. "So what happened?" Luania asked.

"I don't know, Lu. I was explaining about Cara," she said, looking down at her hands, "and why I didn't feel up to going to the party, and he just...lost it. It's like he didn't hear a word I said other than I wasn't going. His eyes...they were different, Lu."

"I don't understand," Lu interjected. "You've warned me of impending danger many times. Does it work differently for yourself?"

"Not normally. I've always been able to anticipate Zackary's behavior, and although I've recently had dreams, none of them have been relevant to my life or...Cara's."

"So what happened to Zack?"

Jennifer opened her mouth to explain but remembered Locknoff's words to Taren. "We aren't sure what she may have said to her while under the orb's influence. But thanks to you, we can find out."

If I tell her anything, she could be killed. I can't risk it. I can't tell anyone what's happened. At least not yet.

"Yes?" Lu prompted.

"It was someone else. I didn't know him, and there was so much blood. I thought he was going to kill me, Lu. I blacked out as he came toward me, and I woke up in the park, miles away."

Lu raised an eyebrow briefly. "Why didn't you press charges?"

"Because whoever it was defended me. What happened next I couldn't say, but Zack got what he deserved, and I am not so sure he was responsible for where I ended up."

"And you think a restraining order will keep him away if he intends on finishing what he started?"

"No, but I depend on the brotherhood to keep him away from me."

"Fear of dishonor is a pretty good motivator. Did he rape you?"

"No—at least, I don't think he did."

"And you think it may have been someone else from Sigma Phi who kidnapped you?"

"Or a rival," Jennifer replied with a shrug. "Either way, a restraining order keeps him away from me and the brotherhood off my back. Or so I thought," she said, looking at the door.

"Don't worry about Joshua. I'll handle him." Lu got up then and retrieved something from her kitchenette cabinet, along with a glass of water. "Here," she said, placing the glass of water in front of Jennifer. She put a little blue pill beside it. "Just in case." Luania then returned to her seat. Jennifer did not want to give her cause to be suspicious, so she swallowed the pill without a word.

"Now," Luania continued, "I've spoken to Cara's aunt Brenda. She has flown in to conduct the funeral arrangements. Although many of your sisters will attend the ceremony, I expect you'll want to return immediately."

"Yes."

"Are you sure you feel up to it?"

"I'll be all right, Lu."

"All right then, if there is nothing more you wish to discuss, I suggest you change into something more suitable and be on your way."

Jennifer looked down at her attire and smiled. "It's better than what I left in."

Lu looked at her disapprovingly.

"Yes, Mother," Jennifer said, lowering her eyes. She stood to leave, but Lu grabbed her wrist.

"Be careful, Jennifer," Lu warned, looking into her eyes. "From this point on, be very careful."

"I will, Mother."

Lu nodded and released her.

Jennifer walked into her room and sighed. Everything was in disarray. She would need to get on the road soon, but first she had to find her things. She didn't take much time to unpack before, so it shouldn't be difficult, but where was her suitcase, she wondered. From where she stood, Jennifer could only see a massive pile of crap. She gave up on walking right out the door and began tidying up her room. As she did, she couldn't help thinking about how the mess came to be and how an alien saved her. Yes, it was done for his own reasons, but what would have happened if he hadn't come in when he did?

Jennifer pulled out the ten thousand dollars and stared at it for a long moment. *A direct flight to New Mexico will be faster. I'll just have a cocktail or two before we take off.* With the decision made, Jennifer shoved the money back into her pants pocket and continued cleaning. Her thoughts drifted, first to Cara and then the others who may or may not be in danger at the moment.

Twenty-Three

The Council's Justice

"You can trust me to room at the hotel, Locknoff," Taren said, walking into another windowless room.

"Not until the council convenes in the morning, I'm afraid." Locknoff pulled the door shut and walked over to the chair. Taren turned slightly and raised an eyebrow. Locknoff pulled out the orb and put it on the seat. "The council has elected to deploy fighters."

Taren's eyes widened. "No, this is madness! We can't hope to wage war on the humans unexpectedly now. Our last drop did not go unnoticed. They are enacting security measures based on recent reports of suspicious sightings."

Locknoff's brow raised briefly. "Your last report," he said while looking down at the orb a moment, "would have been welcomed, Taren, but it was not necessarily a determining factor in the decision to dispatch troops."

"What? Why? Are we now sentencing Elquins to death without considering the totality of the circumstances? The council has no right!"

"We had no choice, Taren! Elquin has lost another 3.52 centimeters."

Taren was quiet for a moment as he looked down at the floor.

"It's time you joined your brethren. Our world is dying, and we no longer have the luxury of time." He picked up the orb and headed for the door, punched in a code, and turned to address Taren once more. "Prepare yourself. The council has decided to consider your request. However, you will be joining us in Elquin form tomorrow."

Taren was livid, and his hands balled into fists. "Why?" he growled through his teeth.

"It's time you distance yourself from the humans. Consider it the council's justice."

"The council's, Locknoff, or yours?"

Locknoff closed the door without another word, and Taren retreated to the mattress, put his head in his hands, and sighed. This would make it harder for him to keep his word to Jennifer, because there would be no way to keep her out of this when Sariah discovered her gift, but he would certainly try.

Before long, Ahdortee, Rashanah, and Fandore came to retrieve him. Taren looked at the women all dressed in black-and-white fatigues and wondered if Locknoff assumed he would try to hurt the men. He chuckled, offering no resistance as they escorted him to the large glass room where he now lay, dressed in a white gown, unmoving on one of the tables. Sariah demanded that everyone leave. She began preparing tools, vials, and needles to perform the transformation. When they were ready, she walked over to Taren and looked him in the eye with a slight sympathetic smile.

"I'm so sorry about this."

"It's OK, Sariah. Just promise me one...ouch...thing." She'd pricked his skin, inserting a thin vial of orange liquid.

"Sorry," she said, holding up the needle. "The anesthetic will kick in shortly. Anything, Taren. What do you need?"

As she spoke, his vision began to blur, and his thoughts became clouded. He tried to focus but found it difficult. "What is it, Taren?" Sariah asked, concern in her eyes now.

"Girl..." he said, "don't...let...kill..." He was asleep before finishing his statement. Sariah's eyebrows lowered.

"What?" she said. "You can tell me when you're awake." Sariah removed his gown and walked to the spiderlike, metal machine. In each arm, she deposited one of the vials she'd been working on. The vials had been filled with a liquid ranging from reddish brown to orange. Afterward, she walked to the other side of the room and stood behind a large crescent-shaped desk. She pushed several buttons on the desk, and a standing image of Taren's human body appeared. She pushed several more, and the one image split into several different images.

One of the images displayed the human skeletal system Taren's body had adopted. Another showed the other layer of skin covering the body. Another depicted the muscles within the body. The final image showed Taren's hearts, one of which had been altered slightly into the shape of a human liver. On each of the floating images, Sariah placed a digital image of one spider's arm. Each one was placed on a different part of his body so as not to overlap one another.

Once each image had its instructions, they were slammed back into the original image. The spider arms that were connected to the individual images now resembled a large claw. Sariah looked up at Taren's naked body, sighed, and pushed another button. As she did, the machine began moving. It positioned itself over Taren's body and inserted each arm as directed. Once the image depicted empty syringes, the spiderlike machine released Taren's body. His body immediately responded, his breathing became labored, and Sariah watched his chest rise and fall with the effort.

She watched in awe, clutching a syringe full of liquid in each hand close to her chest, while Taren's body crunched, shifted, twisted, and bent under its new demands. It moved effortlessly, almost as if it was made of putty. When all was still and Taren's breathing returned to normal, Sariah dropped the syringes where she stood and ran to his side.

"Oh, Taren," she said, grabbing a tiny flashlight and looking at his pupils. "OK," she said, "you're OK." She looked down at him briefly and immediately grabbed a sheet to cover his body.

Just then, Locknoff entered. "Good work, Sariah; the council will be pleased."

"I'm not so sure about that."

"Oh?"

"This was an extreme judgment, Locknoff." He raised an eyebrow, and Sariah continued. "I'm just not sure if it was the right one. We have no way of knowing how recent events will affect him in this form."

"You let me worry about that, Sariah. How long before he wakes?"

"Within the hour."

"Good. Here," he said, handing her the canister of Jennifer's blood. Sariah looked at it curiously. "It's the girl's blood. She was on the brink of death when we found them."

Sariah's eyes grew. "Thank you, Locknoff."

"I'll need a report for the council. There are a number of questions I need answers to."

"I will deliver it personally."

Locknoff turned and walked out of the room. Sariah walked over to the desk and pushed several buttons. A slim compartment rose from the desk, and she placed the syringe into it without the casing. The compartment lowered, and a thin, semitransparent screen appeared over the desk. The screen was roughly the width of the desk. Instantly, a thick DNA strand dominated the screen. It rotated slowly. Sariah moved very fast, pushing buttons behind the desk, which resulted in a rotating image of Jennifer from her head to her upper arms.

The image was much like the security print out, only it had much more detail. The eyes were a darker blue, her cheeks had more color, and her hair went past her arms. Sariah stopped and looked up.

"Girl," she said aloud.

"Yes," replied Taren, "and her hair is slightly shorter."

Sariah pushed another button, and Jennifer's hair became slightly shorter, just past her shoulders.

"Perfect," Taren said much too loudly. Sariah jumped slightly and turned toward him.

She could see him staring at the image. No, he was staring through the image. It was like her face was a magnet drawing his attention in. His eyes were full of wonder and elation. Sariah gasped, her jaw dropped open, and she looked several times between the image and Taren. It wasn't until she heard someone entering the room that she quickly pushed a button, removing the images from the screen. Taren looked at her, first with anger in his eyes, then gratitude when he heard the sound of someone entering the room.

Sariah walked over to him holding what looked like a handheld ultrasound machine. She lifted the arm and pushed a button. Blue light showered Taren as she ran it along his body.

"How do you feel?" she asked, looking into his eyes.

"Exhausted and confused."

"It will pass. You just need a good meal and some rest. Your body is weak because of the transformation. But you should be back to full strength within a week." She motioned for two of her assistants to help and suggested he try sitting up.

Taren grunted with the effort. "A week!" he growled, falling back into the arms of the assistants.

"Yes," she replied sternly, "if you can manage to keep it together. Your emotional health plays a key role in your recovery, Taren. You must take care to keep your emotions under control."

He looked her in the eyes a moment and then nodded. With great effort, Taren stood. The assistants each grabbed an arm, and he walked two steps, stopping in front of a wheelchair another presented. He looked up at Sariah, silently protesting.

"It's just across the hall," she said in response. When his expression did not change, Sariah motioned for the assistant to take the chair away.

After several minutes of grunting and sliding his feet across the floor, Taren found himself face to face with Ahdortee, who immediately looked at Sariah accusingly.

Sariah simply tossed her hands up in defeat and walked away. "We will follow," Ahdortee said to the men on either side of Taren and moved slightly to get out of their way.

Taren noticed another female with Ahdortee, but he did not focus on her. He made his way slowly across the hall and found a much different scene than he had the first time he'd been in this room. *Or is it a completely different one?* he wondered.

The room was white. On one side was a bed with a pair of white scrubs folded atop it. The bed was set very low to the floor. On the other side of the room was a door leading to a bathroom. Taren made his way to the bed, and the assistant held the sheet in place until he sat down.

Ahdortee came into view then. Bending to eye level with him, she placed something into his palm. "I am to give you this," she said. Taren looked down as she added, "Get better soon, Master Vishnu. We await your orders in the field."

Taren frowned slightly but thanked her and closed his hands over the object. Ahdortee stood and went out the door, followed by Rashanah and Fandore.

"Do you need anything else?" one of the assistants asked as the others left the room. Taren noticed who it was then.

"Elious…I apologize for my behavior before. I trust your health is well?"

Elious looked at him a moment and then spoke. "Yes, thank you, and don't worry about it. I'm not sure exactly what happened, but I'm fine now."

Taren nodded. "Will you get Sariah for me?"

"Sure," Elious said and then turned and left the room.

◆ ◆ ◆

Sariah was deeply engrossed in what she'd been doing, when she was interrupted by one of her assistants. She quickly pressed a button to close the screen she'd been working with. Her assistant apologized for the interruption.

"Nonsense, Yakema. What can I do for you?"

Yakema smiled. She was a short woman with a milk-chocolate complexion. She had long, black hair and thick eyebrows. Her eyelashes were to die for, and the white scrubs she wore elongated her features.

"Well," she said nervously, "I've been asked to inform you that Master Vishnu wishes to see you."

"Asked by whom, Yakema?" Sariah looked on with lowered brows, one hand on her hip.

"Elious."

Sariah took a deep breath. "Thank you, Yakema. In the future, please inform Elious or anyone else who would seek to use your kindness for their own purposes that they must carry out their own duties, not charge you with the task."

"Yes, Master Sariah," Yakema responded confidently.

"You may inform Master Vishnu that I will join him shortly."

Yakema nodded and disappeared. Sariah returned to her work. Roughly an hour later, she sighed heavily, turned off the screen, and left the room. She rounded the corner and slammed right into Locknoff's hard frame.

"Ouch…Master Locknoff," she said, rubbing at her temple, "I was just on my way to see you." Sariah lifted a thin silver strip between her fingers. "You'll want to review this personally before the council convenes tomorrow."

Locknoff raised an eyebrow but nodded and took it, walking away without a word.

Twenty-Four

WONDERS OF THE UNIVERSE

Sariah walked into Taren's recovery room and found him staring intently at the ceiling. She half- smiled, moving toward him.

"How are you feeling?" she asked.

Taren inhaled deeply and closed his eyes. "Like I've been training for a raid on Gala-4 for the past seventy-two hours."

"It will pass," she promised. "Taren," she continued, "I've completed my analysis on the girl's blood."

"So!" he responded much too loudly.

"Sooo…" she said dramatically, "I've discovered why the orb affected her so much faster than the others."

Taren blinked and then turned toward her while pulling himself up onto his elbows.

"Based on the orb's recording of the girl's theta wave readings, there is a 99.735 percent chance that she had precognitive abilities. It would take an official reading to confirm, of course, but—"

"Had?" Taren interrupted angrily.

"Well, yes," Sariah responded skeptically. "Locknoff said she was close to death when he found you. I can only assume she didn't make it based on his description of the situation."

The anger disappeared completely from Taren's features.

"All right," he said calmly.

Sariah's brows lowered. "Taren, you understand the implications if she's survived."

"Enlighten me," he responded with a smirk.

"She could be aware of us, for one thing, and who knows what effects the orb has had on her. The orb readings alone are astronomical. It didn't just review its inherited knowledge, Taren; it scanned for responses to its parentage." When Taren's expression did not change, Sariah continued, "Taren, she may have seen the orb as it was created."

His eyes widened slightly, and for such a brief period, that Sariah thought she'd imagined it.

"Taren, we have to know how she was affected by it."

"Sariah, please, this isn't her fight."

"I didn't bring her into this, Taren, and based on the findings, it's now a decision for the council. Perhaps you should consider the benefits her presence will bring to our efforts."

Sariah watched as Taren's features went through several different emotions before settling on acceptance. It was then that she remembered his reaction to the image.

"Taren," she said, kneeling and looking into his eyes, "I will not let harm come to her."

He nodded and lay back down.

Sariah smiled. "This isn't exactly what I had in mind, Taren," Sariah said, getting to her feet, "but I suppose it will do."

"I have no idea what you're talking about, Sariah. And why can't I have normal quarters?"

Smiling, Sariah moved toward the door. "This room is temporary, Taren. It has been discovered that our mental recalibration is better stimulated by this color during the first few hours after a transformation. Don't worry. You'll be able to get under the council's skin from your own station soon enough."

She then left the room in search of Locknoff. It didn't take her long to find him. He'd been so demanding about a workspace that she'd given him the first thing she could think of. It didn't matter that it wasn't suitable for a master of his stature, but she guessed it would have to do for now. Besides, it was on the other side of the building and out of her line of sight and hearing.

"Come in, Sariah," Locknoff said from behind his desk. "I've just been reviewing your analysis."

His office was simple. There were a few cabinets, a computer, a large mirror mounted on the wall, a phone, and three chairs. Locknoff sat behind the desk, staring intently at the computer screen.

"Please sit down," he said, gesturing to one of the chairs on the other side of the desk.

"I apologize for the condition of this office, Locknoff, but you were quite insistent on having something immediately."

"Nonsense, Sariah." He smiled. "It will do nicely. How is Taren?"

Sariah raised an eyebrow, instantly suspicious of his tone. "He is progressing nicely. I imagine he will be strong enough to attend the council meeting tomorrow, but there isn't much I can say for his emotional strength."

"He's stronger than you think, Sariah. He'll do fine. Your evaluation of the girl's blood was quite thorough. I imagine the council will appreciate your report firsthand."

"I have already submitted my findings to Zeeporah, Locknoff. I'm sure she's quite capable, but thank you for the invitation."

Locknoff sank deeper into his chair and smiled. "Your abilities with the orb have proven invaluable, Sariah, as well as the contributions you've made to Elquin. I believe a consideration of my invitation is in order."

"No, thank you, Locknoff. I am quiet satisfied with my current station."

Locknoff was quiet for a moment, seemingly contemplating as he tapped his fingers on the desk, and then added, "I can respect your decision, Sariah. May I suggest then that you ready your station?"

"For what?" Sariah asked, taken aback.

"A human. I'm no reader, but I would guess the council will want to know more about this precog."

Sariah's eyes widened, and her lower lips formed an *O* as she gasped audibly. "I thought she was dead. You…you told me that she—"

"As did I," Locknoff interrupted, sitting up. He turned his computer monitor around. "But there she is, alive and well."

Sariah looked at the screen expectantly, scooting to the edge of her seat. On the left side of the screen was a map. The right was split into two. The top half was the image Sariah had submitted in her findings and the bottom was a composition of Jennifer's name, vital signs, and location.

"You placed a tracker," Sariah asked, surprised.

"It was necessary at the time."

"She lives," Sariah added.

"For now," Locknoff said, more to himself while reaching to recover the monitor.

Sariah was shocked. Immediately she was reminded of Taren's behavior not so long ago. *He must have known.* "I will attend the council meeting if you require my assistance, but my decision to join stands."

"Then I will see you there."

The rest of the day passed uneventfully, and the council meeting came all too quickly for Sariah, who sat at the table, calmly watching Taren for signs of physical or mental fatigue. The council would be joining them soon, and Taren had already experienced two emotional out burst that seemed to weaken him. The first was when Locknoff brought up the subject of Jennifer's tracker, and the second was when Sariah reminded Locknoff for the third time of Taren's frail emotions and the need for him to get better.

"How long will this take?" she asked a frustrated Locknoff, who only tried to pacify her.

"It has never taken this long before. I'm not sure what's going on, but I'm sure they'll be joining us shortly." As he completed his statement, the small conference room became quiet as everyone turned their attention to the flickering screen above the table.

Also in attendance was Feleet, who could not stop giggling and complimenting Locknoff, and another male Sariah remembered meeting only once and for a brief moment. His name was Ryous. He was a coordinator of sorts, responsible for troops being where they were needed mostly. He was tall and had a muscular build. Ryous never seemed to carry on much of a conversation with anyone, but he was often sought after for council when there was a problem Locknoff couldn't or wouldn't address. Even Locknoff sought out Ryous at times, which only added to the mystery surrounding him. Sariah returned her attention to the flickering screen.

The gathered watched intently as it came into focus. Sariah's gasp was echoed by nearly everyone else in the room. The entire council had convened. Not just those on Elquin, but every council member stationed on every farmed planet throughout the galaxies. They had each logged on. In the center of the screen was the Elquin table of council. The other thirty-eight council forums were framed around them.

"Welcome, council masters," Elitar said while standing. He'd aged, Sariah noted. The white ceremonial robe he wore now seemed to be a burden to him, and his crown did not fit as snugly as she'd remembered. It had contentiously grown to represent the planets under Elquin charge. *He's tired*, she thought. *His moons are catching up to him.*

"You have all been called to weigh in on the future of Elquin. Our planet is dying. We no longer have the luxury of implementing containment measures. The status of our shield proves only one thing. We must leave this world, or accept extinction. We have searched the neighboring galaxies for a suitable replacement for our planet and found only one: Earth. The current cycle of this star suggests that the planet is safe from implosion for another two hundred fifty bokorah. Based on our history with the current inhabitants of this world, the question before you today is whether we should conquer their world or seek cohabitation."

Gasps could be heard throughout the council.

"Before you weigh in, we shall hear the facts. Bathmantu," Elitar said, gesturing for him to stand. Bathmantu pushed several buttons in front of him on the table before standing. Two 3-D images of planets were projected.

"This is Earth," he said, pointing to the green green-and and-blue world. "Compared to Elquin, this world shows the most promise for mining potential. The cerium deposits are uniquely plentiful on this world. Research reveals a structure not that dissimilar to our own." He pushed a section of the 3-D images of Earth, and it began spinning slowly as he spoke. "There are rivers, streams, mountains, and valleys. The perfect ingredients for life are astronomically abundant here. The only challenge we currently face is an acclimation to its shield. Like Elquin so many epochy ago, Earth's shield is strong and unique, providing its inhabitants great benefits. The cycles of life on Earth are all governed by the shield's influence. Research suggests that our life cycle will acclimate over time. This will allow our current disadvantages to diminish greatly. If research proves correct, our cycles will acclimate within five generations."

Shock covered the faces of so many that Sariah had a difficult time focusing on Bathmantu's words.

"Locknoff, if you will," Bathmantu said, redirecting her attention.

Locknoff stood as Bathmantu sat. As he moved, the screen focused on their gathered party for a brief moment, then on what he was doing. Locknoff pulled up Taren's report and pinpointed several sections of it before removing parts he did not want.

"Military intelligence has been made aware of our presence, making a surprise approach impossible. If we vote to remove the dominant species here, an all-out attack is recommended."

Sariah turned sharply to check on Taren, who seemed to be growing angrier with every word spoken. A sharp look from her, and his breathing came easier.

"What options do you believe would work best, Master Ryous?" Locknoff asked, reclaiming his seat.

Ryous stood. "In war, the best strategy is the element of surprise. Because we no longer have that, I would suggest attacks from both land and air, running consecutively and/ or concurrently as needed. Perhaps a large contingent of unmanned deployments to begin."

With no questions to address, Ryous returned to his seat. Moments later, Nesset addressed the council. "Although war is effective in conquest, let's not forget the capability of our opponent. Elquin has suffered great losses at the hands of the humans, and it appears we are prepared to lose more. I propose we consider Master Vishnu's request for a diplomatic solution to our endeavor."

Whispers could be heard throughout the council, as individuals began to weigh in among themselves.

"Through trial and error," Nesset continued, "we have come to understand our own strengths and limitations on this world." She looked at Locknoff briefly. "Recently, we've been made aware of miraculous possibilities between our species and the human race. Master Vishnu of Ateenn blood has risked everything. His recent mission has led to the unexpected creation of interspecies offspring."

Audible gasps swept throughout the council. Some Elquins covered their mouths, while others placed hands to their chests.

"This possibility," she continued in a more sturdy tone, "suggests that our future can include humans and decreases the need to completely destroy them. Madafski, Skyke, please share with the council what you have discovered with regard to this matter."

She looked at Taren and smiled when she saw acceptance in his eyes. Skyke and Madafski stood facing each other from opposite ends of the table. Simultaneously they pushed buttons on the table surface to reveal chromosomes.

On one side of the table was the projection of a human male. Next to him was a composite of twenty-three pairs of chromosomes. On the other side of the table was an image of an Elquin male and twenty-three pairs of chromosomes.

"As you can see," Madafski began, "both humans and Elquins share the same number of chromosomes. There are only seven sequence differences, which is what allows us to manipulate them for a brief period of time." The seven chromosome differences were outlined on the screen for all to see. One of pairs 2, 6, 10, 12, and 21 was shaped slightly differently, and both the X and Y chromosomes shared a similar difference.

"Research shows that while binding the two is possible, any offspring will inherit its chromosomes from the original microbe design."

"This is because," Skyke added, watching the facial expressions of several council members, "the manipulation is temporary, and the chromosomes begin regenerating themselves instantly. The process takes seven years to complete, or roughly one year per chromosome. Because they regenerate simultaneously, the outward changes all happen at the same time." Skyke looked at Madafski, who continued.

"What this means is that a young one could be born with a combination of human features and Elquin interior, or vice versa. The only difficulty we now face comes when we enter Earth's atmosphere. Zeeporah will better explain the challenges every one of us will face when entering Earth's gravitational field."

Madafski sat and all turned to Zeeporah, who stood regally in her council blue, wearing her crown of braids so full of gems that one could hardly see the white of it.

"Our advantages, or disadvantages, depending on how you view them, involve the emotions. It appears that our emotional state is greatly intensified on this planet. Its effects are far greater than anything we've ever encountered. For example," she said, looking at Taren, "you have lost two young ones on this planet, Master Vishnu." Sariah gasped and looked at Taren. "Do you think it wise to attempt the creation of another, or would you agree that any unborn Ateenn on this planet is destined to meet an untimely demise before they are even born?"

"Zeeporah!" Sariah shouted, leaping forward to catch Taren as he fell to the floor after leaping to his feet, growling.

"No, Zeeporah," he barked. "I believe you are destined for destruction by my hands the moment you step foot on this planet for making such a misguided prediction against my bloodline."

Gasps filled the council, and individuals spoke among themselves briefly. "Master Zeeporah of Tisha blood," Nesset interjected angrily, "you go too far! He has been through enough."

"You will make your point without further insult," Elitar interrupted.

Sariah returned to her seat at Taren's request once he'd been seated.

"My apologies, master council. I only meant to outline the importance of the decision we make today. We must take into account the totality of the circumstances prior to moving forward."

"Point made," Sariah said angrily.

"Not quite. As you can see," Zeeporah continued, "being in human form dulls the intensity slightly, but working with the humans may mean we must work as Elquins and in our native forms." She shook her head. "It may become easier over time, but we must take into account the immediate disadvantage."

"Excellent point, Zeeporah," Elitar said. "Do you have more to add?"

"No," she replied matter- of- factly as she took her seat.

"Then the decision we must make first is to the issue of abandoning our home. Does anyone have any questions regarding this matter?" Silence ran throughout the council for a while until Elitar asked, "Then may I have your vote?"

One by one the council members spoke. "To Earth," they each voted in turn.

When it came to Taren's turn, he was still visibly distressed. Breathlessly, he spoke, "To Earth."

"To Earth," Elitar repeated and looked to Sariah. "I know your decision to join the council is still under consideration, Sariah, but may we have your vote?"

She looked at Locknoff with a scowl and then turned to Elitar saying, "To Earth." *Far be it for me to go against every other individual here*, she thought.

Twenty-Five

Diplomacy And War

"A decision has been made, yet more must be decided. Let us now focus on how best to proceed. Based on the facts presented, does anyone have any questions?"

"Yes," came a soft voice.

"Master Dalani," Elitar said pleasantly, "what have you to share?"

Dalani had young features. Although her crown was full enough to completely cover the skin on her forehead, Sariah always thought it was hard to tell how old she really was by looking at her.

"This Earth we've claimed as our new home, how can we keep it from suffering Elquin's fate?"

"The star's fate will be that of our own," Bathmantu clarified. "This we cannot change, but the knowledge we carry from this world will better prepare our children for what is to come in the distant future."

"If the decision to live among these beings is made here today, what knowledge have we of their bonding capabilities?" a harsh voice added.

"Bonding?" Skyke asked.

"Yes. If we are to live among them, could it be possible for us to find a heart song with them?" The question came from a male who seemed to be the same age and build as Taren. His long, white hair was waist length, and he wore his traditional blue robes with a sash that displayed a large orange-and-blue fire jutting out of a rosebud.

"Well," Skyke replied, "a heart song can be found anywhere, I imagine, but the council will need to retain approval prior to any bonding. Genetically speaking, our bonding process could be done with a human female's blood rather than her sweat glands, but a male would need to undergo a complete transformation."

"Bonding! Living among the humans! Have you all lost your minds?" a female shouted angrily. "Have we forgotten what they did to our council?"

Sariah looked at Taren and was pleasantly surprised to see that he wasn't doubled over in pain.

"That tragedy will live on in our histories for all time," Madafski said, "but there is no reason to kill all of them because of the actions of a few. I suggest we give them an opportunity for redemption before deciding their fate."

All was quiet for a moment, and then Elitar spoke again. "Madafski brings up a valid point. Death and destruction only beget more death and destruction. We should not threaten our new resources with such actions. It will take a pieleen or more to clean up after such an event. Master Vishnu, what course of action would you suggest?"

Instantly his breathing became more difficult, but he spoke as loudly and as confidently as Elitar had.

"We have just voted to abandon our home world, all that we hold dear, in the hopes of a new beginning. To start that beginning with the annihilation of an entire world without provocation only suggests that we are barbarians. Yes, they have brought great grief to our world, but like many others, they made that choice out of ignorance." He leaned forward and began gasping. Sariah came closer to aid him as best she could. "I'm fine, Sariah," he said holding a hand out to her while returning upright.

"My suggestion would be to stop mining projects at once. Transport those who are unable to fight for the time being, mobilize the fighters and ERT, and develop a council team to represent Elquin for initial contact with Earth's leaders. Give them an ultimatum with the promise of gain, and lay siege if they refuse."

Locknoff looked at him with a raised brow and smiled slightly.

"I second the motion, council master," Elitar said. "Does anyone have any objections?" All were silent.

"We must decide now," Skyke said. "Our star is running on its last leg. There is no telling how much time we have left."

"I second the motion," Locknoff said, standing.

"And I," Feleet added, getting to her feet.

"And I," Ryous said, joining them.

"And I," came the voices of others.

Elitar stood once it was declared. "As decided, so shall it be. Ready your stations for the changes. We shall meet again in two weeks when the remainder of our fighters reach Earth's moon and the council is ready to make contact."

Locknoff logged off the screen and looked at Taren. Everyone in the room was speechless.

"Taren…"

"Please, Sariah, not now."

As she stood to help him, the Elquin council came into focus with only Elitar and Nesset in view.

"Master Sariah."

She sighed and turned to the screen. "Yes, high council master?"

"Your work in this transformation process has not gone unnoticed. You will follow up with Master Tomahbare and study the girl's reaction to the orb as best you can. Please keep us informed of your progress, and be prepared to begin transforming key members of the council mission as their identities are made known to you."

"I shall," she replied, reaching for Taren's arm to get a better grip.

"Honor, Ateenn," Elitar said, looking at Taren. He paused and looked up at the screen. "I know you have been through much, Vishnu, but I fear I must ask one more thing of you yet."

Taren sighed. "And what would that be, Elitar?"

"I want you to replace me as high council master when the time comes."

Taren was speechless, Sariah and Feleet gasped, Locknoff lowered his eyebrows suspiciously, and Ryous just smiled and nodded. But before he could respond, Taren collapsed onto the floor.

"He has been through much, Elitar. Please allow him to rest now. I'm sure he'll have your answer soon. In the meantime I shall prepare for what is to come," Sariah proclaimed.

"Excellent. Feleet, you too will need to make preparations." Feleet nodded, and the pair logged out. Sariah looked at Locknoff, and he bowed his head slightly.

"I shall retrieve the girl," he said, bending to help Ryous with Taren. Sariah nodded and gathered herself for the upcoming task.

Jennifer sat comfortably in her first-class accommodations, awaiting takeoff aboard flight 5734 to Ruidoso, New Mexico. Though no longer a nervous wreck, she'd stumbled through check-in so nervously that she was pulled aside by airport security and questioned. After explaining herself, she immediately found a bar and stayed there until the idea of flying no longer bothered her. Jennifer closed her eyes in the hopes of getting some much-needed rest. A four-and-a-half-hour flight would not be much, but it might help.

Closing her eyes, Jennifer was asleep in no time.

She was staring at Cara's lifeless body in a casket, tears running down her face. She felt like screaming.

"I look peaceful, don't I?" she heard someone say—and snapped her head up at the sound of her friend's voice.

"*Cara!*" Jennifer exclaimed, wrapping her arms around her.

"Oh," Cara responded and gently embraced her friend.

"But you're...I'm...how did I..."

"Shhh..." Cara placed a finger on Jennifer's lips. "It's OK. I'm all right."

Jennifer looked at her in surprise. She then noticed that Cara was dressed like Billie Holiday, her favorite artist. She smiled and wiped at Jennifer's tears. Her white cocktail-style dress matched the large bunch of chrysanthemums on the left side of her hair. Jennifer looked down at the casket and cried openly.

"Shhh...it's OK, Jen. You don't have to be sad for me."

"But your...I didn't..." Her shoulders slumped, and she sobbed with her head in her hands.

"Jennifer, my journey has come to an end on this path."

"But"—sniff—"what happened...how...I don't understand." She stopped talking and just cried.

Cara inhaled deeply and placed a hand on her friends shoulder. "I allowed someone into my home who wasn't what they appeared."

"I'm so sorry, Cara. It's all my fault."

"Your fault?" Cara repeated with a raised brow. "No, sister, you could not have warned me of something you didn't know was possible yourself."

"But my dreams..."

"It's all right. It was simply my time, sister. Your warning would not have changed the outcome."

"I'm so sorry," Jennifer said again, shaking her head.

Cara took Jennifer's hands and looked into her eyes. "Jennifer Braxton, you are beautiful, even when you're not perfect."

Jennifer smiled and sniffed. "So…" she said, and they both chuckled.

"Sooo…" Cara responded, looking down at the casket. "You're coming to the funeral?"

Jennifer shook her head. "I wouldn't miss it for anything." She closed her eyes and inhaled deeply, taking in her friend's scent. When she opened them, she was standing in a white room.

Someone lay on a bench in front of her, moaning in pain. For some reason she felt compelled to reach out. As she did, she heard her name in a rough voice. Curious, Jennifer moved closer and touched the person's shoulder. When she did, he turned slightly and she could see his features. It was Vishnu…or Taren, but in Elquin form. Her eyes bulged, and she gasped. He was weak, unlike she'd ever seen him before. He almost looked sick.

"What have they done to you?" Jennifer asked no one, reaching out to comfort him. She felt sick. As her hand made contact, she fell to her knees in pain. She could hear voices in the distance, calling to her. "Ma'am…miss…are you all right?"

"Ugh," she said aloud, coming to.

"We've landed, ma'am. Do you need a doctor?"

"No," she replied, shaking her head slowly. She blinked several times, remembering where she was. "Thank you," she said, getting to her feet. *I guess I was more tired than I thought.* She half smiled and looked around for her carry-on items. The flight attendant smiled as Jennifer headed out the door in search of baggage claim.

Twenty-Six

Passing Through

When Jennifer reached the right conveyor belt, as determined by her recognition of the people from her flight, she noticed the belt hadn't started yet. Groggy and a bit disoriented, she made her way to a restroom. After relieving herself, she washed her hands and face and saw a woman she recognized from the plane standing next to her luggage, reapplying makeup. *Crap*, she thought and headed out in search of her own.

Her eyes were glued to the conveyor belt when she came out, so she didn't recognize him until she ran him over.

"Josh! Sorry," Jennifer said, helping him up.

"Jennifer," he replied, almost formally, as he picked his things up. Then he walked away without another word. She lowered her brows but decided against pursuing him when she remembered his friendship with Zackary. *He must be angry about the protection order.* After retrieving her bags, Jennifer headed for the rental lot. She wasn't interested in being anywhere except Cara's home. But she would not depend on anyone to get her away if there was trouble, nor would she put any more of her friends in harm's way.

The house was a bustle of activity when she arrived. Emily, Amy, and Kim were all sitting on the couch, watching old home movies of

Cara. Nancy and Cara's aunt Brenda were in the kitchen, making coffee and chatting. Several others Jennifer had never seen before were gathered around the small dining room table. Everyone stopped when she walked in. The silent gasps were deafening, and then she was surrounded.

"Oh, Jen, are you all right? We heard what happened. We were all so worried. Where have you been?"

"I'm fine, guys. Don't worry about me. I just had a little trouble with Zackary, is all." She stopped abruptly when she saw Brenda, who looked relieved. She went to hug Jen, who was suddenly in tears.

"I'm so sorry I left her. I didn't know..."

"Nonsense, child. You would have met the same fate. Now come. Sit with us and have some tea."

After a couple of hours chatting, planning, and catching up, Jennifer excused herself. "I'm gonna try to get some sleep," she said after learning of her friends' encounter with the hotel security and the technological problems that followed. She was immediately reminded of the car trouble she and Taren had.

"Yeah," Kim explained, scrunching her face into an unrecognizable expression. "It was weird. We got off the elevator to check out, and my phone rang suddenly. I had over a hundred and fifty messages. Total shocker after hours of being in the twilight zone."

"Yeah," Emily said, "and we still can't get you off it."

"I'm just afraid it will die on me again," she replied, her fingers moving across the keys with lightning speed.

Jennifer was convinced—her friends were not safe around her.

"I'll leave after the funeral," she declared to no one as she closed the bedroom door. Her cheeks glistened as she looked over the room she'd shared with her now-dead friend not even a week ago. Cara's room was an extension of her heart, displaying her love for black bears. Her bed, dresser, and nightstands were made of darkly stained oak with black bears and flowers carved throughout. Her comforter was a canvas of woods and flowers. It displayed a mother bear lying with her twin cubs. The edges were lined with black bears.

She had pictures, posters, and trinkets of the lovely beasts. The throw pillows on her bed were a variety of black teddy bears. Jennifer noticed one particularly large bear on the nightstand. She picked it up and traced the bear's facial features, stopping at its eyes. She never could figure out Cara's love for these creatures. Jennifer thought they were wild killers, but in this moment, she could see the joy in its features and smiled through the tears.

Jennifer lay down, clutching the bear as she cried. Letting go of everything finally, she cried for the friend she'd lost; she cried for the friends she would now have to say good-bye to; she cried for the stranger who'd saved her; she cried for humanity; she cried for herself. Sleep was long in coming, but eventually it found her. Jennifer slept through the night in that spot and awoke feeling refreshed. She had no nightmares or dreams of any kind, only memories of joyous times with Cara.

Jennifer was confident that her friend was at peace, but was saddened that she would no longer be able to share a meal with her, laugh at her jokes, or express her disapproval for her strange obsession with black bears. Today she would say good-bye and dedicate the rest of her life to keeping the rest of her friends safe—even if the remainder of her life turned out to be an incredibly short period of time.

◆ ◆ ◆

The viewing was set for that evening, but Jennifer promised to accompany Brenda to the funeral home. She wanted to ensure that preparations were made according to order. After hours of deliberating changes, overseeing them, and incorporating new specifications, Jennifer needed a break, so she stepped outside for a breather. She spent twenty minutes sitting in the funeral home's floral garden and then decided Brenda might be looking for her, so she headed back in.

As she passed the main office, Jennifer heard a name that stopped her dead in her tracks.

"Lillian Waters," the feminine voice said. "I came by here yesterday, and they told me it would be ready for viewers by eight o'clock in the morning."

"What was the name again?" Jennifer heard the administrator ask.

"Lillian Waters. The funeral was last night at eight fifteen."

"Oh, the military chick. Yeah, they finished that one about an hour ago. Give me a sec."

Jennifer backed up slightly and looked into the office. She could see the back of a dark-skinned woman's head. Her hair was pulled into a thick bun, and she was dressed in a denim one-piece with a black belt and pumps.

"Row K34, plot 7428."

"Thanks."

As the woman turned, Jennifer was distracted by the sound of her name.

"There you are, Jen. I've been looking everywhere for you," Brenda said, relieved. "The viewing is set for seven. I guess we should get back and see if they need any help."

Jennifer turned to see the dark-skinned woman leaving and said, "I'll be ready in just a second." She followed after the woman before Brenda could object. When Jennifer reached her, the woman was getting into her blue Volkswagen convertible.

"Excuse me, but did you say you were looking for Lillian? Lillian Waters?"

"What's it to you?" she asked, shutting the door and starting the car.

"I'm sorry, but I didn't realized she'd passed," Jennifer said.

The woman stopped what she'd been doing and closed her eyes. "I'm sorry…did you know her?" she asked, wiping the tears from her cheeks.

"I knew her brother-in-law, Locknoff."

The woman froze. She looked up at Jennifer with lowered eyebrows, and her expression changed instantly. Her eyes grew about two inches as she noticed the bruises on Jennifer's face.

"Locknoff?" she repeated. Jennifer's interest piqued. *Could this be Anna?* she wondered.

"I'm Jennifer, by the way," she said, holding her hand out. The woman was stunned; she looked at Jennifer with pitied eyes.

"Anna Desai," she replied in greeting. Jennifer's eyes bulged; even though she was ready, the confirmation still surprised her. "What?" Anna asked.

"I'm sorry…it's just…he talks about you a lot."

Anna looked around somewhat nervously. If she was surprised or flattered by the comment, she didn't show it. "Look," she said and pulled something out of the center console. "I can't talk now. E-mail me, and we'll chat." She put the car in gear and pulled out while Jennifer reviewed the card.

It was just an e-mail address in the center. Jennifer looked up to see Anna turning into the cemetery and was interrupted again by Brenda before she could do or say anything else.

"Are you OK, Jennifer? Who was that?"

"Yes, I'm fine," she replied distantly. "That was just an old friend. Let's go."

Brenda's expression was doubtful, but she didn't inquire further.

Jennifer was in a hurry to get to her laptop after the viewing, so she headed straight for her things. She dropped to the floor next to her bag and pulled out her laptop. The others wondered silently what she was on about but didn't ask.

She logged in to her e-mail and typed a message: *Anna, I'm sorry for bombarding you at the funeral home today. I just had a few questions for you about Locknoff.* She pushed Send and then watched the screen. After only a few minutes, a reply came.

Go to 5732 Avenue Drive. Come before 6:00 p.m. tomorrow.

Jennifer sighed and shut the computer. She desperately wanted to be on the road tomorrow after the burial, but she had to talk to Anna first. She needed to know everything she could about Locknoff if she was to outrun him. She rubbed her leg where he'd shot her and sighed. Jennifer didn't want to put Anna on his radar. "Not after what she did to get away from him," she said aloud.

"Get away from whom?" Nancy asked, sitting down next to her on the floor.

"Zackary," she responded much too quickly.

"I'm so sorry about what happened. Are you OK?"

"No." She shook her head and then half smiled. "I will be though—don't worry."

"I'm glad you filed charges against him. I never would have thought a Sigma would be capable of doing something like that. Don't worry. He can't come within a thousand feet of you now, right?"

"Yeah, that's right."

The friends embraced and got up to join the others.

◆ ◆ ◆

The funeral was surprisingly short for the number of guests gathered, but Jennifer was determined to be on her way as soon as possible, so when the last prayer was uttered, she said her good-byes and left. She drove directly to 5732 Avenue Drive. The dashboard clock read 12:50 when she arrived, so she got out and headed to the front door. Anna's home was the last unit of an attached home community. Two baskets of flowers hung on the porch.

As she reached for the doorbell, Anna opened the door.

"Welcome, Jennifer. Please come in."

"Thank you," Jennifer replied, stepping clear of the door.

Anna's thick curls swung freely, sweeping her lower back. She smiled politely and secured the door, then led the way to the living room. Her home flowed in an open floor plan. There was a thick column separating the living room from the small dining room, with a lovely arched doorway leading into the kitchen. There was a small table in the breakfast area under the bay window. The stairs arched slightly, revealing part of the second-floor balcony.

The couches were a green-and-white flower pattern that was carried throughout the bottom floor. On the opposite side of the living room was a sliding-glass door that led to a small outside living space. The home didn't scream bachelorette, but it wasn't exactly child friendly either. The walls holding the sliding doors were decorated with several weapons, swords, knives, and even a bow and arrow. No doubt from Locknoff's experimental rampage, Jennifer concluded.

There were several decorated pieces of art adorning the room's walls, but Jennifer's eyes settled on a cordless digital photo frame that had rotating pictures of Anna spending time in what could only be London.

"A vacation I took about six months ago," Anna said, looking at Jennifer. "Well, most of them are." She stopped as the rotation hit several sonogram photos before moving on to more of Anna with friends.

"Oh, I've always wanted to go there."

"It was a blast. You would enjoy it. So what would you like to drink? I have soft drinks or juice, but I was about to have some tea, when I noticed you walking up."

"Tea is fine," Jennifer replied eagerly, her attention returning to the rotating photos. She saw one of Anna and Locknoff at an amusement park. As she studied them, it was like she was looking through them.

She could see Locknoff and a dark-haired woman driving past a children's park. She recognized the woman and two of the men in the car that followed. They were there when Locknoff found her and Taren. She gasped as she recognized the direction they drove. It was Anna's neighborhood. Instantly she was on her feet.

"I didn't know how much sugar you wanted, so I just filled a cup." Anna stopped where she stood, holding a tray of steaming tea.

"I'm so sorry," Jennifer said, looking at her with tear-filled eyes. "I have to go." She ran out the door.

Anna looked at the frame with lowered eyebrows and noticed the rotation of photos. She sighed and put the tray on the table. "Jennifer, wait." She looked out the window and could see that Jennifer had stopped halfway down the driveway. She seemed to be speaking with someone. Anna had never seen the man before, but she could see that Jennifer was clearly nervous.

◆ ◆ ◆

"You shouldn't encourage her, Ahdortee," Sariah said as the two women entered an elevator. The floor they were on looked like a business suite with numbered doors throughout the hall. "He obviously isn't interested."

"I'm not encouraging," Ahdortee said, holding her hands up defensively. "I only suggested Locknoff share a meal with her since she's obviously not going to quit. Who knows...he may actually discover that her company is pleasurable."

"Locknoff is single minded more often than not on the subject, Ahdortee, and I don't think you'll be able to sway him on it. But keep trying. There's nothing like a lost cause."

Ahdortee shrugged. She pushed the ground button on the elevator, and the doors closed. "Besides," she continued, "if I'm going to encourage anyone, then I have the perfect woman in mind for Vishnu." She smiled, satisfied with her new interests.

"Who?" Sariah asked suspiciously.

"Naeefah," Ahdortee responded matter of factly.

Sariah's mouth fell open. "I don't think he'll even see her, Ahdortee."

"Oh, I'll be sure he sees her. Don't worry about that part."

The low ding as they came to the ground floor made Sariah smile. "But that too would be interesting to watch," she said.

"I know he's lost much," Ahdortee said, "but everyone's capable of healing. I would love to see—" She cut off abruptly when she heard her name called.

It was Locknoff. "We're heading out. I want to be back before Porock returns."

Ahdortee nodded sharply, smiled at Sariah, and quickly made her way to where he stood waiting.

Ahdortee opened her notebook the moment she closed the car door.

"Good morning, Ahdortee. How may I..." the computer's voice said before she silenced it. "Vitals are strong. She's five miles from... here," Ahdortee said, lowering her eyebrows.

"Hmm," Locknoff commented. Ahdortee looked at him, her brow still lowered, to which he responded, "I didn't think she'd be back so soon. But some human ways are still a mystery to me."

When he didn't go on, Ahdortee returned her attention to the computer screen. There was a split screen account of Jennifer's photo from Sariah's report, and vital signs underneath. A map of the immediate area was on the other side of Jennifer and displayed her location and movements.

After a few minutes, Jennifer's vitals began to blink. Ahdortee pulled the information into focus. "Her heart rate just went up."

Locknoff spoke as if a crowd had gathered. "OK. Look sharp. She knows we're coming. Break off, and we will descend on her location together, covering every possible escape route."

"I don't get it," Ahdortee said after a moment, shaking her head in confusion.

"What?"

"She's not moving."

"Are the authorities with her?"

"No."

"Good. It will be less difficult this way."

Ahdortee studied the screen as others reported their positions through the car's speakers. Suddenly, Jennifer's vitals accelerated briefly on the monitor, then began to drop rapidly.

"Something's wrong. Her heart rate is dropping fast."

"Is she still at the same location?"

"Yes."

◆ ◆ ◆

The man who was talking to Jennifer, Anna noted, seemed to be asking her questions about the house. Anna's brows lowered a moment, and she shook her head, seeing the man grow angrier with every word. She stepped outside to speak on Jennifer's behalf, when the man suddenly struck Jennifer. Anna's jaw dropped in horror as he moved in and started punching and kicking Jennifer repeatedly when she refused to get up. A car parked directly across the street suddenly pulled away. The tires were moving so fast their marks were burned into the road.

Anna rushed to the phone and dialed 911. Meanwhile, Jennifer was clawing for the safety of her car. Bruised and bloodied as she was, Anna thought it was a miracle she could even see her car. She rushed back out to Jennifer's aid and saw that the man had pulled her to the lawn and was undoing his pants. Jennifer wasn't moving.

"Jennifer!" Anna screamed and ran to push the man away from her. Her tiny frame slightly nudged the man off balance. As she did, he grunted and turned. Without a word, he landed a backhand across her face so hard that she hit the ground.

◆ ◆ ◆

Locknoff rounded the corner and pulled up to Jennifer's location the same time as the other three vehicles. As he did, he could see why Jennifer's heart rate had suddenly dropped. A man was beating her senseless. She was clawing at a nearby car, and he'd pulled her away by her hair. Her face was bloodied and swollen. She abandoned her efforts at the car when the man landed a kick to her midsection. He then grabbed her and pulled her onto the lawn and then started fumbling with his pants.

The man was so engrossed in what he was doing that he didn't notice the vehicles pulling up to the curb.

"Ahdortee..." Locknoff noticed a small woman looking anxiously out the window at Jennifer. He was frozen where he sat. Ahdortee had begun getting out of the car but paused momentarily as he did. She looked over at him and saw that his facial expression was absolute euphoria.

Locknoff could see the olive brown of her skin, her dark-brown eyes, and the long curls that swung wildly at her movements.

"Anna," he said in amazement.

Ahdortee was rigid; she knew that name. Anna kept him up most nights. Her whereabouts tormented Locknoff for over three years now. She knew he didn't notice her intuition on the subject, but he'd seemed to be getting better recently.

Anna ran out of the house, and his eyes were locked on every move she made. As Ahdortee resumed movement, Anna fell to the ground. Locknoff stopped Ahdortee's advance with a sturdy hand on her arm. His eyes blazed with anger, and he ran toward the man without another word.

◆ ◆ ◆

It took Anna a minute to pick herself up. Her head was spinning. But when she finally did, she saw a man coming toward her with blinding speed. She looked into his eyes and saw a rage like no other. She knew him at once. The last time she'd seen him, he was angry as well. But this was different. He was furious, maddened. As the reality of his identity dawned on her, everything went dark.

◆ ◆ ◆

It all happened so fast that Ahdortee only had time to see him standing over Anna with the bloodied knife. The man's head rolled to the ground; his body fell after. She hadn't even noticed him grabbing the sword.

"Search the house!" Locknoff yelled while bending to pick up Anna's unconscious body from the ground. Three men followed Ahdortee into the house.

"Bring her," Locknoff ordered, gesturing with his head to Jennifer as two more ran toward the house. One bent to pick Jennifer up while the other ran ahead to get the car door. Locknoff heard sirens as he gently placed Anna into the backseat.

"Put her here. We're out of time."

"Ahdortee," he shouted over his shoulder, not taking his eyes off Anna. "The police are on their way."

Twenty-Seven

BRIDGE

Ahdortee was visible within seconds. She got into the car and shut the door as Locknoff pulled away. Ahdortee turned to see both women in the back, and her brow lowered briefly. She opened her notebook and said, "She's alive…barely, but we'll need to get her to Sariah quickly."

She started pushing buttons and, after a moment, looked at the screen intently. She moved her head slightly closer to the monitor with widened eyes. Ahdortee looked at Anna with shocked confusion on her face.

"What!" Locknoff demanded.

"She's carrying a tracer."

His eyebrows lifted in surprise. He turned to look at Anna briefly and then back at Ahdortee. "Scramble it, and inform Ryous of its origin."

Ahdortee nodded and turned to comply, pushing buttons so fast that her hands were almost a blur.

"Ryous," she spoke into the phone several seconds later, "we've got a problem."

When they arrived at the compound a short time later, both women were still unconscious. Locknoff carried Anna as if she were a delicate flower, and Ahdortee grabbed Jennifer before anyone else could get to her. Ryous met up with them as they approached the building.

"The signal came from a federal building. It's a local operating unit for a federal investigation team."

Locknoff slowed briefly but didn't stop. He frowned and looked down at Anna as they headed into the building.

"Your assessment?" he asked Ryous.

"We can keep the signal blocked, but they'll send patrol units out if they can't get a fixed read on her."

"I don't want them within a hundred miles of her!"

Ryous called one of the men over.

"Plant the tracer in the desert," Locknoff demanded. "Make sure the signal leads back to their tracer only after the scout is ten miles clear of it."

Ryous nodded as they moved along the building. He waited in the hall with another man while they carried the women into the medical bay, where they interrupted Sariah's conversation with Yakema.

"Were the spikes removed?" Yakema asked and then stopped talking instantly when she saw the party enter.

"What happened? Two of them?" Sariah asked, rushing over to Jennifer and looking into her pupils.

"Her heart rate is very low," Ahdortee said.

Sariah walked over to Anna and repeated the examination. "What happened?" she asked again.

"She fainted," Locknoff responded immediately.

Anna began to stir, and Sariah immediately replaced the flashlight with a sedative. She injected it into Anna's shoulder and went back over to Jennifer.

"What happened to *her*?" she asked, gesturing with her head while pressing buttons at the foot of the table. The arch moved toward the head of the table. Sariah walked around to inject something into Jennifer's arm. When she finished, she looked at Ahdortee accusingly.

Ahdortee raised her hands defensively and shook her head. "We pulled up on a beating in progress. If it wasn't for Locknoff, the girl would be dead now."

Sariah turned to her with a quick response ready, but she noticed Ahdortee's line of sight was on Locknoff.

"She has a tracer we need removed immediately," Ahdortee said as she turned her attention back to Sariah, her face a mask of professionalism.

A 3-D image of Jennifer's body appeared over the table, and Sariah looked at Yakema, who shook her head. "She's a human. I...I don't know how to treat humans."

Sariah raised a brow questioningly and then opened a drawer under the table and pulled out a syringe. She filled it with a blue liquid. "There isn't much difference, Yakema. Just pretend you're removing a thorn."

Yakema gulped and took a step forward. She pulled a small wand with a white rounded tip out of the table underneath Anna.

Locknoff's head shot up instantly. His eyes were glued to the object in Yakema's hand. Yakema looked at Sariah, who had just injected the last of the syringes into one of several spots on Jennifer's body.

"Get out of the way, Locknoff. Do you want the bug or not?"

Locknoff looked back and forth between Yakema and Sariah several times before finally stepping back to join Ahdortee.

Yakema moved fast, pressing buttons on the side of the table. A green light illuminated from the table's head, and it moved downward scanning every part of the table. After a moment, a small section under Anna's left ankle lit up. Yakema moved to the other side of the table and placed a rod on Anna's skin directly in the center of the green light.

A yellow light glowed from within the rod, and Yakema removed it. Blood ran down Anna's leg, and she wiped it lightly, aware of Locknoff's glare behind her. There was a small puncture wound, and Yakema wiped a green paste across the top of it and then covered it with a Band-Aid.

"Good as new," she said, satisfied with herself. She turned to Locknoff and held out the glowing rod.

Ahdortee took it and gladly left the medical bay. Moving to Anna's eye, Yakema wiped more paste along her bruises and checked for other signs of broken skin or bruising. Finding none, she went to clean her hands of the paste. Once finished, Yakema grabbed a pair of gloves and looked at Sariah, who smiled proudly and gestured for Yakema to join her. Jennifer's digital image showed a stronger heart rate than before and what looked like thousands of tiny bugs crawling all over her insides. Locknoff sighed, looking over Anna again.

"Who is she?" Sariah asked curiously, attending to her patient's outward blemishes.

"Her name is Anna Desai," he responded, turning to leave the medical bay.

Shock covered Sariah's face, and she was momentarily distracted. Yakema's voice reminded her of the task at hand.

"Who's Anna Desai?"

"Trouble," Sariah answered as she returned to her task. They continued their work in silence and had the women moved to an observation room across the hall when they had done all they could.

Yakema was elated when she saw Deverah. Her presence meant Yakema's shift was over.

"Oh, good," Sariah said, stepping in front of her work desk. "I have to make a few arrangements, but I'll be back soon. Continue your duties as normal, but no one is to address the humans until I return."

"Humans?" one of the assistants asked, puzzled. Deverah nodded and moved behind the desk. She began pushing buttons but stopped when Sariah spoke again.

"Yes, we have two human guests in recovery. I shall return shortly."

A few feet down the hall, Sariah saw Locknoff and Ahdortee chatting outside the recovery room. Ahdortee handed him something and trotted off angrily. Sariah was confused by the exchange but decided not to inquire. She had much to do, so she went in search of a private place to make her arrangements.

Locknoff looked down to see an SD card in his hand. His brows lowered, and he looked through the door's small glass opening at Anna once more. Sighing, he closed his hands around the card and walked away. His office was surprisingly quiet despite the noisy activity outside. *The council certainly knows how to liven up a campsite*, he thought, putting the SD card on the desk. He leaned his chair back slightly and closed his eyes. He was so exhausted. These past few days had been draining. *But these next few weeks*, he thought as he put his feet on the desk, *will be even tougher*. He drifted off to sleep effortlessly.

Moments after he closed his eyes, or so it seemed, Sariah was waking him up. Four hours had passed.

"She's awake."

"How long?" he asked, clearing his throat. His voice was groggy.

"Nearly an hour."

Locknoff looked at the SD card on his desk for a second. "I'll send for her shortly."

Sariah turned to leave, and he sat upright. He put the SD card into the computer and waited.

"How did you find her?" Sariah asked curiously, standing at the door.

"I didn't. She was with the girl."

Sariah continued on her way, her eyes wide with shock.

Locknoff turned his attention to the screen. His own eyes grew as the pictures began to flow. At first, they were just photos of Anna with friends. Then the scenery changed. Locknoff only recognized them because he'd been dragged to a coworker's baby shower once where there was an entire game dedicated to the sonogram photos.

"Impossible," he said aloud. "Anna's a mother."

He read the information next to the photo: Anna Desai, 14 weeks, baby girl, September 3, 2007. Estimated date of delivery: July 10, 2008. He moved closer, shock clear across his features. He stared at the screen for several more moments, and Ahdortee's words were forefront in his mind.

"She's poison for you, Locknoff. You should return her now."

"That's out of the question, Ahdortee. We need to know what she's involved in."

"I never thought I'd see the day I'd be betrayed in my hatred for these creatures. Not by you. If you are going to keep her," she'd said, placing the slim card into his hand, "you'd better take a look at this."

He looked at the sonogram photos a bit closer then and could see the outline of the fetus perfectly. He could hear the ultrasonic waves bouncing off the fetus, could feel its hearts. There were two, and they were both beating rhythmically, almost in synchronization. "Impossible," he said again and got up from his seat so fast that it shook under the demand.

"Ryous!" Locknoff shouted, storming out of his office. He spotted him speaking to a young scout less than fifty feet outside his door.

Ryous turned to him. "Yes. The scout returned safely, but I received word that you were resting, so I—"

"This isn't about the scout," Locknoff said much too loudly. He shook his head vigorously. "You have young ones, right?"

"Yes…" Ryous replied skeptically, raising one eyebrow. "Three."

"Tell me of the bond."

"Don't tell me the famous heart crusher is considering settling down. Who's the lucky female?"

When Locknoff's expression did not change, Ryous continued, "Well…it's simple, really. It's like you're aware of a completely different part of yourself. Almost like an extension of your soul. You can feel them, but they are not a part of you. It's different than a bonding."

"How so?"

"With a bonding, you take in each other's essence or being, if you will. You become a part of them, and they become a part of you. With a young one, it's like there an extension of you. Why?"

"I'm not entirely sure," Locknoff said mechanically, looking back toward his office. "Thanks."

"Anytime."

Ryous returned to the task at hand, and Locknoff went back to his desk. He printed off a copy of the sonogram photos and headed to the medical bay, where he barged in and slammed the pictures on Sariah's desk.

"We need to speak with her." Sariah looked up at him briefly and then returned her attention to her papers.

"What…afraid you've barged in on her life unwanted?"

"It has two hearts!" he said, ignoring her comment.

Sariah looked up at him suspiciously and grabbed the photos. She looked through them briefly and then back up at Locknoff, a bit confused. "Deverah, move the long-haired female…"

"Anna," Locknoff interrupted sternly.

"Anna," Sariah repeated matter of factly, "to a single observation room please. The rest of you, give us a moment."

Deverah nodded, and everyone else left the bay in somewhat of a hurry. Sariah took the photos from the desk and examined them carefully. She turned the pictures sideways as she neared the front of the stack.

"Locknoff, these are splotches on a page. What makes you think it has two hearts?"

He sighed. "Because I can feel them beating," he replied tiredly. "I can see its features, Sariah. For a minute, I thought I could even hear the ultrasonic waves bouncing off her."

"Her?" Sariah asked, looking down at the photos again. She was quiet for a long moment and then said, "Well, it appears we should have a chat with Ms. Desai."

◆ ◆ ◆

Anna awoke somewhat groggy. She looked around and figured she was in a hospital room. She closed her eyes tightly and reopened them. *Yeah, a hospital room*, she said to herself. The walls were white, and the beds were slightly uncomfortable. There was a closed door across from her bed, and on the other side of her was another woman.

There was no curtain separating them, so she could see the female's features clearly. Her battered features.

"Jennifer," Anna called out, remembering what happened. She brought a hand up to her head, expecting to recoil from the pain, but felt completely fine.

Looking around, she saw a neatly folded pile of white clothes at the foot of both her and Jennifer's beds. She looked down at what she was wearing and frowned. It was a hospital gown. She pulled the covers back to get up and froze when she saw that one of her legs was bandaged. Her eyebrows lowered as she tried to remember getting hurt there. But nothing rose to the surface.

Snatching the clothes, Anna got out of bed and headed for what could only be the bathroom. She came out a short time later, confused. There was nothing in there but a toilet and sink. No shower, mirror, toothbrush, or even towel. She was somewhat surprised to see toilet paper. Upon returning, she noticed that the beds had rails but nothing else. There were no phones, buttons to call for help, or oxygen hookups, or anything. The door didn't look like it had a knob either, but there was a keypad where it would normally be.

She looked over at Jennifer and noticed there were no monitors or other hookups or anything attached to her. She remembered the oddity of the clothing she now wore. *Scrubs...who gives scrubs to patients?* she thought, and stress covered her features. She remembered Jennifer's words and running out to help her. Then she remembered seeing Locknoff. Immediately she ran to Jennifer's side. As she reached out to check Jennifer's pulse, the door opened and a blond woman entered.

"Your friend won't be awake for a while, I'm afraid. But you'll need to follow me, please." The woman was dressed in the same white clothes as Anna was.

"Where am I? What do you want with me?"

"All your questions will be answered momentarily, ma'am. Please follow me."

Anna followed without another word, but skepticism ran through her bones. They walked into another room.

"Just wait here. Someone will be with you shortly," the woman said and left before Anna could object. The room was simple. There was a bench with a thin mattress on it and a chair that seemed to be bolted to the floor.

Anna paced the floor in her white socks, wondering just what was going on here, until the door opened and a woman with dark-brown hair and gray eyes entered with Locknoff close beside her. Anna paused, her eyes grew about two inches, and she backed up slowly until she ran out of room. She then sank to the floor with an audible thump and stared at the pair. As they made their way further into the room, Anna's eyes were glued on Locknoff. She didn't even hear the woman speaking until Locknoff turned his head to look at her.

"Sariah," the woman said and then knelt down next to her.

"How are you feeling, Anna?" Sariah asked, reaching a hand out to help her up. She continued speaking as they walked to the mattress.

"What?" Anna asked, her attention now on Sariah, who sat in the chair.

Sariah smiled warmly. "I was wondering how you're feeling, dear."

"Confused," she replied honestly, returning her attention to Locknoff.

"Anna, do you have any idea why—"

"Anna," Locknoff interrupted, giving her the sonogram photos. His face was a hard mask when he looked at her. "Explain."

"Where did you find these?" she asked, looking over the photos. Anna was quiet for a moment as she reviewed each one of them, and then she sighed and lifted her head. Her cheeks glistened, and a teardrop fell onto the photos. The sadness in her eyes didn't touch her voice as she spoke.

"You told me to get out. You didn't want me. Why do you care now?"

The hard mask evaporated completely, and Locknoff was on his knees before her. "Anna, I have never stopped wanting you. I didn't want you to go. I never wanted to spend one minute of my time away from you. Not then, and certainly not now."

"But you kicked me out," she said, confused. "You told me not to ever come back."

"I'm so sorry, Anna. I didn't mean a word I said that night."

Sariah was shocked. The look she gave Locknoff suggested that she'd never seen him like this before, never heard him apologize for anything.

"And I certainly didn't mean to hurt you. My behavior was inexcusable. I beg you to forgive me."

Anna was quiet for a moment as she looked at him. She then blinked and redirected her attention as tears fell down her cheeks. "I've really missed you, Locknoff." She quickly wiped at her cheeks. "You've missed a lot"—she sniffed—"and I could have really used your help."

"Anna, if you'll let me, I will spend the rest of my life making it up to you, and I will never let you go again."

Anna leaned forward and kissed him on the cheek. "I can forgive you, Locknoff," she whispered, conscious of the other woman in the room. She leaned back into her original position. But Locknoff followed her as she moved. He was so close that the only features Anna could make out were his gorgeous brown eyes. She grabbed him around the neck and pulled herself closer, crushing his lips. His response was immediate. He wrapped one hand around her waist, pulling her closer, and the other braided into her thick curls.

Their lips were a fury of movement. They moved feverishly together, and when they were both out of breath, Locknoff moved on to her neck. By their actions, it was amazing either of them heard the loud "ahem" from Sariah. Locknoff froze immediately, his eyes widened, and he looked over at her apologetically. He must have completely forgotten she was there. Anna blushed, and Sariah smiled.

"There are rooms available for that sort of activity if you can make it there, but we really must know about the child, Anna."

"Yes," Locknoff agreed breathlessly. He looked at Anna hopefully.

Anna looked down at her hands and spoke while twirling her fingers.

Twenty-Eight

TROUBLE

"I found out three weeks after arriving in Turkey." Anna laughed humorlessly, looking into the distance. "I was at a company fund raiser one night and had to be rushed to the emergency room after eating trout." The smile was back as she looked at Sariah. "I've eaten trout my whole life without incident." Sariah winced slightly. "But I was allergic then…violently allergic. I had hives all over my body, my hands itched, and I couldn't stop vomiting. They put me on intravenous fluids once I finally stopped. They were afraid I was dehydrated. Apparently I also had food poisoning."

Locknoff sat down next to Anna on the bench and held onto her hand firmly. She smiled and continued.

"They gave me an epinephrine injection and ran some blood work. The next morning when my color returned, they told me I was pregnant. They explained that the pregnancy could have been the reason for my sudden allergic reaction. I went back to work and tried to be careful of what I ate and paid attention to how my body reacted. When I was twelve weeks…" She paused and took a deep breath. "When I was twelve weeks, I went in for a routine checkup and was told that I would be having twins. They said they could hear two heartbeats. Suddenly I was high risk. The company offered to send me home, but it wouldn't have mattered." She looked down at the hand Locknoff was holding and put her other one on top of it.

"I had to wait another couple of weeks for the ultrasound, but when I did have it, everything changed. There was only one baby. They said it was developing abnormally. The doctors were baffled." Locknoff sighed and wiped the tears away from her cheeks. "There was only one lung. It was a bit large and right in the center of her chest. The two heartbeats they heard before had come from opposite sides of the body. They concluded that I'd had twins, but at some point in the development process, perhaps one of the babies was absorbed by the other or my body. They advised me not to carry the baby to term."

Sariah gasped audibly. Locknoff sighed and pinched the bridge of his nose with his free hand. Anna continued, "They said it wouldn't be healthy. That it might not even survive the pregnancy. So I set the date." She paused a moment and then continued, "I went into the hospital that morning and got changed. While I was lying there waiting for the nurse, I thought I could...feel her presence somehow, like she was already in my arms.

"It was like I could feel her fear, almost as if it was an echo of my own. I couldn't move. It was hard to even breathe. I didn't know what would happen if she was carried to term. But they didn't know either. I suddenly didn't want to be doing it. I started to panic, and I just wanted her safe for as long as I could make her so. She was alive in me, and that was enough for now. I didn't care if she made it to term then. I didn't care if she died minutes after she was born. She was mine, and I would take whatever time I was blessed to have with her."

She laughed humorlessly again. "They wouldn't take the risk though, so I was sent back to the United States. I thought it would be a better situation here. I figured doctors would be more reasonable, but they came to the same conclusion after only a few weeks of observation. They were convinced that if the baby made it to term, it wouldn't live long after birth. But I was determined to carry my baby for as long as I could.

"I found a midwife who agreed to deliver the baby. She understood what was at risk and did not require anything of me. She advised me to get counseling and make arrangements for afterward, but was otherwise supportive. I carried the baby to term without any further intrusive examinations and went to the midwife when I was in labor.

"I walked in that day, and she smiled at me. I was a bit numb," she said, shaking her head. "I didn't know what to expect, but I was prepared for the worst. I'd hoped to hold my baby once before it passed away, and the midwife said it could be possible. She explained that as long as the baby was still attached to the placenta, and it to me, it wouldn't need to do much work for itself. So I would hold my baby until the very last moment possible.

"The delivery was difficult at first because I couldn't find a comfortable position, but after moving to the water, every part of my body responded with relief. The baby was born within an hour of my being in there. When she came out, the midwife hesitated before placing her in my arms." Anna smiled. "It seemed like a lifetime before I got her, but when I did, there was nothing else. She was so beautiful, and the first thing I said was, 'Leanah.' It just...fit." She shrugged.

"I'd never allowed myself to hope that she would live long, but when I saw her, I couldn't picture my life without her. Leanah was definitely different." Locknoff and Sariah shared a brief look and then returned their attention to Anna. She was smiling into the distance, remembering.

"I noticed it when I pried my eyes away from hers. Her lashes were white, and her skin had somewhat of a greenish pigment to it. She was covered from neck to ankles in the same light green, then a darker green color. It was like a pear green mixed with a darker olive pattern.

It swirled outward from her umbilical cord and wrapped around her little body. The pattern didn't seem to have a beginning or an ending other than the umbilical cord. Her fingers and toes had the same pear green as her face. The bridge of her nose was covered in tiny scales. I was somewhat surprised at first to see that her ears were shaped like mine.

"The shock must have been clear across my face as I took her in, but the midwife said nothing. She just…watched. After a while she said we needed to cut the cord. We both looked at Leanah and smiled. 'I don't think anything is wrong with her,' the midwife said and reached her arms out for Leanah with promises to return her to me shortly. She looked her over intently, checking both her hearts, and making sure her lungs worked, checking her reflexes and the flexibility in her limbs."

Anna chuckled distantly. "It took her a while to finish. She spent a little time looking over Leanah's skin, eyes, nose, and ears. After a bath, she returned her to me and offered her help getting Leanah to nurse. I took her home the next day when we determined she was perfectly healthy, but the midwife suggested that I keep her indoors for a while, just until she had a stronger immune system. I agreed and took a little time off of work." Anna's voice took on a sad tone then. "Two days later I got a knock on the door." She looked up at Locknoff. "It was the FBI." His eyebrows lowered. "They took her, Locknoff." The words came out in a rush then.

"Four days was all I got with our daughter when they barged in and took her away and arrested me. I suppose I should have known they would come, but I wasn't ready for them. They ran all kinds of tests on me and asked dozens of questions. Some of them were normal, given the situation, but others were just odd. They wanted to know the father. They seemed angry when they could not find anyone in my life that wasn't human. They told me to forget about Leanah and keep my mouth shut. They claimed that it was a matter of national security and that Leanah would be in danger if I told anyone about her. In the end they promised to return her after they did their tests...I should have known better. They said they needed to determine if she was a danger to humans. As if she could be anything other than a baby. It's been over three years, and they refuse to even discuss her with me. I thought they were bringing her back to me a few days ago, but they just wanted to know if I knew where your brother was and if I had any idea about how Lillian died. I didn't even know she was dead."

The tears came freely then. Locknoff pulled her into his chest.

"Anna, I will get her back," he vowed.

"No!" she shouted, looking up at him. "You can't. They'll take you away too and do all kinds of experiments on you and..."

"Anna, I'll be fine. I won't rest until she's in your arms again."

Sariah sighed and stood to leave. As she reached the door, she turned and said, "Anna, I'm terribly sorry for what has happened to you, but I'm afraid I will have to run a few more tests." She looked at Locknoff's expression then and added, "Perhaps tomorrow."

Anna looked up from Locknoff's massive arms and nodded. Sariah smiled as she looked on, noticing the size difference between them. Anna really did look like a child in his arms.

"I am going to take a quick nap. If you need anything, be sure to wake me, Locknoff." Sariah then headed out the door.

◆ ◆ ◆

Anna was confused as Locknoff pulled her through the busy building. Had he not been holding her hand, she may have become lost. Everyone they passed took a moment to stare. She felt like she was back in fifth grade and all the kids were staring at her because she'd started her period unknowingly.

"Don't worry," Locknoff said, noticing her panicked expression. "Everything will be all right."

They stepped into the elevator and Anna sighed. "I feel like they all know I'm human."

"How could they?" Locknoff asked, pushing a button on the elevator. "We all look the same."

"Yes." She said, exasperated. "Why is that?"

"I'll tell you later." He pulled her close and hugged her gently.

The elevator door opened, and three men entered. They were almost as big as Locknoff and were wearing the same cargo trousers. But their shirts were a different color. Locknoff's was black with white writing on it, and the others were brown with white writing. They looked at the two of them with questioning expressions. Anna thought they looked shocked. *They have to know,* she thought.

"Locknoff," one of them said, nodding.

"Marcus," he replied, holding Anna closer as she gently tried to pull away from his embrace.

"That's it," she said, turning to face him when they got off the elevator.

"What?"

"They know something."

Locknoff half smiled and kissed her just above the left eye. "You'll see in a minute."

She sighed as they walked off the elevator. Only three doors down, they stopped in front of an office door. Anna looked at him questioningly, but he kept moving, pulling her along. When they walked in, Anna gasped. It looked like a five-star hotel room.

There was a huge crystal chandelier hanging in the middle of the room. The walls were a mixture of white and very soft gray. The huge bed was centered between two white pillars that looked to be part of the wall. A canopy of green and gray hung down from the ceiling at the head of the bed and flowed down and outward behind the bed. On each side of the massive bed were white nightstands with green lamps sitting on top. The bed was covered in white. On the bed skirt was a thin strip of green.

The floor was covered in thick carpet that matched the soft gray on the walls. There was a large painting on the wall. It was of a body of water surrounded by tall grass and several trees. Behind the water was a gray sky that flowed into the gray of the water. On the far wall, there was a wooden dresser with a seashell pattern carved into it.

"Is that a bathroom?" Anna asked, pointing to a closed door on their left.

"Yes." Locknoff walked over to the dresser and pulled out a huge, white bathrobe. "I'm sorry we didn't have time to get any of your things." He held it out to her.

"Hmm," Anna said, distracted. She looked at him then and the robe he held. "Oh," she said, taking the robe with her into the bathroom.

It was an extension of the beauty in the bedroom. She put the bathrobe down and looked at herself in the mirror. Her eyes grew about two inches, and she inhaled sharply. There was a huge black-and-purple bruise on the left side of her face. It extended down past her cheekbone and up into her hairline. She could even see bruising on the tip of her ear. She touched it, cringing for the pain, but was pleasantly surprised by the lack of it. She remembered getting hit there. Whatever Sariah did to her took away everything except for the discoloration. "Hmm," she said aloud, remembering the trip here and all the stares they got. *They probably think he beat me up or something*, she concluded.

It felt like she was in there forever, but when she came out, Locknoff was putting a tray of food on the foot of the bed.

"I thought you might be hungry," he said.

"Thanks," she replied, smiling.

He disappeared into the bathroom then, and she sat down. Anna was famished and tried a little of everything on the tray. Once finished, she looked at it and wondered if she'd even made a dent in it at all. *He must be hungry too*, she thought and replaced the covers before setting the tray on the dresser.

When she turned around, Locknoff was standing there in a robe that looked like it was made for a child. She smiled.

"Not hungry?" he asked.

"No, I've had enough," she responded.

"Anna," Locknoff said distantly as he walked over to the bed. "There's something we need to discuss."

"Later," she said, dropping her bathrobe onto the floor. Locknoff turned to her, opening his mouth to protest, but stopped as she moved closer to him. She was beautiful. Her luscious brown body was perfect at every curve. He'd forgotten what he'd intended to say and closed his mouth, swallowing.

Without another word, he scooped her up and began kissing her. His hands moved hungrily over her body, and she couldn't help but snatch his robe clean off. They fell onto the bed mechanically, and Locknoff's hands caressed her neck and then her breasts and her back as he pulled her closer. He replaced his hands with his lips as he explored her entire body. He was lost in the essence of Anna as she kissed, caressed, and pulled at every part of him she could reach.

He gently pulled her legs apart and put his head in between them. A low moan escaped Anna's lips as he gently kissed her inner thighs. Her breathing slowed, and her moaning increased. She braided her fingers in his hair as he began pleasuring her. When her legs shook and moans became deep cries of pleasure, he moved to position himself on top of her. Every muscle worked as he scooped himself deep into her inner core. She pulled his body closer with eager anticipation as he inserted his penis.

Their bodies moved like a well-orchestrated symphony as they made love. Everything was forgotten for the moment, and together they explored one another. Anna grabbed his buttocks, thrusting him forward as she came closer to climax.

He growled and whispered, "I love you, Anna."

She let out somewhat of a moan and a wail, and her entire body shook underneath him.

When her body was still, Locknoff's breathing became short moans. He moved slightly faster, holding Anna's upper thighs.

After a minute she spoke, "Not yet."

"What?" Locknoff asked, pausing.

"Not yet," she repeated. He growled as she squirmed under him, but he lifted himself off her slightly. Anna turned over, and he entered her again. The pleasure of being inside her again was clear in his breathing.

She leaned forward slightly, reaching her hand in between her legs, and Locknoff adjusted by moving deeper inside her. She grabbed his testicles and massaged them gently. Locknoff moaned and paused briefly. Anna didn't stop. She placed her middle finger directly in between his testicles onto his urethra and moved it in a circular motion.

His moaning was slightly louder, and then his thrusts were faster, harder. His body shook slightly, but he continued thrusting forward with vigor until he reached the point of release. He let out a growl so loud it echoed throughout the room. Their breathing was heavy and uneven as they lay side by side, unmoving, sweaty, and breathless. Sleep found them shortly thereafter.

Twenty-Nine

PRECOG

Sariah opened her eyes to find a dark-brown-skinned man's face not ten inches from hers.

"Tomahbare," she exclaimed, reaching out for him. He joined her on the bench mattress and hugged her tightly. "I've missed you fiercely."

"I've missed you too, my heart." They kissed sweetly. As he started to pull away, she grabbed the back of his head and pulled him closer for a more intimate kiss. When they were both out of breath, Sariah moaned slightly and said, "Oh, how I've missed you."

"It's only been three days," Tomahbare exclaimed.

"Exactly," she replied, pulling him closer for another kiss. He laughed and continued kissing her.

A knock on the door interrupted their reunion. Sariah closed her eyes and inhaled deeply, calming herself.

"They mean well."

"I know," she said, exhaling. "I wonder what it is this time."

"Your human. She's awake."

"Really," Sariah said, barely containing her excitement.

"That's why I came to wake you."

"I'll be right there," Sariah yelled at the door. Her brows lowered slightly. "How long have you been here?"

"About twenty minutes…I didn't really want to disturb you."

"Oh. Well, I guess we should go see her then."

Tomahbare stood and held his hand out to help her up.

"How long has she been awake?"

"She's been in and out for a while, shortly after I arrived."

"Hmm," Sariah commented, opening the door. She stepped out only to be yanked back almost violently by Tomahbare less than a second later. She had time only to look at him questioningly before a cart full of supplies slammed into the frame, dropping fighter gear everywhere.

"I gather the fighters have arrived?"

"Just the initial wave. Masters are working to normalize the area activity before the locals decide to investigate."

"How many?"

"Seventy-five hundred. The remaining fighters will be in Earth's atmosphere within ten days."

"Sorry about that," a young fighter said nervously, picking up the supplies. "I guess I should slow down a bit."

"Yes," Sariah agreed, shock still across her face from Tomahbare's statement.

"Are you all right, my love?" Tomahbare asked, concern creasing his features.

"Yes…I just…I can't believe it's almost over. Earth…" She swallowed. "Our new home…"

"Yes," Tomahbare agreed excitedly. "It will be good to be back in our own forms again."

He hugged her tightly and kissed her neck. When the fighter was done picking up the things, they made their way to the medical bay. Sariah thought of Taren and hoped her and Tomahbare's transformation would be less complicated.

They were not needed at the medical bay, so they headed for Jennifer's room. When they reached it, they could see from the small window that she was sitting on the bed, dressed in the white scrubs, hugging her knees. Her head was facing the walls, and she seemed to be rocking slightly.

"Has she said anything, Elious?" Sariah asked.

"No, she's just been sitting there like that, staring at the wall."

She nodded and typed in the entry code. As the door opened, Jennifer turned toward the sound. Her eyes were questioning, but she said nothing. Sariah and Tomahbare walked in and stopped at the foot of the bed.

"Hello, Jennifer," Sariah began. "How are you feeling?"

If Jen was surprised that Sariah knew her name, she did not show it.

"I'm fine, thank you," she said, looking intently at Tomahbare.

"My name is Sariah. This is Tomahbare," she said, gesturing to him. "We have a few questions for you."

"What kind of questions?" she asked, folding her legs underneath her.

"Please come with me. It will be easier to explain in my office."

Sariah turned for the door, but Tomahbare stayed where he was, watching Jennifer. When she got off the bed and followed, he moved behind her. Sariah showed Jennifer into the room with the large, metal, spiderlike claws in the corner. When Jen walked in, her eyes went directly to the machines. She stood unmoving for several seconds before continuing on. Sariah looked at Tomahbare briefly and then gestured for Jennifer to sit on one of the tables. Afterward, she walked over to the desk and began pushing buttons.

◆ ◆ ◆

Jennifer watched silently as Sariah pushed buttons behind the large desk. So this is how it ends, she thought. Suddenly, a large 3-D image appeared over the desk. One side was of her face and shoulders. On the other were several rows of squiggly lines that reminded Jennifer of a heart rate monitor, only the lines were very thick. Jennifer was surprised to see herself so clearly, but she wasn't shocked.

"This," Sariah began, pointing to the lines, "is a composite of your theta brain wave activity at the present. It's quite higher than a normal human's." Jennifer raised a brow at her words but did not respond.

Sariah pushed a button, and the lines changed. There were several rows of overlapping lines that almost looked like an elaborate weaving design.

"This is the reading we recovered from the orb that pertains to you."

Jennifer closed her eyes. A tear ran down her cheek, and Sariah and Tomahbare shared a look.

"I'd like to know if you could tell me what, if anything, you remember of us."

Jennifer inhaled deeply and then exhaled. When she spoke, her words came in a rush. "I remember everything I saw. It was mostly battles, but some of the visions were about your world. I saw when you created that...thing and how you get it in people."

Sariah nodded.

"Are you going to kill me?"

Sariah's expression was shocked. She found it hard to believe that Jennifer would come to such a conclusion.

"No," she responded, shaking her head.

"Then what do you want with me?"

"Your reaction to the orb was unique, Jennifer. We just need to understand why." She nodded at Tomahbare, who walked further into the room to stand directly next to Jennifer, who then froze.

"Tomahbare is something like you, or what your kind would call psychic. He will assess your mental ability to determine if you are a precog and if you pose any danger to us."

"I wouldn't tell anyone anything," Jen said, shaking her head fiercely. "You already killed my best friend. I wouldn't put anyone else's life in danger by saying anything."

Sariah lowered her eyes and apologized. "Our protectors are trained to neutralize any threat. I'm sorry about your friend."

"And if you discover that I pose a threat to you?"

"We'll cross that bridge when we get to it, dear." Sariah smiled halfheartedly. "Tomahbare's assessment will help us decide."

Jennifer looked at him then as he walked over to the other table in the room and sat down. Her expression was pleading.

"I will not harm you in any way, child. All you have to do is relax and answer my questions."

Jennifer's brow rose slightly, but she pulled her legs up onto the table and lay back. The table lit up a bright green, and Jennifer started to move but thought better of it when she saw Sariah come around the desk.

"It's all right," she said, adjusting Jennifer's leg farther onto the table. "I just need to monitor your brain activity. Close your eyes and try to relax."

Tomahbare lay down then, and his table lit up the same way. Jennifer closed her eyes briefly and took a deep breath. She was scared out of her mind but knew there was no point in trying to run. *Five times stronger*, she thought as she remembered Taren's words. Sariah walked over to Tomahbare's table. She smiled and kissed him on the head.

Sariah then returned to the desk and started pushing buttons as he began.

"Tell me about the first time you noticed that your dreams were something more."

Jennifer nodded and closed her eyes as she spoke. "I was at a party. It was just after my thirteenth birthday, at a friend's sleepover."

Suddenly a memory of her parents and younger sister took center stage in her mind. She could see the sand on the ground, hear the ocean, and feel the sun's heat on her back. She looked up and could see the water.

"This," Tomahbare said, walking up to her, "is your first memory. Please be honest with me. It will make things easier." Jennifer was speechless. *How could he know?* she wondered.

"How?" she said aloud.

Tomahbare smiled. "I only need you to think of the memory. I can focus on your thoughts and project myself wherever you are mentally."

"I don't want to be here. I don't want to remember this."

"Which is why you won't have to be."

"Huh? What do you mean?"

"I will witness what you experienced with your past self."

Jennifer was confused. She looked over at her younger self playing in the sand, her father watching close by.

"What?" she repeated, turning to look at Tomahbare, but he was gone. She looked down at the ground and saw her reflection in the sand. She was a little girl again. She tried to think of what she was doing before, but she couldn't remember. She wore a red bathing top with spaghetti straps and red swim shorts with little pink hearts on them.

Her long, brown hair was tied up in pigtails, held back with two big, red ribbons tied into bows. She smiled at the toys in the sand and reached for the one that resembled a little crab. After a few minutes, she looked up to see a tall man. She squinted her eyes a bit.

"You're not him," she said, shaking her head. "The eyes...they're all wrong."

"Can I stay anyway?" the man asked.

Jennifer scrunched her mouth at the corner for a minute and then said "OK" with a shrug. The man sat down next to her and started playing with sand too. He was Tomahbare's size, but with Taren's features.

Jennifer's mother screamed, and everyone looked up. The second sound came out more like a screech of panic, and her father ran into the water after her. Jennifer watched with knowing eyes. Her father came out of the water, carrying her mother as she screamed in agony. The lifeguard met them at the water's edge and helped tow her to the sandbank. Her legs were covered in red marks and purple splotches. Multiple jellyfish had stung her.

Jennifer's father looked over to where she stood and frowned.

"I told her not to go in the water," Jennifer said, reaching for Tomahbare's hand. "I felt them bite me in my dreams."

"I know," Tomahbare said, taking her little hand.

When his hand closed completely around hers, the scenery changed. They were at a school playground. Jennifer had aged slightly. She let go of Tomahbare's hand the second she saw the swing.

"Can you push me?" she called to him.

"Sure," he said and came to help her up on the swing. Jennifer played there for a while, ignoring the other children's demands to have a turn, until she saw an ice-cream truck pull onto the street. She got off the swing and walked over to grab Tomahbare's hand.

"Can they see you?"

"No."

"Good, come with me."

She led him around the playground to where one of the teachers stood talking to a student. She pulled lightly on the teacher's green-and-black skirt. The teacher smoothed her skirt down, grabbed Jennifer's hand, and held out a finger to her. She released Jennifer's hand and continued her conversation. As Jennifer pulled harder, the teacher concluded her conversation and turned toward her.

The teacher's eyes were scolding, and she reached down to touch Jennifer's shoulders. "What is it, child?"

"I thought you might want to know."

"What?"

"That a man is about to kidnap that little girl."

"What little girl?"

Jennifer pointed to a girl in a pink-and-white dress with laced ruffles on the bottom. In her hair was a blue ribbon holding her ponytail up.

The teacher squinted and asked, "What man?" When Jennifer pointed to the man driving the ice-cream truck on the far end of the road, the teacher put her hand on her hip and said, "Now, Jennifer Braxton, where ever did you get an idea like that?"

"I dreamed about it," Jennifer replied matter of factly. The teacher looked up again and saw the little girl jump off the swing and head to the sandbox. She sat down and started playing. At the same time, the boy the teacher had been talking to looked at Jennifer and said, "You're not supposed to tell lies."

"It's not a lie!" Jennifer shouted, reclaiming the teacher's attention.

The ice-cream truck began down the road just then, and the children all ran to the fence.

"You don't have to yell, Jennifer," the teacher said and then turned to the little boy. "Daniel, we just discussed your accusing nature."

"But she told a lie," he continued defensively.

"If I lied," Jennifer interrupted angrily, "then why is she getting into that truck with him?"

The teacher stood up abruptly and saw the man holding the truck door open. The little girl was indeed climbing up into it.

The teacher screamed at the top of her lungs for security. She pointed out the issue, and they were off. All the children were abruptly ushered inside the building, and security vehicles could be seen chasing the ice-cream truck. Not long after they were back in their classroom, the security guard returned with the little girl, who ran to Jennifer and hugged her tightly.

"Thank you," she said. "My name is Cara."

"Hi, Cara," Jennifer replied. "I'm Jennifer."

Abruptly the scenery changed, and Jennifer seemed older yet again. Tomahbare was different too. He was a bit shorter and had a head full of long, white hair.

◆ ◆ ◆

As Tomahbare explored Jennifer's memories, Sariah worked frantically behind the desk. When one of her assistants arrived, she breathed a sigh.

"Elious, excellent. Regulate his vitals," she ordered, bolting to Tomahbare's side. She looked at his pupils with her small flashlight and pulled a syringe out of her scrubs pocket. Elious's brows lowered, but he moved behind the desk and started pushing buttons.

"What's wrong?" he asked finally.

Sariah leaned down, ignoring his question. "Tomahbare," she whispered into his ear, "this cannot continue. You must sever the link."

She looked up at Elious, who shook his head, an indication that Tomahbare did not show any signs of change. Sariah nodded and injected the clear contents into his arm.

"This is taking too long," she complained aloud. "He's been in there for over five hours, Elious. He should have an answer by now. His vitals are sporadically dipping into dangerously low territory. I'll have no other choice if this does not end."

Elious's brows lowered, and he went back to pressing buttons without a word.

Thirty

TWISTED MINDS

Taren opened his eyes to a room decorated in blue and gold. Golden curtains hung from the windows and along the four posts on his bed. Over his head were dark-blue slits of fabric that wove between thin, golden strips. He raised an eyebrow and sat up. The bed was covered in more blue than gold. The nightstands beside his bed each had a blue lamp, and alongside a small, white table there were two blue chairs with golden strips of fabric around the seats.

The wall opposite his bed had a large piece of artwork depicting the capital city in Elquin. He smiled briefly, took a deep breath, and got out of bed. On his way to the bathroom, he noticed the date on the alarm clock. He considered a moment as he examined it. More than two days had gone by. The loud growl from his stomach suggested that more than a month had.

After showering, he looked in the closet and found a rather large selection of Elquin-style clothing. He exhaled heavily and grabbed the first things he saw—a brown-and-white sleeveless shirt and a pair of black cargo pants. The black-laced boots would fit any outfit he put on, so he grabbed them too. He reached for a white sash bearing his family crest, but he thought better of it when he saw the green swirls on his arms and realized everyone would know who he was without it.

He went to the cafeteria in search of something to eat and was surprised by the level of activity around him. When he was on the elevator, a young fighter had a hard time keeping his eyes off him. Every time he looked up, the fighter would put his head down until finally he said, "I'm sorry. It's just you're the first one I've seen in Elquin form since we arrived, and I'm kinda homesick already."

"Arrived? When did you get here?"

"Yesterday."

Comprehension hit Taren like an anvil. *The first wave*, he said to himself. His stomach started to turn and twist. He wasn't sure if his meal would stay down, but he had to try; he was famished. Taren was numb as he took his place in line, and he wondered if leaving was a better idea. Before he could make the decision to walk out, the meal master asked, "How can I serve you, Master Vishnu?"

"Something light," he responded. It didn't really matter what or how he said it, all eyes were on him, so he found a small empty table in the front of the room and tried to enjoy his meal. On his way out, he practically ran into Ahdortee as he yelled greetings and well-wishes to others.

"Taren!" she said in greeting, rather surprised to see him about.

"Forgive me, Ahdortee. My attention is diverted today."

Ahdortee smiled. "I understand. This," she said, placing both hands on a woman who stood almost neck and neck to him, "is Naeefah."

Naeefah was dressed in a tight-fitting, strapless shirt and pants combination that looked more like it was taped on her rather than put on. The sides of the outfit were black with hundreds of tiny, silver moons. The middle was sky blue and also covered in miniature silver moons. The shirt looked more like a corset than a top. She wore a silver necklace with a locket, which hung loosely in the middle of her breasts. The locket was of a blue, polished gemstone with tiny black splotches throughout and a silver, bursting sun behind it.

"Hello, Naeefah," Taren greeted her.

"Greetings, Taren," she responded, smiling.

Ahdortee beamed, proud of herself. "Would you like to share a meal with us, Taren?"

"Thank you for the offer, Ahdortee, but I have already eaten."

"Perhaps another time then," Naeefah said, smiling much brighter than before.

"Perhaps," Taren agreed. He continued on his way, and the women did the same. Less than ten steps later, he heard a group of fighters discussing Locknoff and the human girl.

"She was sporting bruises all over her face."

"Yes, but I heard she was the key to some big project."

Human. . . Sariah must have found Jennifer, he thought.

His stomach was suddenly in knots and threatened to expel his light lunch. *I have to get a hold of this*, he told himself. *Maybe Sariah can do something.* He headed in the general direction of the medical bay. When he arrived, Churvack greeted him eagerly.

"Master Vishnu, it's wonderful to see you. How are you feeling?"

"I've been better, Master Churvack. Where is Sariah?"

"She's with Tomahbare and Elious, monitoring an official reading."

Taren's brows lowered. "Since when does medical have to monitor an official reading?"

"Well. . .never," he said, "but it's on the human, so. . ."

"Human?" Taren interrupted. "What human?"

"One of the women ERT brought in last night."

"One of the women?"

"Yes, I believe the other is with Master Locknoff."

"Locknoff? Where?"

"I don't know, but Sariah may. She's in the observation bay."

"Thank you, Churvack."

Taren walked away in search of Sariah. When he reached the observation bay, the blinds were down but not completely closed, so he looked closer and saw Jennifer. She was bruised from head to toe. She looked much worse than she had when he'd left her. He walked into the bay and demanded to speak with Sariah.

"I'll be with you in a moment, Taren," she said, pressing buttons.

He walked over to Jennifer and squeezed her hand gently. Instantly, he dropped to his knees. As he tried pulling himself up, her hand closed around his, and he fell to the floor.

"Taren," Sariah shouted. He was unconscious. "Get Locknoff!" she barked.

As Elious reached the door, Tomahbare's vitals stabilized. Sariah exhaled audibly.

"Go, Elious. I don't know how much longer we'll be able to keep this up."

She sent him for Deverah and Yakema the moment he returned unable to locate Locknoff.

"But Ahdortee has sent for him," Elious added.

Any other time she would have scolded Elious for turning his responsibility over to someone else, but today it was helpful.

"Good," she said. "We'll need your help as well."

When he returned with the women in tow, it took all four of them to transfer Taren—who was still half sprawled on the floor, trapped by Jennifer's clutched hand—onto a table, which had been brought in by a couple of fighters. Sariah was confused but grateful for Taren's interference. Whatever he'd done had eased the stress on Tomahbare's hearts.

"How is this possible?" Deverah asked.

"I don't know, but when they make it out of there, I intend to find out."

They all set about their individual tasks with renewed motivation as they awaited Locknoff's arrival.

◆ ◆ ◆

Jennifer was clutching Tomahbare's hand as she watched the bleachers fall one after the other. She had tears in her eyes. "I asked him to check the bolts yesterday."

"I know, Jennifer. I'm so sorry."

"Why is it that no one will—" She stopped abruptly and turned her head to the far right side of the football field. Her hand came out of Tomahbare's hand swiftly, and he abruptly returned to the appearance he had when she'd agreed that he could stay.

"What's that? No…Jennifer, wait."

But she was already gone. Tomahbare closed his eyes and inhaled. When he was calmer, he exhaled slowly and opened his eyes. He was back on the beach 370 yards away from a fully grown Jennifer and Taren, who stood there in Elquin form. They were staring at each other and standing within an arm's length of one another.

Tomahbare gasped. "Impossible," he said aloud. Although he was several hundred yards away, he could hear their conversation as he made his way closer.

"Hi," Taren said.

"Hi. Who are you?" Jennifer replied.

"My name is Vishnu…or Taren," he uttered, half smiling.

"You have two names?" she asked skeptically.

"No, one is…you can call me whichever you like."

Jennifer looked at his huge, brown eyes for a moment, seemingly calculating, and then she smiled brightly. "I like Vishnu," she said. "That was your name before, right?"

"Right," he responded, smiling brighter now.

"Vishnu it is then. How did I get here?"

"I don't know, but will you stay?"

A low humming filled the air.

"What is that?" Jennifer asked, putting her hand up to shield her eyes from the sun as she looked into the distance.

"It's me," Vishnu said, taking her hand as she returned her attention to him. He placed it directly over his left heart. "It's me," he repeated. "I'm pleased to be here with you." He gazed into her eyes, and she smiled. "It's what happens when my kind find someone they…enjoy being around," he said with a smirk.

"You enjoy my company?" Jennifer asked, elated, while her other hand reached up to touch his face.

"Very much so," he replied, grabbing her other hand. He held them both in the middle of his chest and gazed into her eyes.

"I enjoy your company too," she said, blushing a bright red. The humming turned into a low buzz, and his ears twitched slightly. Jennifer didn't miss the movement.

"Are you all right?" she asked with lowered eyebrows.

"Better than all right. What is it?" he asked when her expression didn't change.

"Who are you?" she asked, touching the bridge of his nose. His lips frowned slightly at her question, but the words came smoothly as he braided his fingers through hers and turned to walk the beach.

"My name is Vishnu, and I was born of the Ateenn bloodline. We are Elquin."

"Elquin?"

"It is a planet several thousand light-years away from yours, and we are in dire need of a new place to call home."

"Why?"

"Our star has reached the end of its life cycle. If we do nothing, we perish. Scientists noticed the potential problem almost seven hundred years ago and tried to save our world by developing something of a shield. It didn't work as they intended though, and we are now out of time.

"My world has explored the galaxies in search of a suitable and permanent source to run the shield generators for many years now. Initially, it was believed that the shield would interrupt the star's gravitational pull on the planet, and perhaps we could drift away from the star slowly. But after years of trial and error, the decision was made to focus the shield's efforts on preventing the star's rays from destroying life on our world.

"In order to do that, however, we needed resources that were either rare or nonexistent on Elquin. So the council voted to begin farming other worlds. Initial efforts yielded vast amounts of resources, and our world flourished. But as time moved forward, the generator needed more as our planet was slowly pulled toward its star. Elquins, young and old, were drafted to save our world. I joined them shortly after my general education, and have remained."

"How old are you?"

Vishnu smiled. "By time generated in your world, I would be... about thirty-one."

"And your world?"

"More like one hundred ten, but an Elquin life cycle can be well into five hundred."

"Wow. How did you find our world?"

Vishnu stopped talking then and looked off in the distance.

"What is it?"

He looked down at Jennifer briefly and then lightly brushed the back of her hand. The buzzing dulled slightly, but with the silence, it was deafening. Vishnu smiled.

"The council found resources here that bested any we'd ever come across. But mining was not an option, and our planet took a turn for the worst."

"How so?"

"Well, rather than losing centimeters once every few years, it happened two or three times a year. More recently, it's become a weekly event. If Elquin does not find a suitable replacement, every one of our lives would be forfeit."

Jennifer gasped audibly, and the scenery changed. They were back in the conference room, standing behind Bathmantu, looking at the two planets that hung suspended above the table.

"My world. You found Earth."

Vishnu was slightly taken aback by the change but accepted his inability to control the situation. "Yes," he admitted. "We found Earth."

"Will you take it from us?" Jennifer asked, looking into his eyes.

"We wish to share it with you."

Jennifer smiled, and they were back on the beach. Vishnu blinked several times at the change and brightness.

"I would like that," Jennifer said, pulling herself into his chest. The buzzing sound became a loud hum, and Vishnu wrapped his arms around her.

"Taren," a familiar voice called. They both looked up to see someone coming toward them. "Tomahbare?" Vishnu asked, confusion lacing his voice. Tomahbare had returned to his own human features. "What's happening here?"

"You've interrupted an official reading."

"My apologies, Tomahbare. I have no idea what happened. I just wanted to offer my support when I touched her hand."

"Yes. Well, you have clearly found a heart song in her. That kind of pull has an effect on the subconscious. It really would not have mattered if you touched her. Your presence alone would have been enough to pull you in. She could sense you when you entered the room."

"Sense me? What does that mean?"

"It means she likes you back."

"Why do I feel so…"

"Because we're in *her* mind," Tomahbare interrupted. "The feelings you naturally have for her are intensified by the intimate bond here." He shook his head. "You've said too much, Taren. She will remember everything you've discussed when she wakes. And what about Youkoni's memory?"

"Youkoni will always be a part of my soul." He looked down at Jennifer and smiled. "But I can't deny what I feel for her, not here." He looked up at Tomahbare. "I feel like I have to speak when she asks me a question. Why is that?"

Tomahbare was breathing heavily with his hands on his knees. He stood upright before speaking. "That's due to the nature of this reading. Normally I ask the questions, but one always feels compelled to respond. We must get back; I can feel Sariah's panic. This reading has taken several unexpected turns. Jennifer," he said, looking down at her, "there's one more memory we must explore, but I'm afraid you will have to experience it as you are. I lack the strength to change you." Jennifer grabbed Vishnu's hand and reached out for Tomahbare's. "I need to see the memory of your father's crash."

Jennifer shook her head quickly from side to side, concern dominating her features. "Don't you have enough," she protested but was pulled into the memory almost violently. She took a deep breath and looked directly ahead. Vishnu eyed her reassuringly and gave her hand a gentle squeeze.

The scenery shifted, and they were standing on a runway. "After everything I'd told him and all that had come true, I don't understand why he took that flight," she said as a huge 757 came into view.

They could see the tires come down. As they touched the runway, however, the tires under the nose broke off and sent the plane hurdling across the pavement. Jennifer released them both, closed her eyes, and put her hands over her ears seconds before the airplane was ripped apart and engulfed in flames. Vishnu grabbed Jennifer and pulled her close. Every part of her body was shaking, and he screamed, "Tomahbare, enough!"

◆ ◆ ◆

Locknoff opened his eyes to a blushing Anna. He smiled and pulled her on top of him. "I've really missed you, Anna."

She smiled. "I've missed you too."

He grabbed the back of her head and gently pulled her closer for a kiss. After a moment, he pulled back.

"What?" Anna said, lowering her eyebrows.

Locknoff pulled himself into a sitting position, still holding her with one arm. "Anna, there's something we must discuss before another word...or act is done."

"What is it?" she asked, sitting up.

"Your friend Lillian."

Anna closed her eyes briefly and then spoke, tears brimming.

"What about her?"

"I'm responsible for her death."

Anna's eyes bulged. She backed away from him slightly and looked at him with horror-struck eyes. "What? Why?"

"I'm sorry, Anna. I was under the impression that she'd put our entire mission at risk."

Anna was shaking her head. "I don't understand. How could you? She was my best friend."

"I got a message that suggested Taren was in distress. When I arrived on the scene, it appeared that Lillian was the cause of it all. I followed protocol, Anna...I eliminated the threat."

"You mean, you killed her."

"Yes...it wasn't until later that I understood the situation."

"And what was that?" she asked with tear-filled eyes.

Locknoff reached for her cheek to wipe the tears away, but Anna backed away from him. He dropped his hand and inhaled deeply. After letting it out, he continued.

"Anna, Taren abandoned his post without explanation. He sought to express his opinions about our mission here in an unauthorized manner, and I reacted as I was taught. I'm sorry to have caused you more grief in this—sorrier than you could ever imagine. I will keep my vow, Anna. Leanah will be freed from those who have kept her away from you for so long. You do not have to feel obligated to be near me. If you would rather I walk away, I'll never bother you again."

Anna was unmoving. Locknoff sighed, got out of bed, and went into the bathroom for a shower. When he returned, Anna had shifted slightly, deep in thought, he figured. When she looked up at him and spoke, her eyes were void of emotion.

"I do not agree with how you handled the situation, Locknoff, but I suppose I can understand duty. I had the opportunity to save my world from...whatever it is you're doing here, and I chose to protect our daughter. To protect you." She looked up at him as he sat beside her on the bed with a huff.

"Anna..."

She held a finger to his lips and continued. "Locknoff, I would ask that you take better care in the future, but I never want to be without you again." Her eyes were almost hopeful as she gazed at his. Locknoff reached up to wipe the lingering tears from her cheeks.

"Anna, you have my word, and I'm with you until I am dead."

He hugged her tightly and kissed her on the head. A frantic knock at the door redirected their attention. Locknoff answered the door with his towel still wrapped around his waist. It was Ahdortee.

"Locknoff, Sariah needs you. There's a..." She stopped midsentence when she noticed Anna and his attire.

"There's?" he prompted, ignoring her look of disgust.

"A problem with Taren. He's in the observation bay."

"I'll be there in a moment."

He disappeared briefly into the closet. When he emerged, he wore black cargo trousers and a black T-shirt. Ahdortee was looking at Anna disapprovingly.

"Locknoff," she said, confused, "have we a mission today?"

Locknoff looked at Anna briefly and then back at Ahdortee and said, "Yes. I seek my young one—Anna's government denied me the opportunity to know Leanah shortly after her birth."

Ahdortee was speechless; her eyes grew at the news. She looked back and forth between them several times before exhaling.

Locknoff walked over to Anna and kissed her on the head. "I won't be long," he said and walked away. After three steps he turned to Ahdortee and said, "Ahdortee, make sure she gets something to eat and some clothing, please."

Before Ahdortee could respond, he was on the elevator. She turned slowly to Anna, who sat on the bed, holding the white sheets up to her chest.

Ahdortee was visibly upset and disgusted. *Guess I'll be staying in bed hungry today*, Anna concluded. Her thoughts were confirmed a few moments later when Ahdortee slammed the door shut and stomped down the hallway. Anna didn't breathe until she heard the elevator doors close. She pulled the covers over her head and stayed there until she heard a loud crash. She jumped up and saw Ahdortee standing at the foot of the bed. She'd slammed a tray of food on the desk.

"I am Ahdortee," she said, tossing something at Anna. "If you wish to stay, you must get out of bed. I don't know what kind of life you've been used to, but here we work in the daylight, and we've much to do. Put that on. The fewer who know you are human, the better." She spat the last words.

Anna inhaled deeply and looked at Ahdortee for an immeasurable moment. She then stood and let the sheets fall to the floor.

Ahdortee was appalled. "Get dressed," she ordered, scrunching her nose at Anna.

"I will do no such thing. This form you obviously find appalling..." She slowly walked to the plate of food, lifted the lid, grabbed a few grapes, and looked Ahdortee in the eyes while she continued speaking. "Has found favor with your Master Locknoff. I'm sure you understand that he can be tempted, tamed, and influenced by these curves." She ate several of the grapes. "I would consider that the next time you see fit to belittle me. He has chosen to stay by my side, and I will remain by his for as long as he lives. Thank you, by the way," she said after finishing the rest of the grapes, "for the food and clothing." She grabbed the wad of fabric Ahdortee had tossed. "If it makes things easier for you, I would be happy to work together, but do try and remember I will not be treated as an inconvenience."

Ahdortee was quiet for a moment and then raised one eyebrow and said, "When you are strong enough to run your own errands, I will consider your request. For now, please get dressed. We have much to do."

◆ ◆ ◆

Locknoff stepped off the elevator hastily—he needed to get back to Anna. *Who knows how Ahdortee will react once she comes out of shock*, he thought. *Anna will probably be starving by the time I'm done. Sariah does have a tendency to linger.* When he walked into the medical bay, he felt like he was in a war zone. Tomahbare, Taren, and Jennifer were all lying on tables, and medical staff worked frantically on each of them. Locknoff could see digital images of all three. Taren's hand was clutched to Jennifer's, and his hearts were humming away.

Locknoff's brows lifted. Eyeing Sariah, he walked farther into the room. "What is it, Sariah, and what in the name of the bloody moon of Elquin is going on in here?!"

Sariah stopped what she'd been doing abruptly and came over to him. She swallowed and then spoke softly, knowing what she needed to address. "Locknoff, Tomahbare has been conducting an official reading. I have no idea why, but Taren showed up out of nowhere. He touched Jennifer's hand and is now trapped."

"What? How is that even possible, Sariah?" Locknoff interrupted.

"The problem," she said as if he hadn't spoken, "is that both Tomahbare's and Taren's vitals have been sporadic." Sariah shook her head. "I don't know how, and I've been trying to get through to Tomahbare, but he is not responding to me.

"I cannot say when, but there is only so much we can do on this side. At some point I may need your permission to decrease the girl's heart rate until they are able to end the reading."

"Decrease her heart rate? She only has one heart, Sariah—won't that kill her?"

Sariah sighed and shook her head. "It may, if they do not get out of there soon after, but it's the only option I have left."

"Sariah, you can hear that just as well as I can. If she dies, there may not be a Taren worth saving."

"It's a reading, Locknoff. We don't know what that's about, and I will not lose them..."

Just then, Tomahbare's and Taren's vitals decreased, triggering alarms to sound. The staff moved to their stations and began evaluating them immediately. Locknoff looked over at Sariah's pleading eyes.

"Agreed," he said, and she injected a syringe of blue liquid into Jennifer's chest. She then went to the foot of the table and began pushing buttons. Jennifer's heart rate started to drop. After a few moments, Tomahbare and Taren gasped simultaneously as they sat up. Everyone sighed. Sariah pressed several more buttons, nodded at Yakema, and ran to Tomahbare's side. She hugged him tightly as Yakema continued to work. Vishnu looked over at Tomahbare for a moment and then down at Jennifer. Yakema's frantic button pushing quickly gained his attention.

"Why isn't she awake?"

"She has to resend the order," Elious responded.

"Order, what order?"

"The one that saved both your lives." When Vishnu's confused expression did not change, Sariah cleared her throat. "About two hours after you touched her, both your and Tomahbare's vitals began to drop significantly. We had no choice but to manually decrease hers until you both were out of the reading."

"What!" he asked angrily, half falling off the table.

Yakema exhaled audibly and sank to the floor. Vishnu looked at Jennifer and asked, "What. Do. You. Mean. Sariah."

She was at his side at once. "Taren, we..."

"I do not believe that name is appropriate any longer," he interrupted.

Sariah looked at Tomahbare briefly and then nodded and continued. "Vishnu, we were losing both of you. The only way to get you back was to decrease her heart rate."

Vishnu was on his knees, gasping.

"It's all right," Sariah assured him, bending to be at eye level with him. "Yakema has gotten her heart rate under control. She'll be fine."

"Then why isn't she awake!"

"She's exhausted. You all are. She just needs rest. This isn't easy for her. Don't worry. She'll be fine."

When he didn't move, Sariah ordered Locknoff to get him into a recovery room immediately. "And keep him there." Locknoff nodded, and Elious helped Vishnu to his feet.

By the time they returned, Jennifer's heart rate was stabilized, and she was resting comfortably.

"It's a decision for the council, I'm afraid," Tomahbare explained when Locknoff asked about the findings. "Due to his interference, she now knows too much. Her ability could be damaging in the wrong hands."

Thirty-One

Trial Of A Brother

Locknoff barged into the room, causing Ahdortee and Anna both to jump. He went directly to the closet. The women shared a look and stood. When he came out, Ahdortee froze. Her face took on an expression of stone—for in his hand was a sword. Ahdortee's eyes were drawn to it. Its edges were sharp. On both sides of the blade were tiny, sharp, barbed-wire ribbons that went from just under the pommel to the tip. Anna was puzzled as she watched.

"Ahdortee." Locknoff went before her, putting the sword in between them and resting his hands on the hilt. "You believe I have wronged you in my choice of a mate." He shook his head. "I assure you, sister, that was not my intention. I ask for your loyalty as a master in spite of my choice, for I know not why the hearts have decided on this path. But it is one I shall take fully. What say you?"

Ahdortee looked at Anna briefly and then back to Locknoff. Her expression did not change as she spoke. "Locknoff, you ask for my support of something I do not like nor understand. However, it is my hearts' desire to see you successfully bond with a mate. If this is truly your choice, then I will support you on one condition. You must prove your hearts' desire and bond with her at the first opportunity." She looked at him, expecting his resolve to falter at the thought of bonding, but was completely taken aback by the words that followed.

"It cannot come fast enough," Locknoff said without a pause.

Ahdortee lowered her brows and looked over at Anna briefly. "Then I am with you, brother." Locknoff sheathed his sword and turned to Anna.

He closed his eyes and exhaled loudly. "Good. Then I will need you to fulfill my vow to her if I cannot, for what I do next may claim my life." Anna looked between them both, growing more confused by the second. "Anna, I…" He stopped talking and really looked at her. His eyes grew as he took her in.

She was dressed in a pair of skintight black leather pants. Where they ended, a black pair of six-inch heels met the floor. Her top was a black leather corset with a thick, embroidered rope along the top and bottom, which blended into the pants. Locknoff cleared his throat.

"Anna," he said, looking into her eyes, "Ahdortee brings up a valid point, which I will explain later, but right now there is something I must do."

"What is it?"

"I must seek forgiveness from my brother, whom I've wronged greatly."

"Why do you need the sword? I don't understand."

"I know, love, and I promise to help you understand when I get back." He hugged her tightly and turned to walk away.

"You mean, if you come back, Locknoff. He could kill you," Ahdortee added.

"What?" Anna interjected.

He stopped, looked straight ahead, and said, "I'm aware of that, Ahdortee, but it must be now."

"No!" Anna screamed and started after him.

Locknoff disappeared as Ahdortee caught her around the waist. "If you care anything for him, human, you'll let him go."

Anna stopped fighting her grip and turned her head around, prepared to confront a mad woman, but noticed tears falling from Ahdortee's eyes.

Ahdortee released her and dried the tears on her cheek.

"Where is he going?"

"To seek forgiveness or death from his brother."

"Brother?"

"Not that kind of brother."

"Why?"

"You lost a friend, gained a mate, and possibly a daughter. Taren failed an assignment, lost a child, and possibly started a war. Locknoff has much to ask forgiveness for."

"Lillian was pregnant?" She gasped.

"I do not know her name, but yes, his human mate was pregnant."

"Oh," Anna said, looking at the floor. "Is there nothing we can do?"

"No, he must confront his brother alone, according to Elquin tradition."

Anna was quiet for a moment. "I...am...not...Elquin," she said sternly. "I refuse to stand by and do nothing. If you wish to stop me, kill me." She turned and headed for the elevator.

After a moment, Ahdortee followed. "Anna, Anna, wait. You have no idea where you're going."

"I'll follow my heart," she said sarcastically and pushed to call the elevator.

◆ ◆ ◆

"Locknoff, what are you doing?" Sariah asked as he walked toward her followed by two fighters. She was coming out of a recovery room.

"I must speak with him."

"No! Locknoff, please, let him rest. We just got him calm enough to rest. His ordeal has made him very weak."

"Sariah, he has been sleeping for almost three days. I must do this now."

Sariah sighed. "Look at him, Locknoff," she said, tiredly gesturing to the small window.

Vishnu was curled up on the mattress, facing the wall. It looked like he was rocking.

"Sariah, I understand your concern, but he's stronger than you think, and I must do this now." He paused. "It will not matter later. Vishnu's purity in this moment will decide my fate."

Sariah looked into his eyes for a moment and then at the two ERT standing behind him. She input the code to open the door. Without another word, she walked back to the medical bay, closed the blinds, and took a seat behind her desk. Locknoff turned to the men at his side. "Do not let him leave this room with the sword." He then entered the room and secured the door behind himself.

He took three large steps and pulled the sword from its scabbard. Instantly Vishnu was on his feet—all signs of fatigue and stress gone. Locknoff grabbed the hilt with both hands and raised the sword as far over his head as his arms would allow. He then drove the sword into the floor between them. The point did not penetrate the floor very far, but Locknoff released the hilt anyway and dropped to the floor in a deep bow.

"Brother," he began, "I am sorry for what I have done to you. For the hurt I have caused you and for that which you must endure now. From the deepest part of my being, I humbly ask your forgiveness."

Vishnu moved closer and removed the sword. He began pacing in front of Locknoff. Every muscle in his body was tense. He had a death grip on the sword as he moved from left to right. He swung it closer and closer to Locknoff's head with every pass. When there was no more room to swing the sword, Vishnu stopped.

"Why now, Locknoff? What's changed in you?" His eyes were skeptical, his jaw tight as he waited for Locknoff's reply.

"If it pleases you, brother, I'd rather answer your question after you have made your decision and before you carry forth your judgment, for the answer may sway you one way or the other."

"My decision is made!" Vishnu seethed.

Locknoff lowered his head even further before speaking.

"I am prepared to embark on a mission that may claim my life, and I wish you to find honor in my name should I not return."

"What mission?"

"My young one has been taken by this planet's authorities, and I intend to retrieve her."

Vishnu was dumbfounded, his demeanor loosened. "Young one," he said to himself, looking at the sword.

He shook his head slightly and gripped the hilt with both hands. He raised his arms high above his head and brought the sword straight down, stepping back slightly, taking a knee as the sword reached the level of Locknoff's bare neck. The weapon was just inches away from his head. The tip of the sword was embedded a good two inches into the marble floor.

"Your life means more to me than your transgressions, brother. Rise. You are forgiven. We will speak of this no more. Your honor stands."

Locknoff stood and removed the weapon, sheathed it, and looked at Vishnu.

"Tell me of your young one, brother, and how the authorities came to know of her," Vishnu said, holding his hand out.

Locknoff grabbed Vishnu's forearm firmly and pulled him in for a hug.

"I only recently found out about her. She was born almost three years ago to Anna Desai."

"Anna?" Vishnu asked, astonished and suspicious at the same time. "How? When did you find her?"

"I didn't—Jennifer did."

"Hmm," Vishnu agreed. "That one is surprisingly resourceful."

They walked to the door, and Vishnu knocked three times. When the door opened, Anna bolted through and went straight into Locknoff's arms. She was in tears. "Don't you ever do that to me again."

Vishnu's eyebrows lifted questioningly, and Locknoff wrapped his arms around her. He lifted one hand to her cheek and wiped the tears away. "I'm sorry," he said, kissing her gently on the lips.

"I see all is well," Sariah said, coming into the open door. Anna and Locknoff turned to the sound of her voice.

"Oh," Anna said, looking at Vishnu for the first time.

"Hello, Anna. It's good to see you."

"Hello," she said distantly, looking over his features. She turned to Locknoff and smiled. "Is that what you look like under there?"

"Well, not as handsome, but similar, I suppose."

Vishnu laughed.

Anna looked at Locknoff and asked, "Will I ever get to see?"

"Soon," he replied.

"Sariah, I need to speak with you," Vishnu announced, walking alongside her.

She stopped. "Vishnu, you're free to rest in your own space if you like. Just remember to eat something, but please, please, can we discuss your concerns tomorrow?"

She looked exhausted, both physically and mentally.

"Of course. I shall return after sunrise."

"Thank you," she said and continued on her way.

"Locknoff," he called out.

"Yes, Vishnu."

"I look forward to meeting your young one soon."

"Leanah," Anna interjected.

"Leanah," Vishnu repeated, looking at her. "That's quite a fitting name."

Anna smiled. "Thank you."

"Rest well, brother," Locknoff said as Vishnu walked on. "We will need your strength in the days to come."

"Indeed," Vishnu said, disappearing into the hall

"What does he mean by *fitting*?" Anna asked with lowered brows. "You said the name just came to you when you saw her?"

"Yes, I liked how it sounded. It never occurred to me that there might be more to it."

"In the ancient language, Leanah means bridge."

"I named our daughter after a structure."

Locknoff laughed and pulled her into his chest.

"Perhaps she named herself. I have heard it said that young ones are known to do such things. Even human children," he added matter of factly.

"Are we going to get your young one now?" Ahdortee interrupted. "Or have you decided to make another one right here?"

Anna turned to her with a look of shocked disbelief, but before she could say anything, Locknoff responded, "Perhaps later. Now we move out."

He grabbed Anna's hand and followed the others out.

Ahdortee looked at him rather suspiciously.

Locknoff laughed and kept walking.

Thirty-Two

YOUNG ONE

Tom Davis sat behind the desk anxiously awaiting his replacement. His 360-degree view of the strange toddler's room offered little in the way of entertainment. His tests were winding down for the day, and scientists were already leaving. The night was young, and his football game was scheduled to start in roughly fifty-seven minutes. He looked down at his watch.

"Come on. Come on," he whispered, tapping his foot under the desk. A few seconds later, the air-lock door opened behind him.

"Yes!" he said, eagerly jumping to his feet.

The woman coming into the room jumped at his outburst. "Hey, Tom."

"Hey, Candace, got a—"

"I know. I know."

"Game," they said in unison and then laughed. He grabbed his little black gym bag from under the desk and bolted for the door. "Night." He waved over his shoulder.

"Good night," Candace responded, securing her identification card into place on the keyboard. The day's events popped up on the screen.

"It seems you've had a long day, my little, green friend," she said, looking out the window observatory. The remaining scientists were leaving, and the night nanny was beginning her evening ritual. The little girl looked exhausted, but the computer readouts of her brain waves suggested she was excited.

"Hmm," Candace said aloud, looking down at her. "I wonder what's on your mind, little one."

Her desk was located directly in the center of the small room, which was something of an oval shape. The walls were twenty-four inches of thick glass, which was carried through to the ceiling. The crescent-shaped room was covered from every angle to show the girl's behavior and whereabouts. The walls were encoded to pick up readings from her clothing that reported her vitals, brain waves, and heart rate. It was crucial that every aspect of her existence be recorded in order for the government to learn more about this creature. Candace thought it strange that the team was not there every day, because she thought the girl changed every time she saw her, and Candace was there practically every day.

It was only when something changed drastically that a team was sent in to evaluate her. She was always put through a gruesome routine, like today's, which involved eating, exercising, and guided play. It only happened twice as long as Candace had been working here. The first time Candace was only an intern and didn't understand why they did it. This time she had been the one to point out the minor change in brain-wave activity.

It seemed like she'd become more alert within the past few days, because her brain waves were off the charts and her physical appearance did not suggest anything different had taken place. Her behavior was perfectly normal. The observation team was baffled, so they called for a round of tests and evaluations. The little girl yawned as her nanny brushed her long, white hair.

"No curls," she said, hitting the large rollers on their way up. The woman looked at her for a moment and then said, "OK, but just for tonight."

"MaryAnn," Candace called over the loud speakers.

"It's just for tonight. They had her hooked up and tested all day. I don't think anything will change between now and the morning. Why not let her rest now?"

Candace thought on it for a moment, sighing. "You'll be the death of me, MaryAnn."

The woman smiled and tossed the huge curlers on the floor. "No curls," the little girl said again as MaryAnn continued brushing.

"Only for tonight, Lee."

"And if they ever hear you call her that, you'll be fired," Candace added.

"Bah," MaryAnn replied, tossing the brush as well. "As if I would ever call her Alien Species Test Subject 017 or anything else of the sort. It was her mother's only wish, and I like it. Besides, I've shortened it enough to where they wouldn't care anyway. I could always tell them it stands for *leave us in peace*."

Both women laughed, and Lee climbed off the bed to get a book with bright colors for MaryAnn to read.

Not long afterward, MaryAnn was tiptoeing out of the girl's room. Lee had fallen asleep clutching a teddy bear. The room was dark, but Candace could see her with the night-vision cameras.

"Do you think there are more?" MaryAnn asked Candace after a while. "I mean, if she is 017, what happened to the other sixteen?"

"There is at least one more, but he hasn't shown any interest in the child or her mother. It's unlikely but possible he never knew about her."

"Are they still watching her? It's been what—almost three years now?"

"I know," Candace said, shrugging, "but you never know. I just wish I knew what the big deal was all of a sudden. They didn't behave like this the last time she had a mental spike."

"The last time she'd seen her mother, Candace. The reason was clear."

"Guess so."

MaryAnn said, "But we know she hasn't seen anyone this time around, because she's been inside for the last month."

"Your guess is as good as mine. I just work here."

The women shared a laugh and sat quietly watching the monitors well into the night.

◆ ◆ ◆

"Are you all right?" Locknoff asked Anna as they sat waiting in the back of the delivery truck across from the federal building where Anna's tracker signal originated from.

Anna didn't know who, but someone was outside the truck taking crates of bread into a store she was sure already had more than enough. "Yes, I'm just a bit nervous. I have no idea what I'm doing."

"Don't worry, Anna. I'll guide you through it. The only reason I'm not the one doing this is because I've never seen her. She exists for me only through your memory. That will change, of course, once I meet her, but for now your connection is much stronger."

Anna inhaled deeply and then exhaled. She looked straight ahead.

"Almost ready, Locknoff," came a voice from the front of the truck. Locknoff turned to Anna and took both her hands.

"Are you ready?"

"Yes." She gripped his hands tightly and closed her eyes.

"The teams are in place. Whenever you're ready," said the voice.

"Anna, think back to the day when you first felt Leanah's emotions, when you decided that you wanted to keep her."

"OK." Anna nodded.

"Remember what it felt like. Let yourself feel now what you felt then."

Anna gripped his hands firmer. Her breathing changed to one of a meditative state. Locknoff looked over at Churvack, who nodded encouragingly.

"Good," he continued. "Now think back to the day she was born. When you could see her, feel her, and hear her hearts beating. Let the memories take center stage in your mind, Anna, and feel her hearts as you feel your own."

Anna's hands began to shake, and she opened her eyes.

"Where is she?"

"On the second floor of that building, near the northeast corner."

Locknoff gave her a tablet with a digital image of the building's second floor. Anna pointed to the last room on the right side of the tablet. "Here," she said and looked up at him.

"Ryous," Locknoff called in a firm voice, turning his head toward the truck's cab. "We have it."

"Locknoff," Anna said, reclaiming his attention.

When he looked at her, his brows lowered at her expression. "Yes."

"She's afraid, Locknoff. She's very, very afraid."

"Don't worry," Churvack said. "She's just becoming fully aware of you. She'll be fine. Try to stay calm, and send her reassuring thoughts."

Anna nodded. "I'll try."

They all listened as the operation began.

"Prepare for primary power break," Ryous's voice whispered. A moment later the entire grid was cut, but the building's power remained. "Secondary power break in three, two, one..."

The building went black. Anna could hear voices, scuffing, both muted and unmuted screams of agony, which turned her stomach into knots. Locknoff held her close, and she closed her eyes.

Suddenly all was quiet, and Ahdortee spoke. "We need power in the northeast corner."

◆ ◆ ◆

Candace and MaryAnn both jumped at the sudden beeping of the monitors. Lee's heart rate was through the roof.

MaryAnn was on her feet at once. "What's wrong with her?" she shouted, heading for the child's door.

"I couldn't be sure," Candace replied sarcastically, pushing buttons on the keyboard, bringing up her heart rate. "Someone didn't put the rollers in."

MaryAnn raced to Lee's side just as she sat up.

"It's OK, little one," she said, holding her arms open.

Lee jumped into them with wide eyes. Her breathing came easier as she looked into the distance. Before MaryAnn could begin with the rollers, the power went out. Lee clutched MaryAnn frantically, and MaryAnn held her closer. The quiet was eerie as they sat waiting. Before long, they heard voices.

"Who are you? What do you want? You can't be in—" The voice cut off.

MaryAnn clutched Lee tighter as more questions became muffled or muted altogether. She heard screams and muted thuds, and then she heard footsteps...heels. *What's going on out there?* she wondered. The lights came back on, but she couldn't see into the observation room.

"Candace, what's going on out there?" she asked, her voice laced with panic. There was no reply. She stood and walked closer to the large glass windows to have a better look, but she could see nothing. The lights returned, and she heard the air locks pop. The doors to Lee's room swung open.

MaryAnn could see several dark figures. Then the woman in heels came in. She was dressed in black from head to toe, and her heels were a good five inches off the ground. She was beautiful. She reminded MaryAnn somewhat of a supermodel. She noticed then that the woman's heels were bloody; she gulped and held Lee closer to her chest. The woman just stood there for a moment. It was like she was in shock or something. Her expression reminded MaryAnn of the first time she'd seen Lee.

The woman looked back and forth between Lee and MaryAnn several times before speaking.

"Who are you?"

"The night nanny."

"Put her down."

MaryAnn tried, but Lee would not release the death grip she had on her. She looked at the woman with fear-struck eyes.

"It's all right, little one," the woman cooed. "I am Ahdortee. I will take you to your mama and papa."

"Mama..." Lee responded with a smile, releasing her grip on MaryAnn.

"Yes."

MaryAnn began to protest but stopped at the look in the woman's eyes and gently placed the little girl down. Lee walked over to Ahdortee and took her hand. Moments after they walked out, the door shut, and the power went back out. MaryAnn released the breath she'd been holding and hit the floor.

◆ ◆ ◆

Ahdortee and Lee followed the others out of an energy-blasted front entrance and jumped into the waiting SWAT truck. All was silent as

Ryous and others looked at the little Elquin, who suddenly climbed onto Ahdortee's lap.

"Let's move," Ryous said as he heard Locknoff's warning over the radio of approaching government vehicles.

When they reached the warehouse, Ahdortee and Lee were the last to get out. They went directly into the medical bay to await Locknoff's return. A fighter came along to hold a constant signal blocker against Lee's transmitter.

Locknoff burst through the doors with Anna in tow.

"Where is she?" Anna asked breathlessly. "Where is Leanah?"

The little Elquin's face lit up brightly when she saw her.

"Mama," she said, holding her arms out to Anna, who turned at the sound and exhaled audibly.

Leanah was more beautiful than she'd imagined. She had grown so much, and her hair was just past her elbows. Anna scooped the little girl up into her arms and held her tightly.

"Oh, thank you, Ahdortee," Anna cried.

Ahdortee half smirked at Locknoff and walked out of the medical bay.

Locknoff's eyes went from Anna to Leanah several times before he stepped closer and hugged them both. Leanah looked up at him then. Her huge, brown eyes made him feel like she could see right through him. His breathing slowed down, and everyone else in the room became background as he took in his daughter. He could feel his hearts racing independently as they acclimated to the new extensions. Leanah's heartbeats were slightly faster than his own, but independently beat just milliseconds after his.

Leanah was a part of him, now and always, and she was finally home. He smiled at her warmly and held them both close. All too soon he was reminded of the others in the room as Churvack spoke.

"Locknoff," he said nervously, walking over toward them. "Would you mind if I took a quick scan of your young one?"

"Not at all," he said, looking at Anna. "We need to remove the tracker anyway."

"Yes, but I'm more concerned about this."

He pulled her long, white hair aside to reveal the back of her neck, which was glowing a dim orange. He and Anna both looked at the spot and gasped.

"Get Sariah," Locknoff yelled to one of the assistants.

Anna gently laid Leanah down on the table.

At first, it seemed to her that Leanah was asleep because her limbs had suddenly gone limp. But when Anna laid her on the table, she could see that her eyes were wide with fright, and there were tears rolling down her cheeks.

"Locknoff," Anna cried frantically.

"Yes," he said, redirecting his attention. Just as he began investigating Leanah, the table arch moved. Simultaneously, the green light came on under it and began to scan her little body. The tracker was in her ankle.

"Locknoff, why can't I feel her anymore?"

"I don't know, love. Something's wrong."

The arch returned then, and an image of Leanah's little body was displayed with the layers of skin and muscle removed to show thousands of tiny wires attached to her spinal cord, releasing a steady stream of strange orange liquid into her body. The source was a tiny computer chip attached to the base of her brain. Wires ran from the chip into two surgically implanted pouches that sat on either side of the chip. The liquid was making its way throughout her bloodstream.

"What is that?" Locknoff asked.

"I have no idea," Yakema responded.

Just then Sariah arrived.

"All right, Locknoff, what's the big…oh," Sariah said, taken aback. She looked up at the image, squinting as she moved closer. "Stop, Yakema. We don't know what that will do just yet. Bring me a sedative," she ordered, looking at the little Elquin's eyes. Churvack moved faster, already at her side with one.

"Sariah, what is it?" Locknoff asked.

"I'm not sure yet. I'll have to run some tests."

She injected the sedative into Leanah's arm and moved behind the desk only after the girl closed her eyes. Sariah wasted no time as she started pushing buttons. After a moment, she looked up and noticed the other patients in the room.

"Churvack, I think it would be better if we moved the others for a while."

"Right," Churvack responded, moving to gather the others in compliance.

"Well, Locknoff," Sariah said after a few moments, "you've certainly given the council much to consider."

Locknoff looked at her for a moment and then smiled.

"It's now our home too, isn't it?"

"Indeed. She's beautiful, by the way."

"Will she be all right?" Anna asked, stress lacing every word.

"I will do all I can for her," Sariah responded.

Ryous entered the bay then and instructed the fighter to wait outside for a moment. He took his tablet and looked at it briefly before setting it down with lowered brows.

"Sariah, I have something for you." He walked over to her and handed her a thin strip. "It contains the names of those needing transformation. The order is to be completed within forty-eight hours. The council wishes to take advantage of recent events. First contact is scheduled for three days' time, during the world leaders' summit in the United States. The council will convene in forty-nine hours. Your presence is requested. There are even…" He stopped. "What is that?" he asked, pointing to the floating image.

"That's the command center for the distribution of this liquid into the young one's bloodstream."

"Leanah," Anna interjected.

"Leanah's bloodstream," Sariah corrected herself.

Ryous ran to the tablet and took a closer look.

"Hmm. This may be more difficult than it looks."

"What do you mean?" Locknoff asked.

"Well, look here," he said, pointing to the image. "There is a constant signal between the two chips, almost as if it's communicating somehow."

Sariah gasped. "No," she said loud enough to make everyone jump.

"What is it?" Anna asked.

"No, no, no!" she repeated again, shaking her head back and forth as she moved her hands frantically around the desk. Everyone looked at her and waited. "The liquid-filled patches are a marine biotoxin," she said, racing to Leanah's side. "It contains a highly concentrated form of domoic acid, and it's headed directly for her hearts."

Sariah injected a blue liquid into several places along Leanah's body. When she looked up, everyone was still staring at her strangely, so she continued with her explanation while walking back over to the desk. She picked up a syringe that popped out of it, returned to Leanah's side, and then injected the liquid into her arm.

"It's a shellfish serum. From what I can tell, several different types of shellfish actually, obviously designed to control her."

The gasps were audible throughout the small group. Sariah pulled an IV bag out of the table and quickly attached it to Leanah's arm. "If what Ryous says is true," she explained, "it seems they figured out a way to derive the serum when they learned of her reaction to it. If you look at the rate of distribution," she said, pointing to the image above the table, "you'll see it's quite small for the moment. The signal between the two chips suggests that the dosage was controlled, perhaps paralyzing her until she could be found, if ever she escaped. I would bet anything that removing the tracker will trigger the main housing unit to release the full supply.

"I'm guessing they assume you have her, Anna, and will bring her back for the medical attention she desperately needs. With the chip in place, they can still control the level of release. If they are capable of monitoring her, they will soon discover that I have increased her white blood cells, which means we don't have much time."

Sariah injected more of the blue liquid into Leanah's scaly nostrils at the bridge of her nose and paused, exhaling audibly. "That could spell disaster if they release the remainder before I am ready." She cut through Leanah's pajamas, tossing them on the floor, and covered her with a sheet.

"What can we do?" Anna asked.

"We have to take that chip out," Sariah responded, looking up at the tiny bugs working their way through Leanah's little body. The ones she'd injected into her nostrils were moving across the base of her brain toward the chip.

Thirty-Three

First Contact

The little bugs made Anna cringe, but she knew they were only there to help. She watched as they moved through the nasal cavity to the back of Leanah's head, surrounding the little chip. Collectively, they moved to strike. If Anna had blinked, she would have missed it. One minute they were all gathered around the chip, and the next, it was gone.

Sariah immediately moved on to the tracker, removing it with ease. The bugs moved down toward the spinal column to join the others who were individually cutting off the flow of serum to the nerve endings and bloodstream. It looked to Anna like this would take a while, because there were hundreds of them, but at least she could breathe easier now, because no more serum would make it to Leanah's hearts, which Anna was desperately beginning to miss the feeling of.

"My work here is done," Ryous said, grabbing the tracker and signal tablet.

"Ryous," Locknoff said with a hand on his shoulder, "return it to them."

Ryous smiled. "I'll deliver it personally."

Locknoff nodded, and Ryous left the medical bay.

"This is going to take a while, guys," Sariah announced. "Although you are welcome to stay, you will know before I do when she's feeling better no matter where you are. Why not make the best of your last child-free night?"

Locknoff and Anna looked at each other and smiled.

"Actually," Locknoff said, "I have to run a few errands. Will you be all right, Anna?"

"Yes," she replied without taking her eyes off Leanah.

"Then I'll be back shortly."

He kissed her gently on the head, and then Leanah, and was on his way. Anna had so many questions but wasn't sure which one to ask first, or if she should even engage Sariah in conversation at the moment. But after a while, curiosity got the better of her.

"Sariah, why is shellfish so dangerous to you all?"

"Our immune system is slightly different than yours. The biotoxin normally found in shellfish triggers the release of chemicals that mixes with our blood and becomes fatal."

"Ryous mentioned something about transformers, and I've seen Taren...Vis...Vich..."

"Vishnu."

"Vishnu, as human. How is it that you can look like us one day and Elquin another?"

"It isn't exactly that simple, and it takes a lot out of us every time it's done. But the process involves a matter of manipulating the chromosomes slightly. Because our chromosomes are so similar, the process can be done on either species."

"You mean, humans can be turned into...I mean, look like you?"

"The change isn't permanent, and the chromosomes begin to re-align themselves immediately, but yes."

"Oh."

"Is it safe for…children?" Anna asked, looking down at Leanah. "I love her the way she is, but it will be difficult in a year or two when she needs to start school and will be around other kids."

"More research will need to be conducted before I would suggest something like that for Leanah, only because she's a carrier for both DNA types. We just don't know how her chromosomes will react. I wouldn't worry about the next couple of years though."

Anna wondered why, but Locknoff came in before she could ask.

"How is she?"

"About ten percent of the delivery pathways have been decommissioned. But there hasn't been another release, so she should start to feel better as the white blood cells make their way throughout her body."

"Thank you, Sariah. I know you have already made your decision about the council, but I would consider it a privilege to serve with you."

"I have not yet submitted that decision, Locknoff," she said, focusing on her work.

Locknoff smiled and looked down at Anna. "Anna, why don't we let Sariah work freely for a while? I have something I want to show you. And she's right. We will know how Leanah's doing before anyone else does."

Considering his words for a moment, Anna turned to him and half smiled. "All right," she said. Releasing her hold on Leanah, she kissed her on the head and stood. "Thank you, Sariah."

"My pleasure."

Locknoff led Anna to a room on the top floor of the building. It was similar to the one they'd shared last night, only this one was much bigger. It had an entire section added on that was big enough for a toddler bed and wardrobe. The bathroom was humongous and had a Jacuzzi for a bathtub.

"We won't be able to get any of your things for a while, but I had a few things brought up for you and Leanah. If they are not satisfactory, we can get others. It's not much, but it should do for a little while."

"It's beautiful," Anna said, delighted. "Thank you."

"I know you have many questions, Anna," Locknoff said, pulling her over to a table set with food and candlelight, "and I promise to address every one of them, but first we eat." Anna smiled and walked around the table once before taking a seat. "By the way, you look positively drop-dead gorgeous in that outfit," Locknoff confessed. Anna blushed so deeply that her normally brown cheeks turned almost purple.

After dinner, she was anxious to check out the Jacuzzi, so they climbed in the bath and turned the jets as high as they'd go. They took turns sponging each other while Anna asked question after question. Sometimes her questions came so fast that she couldn't possibly have heard the answer Locknoff gave before asking another.

"How did they pick Earth?" she asked, pausing after a long string of questions.

"Our scientists found your planet many ages ago while conducting field research. It was outlined then as a potential source of resources." Locknoff pulled Anna into his arms and sponged her back slowly, following the natural curvature of her form down to her hips.

"It wasn't until much later that a more independent evaluation was conducted. It was an unmanned shuttle that made first contact with Earth," he said, smiling. "Its job was simple—collect data. It was deployed to different parts of the globe, where it gathered samples."

"How?" Anna interrupted, her brow creased with confusion...or suspicion. Locknoff wasn't sure which.

"Data sensors were released onto the subject of interest. They returned with the genetic makeup of the object."

When her expression did not change, he continued. "An example would be if you were the subject of interest...or a tree or bush or anything. Data sensors would be released from the shuttle onto you, or it. They would look like tiny sparkles of light to you, or hundreds of lightning bugs."

Anna smiled.

"They would read your genetic material and return to the shuttle. It was a long process because Earth holds such a vast amount of resources, some of which our scientists have never come across before. Evaluating your planet was important at the time, because we were searching for a way to save our planet from destruction."

"And now?"

Locknoff shook his head.

"It's too late to save our world. Elquin's star has reached the end of its life cycle. It is uninhabitable. It will implode soon. Once the inevitable was discovered, Earth became more appealing for different reasons."

"I take it you're not in construction then?" she asked sarcastically.

Locknoff laughed. "Not exactly. I'm a special operations fighter."

Anna swallowed and repositioned herself so she could look him in the eyes. "Like combat operations?"

"Something like that, yes. Does that bother you?" He raised a brow.

"Not really, considering the average life expectancy for a combat fighter today is about twenty years."

Locknoff chuckled. "Well, I think I might have an average human beat, considering my strength, abilities, skills, and years of experience."

"How many years?"

"Are we talking human years here or Elquin?" he asked with a smile.

Anna's brow arched, and she reached up slightly to kiss him on the lips. "How many?" she asked again, pulling back to look him in the eyes.

"Forty-three of your human years," he responded, pulling her closer. She kissed him again and pulled back a little.

"And...Elquin years?"

His breathing was becoming ragged. "Two hundred ten," he responded and braided the fingers of his left hand into her thick curls and pulled her closer, crushing her lips. The conversation was over for the night.

When Anna woke up, Locknoff was propped up on an elbow, smiling. The white sheets were pulled up to his waist, and he had a bright smile across his features.

"Bond with me," he said, smiling confidently.

"What?" she asked, sleepily blinking to adjust to the light.

"Bond with me," he repeated.

"Am I supposed to know what that means?"

"It's something like your marriages, only a bit more...permanent."

"You wanna get married?" Anna's face lit up with excitement, all traces of sleep gone for the moment.

"Yes, I've al—" He cut off midsentence, and they both looked at the door. "Leanah!" they exclaimed together. They looked at each other briefly before jumping out of bed.

When they reached the medical bay, Vishnu was standing in front of Leanah, speaking to Deverah. He was dressed in a sky-blue, sleeveless shirt and a pair of black cargo pants. His long, white hair was thonged and braided.

"Yes, I believe she may be on to something," he'd been saying when he spotted them. Vishnu reclaimed his hand from Leanah's little fingers and moved toward the end of the table.

"Good morning," he said, looking at the two of them. Locknoff was dressed similarly, only his shirt was a khaki color.

"Good morning," they both responded, taking his place at Leanah's side.

Leanah beamed as she saw them and reached up for Anna.

"Where is Sariah?" Locknoff asked.

"She left the moment we removed the patches," Deverah explained, pointing at the tiny device now resting in a sterile cylinder on top of the desk. "She will be preoccupied for the majority of the day, attending to the council's latest request."

"Good day, Deverah," Vishnu said as he disappeared out of the bay.

Locknoff looked in his direction for a moment and then asked, "Has the danger passed for Leanah?"

Deverah looked at Anna briefly. "As far as we can tell, she's fine, but her blood is still working to fight off the toxins. She will need more rest and plenty of fluids, but she should be free from danger within a few weeks, I gather. Feel free to bring her back if you are concerned, however, because I know Sariah had a few more tests she wanted to run."

Locknoff nodded and looked down at Leanah.

"Good morning, little one." She smiled and reached for him.

"Papa," she said eagerly.

Locknoff pulled her into his enormous arms, kissed her on the head, and shifted her weight to one arm. With the other, he pulled Anna into his side and asked, "Hungry?"

"Famished," she replied, smiling. The three of them turned and left the medical bay in search of breakfast. Deverah could not help smiling at the sight of them. Locknoff really did look like he was the proud parent of two lovely daughters.

The cafeteria was oddly slow, considering the flow of activity around the place. Locknoff found a cozy spot to enjoy the meal with his family, but that did little to ease the string of onlookers and admirers. Locknoff's mood was not spoiled by any of it. He simply smiled back and returned the well-wishes when someone paid them a compliment. Shortly after they'd begun their meal, Ahdortee walked over, shadowed by Naeefah and Rashanah.

Her emotional state was unreadable as far as Locknoff could tell, but even her disapproving skepticism would not ruin his day, he decided. Her eyes scanned them all and settled on Leanah. Ahdortee's smile was surprisingly warm as Leanah spied her.

"Ahtee," she cooed, reaching out for Ahdortee, smiling.

Bridge indeed, Locknoff thought, raising an eyebrow. *Ahdortee hasn't smiled that warmly at anything in over a turier.*

"Good morning, Leanah, Master Locknoff, Anna." She kneeled to embrace Leanah gently.

"Good morning, Ahdortee," both Locknoff and Anna replied. "Rashanah, Naeefah," Locknoff added and then half smiled slightly when he took in Naeefah's attire.

She looked like Ahdortee's blond twin. They were both dressed in black, skintight cargoes with black, high-heeled boots. They wore red shirts pulled so tightly that they left nothing to the imagination.

"Will you be joining us at training today, Master Locknoff?" Rashanah asked, pulling him away from his thoughts.

"I was unaware that my presence was required."

"Oh, no, no," Rashanah said, backtracking. "I just assumed you would be there because Master Vishnu is training."

That explains the attire, Locknoff reasoned. "Perhaps I will make an appearance."

Thirty-Four

HOPE

Vishnu stood in the center of a large ring, holding a wooden version of his fighter blades in each hand. His eyes were shut, and his shirt was removed for the moment. He listened for the sound of an approach. The slight crackle and pressure change under his feet had him moving at the speed of light. His eyes flew open at the same time that he stepped forward slightly and positioned both his hands just right to block an attack from the front and rear of his position.

The attack from the front came from a wooden double-bladed bow staff, while the rear warrior used a wooden broad sword. After the initial block, Vishnu twisted his forward wrist slightly, forcing his attacker back. He then brought his other hand up while twisting to block a quick rebuttal, after which he was instantly in attack mode. He twirled and twisted again and again, blocking and striking so fast that those watching could see only a blur of green and hear the clashes of the wooden weapons.

In a short time, his opponent was disarmed, and the fatal strike made in mock movement as Vishnu pulled one hand from pelvis to throat, after which he immediately turned to block the sword with both hands while taking a knee. He then flicked his wrist inward and brought both arms out and down in a swift motion, following the hilt of the sword.

The action grazed his attacker's hand slightly, forcing him to lower the sword. But he did not release it. He simply switched hands and came after Vishnu more aggressively. Vishnu rolled forward and onto his feet as he attacked, moving closer and closer to his opponent, blocking and spinning so fast that his long braid would have been deadly as it circled around, had a weapon been attached to it, because it came within striking distance several times.

When at arm's length, Vishnu disarmed his opponent with a quick flick of his wrist and drove his weapons into his opponent's hearts in mock movements that had the man gasping for air while picking himself up off the floor. Vishnu's breathing was slightly uneven as he reached down to help his opponent up. The monotone clapping had him searching the gymnasium skeptically. It was an unimpressed Ahdortee smiling from ear to ear.

"But can you stop *me*?" she asked.

Naeefah smiled and stepped into the ring then.

"Or her," Ahdortee continued in a taunting manner.

Vishnu cleared his throat. "I do not wish to give lessons today, Ahdortee," he said, returning his attention to her.

Naeefah's hand came up with a wooden baton. "I wish to train, Master Vishnu."

His brain only had time to register the weapon before she was attacking him. Her blows were direct and precise. He found himself blocking her aggressively as he backed away. She started spinning and bringing her heels around to his neck with every pass. He barely missed the bottom of her shoe again and again, and her baton was there the instant her shoe was not.

After a third pass, Naeefah jumped a few feet off the ground, then spun and came down with a deliberate blow to his neck. Vishnu shifted slightly and caught her arm. His grip was so tight on her that it appeared Naeefah was at a loss the way she slowly released her weapon. Then she bent forward slightly, bringing her heel around for another shot at his neck, but Vishnu blocked it with his free hand and twisted slightly, slamming her into the mat.

"Lesson over," he said softly.

"Then perhaps a meal," she suggested, smiling as she breathed heavily.

"Another time perhaps. It appears I have another opponent."

Locknoff smiled, stepping into the ring.

◆ ◆ ◆

Jennifer opened her eyes slowly, blinking a few times as she adjusted to the light. The sight of two familiar figures had her stomach in knots. She turned her head toward the wall and sighed.

"Are you all right?" Sariah asked, stepping forward and reaching her hand out slightly.

"I'm truly sorry for the way our session ended, Jennifer. It was extremely unprofessional and unjustly painful. I extend my sincere apologies," Tomahbare exclaimed.

Jennifer inhaled deeply, closed her eyes, and then exhaled and turned to face them both as she sat up. "So, let's hear it."

Tomahbare and Sariah shared a look.

"You are a very talented woman, Jennifer Braxton. Unfortunately, your particular gifts pose a threat to our mission here," Tomahbare explained.

"What does that mean?"

Tomahbare sighed.

"I don't suppose it will matter in the long run, but for the moment, you will need to remain here."

"What? For how long?!"

"I do not know. The council will decide when they convene next."

"And when will that be?"

"In approximately seventeen hours."

Jennifer sat farther back on the table, turned her head toward the wall, and began rocking back and forth. Sariah placed one hand on her shoulder, and she froze.

"I'm terribly sorry about this, Jennifer, but I'll need to monitor your theta brain wave activity, and the only way to get an accurate reading is to do this while you're conscious."

"Do what?" she asked, confused.

"Just relax," Sariah said, reaching into the pocket of her ever-present scrubs, pulling out what appeared to be a miniature ballpoint pen.

Jennifer exhaled loudly. *Great*, she thought, *more alien crap in my body. Hope I don't end up with blood poisoning or something.*

Sariah pulled Jennifer's hair aside and placed the tool directly on the edge of her hairline. She depressed a button on the end of it. Jennifer felt like she'd been bitten by a bug. She had to fight the urge to reach up and rid herself of the annoying critter.

"There you go," Sariah said, wiping away the small spot of blood from her neck. She smiled and then frowned at the thunderous rumble that escaped Jennifer's stomach.

"Oh…well, you have been unconscious for almost three days now. I imagine you're famished."

Jennifer didn't respond or move or anything until a knock on the door interrupted what Sariah was about to say. She disappeared to address the intruder, and Tomahbare walked over to Jennifer and asked, "How are you doing with all this?"

"By *all this*, I assume you mean Vishnu."

"You assume correctly."

"I don't know anything about him other than the fact that he is a more-than-capable fighter...and nonhuman. How am I supposed to deal with that? I feel like I've been thrown into the middle of a political war and ordered to pick sides," she added without waiting for a response.

"Funny you should say that."

Before she could ask Tomahbare what he meant, Sariah returned with a disappointed look in her eyes.

"I apologize, Jennifer, but we must speak at a later time. There is an important task I must attend to at the moment. This is Kenozo." Sariah gestured to a short, blond male who entered then. "He will show you to your room." She looked over at Tomahbare and smiled. "You could use more rest too, my heart. I'll be back as soon as I can."

"I'm fine, love. There is no need to worry, and I have the next shift."

"That's why you should rest, my love."

"Later. I'll accompany Kenozo to the dining hall. I could use something to eat as well."

Sariah exhaled audibly. "I'll see you soon then." She walked out of the room without waiting for his response. Her frustration level seemed high, Jennifer noticed. When Sariah was gone, Tomahbare explained.

"She doesn't like it when I take chances with my health. In the past I've needed a full week to recover from an official reading."

Jennifer didn't respond to his words; she only stood. Jennifer was reserved as she walked along the corridors. It was amazing and baffling at the same time. It looked to her as if they'd carved a mountain hollow. The temperature felt oddly cool, but it was the inside of a cave, she noted, and there were vast open spaces attached to long hallways. Jennifer followed Kenozo down a hallway off the medical wing. There were only two connections here she could see.

The left side was smooth and polished, reminding Jennifer of granite. They stopped briefly at the first connection. It was huge. The outlined walls were the same as the hallway, and there were several pillars that went throughout the room. They were polished as well. There were people, or aliens, she guessed, spaced throughout the room. To the far right, there was a large group practicing hand-to-hand combat, although to Jennifer it looked more like they were throwing themselves at each other to no end.

In the far left corner, she noticed others working with bow staffs and weapons she'd never seen before. The rear of the room looked something like a resting area. There were lavatory connections, benches, and water coolers—with a strange-looking, brown liquid inside the cooler rather than water.

As she entered the room, she passed several ropes hanging from the ceiling. Each one was occupied, but her eyes were drawn to the room's center because of a large circle painted on a martial arts mat. Vishnu was in the middle of it, half dressed and fighting...Locknoff.

Jennifer's brows lowered. *This is all wrong.* In her last dream of him, he was so...

No, they weren't fighting, she noted. *They're training*, she concluded, more confused than ever. Jennifer couldn't move; her eyes were glued on him. Kenozo began to explain what the room was used for, pointing and describing this and that, but she didn't hear a word he said. The only thing she heard was the thunderous beating of her heart. Tomahbare just watched and followed her eyes to what he already knew she was watching.

Vishnu was deadly, she'd known, and now as she watched him, she was reminded of a viper striking at its prey. He and Locknoff moved so fast that their movements could barely be analyzed, but she wasn't analyzing. She was mesmerized by Vishnu's swirling colors. His face was the same as she'd seen in her visions of him, but she'd never seen him without a shirt. Under his swirls of moss green, there were beautifully developed muscles.

They were not massive-looking like Locknoff's. They were more proportionate. Jennifer then saw his back as he turned to block a blow aimed at his side. She inhaled sharply, remembering a dream she'd had once when he'd gotten the wound. She blinked, and a tear rolled down her cheeks. Tomahbare cleared his throat, and Kenozo stopped talking. Jennifer looked at him and half smiled. They turned to leave in time for her to catch a glimpse of Vishnu's eyes looking in her direction, which was a mistake because just then Locknoff swept Vishnu's feet from underneath him and followed through with a mock killing blow to his throat.

"Distracted, brother?" Locknoff asked, turning then, like the others, to where Vishnu's attention had gone. But it was too late. Jennifer had already moved on.

"Are you all right, Jennifer?" Kenozo asked in response to her hand movements as they reached the cafeteria. She'd wiped a few tears away. She didn't want to give anyone a reason to focus on her now that her bruises were all gone. Whatever Sariah had done gave her a new face, and she was determined not to draw attention to it.

"Yes I'm fine," she responded too quickly.

Although there seemed to be a lot of individuals here, it did not take long for them to get their food or find a seat. Jennifer ate distantly, only seeing Vishnu's lightning-fast movements. Tomahbare watched but said nothing until the meal was complete.

"And now?" he asked curiously.

"I'm tired...I want to rest."

Tomahbare nodded. "Then perhaps another time." He then turned and headed for the exit.

"Right this way. I'll show you to your room," Kenozo said. Jennifer was determined not to look in Vishnu's direction when they passed the gymnasium again, so she looked straight ahead, seeing nothing.

Thirty-Five

COMPANY

Three floors and six doors later, Jennifer walked into what had to be the most luxurious suite she'd ever seen. There were darkly stained exposed beams on the ceiling and khaki paint on the walls. The beams directly over the bed were draped with a gray-and-white fabric canopy. At the head of the bed, the fabric was draped on either side of the headboard, which had flowers carved throughout. The same gray-and-white pattern was repeated on the bed.

One set of pillows had both gray and white stripes, while another was just white. The comforter was gray, and the bed skirt was white. On the side of the bed were two small nightstands that held chrome lamps. The sitting area had a crystal chandelier and a large, white sofa with gray and white throw pillows. The chair beside it was a sleek and modern-style set in gray.

The bathroom had a similar pattern, but Jennifer paid little attention to it because she saw a pool on the other side of it, accessed through an archway. The water was inviting. There were lights along the side and back of the pool and several circular windows placed high enough to let in skylight. There was ample room for walking, but not much more. Jennifer smiled. *I wonder if there are any clothes in the closet*, she thought. Pulling her eyes away from the pool, she walked back into the bedroom. To her surprise, there were several outfits in the closet, all about her size. There were even undergarments and a few swimsuits.

She spent some time in the pool before showering and then sat and checked out the small collection of books stacked on the dresser. But try as she might, reading them was impossible because she fell asleep after turning the third page of *Electromagnetism and its effects on the Elquin Condition*. It wasn't long before she was dreaming.

◆ ◆ ◆

The background was fuzzy as she stood in Vishnu's arms, staring up into his eyes. She had a hunger for him so strong it hurt. He leaned forward and kissed her. She smiled and kissed him back, feeling warmth spread throughout her body. It felt more than right to her, and the fact that he wasn't human made no difference. She felt several odd emotions run through her. Joy, fear, strength, desire, peace, anger, and...love. She wanted him, needed him, and was suddenly as impatient as he seemed to be. They began tearing at each other's clothing, and Jennifer marveled at his naked body. She followed the contours of his muscles down his chest and toward his hips. As she reached his pelvis and looked over Vishnu's genitals, she awoke with a gasp.

Shock ran through her, and she was drenched in sweat. She sat there for a while, breathing rapidly and staring at the picture on the wall. It was of a beachfront sunset. The sand was blue to match the water, and a red sun so large that it looked like she could reach out and touch it stood out behind the water. When her breathing returned to normal, she decided to have another shower.

Before long, Jennifer was ready for bed. She desperately wanted to talk to Lu, if only to tell her that she was still alive. But she didn't see any phones in this room, nor did she think they would bring her one. She accepted the meal someone left at her door without complaint; she only wished she could have thanked whoever had left it there. She'd heard a knock, but no one was there when she opened the door. After dinner, Jennifer lay down on the huge bed and closed her eyes. Sleep came quickly.

◆ ◆ ◆

Jennifer was standing in the middle of a smoky forest. She coughed several times and looked around. There was something wrong with this smoke, she noted. It smelled like burning wood, but it was white, and there was no sign of a fire. It was uncomfortable to breathe in, but not unbreathable. She decided to get out of it quickly. But everywhere she looked was the same thick, white smoke. She coughed several times more and then heard voices. She pulled her shirt over her nose and headed toward them.

A few steps forward, and she stumbled over something big.

"Ouch," she said, pulling herself onto her knees. The ground was cool, she noted as she checked what she'd fallen over—a body. It was a man she'd never seen before, dressed in police attire with FBI written across the back of his shirt. Jennifer inhaled sharply and looked around. There were more bodies. Some were Elquin, others were human, but they were all dead.

It was curious that the Elquins all had identical wounds on their chests. Carefully she walked toward the voices, stepping lightly over the bodies.

"Stupid invading shape-shifters," a man said as he spat on the body of an Elquin male no more than two feet from him. "Who would have thought they'd be so easy to kill?" the man continued.

"They're not shape-shifters," another said. "They're shape-manipulators. The term shape-shifter refers to a being that can readily shift from one form to another. They can only shift into human form and back. And do you see how many of us they took with them?" he asked, gesturing to the bodies on the ground.

"If we had not gotten their fish bullets in time, there's no way we could have stood a chance."

"Hmm…"

"I tell you one thing: I'll never look at shellfish the same way again."

"Shellfish," Jennifer said aloud. *None of this makes sense*, she thought, looking down at one of the Elquin bodies. She lowered her brows, noticing the bullet holes again. They were all in the same general area on every one of the dead Elquins.

"That has to be it. Their vital organs…but shellfish? Weird." She shook her head slightly, and a coughing spasm began. The smoke was bothering her. She coughed and then coughed again. She coughed so fast and so hard that she woke herself up. It took a minute for her to stop coughing, but then she was suddenly aware of her name being called.

"Jennifer, Jennifer…Jennifer Braxton, are you all right?" the frantic voice asked.

"I'm fine," she said hoarsely, her voice thick with sleep.

Tomahbare was sitting on the bed, and several others were standing around them. He took out a small flashlight and looked at her pupils.

"I just had a dream, is all. I'm fine."

"I'll say. You've been in REM sleep with elevated theta activity now for almost twenty hours, not to mention your anxiety levels. Here, let me see your hand."

Jennifer lifted her hand, and Tomahbare clamped his down on top of it. Her eyes went wide as she was quickly taken through the last dream she'd had. She inhaled sharply as the images fluttered through her mind's eye. It felt like she'd been shoved into a tub of ice water. She panted when Tomahbare removed his hand and the warmth returned to her body. Tomahbare was speechless as he stared into her eyes.

"Wait. Did you say twenty hours?" Jennifer asked, her voice normal now.

"Yes," Tomahbare responded, getting to his feet. "The council has already convened. We make contact in three hours."

"But—"

"I know, Jennifer. You have nothing to fear. No one will be within arm's reach of a human."

Jennifer felt pacified by his reassurance. *Good. No humans will die either*, she thought.

"What about me?" she asked as Tomahbare turned to leave.

He stopped, looked down a moment, and then said, "The answer to that question no longer applies. I'm afraid you must wait a little longer, Jennifer Braxton." He continued on his way without another word and was followed by all but one of his assistants.

"Wait," Jennifer shouted, trying to follow them, but the last one out closed the door before she could get there. Turning, she noticed the other woman and asked sourly as she plopped down on the bed, "What do you want?"

"To help you find your way." Jennifer's brows lowered, and the woman continued. "Around camp, I mean."

"Thanks, but I think I can manage."

"All right," she said and stepped outside the room, closing the door behind her. Jennifer tossed a pillow at the door with a humph and lay back down.

◆ ◆ ◆

Tomahbare was flabbergasted. He left in search of answers before he could even form questions. *This news will need to be addressed*, he thought. "But not now," he said aloud. The camp is under enough pressure with tonight's events. He felt a strong need to be with Sariah. The pressure she felt to join the council was overwhelming. *They were smart to deploy both partners of a bonded pair to this world when they discovered its effects on us.* His thoughts were immediately redirected to the council meeting just a few hours ago.

"Greetings," Elitar had begun.

Sariah was right—he looks fragile. It must be all the stress, Tomahbare had thought.

"Tonight we meet to discuss the best strategy to make our presence known to the humans without losing a single life. I know we are meeting much sooner than we'd initially intended, but let us begin with progress reports. At our last meeting, the decision was made to cease mining projects and commence transport. Master Nesset, will you share with the council where we stand with this project?"

Nesset stayed seated as she spoke, but she was in the center of the screen for all to see. Outlining her frame were only twenty other council gatherings.

"Everyone has been evacuated from Elquin. We have taken only plants and animals that research suggests will survive on Earth. All others have been catalogued and stored for future possibilities. Our strongest stand ready to fight. Upon our departure, Elquin has consistently loss 2.704 centimeters daily. If its current rate of loss persists, our planet will reach fatal distance within six moon cycles. When the shield no longer holds, harmful rays will penetrate the atmosphere, making life impossible for any living thing that still exists there."

All was quiet as everyone took in Nesset's words.

"What of our farmed planets?" Elitar asked.

"Of the original thirty-eight planets farmed," Bathmantu said as his face dominated the screen, "we now hold colonies on eighteen. It was difficult to reach an agreement for many and impossible for others, but as it happened, there were more Elquins willing to fight for our new home than originally anticipated. Of course we have three full waves of fighters on each of those planets, but all the others are en route to Earth."

"How many vessels do we have headed for Earth?" Elitar asked in a ragged voice.

"Two thousand full fleets will be ready to enter Earth's gravitational field in roughly forty-eight hours. Within seventy-two, we should be ready to enter her atmosphere," Bathmantu replied excitedly. "The remaining five thousand will join us within two weeks."

"Excellent." Elitar turned to Locknoff. "I would like to congratulate you on your recent discovery. I presume we will receive an official bonding request soon, Locknoff?"

Audible gasps could be heard from every council gathering. Silent questions filled the room, but Locknoff ignored them all. "As soon as possible, I assure you," he responded proudly.

"Excellent," Elitar exclaimed again, with a bit more energy this time.

"What of the precog?" It was Tomahbare's turn to speak. He inhaled deeply and then exhaled while pushing buttons on the table. Jennifer's picture was suspended above the table.

"Jennifer Braxton is an incredibly gifted precog. Her official reading revealed over 897 accurate predictions. Her gift was born to her, and it is only just beginning to break through to the surface. I believe she can be a valuable asset to our efforts." He looked over at Vishnu for the first time and added, "Or a dangerous enemy."

Vishnu looked annoyed but in control of himself. It was as if he was determined not to let a single word set him off. *Nicely done*, Tomahbare reasoned.

"My suggesting is that we keep her here under close supervision until she is no longer a threat."

"We should eliminate the threat now," Zeeporah interrupted. "This precog has already proven to be more of a challenge than——"

"Not if she can be of use to us," Bathmantu interrupted. "We must consider the tactical advantage she offers."

"To what end?" Skyke asked slightly above a whisper. "You suggest we become like them? Use humans for our benefit, and then dislodged them when we no longer require their services? If we are to live among them, should we not offer her a choice?"

"Absolutely not!" Bathmantu all but shouted, his opposition echoed by several others. "She should be used as any other intelligence source or discarded for the potential danger that she possesses."

Tomahbare and Locknoff both looked at Vishnu as he stood with an exasperated expression.

"Enough!" he said loud enough to gain everyone's attention. All became silent as his features dominated the screen. "Master council," he said, addressing Elitar, "I accept your proposal." Tomahbare looked at Sariah worriedly. Vishnu turned his attention to the group.

"We will do none of the above. This woman has never been a willing participant in our efforts here. She was randomly selected to be of assistance and is now being pulled into a position of political interest. She is not a pawn to be played, but a living being whose life I have unknowingly turned upside down." The silent protest had him lifting his finger. "I'm not finished, Zeeporah. We have a brilliant medical team whose abilities are unmatched by any world we've come across thus far."

Tomahbare did not like the direction Vishnu was headed.

"Perhaps a simple manipulation of her memory could ensure our safety. We can stay true to who we are, and she can return to her life none the wiser."

Sariah, Tomahbare, and Locknoff all looked at Vishnu with raised eyebrows. Feleet was still in shock of hearing Locknoff's words and would not take her devastated eyes off him.

"By doing so," Vishnu continued as if he hadn't noticed any of it, "she can return to her life, and our anonymity remains intact." All was quiet as he sat and exhaled loudly.

Tomahbare thought Vishnu's expression was more one of defeat rather than resolve. *Why is he doing this? It doesn't make any sense. She is his heart song. He will be in agony without her.* "I second the motion," Elitar said, bringing him out of his internal processing.

"And I, and I," came others.

This is all wrong, Tomahbare thought, shaking his head. He could see Sariah agreed with him. After a moment, the naysayers began. They argued for her immediate death. *It's all madness*, Tomahbare thought as he walked along the corridors searching for Sariah. In the end, medical was ordered to identify the safest way to remove her memory and administer it as soon as possible.

"May I suggest we wait until after tonight's events?" Madafski offered as the final votes were tallied.

"Excellent suggestion," Elitar said, effectively ending the debates. "And now," he continued in the same breath, "what is the plan of action for tonight's meeting?"

Tomahbare stopped listening then; it was too much for him. He knew how Jennifer felt for Vishnu subconsciously and he her consequently. If medical succeeded in this endeavor, she would forget about him, but Vishnu would still have *his* memories of her and the pain of her loss. *What was he thinking?!* Tomahbare asked himself. He desperately wanted to read Vishnu, but it would have to wait until after the council meeting. The only problem with that, of course, was Vishnu's disappearing act after the meeting and the alarms that started going off, informing medical of problems with Jennifer.

Tomahbare exhaled slowly before entering the medical bay. He shared the news about Jennifer's health and vision with Sariah, who agreed that it would be better to wait until after the evening meeting with Earth's leaders before bringing it up with Ryous. Additionally, Sariah felt like they both needed to have a long talk with Vishnu before he got away after the night's events. So they plotted to block his escape route and confront him.

Thirty-Six

SUMMIT

The early evening hours drew on slowly as Elquins readied themselves for the night's events. Vishnu felt confident in his decision to let go of Jennifer as he stood with the gathered party. There were seven of them in total, and they were all ready to get this particular stage of the process over with quickly. The decision had been made to broadcast the signal much like a council meeting, only each council gathering would be standing in the frame around the Elquin council representation. The signal would be broadcast through Earth's campsite, with signal scramblers posted throughout.

◆ ◆ ◆

As Vishnu stood awaiting the Elquin council, his thoughts drifted to Jennifer. He would miss her terribly, but he wanted her to be happy. He'd seen her briefly yesterday while sparring with Locknoff. Locknoff had gotten a lucky shot in when he noticed her watching him. He was so happy to finally see her face without all the bruises. Only in her reading had he truly seen her, but it wasn't the same. His mind was so clouded with overwhelming emotions then that the only thing he could focus on was how she made him feel.

In that moment she looked beautiful standing there, even in white scrubs. He'd noticed a tear falling down her cheek and felt a twinge of anger at himself for putting her in this position, though he couldn't help feeling…overjoyed by seeing her. In the end, he'd won the match with Locknoff and congratulated him again before heading on to focus on other training. He'd spent all day at it, redirecting his thoughts while he trained whenever his emotions threatened to overwhelm him. He stopped only when Locknoff returned with Anna and Leanah briefly to remind him of the hour and upcoming events.

By the time he'd closed his eyes that night, his body was already in REM sleep. When he finally woke up the next day, or afternoon, it was to the frantic sound of medical rushing down the hall. *Must be one of the newly transformed council representatives in peril*, he thought and went back into his room to get ready for the day. He was slightly annoyed by the interruption because he'd been having the most intimate dream about Jennifer.

Where have they put her? he wondered and went to shower. He would do whatever he could to take the pain he saw in her eyes away. She'd lost so much since he'd come into her life. She'd lost a friend, been beaten nearly to death twice, kidnapped, dragged across state lines, and shown images no sane human could handle without extensive explanation. She was abandoned in the middle of nowhere, and to top it all off, she was stuck with the images of a dying world she couldn't get rid of. "Or can she?"

He felt the sting of betrayal the same time he considered it. "No," he said aloud, panting and clutching his chest. *I couldn't live without her in my life.* But the pain only seemed to get worse as he considered. It was becoming difficult for him to breathe, so he leaned on the shower wall and took slow, steady breaths. *It's not about me*, he tried to convince himself. *She's not happy here. I have to do what's best for her. I'll have to find another way to manage.* His every thought seemed to pull at his resolve.

The pain was becoming unbearable, so he reached for a towel and got out of the shower.

"Speaking to Sariah should help," he said aloud and thought of her bond with Tomahbare. The council was insistent on his joining her here when they became aware of Locknoff's troubles. "Bonding," he said aloud, panting, "If I bond with someone…else."

He gripped his torso, falling to his knees, and panted while considering it. *If her memories of me were no longer there, she would be free of me and free to live out her life as she wanted. If I bond with another, then I should be free of her.* His body seemed to react better to this line of thought, and he made it to his feet without a shred of pain. *That settles it*, he concluded. *I'll inform the council today.* He finished getting ready and left his room in search of something to eat.

Once in session and as the council meeting dragged on, Vishnu's resolve faltered and crumbled altogether when Tomahbare spoke. But it was the input from others that gave him the strength to speak. Of course, for him to be taken seriously, he would now have to accept Elitar's offer when the time came. So he stood. It was easier to say the words out loud than he thought they would be. But as he spoke, a huge knot developed in each of his hearts, and he knew they would stay there forever.

Movement on the screen was enough for him to focus on the task at hand. The six Elquins behind him were dressed in the same traditional white robes as he wore, echoed by every Elquin on the huge screen before him. The conference furniture had been removed, and the walls and ceiling were covered with the same marble as the caves. It could be seen from every angle of the screen. Directly behind the screen, Ryous sat with an open laptop. He was connected to several others strategically placed throughout the camp. Each one would do his or her part to scramble and block the trace once the broadcast began.

◆ ◆ ◆

Andre Bradshaw was a dedicated agent. He'd spent twenty years as a special operations coordinator in the US Air Force. He'd learned to rely on his sense just as much or even more so than the technology he worked with. There were many cases where he trusted his senses over the equipment and was often proven right. He walked the line restlessly, checking in with every station. He couldn't shake the feeling that something wasn't right.

Everyone was on point, however, as they watched the large crowd of world economic leaders gathered here to discuss the current economic state of the world. *Not sure what good that will do. If they can't agree independently, what makes them think they can come up with an agreement together?* he wondered. He smiled at the irony of it and returned to his command post in the observation room overlooking the conference hall. The G-20 brought in people from all walks of life, and it was his job to make sure they did not kill each other.

Roughly forty minutes after he'd returned, the introductions were complete and the monitors all focused on the US representative who began the session.

"What is that?" Bradshaw asked, looking intently at one of his computer monitors.

"Welcome, ladies and gentlemen," the representative began.

"What is that?" Bradshaw asked again, confusion lacing every word as he moved closer to the monitor.

He pushed several buttons, but nothing changed on the monitor. There were several other agents in the room, who sat or stood behind a computer. They all stopped what they were doing and looked at him.

"What is it, Chief?" a feminine voice asked.

He pointed to a digital ball of yarn that kept blinking in the top right corner of his monitor. Just then, others began to notice it on their screens as well. Bradshaw tried to reboot his system, but small lines appeared on the screen.

"To the thirty-ninth annual world's leaders' summit," the representative went on. Suddenly he was quiet as he noticed the gasps filling the hall. Everyone was looking at the television screens with a variety of expressions across their features. All was quiet throughout the hall except for the rapid breathing of many and the slightly less rapid breathing of others. The representative turned around and saw why they all stared.

Bradshaw was flabbergasted as he watched the screen; he stood mechanically. It held several groups of alien creatures. Their faces were each a different shade of green. Their hair was long and white, as were their eyelashes. None of them had eyebrows, and their noses had a strange scale-like bridge to it. Instead of ears, they all had several rows of arched bands that encircled a triangular shape. Some of the creatures had braided hair on their foreheads.

The one in front wore a thick headband that reminded Bradshaw of a crown. It was beautifully decorated with stars and planets. The white they wore had embroidery along the waist and/or upper left chest. Bradshaw could not help but wonder if the placement of the embroidery determined their sexes. But before he could consider it further, the one standing in front spoke.

"I am Elitar of the Jai bloodline." The phone rang, but no one moved to answer it. "We are Elquin. We have traveled long and far from a dying world to join you once again. This time, however, we seek to live alongside you rather than farm your resources. Our recently abandoned home is currently located forty light-years from here, under the intense gravitational influence of a dying star."

Ring, ring, ring...the phone went on, but no one answered.

"We are prepared to offer you our knowledge and experience in combating this potential threat, as your world undoubtedly faces a similar fate in the not-too-distant future. We are not seeking to enslave or destroy you, but we are prepared to fight if you refuse our request."

Ring, ring…"Bradshaw," he answered mechanically. "Yes, I see the intrusion, but I cannot get a lock on the signal." Others began to thaw out as well and were searching for a way around the wall. "It is unlikely that the signal is coming from outer space because there is a firewall blocking its origin. Yes, I will run a diagnostic. I agree we need to find whoever is responsible for this before…Oh…I see. The reporters are sure to have a field day with this one. Yes, sir. I'm on it." He hung up the phone then and started pushing buttons and shouting orders.

"We await your decision…" the alien continued. "You have forty-eight hours."

The team moved as fast as they could, but it wasn't fast enough. The broadcast was over just as his team bypassed the fifth firewall. Everyone was at a loss for words. The phone rang again, and all the screens displayed the US representative once more. In the hall, the questions began.

"Is this a joke, Mr. Speaker?"

"What is the meaning of this?"

"What does this…"

"Hello?" Bradshaw stopped listening and answered the phone. "No, sir, we cut through several, but were unable to locate the source of the feed. Whoever is transmitting the signal though is earthbound, I can tell you that. I don't understand what…Yes, sir," he responded and hung up the phone.

What the hell is going on? he asked himself. He put someone else in charge, stating he had to leave for McCarran International Airport immediately. Everyone in the room was as shocked and confused as he seemed to be, but he walked out of the door in compliance to an order from the national defense secretary.

They can't possibly think this is an actual alien broadcast coming from some-where here on Earth...but I guess that's why they want me at Paradise Ranch. Perhaps I'll get to assist in the investigation, he resolved.

It was a long night, Bradshaw thought as he sat back on the charter flight to home base. He was exhausted. The live broadcast of alien-streamed nonsense and all the speculation associated with it made traveling all the more difficult for him. The White House had immediately come out with an official apology to the G-20 guests and informed citizens that the stream was an elaborate hoax by an individual or group of individuals here on Earth. Investigations were underway by the federal government.

There were groups of protesters outside the White House demanding the government take the threat seriously because of all the alien activity uncovered over the years. First responders were advised to be prepared for possible public unrest until an official investigation was completed. All in all, the majority of people took the incident as the hoax the government promised them it was. But still, others were not so easily convinced and were confident that the end of the world was at hand. The pilot turned off the seat-belt sign, and Bradshaw decided to get in a quick bathroom visit before he settled down for the flight.

A catnap later, and the plane touched down on Paradise Ranch. Bradshaw and several others were escorted in the building by armed guards. Although he thought it strange, he knew better than to ask questions. As he was led through the building, Bradshaw didn't notice anything that would indicate it as a secret military installation; it just looked like any other government building. There was dark-gray carpet on the floors, pictures of past and current presidents and top military officials on the walls to break up the white paint, and several photo-graphs of trees and ponds. *But overall nothing screams secret*, he thought sarcastically and smiled.

As he walked the long corridors and turned the dozens of corners he concluded were designed to confuse them all, he noticed that every hall had a camera. After a while he gave up trying to remember the way in, and the group came to yet another hall with a single door. An escort opened it and ushered everyone inside. The floor was covered in the same gray carpets, but there was a large, darkly stained rectangular table centered along the length of the room.

Leather office chairs were pushed in all around the table, and the far wall held a built-in television monitor that took up the entire top half of the wall from end to end. There was crown molding along the ceiling and a row of florescent lights that spanned the length of the room. Bradshaw noted there were three built-in cameras, and they were triangular in spacing. One was on each corner of the far ceiling, and another was directly overhead, centered with the end of the table.

The far corners each held a door that was closed for the moment. "Someone will be with you shortly," one of the escorts said, pulling Bradshaw out of his internal evaluation, and walked out of the room, closing the door behind him. There were five others in the room with Bradshaw. Two were women, and the others were men. One woman had her blond hair pulled up into a large bun and wore a dark-blue suit. The other one was also blond and had a very short haircut. Her hair reached just past her ear lobe, and she was dressed in a purple-and-white skirt suit.

Two of the men were of fairly average size and build with brown hair, Bradshaw noted, and one was a bit shorter than him with red hair and a slim build.

"Hi," the redhead said, holding his hand out to Bradshaw after he entered the room. "Tom Davis."

"Andre Bradshaw." The two shook hands, and the others felt compelled to introduce themselves as well. One was Gereled Litebee, and the other was Harald Torstal. The women were Candace Frankford and MaryAnn Cooper.

Thirty-Seven

Strangers Among Us

Shortly after their informal introductions, a large group entered the room from both sides of the corner doors. Some were in military uniforms. Most were air force, Bradshaw noted, while others wore civilian attire. In total, the additions made eight males and six females. There wasn't time for introductions, because a male in uniform began speaking the minute they entered the room.

"Good morning, everyone. If we could all take our seats, I'd like to begin."

Bradshaw knew he was a senior officer—he could see one star along the shoulders indicating such—and the man was obviously on the losing end of his battle against hair loss. Bradshaw would have to face that battle someday, so he'd preempted it by shaving his head when he turned twenty-eight in response to what he thought was a receding hairline. It was the first of many changes in his life, including his military retirement and a rigorous workout routine that prepared him for his special-agent entry examination. He found that more and more women were attracted to his new look, and he vowed to keep it indefinitely.

Everyone took his or her seat at once, and the television monitor came to life. The news displayed a growing crowd of protesters just outside the facility parameters. They asked questions about the broadcast that many were no doubt wondering, such as, "Who were they?" and "What did they mean about farming our resources, and this time around?"

They introduced a solar scientist who discussed the Milky Way and its closest galaxy neighbors. He affirmed parts of the transmission, stating, "The distance mentioned during the transmission does exist, and the resident star is currently a dim replica of its former glory."

The scientist further explained, "Its behavior is not unlike that of other stars of this age that have been observed, and the possibility of it imploding is more a matter of time rather than fact. It's possible," he continued, "that the message could have more truth to it than the government is willing to share."

On that note, the general changed the scenery to a photo of a female airman. Everyone sat up a little straighter.

"This is Major Lillian Waters. She was pronounced dead on arrival at an area hospital less than two weeks ago after entering a dry cleaner down the street from Andrews Air Force Base, where she worked as an intelligence analyst. Autopsy results suggest something other than human is responsible for her death."

At his pause, a woman in civilian clothing said, "Now perhaps there isn't a connection as some speculate, but her death was less than a week after the increase in solar activity began. Consequently, we are searching for her missing or hiding husband. It is likely that he saw or heard something. During the autopsy, it was discovered that Major Waters was pregnant, and it is unlikely her husband is the father."

Before Bradshaw could really wonder, a picture of a young fetus still attached to its umbilical cord dominated the screen. It was fairly small, and...Bradshaw blinked several times and moved his head toward the screen to be sure he was seeing what he thought he saw. The fetus was...green?

Bradshaw's eyes grew to bulging as he recognized the skin tone's similarity to the beings he'd seen at the conference.

"Wait a minute," he interrupted. "Are you saying what happened last night was legitimate? That we could be facing war with an..." It was hard to say. "Alien world?"

"Not world. Beings of a dying planet," someone answered.

"Vagabonds," another added.

Bradshaw was too far past reality to identify who was speaking. It sounded feminine though.

"This suggests," she continued, "that Major Waters was in close contact and possibly providing military intelligence to at least one of them."

"That isn't likely," another person in uniform said defiantly. "Major Waters was a dedicated airman. If she provided anything, it was done without her knowledge. Her scans never suggested a breach in allegiance."

"What she did or didn't do," the general interrupted, "is not the point here. She is dead. We must focus on the threat at hand. We are more than likely being targeted because of our past history with them."

Bradshaw was numb. *Past history—what is he talking about?* "We must take this threat seriously because this isn't the first time they have visited our world, Captain Frankford?"

The blonde with the bun spoke as the picture of a little girl was put onto the screen. She was perfectly healthy, wearing a purple-and-white ruffled dress. There were several gasps throughout the room. The little girl looked almost identical to the summit creatures. The only difference was her ears. They were shaped more humanlike, and both her arms and legs could be seen. Her limbs depicted a swirl that Bradshaw was sure every one of them must have had.

"I believe they have been conducting research to identify their compatibility with our world and our species. I was assigned to the READY project."

"Ready?" someone asked.

"Research and development of extraterrestrial intelligence through analyzing and developing the youth born of interspecies relations." *They sure as hell know how to come up with some acronyms. How the hell does all that equal READY?* Bradshaw wondered.

"Four days ago," Frankford continued, "our facility in New Mexico was breached by a group of humans claiming to represent her parents." She gestured to the screen. "We lost twelve agents that night and have had to shut down the facility for repairs.

"Our attempts at retrieving the child were blocked by the same sort of signal used during the summit," said the general. The room was silent. "There are more pieces to this puzzle," he added after a moment. As he spoke, manila folders were being passed throughout the room.

"Feel free to review those at your leisure. Our objective today is threefold. First, we must find Mr. Waters and identify his connection, if any, to these creatures. Secondly, we must filter the recorded signal and pinpoint its possible origin. Our final goal is to identify the most effective way to deliver the serum without physical contact. The president needs a Hail Mary if they turn out to be hostile."

Serum? Bradshaw planned to review that folder thoroughly.

"Mr. Bradshaw, I believe your experts will prove helpful in the search for Mr. Waters. Mr. O'Brian and Mr. Davis, you will work on the signal. Ms. Cooper and Captain Frankford will work together with my staff here to develop this serum further. Any questions you have are to be addressed to Mr. Buccum," the general explained. One of the men who accompanied him into the room raised his hand. He was a dark-skinned man with short hair and broad shoulders.

"And I am to be made aware of your progress every twelve hours for the next thirty-two." With that, he got up and left the room. He was followed by only three of the people who accompanied him in. Bradshaw, like many others, was shocked by it all and said nothing while quickly reviewing the contents of the folder, when suddenly the reality of the general's words sunk in. He picked up the folder and stood.

"Headed to the airport?" Buccum asked, moving toward him.

"Yes, I thought I'd start at ground zero."

"That's fine, but the folder stays here."

Bradshaw froze. "What. How am I—"

Buccum handed him an SD card. "You are only to view that in a secure area."

"Understood," Bradshaw replied and walked out the same door he had entered. An armed guard was waiting and escorted him back to the airfield. Bradshaw thought it strange that he was still required to be escorted all the way back to the boarding platform. *My knowledge of the current situation should be enough to earn me an independent walk. I mean, what if I had to use the bathroom, for crying out loud.*

As it turned out, the airport had a lounge dedicated to Paradise Ranch passengers. It was equipped with food, bathrooms, and secure meeting areas. So Bradshaw pulled out his laptop and popped the SD card in. While he waited, he enjoyed a ham-and-cheese sandwich with a caffeinated beverage. Afterward, he dove into work. It wasn't long before he regretted that meal, because the images that popped up had him searching for a trash can to vomit in.

The mutilated bodies of aliens that dominated the screen were enough to give a person nightmares. As Bradshaw regained his composure, he decided to review the reports individually and only as needed. The first report he opened was titled Security Detail. There were five pale-green headshots. The next page depicted a picture of the entire body without clothing. They were definitely male. The strange shape of their genitals was not enough to change his recognition of their gender.

Dissected bodies followed the photos. Two of them had most of their insides taken out, while the others only had theirs labeled. Even the heads and faces were skinned and sliced in half. It was strange to see the insides of these creatures. Their livers looked like inflated almonds, and their position in the body was odd.

"They must have very low oxygen on their home world," Bradshaw said aloud.

The hearts were easy to spot, and again Bradshaw was puzzled because they were of average size and shape but oddly positioned, and there were two. Everything else was so similar to a human's that Bradshaw could identify them without the labels. *They're just all in the wrong places*, he thought.

The next report was labeled Council. It held ten head shots. Some had hair on their foreheads like the ones at the summit, and Bradshaw knew instantly that it was a distinction of their genders. The naked body that followed only depicted subtle differences.

It resembled a human female, only the chest and genitals were different. A pattern of colors wrapped around the bodies and extended from the navel and ran throughout, but did not touch the face, hands, or feet. It included every inch of skin in its path. The only indicator used to identify the breast was the small rosebud nipple protruding from the bump. The vagina had about four different slits in it and reminded Bradshaw of an onion.

On the following page, the top half of the body was cut open with vital organs labeled. The vagina lips were pealed back like a daylily to reveal a perfectly normal-looking clitoris. The next dissected body was the hardest for Bradshaw to look at. It had been sliced opened and peeled back delicately throughout.

Her midsection was missing everything and was labeled uterus. With those words, he'd had enough and closed the folder. Bradshaw moved to close the file completely, believing he would find something back in Washington that could help, but saw something that stopped him instantly. Weapons, he reads.

Opening the file revealed several dozen alien weapons and the humans who died by them. There were strange-looking guns, knives, rods, and staffs. There were disks, swords, and oddly colored and shaped weapon cartridges. The explanation accompanying the weapons was no comfort to his mind as he saw all the bodies of dead agents and government employees. Many of them must have died before they even hit the ground, because there was simply nothing there. There were giant holes where vital organs used to be. Bradshaw was glad his stomach was already empty.

At the very end of the file, there were pictures of what must have been left of the aliens' spaceship, because it was just a charred capsule. The only thing recoverable was a faint signal that lasted roughly fifteen minutes after US authorities discovered the ship. It had the same underlying signature of the signal recorded at the summit. The pages that followed were of numerous reports of strange sightings and unidentified flying objects.

Bradshaw sifted through them all until he came to a recent report about an abandoned vehicle found at a city park in Florida. Its engine had inexplicably experienced a total system failure and was not responsive even after roughly 95 percent of its components were replaced. A silver cylinder object half an inch long and a few centimeters in diameter with a rounded point was found sticking out of the rear bumper. It was lodged all the way through the frame. The same type of radiation that was found on the charred spaceship was emanating from the entire vehicle. The rear half of the frame looked like charred coal under the body.

Bradshaw felt like he'd found the Holy Grail and instantly booked a flight to Ruidoso, New Mexico. When he arrived, however, he was disappointed to learn that the owner of the vehicle still hadn't come forward. He decided to track down the park ranger who discovered it and inquire about its owner as well as the condition of the vehicle when found. As it turned out, the owner, a woman named Sarah Middleton, had reported it missing while on vacation, because her neighbor came home from work one day to find it gone. Bradshaw's investigation led him to a college fraternity in Florida and a student named Jennifer Braxton. He wanted to know who these people were and exactly what had taken place in that car.

Thirty-Eight

FORGOTTEN

Jennifer lay there exhausted and frustrated. She was at her wit's end with these beings and just wanted to go home. *What the hell did he mean by, "The answer to that question no longer applies"?* she wondered angrily. *How difficult can it be to make a decision? This is worse than waiting for Congress to decide on a national budget. I should march right up to Sariah and demand that she release me or kill me,* she reasoned, sighing. A shower would be easier.

After showering, Jennifer went into the closet and just stood there. She stared at the unbelievably large selection of clothing with mouth agape. After regaining her composure, she reached out and grabbed the first thing she saw. It was a peach-and-silver sleeveless dress. It had thick rope straps and a small ruffle around the bust. *It's beautiful,* she thought, *and certainly over the top. But Lu would definitely think it appropriate if I turned up in this rather than sweats.*

She laughed and returned the dress and then continued looking. Every piece was more beautiful than the last, and everything still had a tag. Jennifer assumed it was a phenomenon limited to the undergarments, but seeing all the brand-new items in her closet just piqued her curiosity. *Some day one of them is going to have to explain how an alien race can afford all this crap,* she thought.

In the end, Jennifer went back to the peach-and-silver dress. When she removed it this time, she noticed an out-of-place bag on the floor. Curious, she reached down and opened the bag after placing it on the bed. It held the keys to her rental car, the remaining cash, and the ID she'd put into her pocket to get through security faster at the airport. She hadn't wanted a repeat of her last encounter with security.

"Well, at least I know they aren't thieves," she said aloud, putting the things back in the closet. Jennifer wasn't surprised to see the female outside her door, but she was annoyed at the need for her presence, particularly when the guard looked at her attire and smiled approvingly.

"Elanah," she said, holding her hand out in greeting. Jennifer was reluctant but thought it rude not to shake it...even if the woman was an alien.

"Jennifer," she said, reaching out.

"So where to?"

"The cafeteria and then Sariah. I need to speak with her."

"As you wish." The women turned for the elevator.

The cafeteria reminded Jennifer of a huge food court in a mall. There was something from every corner of Earth. It was difficult for her to decide. Some of the available combinations she'd never even known were possible. In the end, she settled for a burger and followed Elanah to a seat near one of the television monitors. Although she could see several from where she sat, they were all tuned into the same program: a live broadcast of the world economic summit.

Jennifer understood the general point of the summit but never paid attention to it—because no matter what they decided, she still had to dig deep when it came to paying for things. It didn't matter what country she lived in. *I guess their finances are affected by it somehow.* She really could not think of another reason they would care about the summit. As she began to eat, another thought occurred to her. "Is there anything here from Elquin?"

"Very little," Elanah responded cheerfully. "A few teas and pastries. Our bodies are adaptable to the food combinations Earth offers. Do you like tea?"

"Some t—" Jennifer stopped midword; she was frozen stiff. The burger fell onto the plate, and her eyes grew about two inches. She was looking intently at the television monitor. The summit was now broadcasting a message from the Elquin council. Jennifer recognized some faces from past visions, but there were so many of them now.

It was difficult for her to focus on the words spoken because she couldn't get past the number of Elquins she saw. Then she noticed Vishnu, and his earlier words rang in her ears: "We wish to share it with you," he'd said. But he'd never mentioned what would happen if the humans did not accept them.

"Forty-eight hours," the one in front was saying, and everyone around the two women rejoiced.

Jennifer was frozen stiff until the broadcast ended. For several moments, Elanah said nothing, and then at the sound of Jennifer's continued breathing, she asked, "Are you all right?"

"Yes…I…I think I'm OK." She thawed out her fingers and lifted the burger once more. The rest of the meal was completed in silence. She couldn't stop the thought patterns racing through her head.

If they're coming out, then there is no need for me to be here. Tomahbare saw my last dream, so they can prepare themselves, and I can move on. If the world now knows about them, then my knowledge of them will not be an issue. They won't have to worry about me telling anyone what I know, and they can always find me if they need to. I'm sure Lu's worried sick about me, and I suppose I'll have no choice but to press charges against Zackary now, but most of all, I can get my classes in order and—

"Did you still want to see her?" Elanah asked, interrupting Jennifer's internal monologue.

"What?"

"Sariah. You said you wanted to see her. Have you changed your mind?"

Jennifer looked down and noticed her meal was done. "No, let's go."

◆ ◆ ◆

Sariah stood next to Ahdortee, waiting for Tomahbare to finish his conversation with Ryous.

"Forty-eight hours will not be enough time to have everyone battle ready. Don't worry, Ahdortee. The council has not issued the order. I believe they're hoping for a diplomatic solution. Besides, if it comes down to combat, I'm sure it will not matter what form you're in."

Ahdortee smiled. "And it will confuse them to see their own attacking."

Just then, Locknoff walked past them.

"Perhaps they will die faster," Ahdortee said, looking in his direction of travel.

"You shouldn't be so hard on him, you know."

Ahdortee looked at Sariah like she'd insulted her. "A week ago, he would have killed any human who looked at him wrong. Now she shows up, and he's prancing about like a young one with his first crush."

"He doesn't prance, and he can't help it, Ahdortee, any more than you would be able to. It will take time for us all to adjust to this planet's pull on our emotions. You should try to be happy for him. Everyone else is."

"I doubt that," Ahdortee responded sarcastically. "I can think of at least one other who is not happy with the situation."

Sariah lifted her brow briefly and then sighed. "Feleet has never been his heart song. She will simply have to accept his decision."

"Feleet has never been able to simply accept his decision. I cannot imagine her doing so now."

"You may be right, Ahdortee, but I don't know how she'll be able to ignore it. He seems happy, and the human's hold on him is more than skin deep." Ahdortee frowned, but before Sariah could ask about her reaction, Tomahbare spoke.

"Please forgive my interruption, Ahdortee. Are you ready, Sariah?"

"Yes." She looked at Ahdortee. "I wouldn't worry about it. I'm sure things will work themselves out."

Sariah and Tomahbare then left in search of Vishnu. It didn't take long for them to find him. He'd been heading to the medical bay.

"Why don't we step into my office," Tomahbare suggested. His office was similar to Locknoff's. Though it was much bigger and there were more comfortable chairs, the biggest difference was the water feature. Behind one of the marble walls was a huge waterfall with dim lighting. A rectangular marble tub with small plants collected and recycled the water.

"Sariah," Vishnu began the moment he was seated, "if I bond with someone other than the human, will my need for her subside?"

Sariah was mortified; she couldn't answer.

"Sariah," he prompted.

"Yes, Vishnu. Medically speaking, yes, but why would you want to do such a thing? She is your heart song. How could you even stand to suggest such a thing? And what were you thinking at council? Why would you want to send her away or make her forget about you?" Sariah was emotional by the time she'd stopped ranting. Vishnu waited to see if she had any more to say before answering.

"Sariah, I have agreed to become high council."

"But——" He held up a hand to silence her, shaking his head.

"We have moved forward with plans to make Earth our home, and she does not want to be here."

"Yes, but you have to——"

"Sariah," Vishnu interrupted sternly. "I have made my decision."

Sariah took a deep breath. "And have you considered the hearts of the one who is to replace her?"

"Leave that to me."

"Vishnu," Tomahbare said worriedly, "would you deny another the opportunity to find a heart song?"

Vishnu was quiet for a moment. "The decision's been made." He then looked at Sariah. "How soon will you be ready to remove her memory?"

"We are ready now, but—"

"Sariah," Tomahbare interrupted, placing a hand on her shoulder. She looked at him with pleading eyes, but he shook his head. She closed her eyes and a tear fell down her cheek. Sariah exhaled audibly. "We will move forward immediately, High Council."

"I am not high council yet."

"Perhaps, but your actions say otherwise, Vishnu." Another tear fell, and she turned her head toward the wall.

Without another word, Vishnu stood. Tomahbare got up and walked over to the door.

"Please excuse me a moment," he said and stepped out into the hall. Sariah and Vishnu looked after him with raised eyebrows until they heard him speaking to someone. Vishnu sighed. "Sariah, there is much to be done. Please do not waste any more time worrying about me."

"I don't understand how you can be so—"

"Sariah," Tomahbare interrupted, his body halfway out the door, "your presence is requested."

Both she and Vishnu walked to the door. Tomahbare held out a hand as Sariah walked past him, touching Vishnu's chest lightly. His brows lowered briefly. "Just Sariah," he said and closed the door.

"Am I a prisoner then?" Vishnu asked, slightly annoyed. "I have made my decision."

"I think it would be wise to allow Sariah an opportunity to address those who have come to call before leaving," Tomahbare insisted. Vishnu's expression became one of suspicion, and he looked at the now-closed door intently.

"Who was that?"

"No one of particular importance. So are you sure of your decision then, Master Vishnu?"

"Undoubtedly."

"Then I will assist Sariah as needed."

"Good. Inform me when the process is complete."

He left shortly thereafter, and Tomahbare headed to medical. When he reached the observation area, Sariah was explaining the procedure to Jennifer.

"It is the council's decision and the only safe way to proceed, but because it will affect your ability, you must decide for yourself."

"And the alternative?"

"You stay here until an agreement can be reached between our worlds. You don't have to decide now, Jennifer. You may take all the time you need," Sariah insisted.

"How long did you say?"

"Roughly three years."

Jennifer was quiet for a long moment, contemplating. Tomahbare interrupted her thoughts by suggesting she wait a couple of days before deciding.

"No," she responded much too loudly. "It's fine. Let's do it now."

"Are you sure, Jennifer?" Sariah asked.

Jennifer looked at Tomahbare, who only stared back blankly. "Yes."

"Then let's get started."

◆ ◆ ◆

Jennifer lay down on the table and closed her eyes. Tears ran down the side of her head as she thought of Sariah's words when she finally came out of that office. Jennifer given her an ultimatum.

"Let me go, or kill me," Jennifer ordered. "You clearly don't need me around anymore, so please...let me go back to my life."

"I'm sorry, Jennifer, but killing you is not an option I'm prepared to consider. But if you are determined to leave us, there is another course of action to take."

"What course of action?"

"One that will leave you without your memory."

"Let's do it."

"Please, Jennifer, let me explain."

Jennifer's brows lowered, and her optimism dwindled as Sariah continued. "Your ability makes it impossible to use the techniques developed specifically for the orb, so a completely different approach was necessary."

"O...K..." Jennifer exaggerated the word, raising a brow.

"We've created a device that can be placed directly on the frontal lobe of your brain. It's a thin web about a quarter of the thickness of a strand of human hair." Sariah pulled something out of her pocket and placed it into Jennifer's hand. It was a tiny square web.

"It will be encoded with a signal that informs the frontal lobe to discard sought-after information pertaining to us as erroneous or irrelevant. In time, any memory you have of us will ultimately be lost. Even new information your brain receives regarding us will be discarded when you try to recall it." The blank stare Jennifer gave Sariah had her explaining further. "For example," she continued, "if the barrier was already in place and you tried to recall this conversation at a later time, you would not be able to remember a word spoken."

Comprehension covered her features, but Jennifer was still confused by Sariah's tone.

"I don't see the down side here," she commented sarcastically.

"It will not only affect your ability to remember us, Jennifer, but because of your subconscious connection to...us, so many of your visions will include us. It may affect how and if you continue to have foresight at all, until the web is completely absorbed."

Jennifer was taken aback. For as long as she could remember, there was never a possibility of life without her dreams. Not even when her father gave her those pills. If Sariah's statement proved true, she would no longer need to prove her sanity to people. She would never again have to explain why she sometimes took an umbrella on warm, sunny days, and she would never have another awkward moment around family or friends. Her life would just be...normal. As normal as any other red-blooded American.

But she wasn't normal. She never had been, and now she just might have to be. How was she going to get through this? Her gift was the most interesting part of her, and it had literally saved her life and the lives of people she knew as well as many she didn't. More recently, her lack of sight almost led to her own death in addition to Cara's.

Jennifer sighed internally and shifted her thought pattern to Vishnu. She would never see him again. She wasn't sure how she felt about being with him, but something about the idea of never seeing him again made her feel empty, so she pulled his face to the center of her mind's eye, first his human and then his Elquin features, and just looked at them over and over again. Before long, everything went dark.

Thirty-Nine

Deadline

Dressed in training gear, Vishnu walked into the observation bay to see a look of despair on Sariah's face. Tomahbare rubbed her shoulders encouragingly. As he entered further, Deverah and Elious left the bay in search of other tasks.

"Is she..."

"She's fine," Sariah assured him, motioning toward a sleeping Jennifer. Vishnu walked over to her, somewhat surprised that she wasn't in white scrubs, and took her hand. He leaned forward and pulled it onto his chest.

He then closed his eyes, and the room filled with the sound of his humming hearts. After several minutes, he opened them and caressed Jennifer's face with his other hand. Vishnu moved close to her ear and whispered, "I'm so sorry, my heart. I will love you forever." He kissed her gently on the lips and stood. After replacing her hand to the table gently, the humming turned to a dull buzz before stopping altogether.

Vishnu walked over to Sariah, who was now in tears, and said, "She may be in possession of a large sum of money that will need explaining. When will she be transferred?" He sniffed.

"Within the hour."

"Good. Be sure to remove the tracker. The deadline draws near, and our ships will begin entering the atmosphere soon. She is not to leave the hospital until tomorrow evening." Sariah nodded, and he continued on his way with a look of determination about his features.

◆ ◆ ◆

Bradshaw was frustrated to no end when his plane touched down in New Mexico. His deadline was fast approaching, and the only thing he'd found out was that Jennifer Braxton had not returned from a grievance leave she'd requested from school. The oddity of it was that all but one other student had returned to school. He felt like this investigation was getting him nowhere fast.

On a more positive note, however, New Mexico was where Mr. Waters was last seen and where his wife's funeral was held. So if he had an opportunity to investigate both before being called back to Paradise Ranch, he may have inadvertently hit the jackpot. With that in mind, Bradshaw tried to be positive and not let all the side conversations he heard about alien invasions get to him on his way to the rental-car pickup.

"Hello, sir, how may we help you?" the attendant asked in a cheerful voice.

"I need a car."

"Will that be compact, economy, luxury, truck—"

"I'll take whatever is closest to the exit," Bradshaw interrupted.

The rental process took less time than he'd expected, and he soon found his way to Cara Johnson's house. It wasn't his ultimate destination but was close enough to his route that he wouldn't be delayed much. When he arrived, the women were more than willing to speak with him.

"She didn't know who the car belonged to," Nancy Peterson explained. "She was kidnapped by someone after being horribly beaten by her boyfriend."

"Someone."

"Yeah, the police are still looking into it, but *I think* it was someone who had a grudge on Gamma Sigma Phi."

"Why is that?"

"Because her boyfriend, Zackary Mason, is a Sigma."

"Did she have any admirers other than Zackary Mason?"

"No."

"And you have no idea where she went?"

"No. She said something about talking to one of Zackary's ex-girlfriends, but nothing about where or who she was."

"Would you like more coffee?" Brenda interrupted, coming toward the table with a fresh pot.

"No, thank you. I really must be going," Bradshaw replied as he replaced the legal pad in his bag.

"Hey, what did he steal, anyway?" Nancy asked.

"I'm sorry?" Bradshaw responded, confusion clear across his features.

"That man you guys picked up the other night," Nancy said, gesturing with her chin to the picture half exposed in his bag. Bradshaw pulled the photograph out and turned it around.

"Him?" he asked, confused.

"Yeah, you guys picked him up in the casino parking lot at the Chess Ling Inn, right?"

Bradshaw lowered his eyebrows, put the photo of Taren Waters on the table, and slid it across to her with one finger. "This man was arrested at the Chess Ling Inn?"

"Yeah, almost a week ago."

"How do you know it was actually him?"

"Because we literally ran into him while he was running from security. He actually had the gall to kiss Jennifer when she tried to help him up, and the actual takedown was one to remember. I don't think anyone will be forgetting that scene for a while."

"Hmm," Bradshaw responded, deep in thought. "You say he kissed your friend?"

"Yeah, it was really weird too."

"How so?"

Nancy took a sip of coffee. "Well," she said, putting the cup down, "she'd never seen him before that moment, but it was like she couldn't control herself or something. He kissed her, said thanks, and then ran out into the parking lot. He knocked a couple of your guys out and then was tackled and dragged away in a SWAT truck." Brenda listened intently.

"SWAT truck," Bradshaw repeated to himself. Nancy nodded and returned the photo to his bag. "I'm sorry, but I can't discuss him with you in detail at this time, ma'am. He's still under investigation." Bradshaw then thanked the women for their cooperation and left.

After an hour and a half of telephone conferences and interviews, Bradshaw sat patiently in his vehicle outside the Chess Ling Inn, watching his computer screen closely. He was awaiting a file transfer from local police. He'd spoken to the FBI and learned that no one from the state or federal government had picked up Mr. Waters. He'd also spoken to Mr. Buccum, who relayed General Henley's orders for him to remain where he was for the moment and follow up on any leads he'd uncovered. Bradshaw was aware that due to recent developments, the United Nations would be holding an emergency session sometime in the near future.

Why that session was necessary became clear when he saw the news. The media was airing a stream of reports that astronomers picked up several unidentified ships orbiting in or around Earth's gravitational field. It was like they'd come out of nowhere, and people could see them through telescopes. Scientists mentioned that the naked eye would write them off as really bright stars. Satellite photos could not detect anything outside of Earth's gravitation field, but those within could be seen clearly.

The low beep indicated the arrival of a new e-mail. After confirming what he discussed with local police investigators, Bradshaw decided to check out local hospitals as well. *It's unlikely she made it very far, based on these photos*, he thought, viewing the message contents the local police sent him. There were copies of photos from the scene at Anna's home, where Jennifer's rental car was recovered.

"But who killed him?" Bradshaw asked no one as he looked intently at the headless body of Zackary Mason. "How is it possible that no one saw anything? It's a neighborhood, for crying out loud. What about the neighborhood watchers?"

As he continued through the photos, an uneasy feeling came over him. Something about the scene was familiar. He couldn't quite place it, but he knew he'd seen it before. It wasn't the decapitated man on the lawn or the trail of blood along the ground. It wasn't the missing victim or her blood splattered all over the car—it was the house. The end unit was barely there in every one of the photos.

Rummaging through his bag, Bradshaw found the disk he was given at Paradise Ranch. A quick scan of the immediate area, and he felt confident opening the files where he sat. Placing the disk into his computer, Bradshaw went directly to the file titled Offspring. The first few pictures were of the dead alien fetus that was pulled out of the council member. Scanning past them quickly, he came across Lillian Waters's fetus and the missing alien child. When he came to the woman of interest, he stopped.

Anna Desai: mother of the only known living offspring. A former friend of the Waters, she broke off that friendship and all contact with the Waters family several years ago, or so it is assumed. Due to the nature of her child's parentage, her life habits, and those of her acquaintances, she remains under surveillance as a measure of national security.

A photo of Anna followed the inscription. She was a dark-skinned woman with long, curly locks. A picture of her current home was also included. *The same home in the other photos...or a very similar one*, he thought. Moving closer to the screen, Bradshaw could see that a yellow-and-black bumblebee wind chime hung on the porch of both photos.

"No," he said aloud. "The exact same house." *What are the odds that two people would have the same house and the exact same wind chime in the exact same place?* He confirmed his suspicions by reviewing the address in the files.

"What were you doing there, Jennifer?"

Anna's file did not suggest that she and Zackary ever had any kind of relationship, so what was the connection here? He looked through the photos of the crime scene once more, following the nagging feeling that he was missing something obvious. The tea serving was for two, he remembered, and the rental car...Jennifer.

"She came here to meet with Anna...but why? And now Anna, Jennifer, and Taren Waters are missing."

He signed and removed the disk and then placed it into his pocket for the moment. Bradshaw got out of the car and went inside the hotel. Someone had to know something about Mr. Waters's whereabouts, because apparently he was arrested on the grounds here. By whom and for what reason didn't matter. His current location was all Bradshaw was interested in.

He walked up to the counter and asked to speak to the manager. He vaguely noticed the attendant, as his attention was diverted to one of the television monitors. A new summit was about to begin, and news crews were camped outside the stadium in London. Speculations ran wild as the media tried to guess at what was being said inside. Bradshaw shook his head and tried to pay attention to the task at hand.

◆ ◆ ◆

"Greetings, world leaders," the speaker began. The noise died down a bit in the large stadium. It was the only place readily available for such a large crowd, but London officials were not thrilled with the need of it. They welcomed the world leaders with promises of alterations before the Olympic summer games were to commence, knowing that after today it would be very difficult to change anything. The games were less than a year away, and they were already running behind.

Leaders from every established country around the globe were present, and even some who demanded attendance even though their independent status was still in question. It was unanimously decided that now was not the time for insignificant bickering.

"In order to be politically correct," the speaker continued, "let's refer to this gathering as the global conference. If necessary, in time we will vote on a more appropriate title." The continued silence allowed him to go on.

"We have gathered together in this place to discuss the threat to our world. For those of you who are unaware, let me remind you of the issue at hand."

The large octagonal shape of jumbo television screens looked like a theater and was centered high up in the stadium, replaying the alien broadcast for all to see. Upon its completion, every individual was quiet.

After the broadcast, a satellite photo of the visible ships was displayed. "Every corner of the globe will be able to look up and see these vessels as they enter our atmosphere," the speaker said. "There are twelve hours left on the deadline they've set. Unfortunately we——"

"That's because the Americans chose to keep the validity of the broadcast a secret until now," the representative from Moscow accused. Several others agreed, but before the US representative could address the accusations, the speaker intervened.

"The validity of their broadcast was made certain when the ships' images came into view. At their current rate of travel, these ships will be above our major cities within six hours. Can we please focus on the task at hand and save the blame game for another day?"

"Yes," the accuser whispered more to himself, and then he spoke a little louder. "We'll save it for our enslavement as we are all hauled off to do their bidding, and we will all remember then who was at fault." When no one else spoke up, the speaker continued.

"The timeline leaves little room for indecision. We must decide now if we are to share our world with these aliens or if we prepare ourselves for war."

"We do not know enough about our adversaries to fight," the Russian representative said with an emphasis on the word *we*.

"But that doesn't mean we are incapable of defending ourselves," the German president added.

"No, it doesn't," others agreed.

"Perhaps we should give them a demonstration of our defense capabilities," the representative from China offered.

"Is fighting the only answer?" the British prime minister asked. "I mean, surely they don't expect us to just hand over the planet. There has to be another way."

"We do not have enough information to determine another course of action to take at this time," the speaker interrupted. "Perhaps we should simply vote on a path and take it."

"It's not that simple," the Australian representative intervened.

"Perhaps…" The US representative spoke for the first time. "Perhaps we should consider a course of action that will buy us more time and allow us the opportunity to discover more about our opponent."

"How so?" the British representative asked.

"I suggest we comprise a small team to meet with the aliens. We can address their claims and request more time to make our decision."

"And who is to make up this team?" the Australian representative interrupted.

"The members are debatable, but their necessity is not. I think we can all agree that more time is necessary."

"Perhaps," the speaker said before anyone could debate that point, "but we must vote on the question at hand in the event our request is denied. What say you all? Do we fight, or do we open our world to the aliens?"

It took a total of fifty-three minutes before the votes were all tallied, but in the end, the majority vote was to defend Earth at all costs. After a quick recess, the delegates were ushered back inside to vote on a five-member team to represent Earth. The seemingly difficult task was fairly easy to decide, as volunteers came up short, many stating their need to prepare for the alternative. In the end, Earth's representatives were comprised of Germany, China, Russia, India, and the United States.

Forty

We Are Elquin

For the first time, reporters were allowed into the conference center. The five representatives were seated to the left of the speaker.

"Welcome," he began, looking intently at the cameras. "This is the Paladin Alliance," he said, gesturing to the closely seated panel. "They have been elected to represent humanity. We would like to extend an invitation to you, Elitar of Jai blood, to discuss your claims and the demands you have made of mankind. We will convene in this place at sunrise and look forward to your party's arrival."

Upon his silence, reporters began asking questions.

"What do these aliens want?"

"Are they preparing to fire at us?" another added.

"How can we protect ourselves?" asked another.

"Where do—"

"Ladies and gentlemen," the speaker interrupted. "Your questions are all valid, but I'm afraid we will not be able to address any of them until after our meeting tomorrow. We will set a news conference for shortly after that meeting, at which time your questions will be addressed in full. Please feel free to return then."

"But people of the world need answers," one of the reporters said with a heavy American accent.

"And they shall have them, just as soon as we do," the speaker responded, gesturing for security to escort the reporters out.

◆ ◆ ◆

Sariah sat comfortably in Tomahbare's arms, looking intently at the night sky. Her long, brown hair swayed slightly as she adjusted. She'd traded her usual white scrubs for a pair of denim jeans and a midnight-blue shirt that was gathered at the waist. It hung off her shoulders slightly and was fringed around the top. Tomahbare, however, wasn't so lucky. The white scrubs he wore as he sat holding Sariah complemented his dark-brown skin. The others surrounding them were in both native and human forms, and every one of them gazed at the sky above.

The ships became visible as the sun started to set, and Sariah found the sight breathtaking. She smiled as Tomahbare hugged her closer. "Did you think this day would ever come?"

Tomahbare inhaled deeply at the nape of her neck. Exhaling, he smiled. She smelled like roses. "All too well, my love…all too well."

"Hmm," she said.

Tomahbare inhaled again, slowly this time, and exhaled before continuing. "And yes," he said knowingly, "I think this is the perfect time to expand our family. I don't believe we'll have to hide much longer."

"Really?" Sariah responded, turning to face him. She didn't even try to hide the excitement in her voice. She'd considered the subject a lot lately, often bringing it up to him, but knowing the struggle their world faced, she didn't force the subject.

"Really," he replied and pulled her closer for a kiss. They watched the ships well into the night, only resting when their eyelids drooped.

Just before dawn, the entire camp assembled. Everyone was at his or her workstation and stood ready as they watched the shuttles descended. The entire world was in audience as two ships descended from one of the spears above and entered the morning sky. The ten-minute trip seemed like a lifetime to Sariah. As she watched, she briefly recalled the pain of her parents' struggle as well as that of so many others who'd paid the ultimate price for this moment to arrive. She exhaled slowly when the shuttles touched down, looking intently at the screen in the medical bay.

◆ ◆ ◆

Thousands were gathered along the perimeter that cradled the convention center. People from all over the world wanted to see the aliens. Police moved into position by the hundreds to block the growing crowd. One row of officers faced the crowd, while two more formed a wall furthering the distance between where the visitors would be passing by and the crowd.

All was silent as the first Elquins appeared. There were thirty of them in total. Ten formed a perimeter line across the front of the shuttles, while others took up positions to the left, right, and rear of the council. The four council members were dressed differently than the rest, who wore black cargo pants and dark-green sleeveless shirts. The council had on traditional blue robes. They stopped several feet short of the building's entrance to address the men and women who came to greet them.

"I am Elitar of the Jai bloodline. We," he said with his arms stretched out slightly, "are Elquin. We have come to answer your invitation. Shall we begin the discussions?"

Sariah looked on and noticed that the alliance members consisted of two women and three men. Each was dressed professionally and wore a look of determination.

"We were not expecting such a large party," the US member said. He was about five feet nine with broad shoulders and dark-brown hair.

His brown eyes depicted the surprise his expression would not allow. As Elitar opened his mouth to respond, a loud commotion caused everyone to turn.

"Die, alien scum," a man yelled after clearing the final pair of legs in front of him. He immediately lifted his arm to throw a glass bottle half filled with a colorless liquid in the direction of the Elquins. Before he could completely rotate his arm, he was taken to the ground so fast that the bobby even had time to catch the jar before it hit the ground. Sariah gasped where she stood.

"Yes," Elitar responded, returning his attention to the representatives. "Well, any act of violence against me or any of my colleagues here will be considered an act of war. Nesset," he called out.

Nesset looked at one of the fighters, who bowed his head and headed into the building with the others. Sariah breathed a sigh of relief as the television screen switched from an outside view to one of the inside. The broadcast now was being provided by the council guard, who accompanied the others inside the building.

Nesset was one of two females to join Elitar and Bathmantu. Sariah thought both her and Skyke could have taken lessons from Zeeporah in the adoration of their crowns for this occasion. She focused as the guest of honor followed the host into a large meeting area. Although there were several cameras visible, no press was allowed inside the building.

The alliance members each stood next to a chair as the American introduced them.

"This," he said, gesturing to the representative from China, "is Miss Feng Teoh." Feng stood about five two and wore her dark hair pulled back and up above the collar of her dress. Her eyes were dark gray; they swept over the seven fighters standing along the far wall briefly before returning to the council before her.

"Standing next to her is Mr. Hadumar Engel." Hadumar was a tall man standing six eight, with short, brown hair and green eyes. He had a star-shaped scar above his right eyelid that was more than noticeable.

"I am Dwight Robinson, and this," he said, gesturing to the woman on his left, "is Ms. Kamala Nizami." Kamala was close to five five and had so much hair that the bun she wore stuck out about six inches from her head. Her light-brown eyes were complemented by the tiny black-and-golden bindi she wore.

"This," Dwight said, motioning to the representative from Russia, "is Mr. Mikhail Bazhukov." Mikhail stood about five nine. He had broad shoulders, blue eyes, and light-blond hair.

"We are the Paladin Alliance. Please feel free to take a seat, and we will begin." Dwight gestured to the chairs on the opposite side of the table. Elitar took a moment to look over each of them before he began.

"This is Bathmantu of the Myopi bloodline." Bathmantu moved behind a chair. "This is Skyke of the Whipki bloodline." Skyke took a chair also but did not sit. "This is Nesset of the Shkatie bloodline." When she moved behind a chair, he continued. "We are council masters of Elquin, and we gladly accept your invitation."

Without another word or gesture, they all sat. The Paladin Alliance followed the Elquin's lead.

"We have invited you here to discuss your transmission," Dwight announced.

"Yes," Elitar said with a nod.

"Well, we were wondering what you meant about this time around, and what exactly you would like to share with us."

Elitar leaned back slightly in his chair, and his eyes took on an expression that suggested he really didn't want to repeat himself. "Well, this time around means exactly that. When our attempts at negotiations failed, your seizure of our council was unprecedented, and that act alone warrants a hostile response.

"Although the event may or may not have been recorded in your world's histories, we are not here to discuss your crimes against our kind. We simply want to move forward. We would like your cooperation in averting a needless war and merging our worlds sooner rather than later. We need to begin protecting this planet from its ultimate fate, as it will surely face the same threat our world faces now."

"Crimes?" Feng interjected. "What crimes? We haven't committed any crimes against—"

"There is blood...precious blood on the hands of your parentage," Nesset interjected, frustration clear in her tone. "Your knowledge regarding the situation or lack thereof makes no difference. We have decided on your planet, so you can choose to join us—or face extinction." She inhaled deeply and then looked over the shocked expressions of the alliance before exhaling slowly.

"Now," she said calmly as if redirecting a child. "We are prepared to offer a compromise in exchange for your cooperation, so let us now discuss this avenue, as the future of both our kinds depend on it."

"Just what are you prepared to offer?" Dwight asked.

"The knowledge of who we are and where we've come from, for starters," Skyke said. "And the ability to make Earth strong enough to survive the death of its star."

"Really," Mikhail said skeptically. "I can see just how *essential* the information was for your world. Perhaps your efforts actually caused the destruction rather than preventing it. Now you want us to allow you access to our planet? I don't buy it."

As Bathmantu nearly began what Sariah knew would be a full-fledged temper tantrum, based on the slight shaking of his hands, Elitar spoke. "We addressed Elquin's problems the moment we became aware of them. Without our action, we surely would have perished long before now. Our actions to combat the threat began much like your own attempts, such as the reduction in greenhouse gases. The problem was that we were too late to devise a permanent solution."

"And you believe you have one?" Kamala asked, intrigued.

"We believe Earth can survive much longer with our help than without it," Bathmantu said.

"Ahh, so you don't have a solution, and you just expect us to let you move into our communities? Send your children to our schools, and shop in our malls?" Mikhail asked.

"We are an entire civilization," Skyke responded. "We would require the same respects as your tribesmen, among others, and full settlements around the globe."

"Settlements?" Dwight asked. "How big are we talking here?"

"Well, a—" Nesset began, but she was interrupted by a clearly disturbed Hadumar.

"Settlements! Schools! Communities! Are you serious?"

Bathmantu smiled slightly, thinking of his protest not so long ago.

"How about we discuss the fact that you have accused us of crimes we are not responsible for."

The loud impact of Bathmantu's fist slamming on the table had the attention of everyone, particularly those who watched the monitors alongside Sariah. "Humanity has sealed its fate. Choose now: extinction or peaceful cooperation."

"And if we decide to allow your kind to live among us," Dwight added, "what guarantee do we have that you won't try to exterminate us the minute we drop our defenses or even disagree with you about one thing or another?"

"None," Skyke said, emotionless, "but rest assured, we will hold true to our end of the bargain as long as you hold true to yours."

"Considering the reality that your entire race has committed to this venture, I can only assume that you've considered this course of action with a great deal of patience," Dwight said.

"What's your point?" Bathmantu asked.

Dwight looked at Elitar. "What you are asking us to do should be objectively considered."

Bathmantu huffed.

"Therefore," Dwight continued as if he hadn't noticed, "we require more time to reach a cultured decision before presenting you with a response."

"How much time?" Skyke asked.

"Three months."

"Too long."

"Six weeks," Feng suggested.

"Forty-eight hours," Bathmantu said.

"One month," Dwight countered.

"You have seven days," Elitar said with a finality that silenced everyone. The council stood in unison, and the alliance members did the same.

"Seven days is not enough time," Dwight said, an edge of frustration in his voice.

"Duly noted. We shall return in seven days for your final decision." Elitar turned for the door, and the seven fighters came to a position of attention.

After just two steps, Elitar stopped and added, "If you decide to fight, I suggest you consider what effects war will have on this planet. We will take it either way, but we would rather heal the wounds already inflicted than bandage new ones in the aftermath of an unnecessary catastrophe."

Without another word, he turned and led his party away. The fighters fell into place one after the other as the council passed them.

Sariah smiled as she watched them board the shuttle. Seven days was not a lot of time, but it was enough for the fleet to get adjusted to the new demands on their emotions. Putting Deverah in charge, she left the medical bay in search of Tomahbare. On the way to his office, she came across Vishnu. He'd walked past her hand in hand with Naeefah. They were smiling and seemed to be having trouble keeping their eyes off one another.

Sariah's eyes grew about two inches, and she gasped slightly. Vishnu noticed her and smiled as they passed her, bowing his head slightly. Sariah was so taken aback that she hadn't noticed Tomahbare standing there until after the third time he'd called her name. He then looked in the direction she'd been looking.

"Are you all right, love?"

"What...Oh, hi." She smiled.

"Are you all right?" he repeated, pulling her closer. "What did I miss?"

"Vishnu," she responded, shaking her head and looking up at him. "Tomahbare, I don't know if I'll be able to get through to him. She seems so happy with him. Maybe I should just..."

"Stop," he interrupted firmly and ran his fingers along her hairline, placing a loose strand behind her ear. "He'll come around. He isn't callous, you know. We will just have to help him better understand with time."

Sariah hugged him tightly. "Do you really think he'll be OK without *her*?"

He lifted her chin and looked into her eyes. "I'm certain of it."

"Is that an official reading then?" she asked with a chuckle. He smiled, hugged her tightly, and took her hand as they continued down the corridor. "I do not need an official reading to know how this will end. Much of it will depend on him. I suggest we allow him the opportunity to try, Sariah." He shook his head. "It could not have been easy for him to let her go, and we have no idea how things will turn out, but for tonight let's just focus on the peace."

◆ ◆ ◆

"You, sir," a man said, pulling Bradshaw's attention away from the monitors. The man was short and stocky. He had short, curly hair and gray eyes. The tag on his left breast pocket read Hostess Management: Steven.

"I'm sorry?" Bradshaw asked, sounding somewhat confused.

"I am Steven Bullock," the man repeated. "On-duty manager. How may I be of assistance?"

Bradshaw showed Steven his badge and said, "I'm looking for a man named Taren Waters. He was last spotted on the grounds here. Is there anything you can tell me about his whereabouts?"

"Please follow me," Steven replied and led him to his office. He sat behind the desk and started pushing buttons on the keyboard. "What was that name again?"

"Waters," Bradshaw responded. "Taren Waters."

"Waatterrss." Steven exaggerated the name as he typed each letter. After several moments, his brows lowered. "Hmm," he said. "I'm sorry, but the only thing I show here is a record of his check-in." Steven frowned. "It seems your Mr. Waters was only here a day." He squinted and moved closer to the screen. "There's nothing else. I don't know what to tell you, sir. It doesn't show him checking out, but that same room was later used for another party only four hours after his initial check-in." Bradshaw looked up. "There is no record of him being moved to another room or an explanation of why he left," Steven added.

"It seems there was some kind of disturbance here that day," Bradshaw said.

"Ahh," Steven replied knowingly, "that would explain it, then." He shook his head. "I can't give you any more information on the subject matter, sir. I'm afraid I wasn't here. You would need to speak to Feleet."

"Feleet?" Bradshaw asked, trying the name out.

"Yes. She was the manager on duty the night Mr. Waters checked in, and she may be able to help you more than I can."

"When will she be available?"

"She is scheduled to work this evening. I can leave a note for her to get in touch with you if you'd like, Mr. Bradshaw."

"Thank you, Steven, but that is not necessary. I would prefer to speak with her in person." He stood, shook Steven's hand, grabbed his briefcase, and turned for the door. "I will return later this evening."

Steven nodded, and they walked out of the office together.

Rather than leave, Bradshaw decided to make himself somewhat comfortable. *This Feleet will be here soon*, he thought, and he could use a comfortable place to rest for a bit. He checked in and retrieved his things from the rental car. When he had gotten somewhat comfortable in his room, Bradshaw pulled out the laptop and set it on the bed. To that he added folders, pads, pens, and pictures. Then he sat and began looking over it all once again. There was a connection here, and he was determined to find it.

Bradshaw searched, looking at the pieces of the puzzle, trying to put them together in his mind. After a few hours, he noticed a few things. Anna and Jennifer must have been working together, meeting in secret for some reason, he concluded. Zackary followed her there, angry about something. Flipping through a few more photos, he went on with his analysis. Lillian Waters and Anna Desi were friends, and aliens impregnated them both. He tapped his finger on the keyboard while looking at one of the photos and then shook his head and contin-ued. Anna's daughter was taken from a heavily guarded federal facility, and someone here blocked the signal from the convention. Here…on Earth, he thought.

His eyes grew wide as the writing on the wall became clear to him. *Taren Waters is aiding the aliens.* He must be—he and other humans like

Anna—and Jennifer must have been impregnated as well. Why else would these two be together? Perhaps Zack…His thought process was interrupted by a knock on the door. Bradshaw quickly retrieved the disk, put it into his pants pocket, and covered the things on his bed with the sheets before addressing his visitor.

Bradshaw opened the door to a lovely young lady with long, black locks. She looked like a supermodel. "You are seeking Taren Waters?" she asked.

Bradshaw raised a brow. "Feleet, I presume?" he asked, holding a hand out in greeting. He did not see any tags on her formfitting outfit.

"Come with me," she said and turned to walk down the hall, leaving Bradshaw to wonder about the common courtesy of the professional staff in this part of the United States.

He had to scramble a bit to get his shoes on, finally taking his eyes off her body long enough to focus. As he rounded the corner, Bradshaw felt a sharp pain in the back of his head, and the floor came up to hit him.

Everything went dark.

Elquin Glossary

Elquin. A planet only eight solar systems to the north of our own galaxy, losing the gravitational tug of war with its star. The star is nearing the end of its life cycle, and its gravitational pull is contentiously distorting the path of planets within its realm. Destruction is the future of this star and every planet within it. A shield generator was created to hopefully weaken the star's gravitational influence on the planet while protecting it from the star's harmful rays. Elquin scientists have been searching for natural resources that can run the generator full time. To date scientists have only found resources to fuel the generator, but they must be replaced more often than not. As the Elquin locate sustainable resources, the idea of reversing the star's gravitational pull on the planet is more of a dream than a reality. When Earth becomes an option for more than farming, the Elquin council moves forward with plans to make it home.

angolore beast. Tigerlike animals that travel in packs. They eat anything that moves and hunt only during dusk or dawn. They are easily confused by sudden high-pitched noises and/or when separated from the herd.

honored elders. Eldest bloodline members of a family, or the eldest survivors of a family in question.

Baiuyo (ba-oo-yo) Forest. A rain forest on Oororah-9 that provides the sustenance for its bordering villages.

Oororah-9. A planet that is visited by the Elquin council in an effort to negotiate terms for mining projects. The Oororah-9 council vote to end the agreement, but hold the Elquin council members hostage. This breach of trust leads to war and the ultimate release of Oororah-9 and the usage of its resources.

Dracora. A tribe bordering the Baiuyo forest, responsible for hosting the next Oororah-9 council leader. Dracora's prized member is Naubo (Na-oo-bo), the village chief's eldest daughter.

Maeeling's protectors. Maeeling is another word for princess. Her full-time protectors include Mickrey (Mc-ki-ree), Kuopo (ku-o-po), Chanta, and others who dedicate their lives to protecting her.

sharuba (sha-ru-bah) tree. When mature, this tree is a multicolored green swirl that dominates the Oororah-9 forest.

thorned tree: This tree gained its name from the spiky thorns that surround its branches and trunk.

merger. A three or more day process of joining the souls and body of a pair, bonding them as partners for life.

heart song. Humming or buzzing of the hearts as a reaction to the recognition of your ideal mate or true love.

heneums (he-nee-ums). Ceremonial drums played only in recognition of the highest honor.

shield generator. Planetary shield created by Elquin scientists to decrease the star's gravitational pull, only it became more useful as a way to reduce its harmful rays. The shield operates with generators powered with natural resources that are mined from other planets.

Resources needed to run the generator: cerium, detritus.

Paladin Alliance. A team developed to represent Earth in negotiations with the Elquin council.

Earth's initial investigation team members: Andre Bradshaw, Tom Davis, Gereled Litebee, Harald Torstal, Captain Candace Frankford, MaryAnn Cooper, General Henley, Travis Obrian, Mr. Buccum.

Chess Ling Inn. A hotel in New Mexico that catered to Elquins briefly after their initial arrival on Earth.

Known Staff Members

Feleet, master of planet affairs, who falls under the communication umbrella and manages room and board at the inn.

Kathrin Brown is one of the humans staffed at the Chess Ling Inn.

Steven Bullock is one of the human management staff members working in the Chess Ling Inn.

Moon cycle—one month
Lenior—one year
Pieleen—ten years
Turnier—one hundred years
Epochy—one thousand years
Bokorah—one million years

Ranking

Each specialty ranking system differs throughout Elquin. However, the highest ranking a specialist can earn is that of a master. High master is reserved for those in charge of a specific specialty group.

ERT rank structure:

Master
Officer
Recruit
Rookie
Trainee

Other known job specialties:

Medical-Master Officer
Officer
Senior Assistant
Guided Assistant
Assistant

*Communications
*Logistics

Ryous

*Culinary Artist—Master Artist

Chief Artist
Specialty Artist
Graduate

Aliases

Ahdortee—Angelia Sylvia
Porock—Gabriel Blackard
Jussalte—Thomas Blackard
Locknoff—Jonathan Grady
Vishnu—Taren Waters
Sariah—Sarah Middleton

Couples/Bonded Pairs

Stofena (sto-fee-nah) and Donoma—bonded
Sariah and Tomahbare—bonded
Locknoff and Anna
Taren and Lillian Waters—married on Earth
Vishnu and Youkoni—bonded
Zackary and Jennifer

Known Bloodlines (family members)

Ateenn
Grendore
Tisha
Albitroin
Grokni
Tocowie
Jai
Myopi
Shkati
Whipki

Known Farmed Planets—Elquin farmed a total of thirty-eight planets before settling on Earth.

Baitorus (ba-it-tor-ous)
Ratier
Tishod
Gala-4
Oororah-9
Starbane

Known Elquin Council Members

Bathmantu (Bath-man-too): male council member nominated after his service on Oororah-9.
Elitar (el-it-ar): male high council master
Locknoff (lock-n-off): male member of military interests
Madafski (med-af-ski): male scientist and council member
Nesset (ne-set): female council member
Skyke (sky-kee): female scientist and council member
Vishnu (Vish-new): ERT and honorary council member
Dalani (da-lane-e): council member stationed abroad
Ahovin: master council member returned from retirement to serve Elquin
Zeeporah (zee-por-ah): master council of medical affairs

Known Lost Council Members

Youkoni (u-con-e): bonded to Vishnu, killed while on a vital mission for Elquin.
Ahovin (ah-ho-ven): Youkoni's mentor, returned to her position to help mining efforts.

ERT

Elquin Recovery Team: Members are trained fighters who protect Elquin and are sent to planets that are being prepared for farming. They are also used to defend against progressively offensive planets. Many times the ERT is called in to keep the council safe or evacuate a planet when negotiations have gone wrong.

Known members

Locknoff: Master of ERT affairs
Ahdortee (ah-dor-tee)
Afenah (ah-fee-na)
Celtine (Kel-tine)
El-aron
Jussalte (juss-all-tee)
Porock (por-ock)
Rashanah (rash-an-ah)
Fandore (fan-dor-ee)
Naeefah (na-e-fa)
Marcose (mar-co-s)

Known Medical Staff Members

Zeeporah (zee-por-ah): high master of medical affairs
Churvack (chur-vk): assistant/master
Elious (e-lie-us): guided assistant
Doram (dor-am): short, unkempt hair, assistant/master
Deverah (de-ve-ra): medical officer/master
Yakema (yah-kee-ma): guided assistant
Sunden: medical officer Sariah replaced on Oororah-9
Tomahbare: medical officer and evaluation specialist
Kenozo (ken-o-zo): senior assistant

Jennifer's Friends

Emily Townsman: California resident and longtime friend
Cara Johnson: childhood friend
Kimberly (Kim)
Amy
Nancy Peterson

Others

Technon (tec-non): Sariah's brother
Kelentar: Baitorus representative
Ryous: military strategist
Zackary Mason: Jennifer's boyfriend
Fraternity: Gamma Sigma Phi
Sorority: Kappa Theta Nu
Elanah (el-ah-na): guard

Acknowledgments

There are not enough words to express my gratitude to all who have contributed to the success of this work, but I will start with this... thank you. Your confidence and vision in my ability and strength, even when I lack the courage and will, have proven invaluable.

To the universal mind, that God mind within and about me, I say thank you. I am humbled and grateful to know you.

To my parents: a big, fat hug, a billion kisses, and more thank-yous than I can express.

To my husband and children, thank you for putting up with me and believing in me.

To my family, thank you. To my SL friends, you're all awesome; thank you.

To the sweetest girl a person could ever know...Sweet Pea, thank you, girl. Your inspiration means the world to me.

To Desire, a beacon of joy, love, hope, light—a friend, sister, and mother, I say thank you.

Kefi…the best tiger in the world, thank you.

To the CreateSpace team, your guidance has been invaluable; your attention to detail, feedback, and patience mean the world to me, thank you.

About the Author

Rose Sweetwater is a veteran, active-duty spouse, student, and homemaker. She lives with her husband and three boys, thrilled to enjoy life as it comes, while sharing her passion for writing with the world. As a student of life and metaphysics, she has inspired many around her and will inspire you too.

Be blessed, and thank you for your time.